False Reality

Within The Darkness

By

Joshua K Andrews

I've heard stories of what this world once was; an untouched paradise filled with life and harmony. I know, it almost sounds like a fairytale. The Human race was once young, but never innocent. Our ancestors were just one of the countless species that walked these lands. We were deemed the fittest. And as so, we hunted the others to extinction.

Caves turned to settlements, then to kingdoms. The fight for survival became archaic for our race, but a lust for blood still boiled in our hearts. That's when the war of men began - a war that would span throughout time and change the world forever.

The prophets state that as the world changed, we were altered also. Suddenly, man couldn't simply defy nature, but the very nature of the universe. They deemed this phenomenon as science and used its power to strengthen our tools, our way of life, into a new golden age.

Technology was far from reaching its peak. However, our intelligence of this continually evolving power was bleak at best. We abused this influence of the gods. And what was our punishment? It was becoming that which we feared, that which we couldn't comprehend. We became gods ourselves, and the planet went to hell…

Bartholomew Barker

0.

Was Only the Beginning

An abyss, a void of pure white, engulfed Sebastian. Regardless of where he turned his gaze, an expanse of emptiness surrounded him. Even when he held his hands to his face, they remained invisible. In this colourless void, there was nothing. Sebastian was nothing. He couldn't move, couldn't even muster a scream. A profound sense of isolation washed over him as he stared into this surreal and disorienting space.

'...Good. You're awake...'

It was her voice. It echoed across the chasm, repeating and overlapping, almost becoming a choir. Sebastian tried calling out to it.

Nothing.

Her melody drifted over the blank canvas like a paintbrush bringing colour to the world. Her words became electric blue and filled the sky. Redwoods sprouted from newly formed grass. Next came gentle rivers, humble hills and a forest surrounded by that thick mist.

She appeared soon after.

Fiery burned orange hair, short and wavy, falling to a carmine hue. Pristine skin like marble formed beneath. Her eyes opened. Sapphires gleamed. Shimmering particles like the salt of the ocean shaped her face. Clothes began to form from the dust, covering her delicate figure.

Sebastian watched her, reaching out a non-existent hand.

Fragments blew in like the wind, constructing a boy with messy black hair, olive skin and a round face. It was Sebastian. He observed the scene, a poignant recollection etched in his mind.

'...I was just taking in the view...'

It was *his* voice, spoken by his painted twin. Once again, the syllables bounced around in warped tones until they became unrecognisable. As the echo of his voice resonated, sharp pillars of rock burst from the ground, surpassing the hills. Bronzed daggers of earth thrust towards the sky, forming a ring around the two of them. The surreal landscape continued to transform, dancing to the whims of their shared dreamscape.

'...Ever wonder what's behind them?...'

The boy asked, turning to her with a hopeful smile. Sebastian shuddered, already knowing her answer.

'...Nothing's waiting for us out there, Seb...'

Like a ghost staring at a photograph, he savoured every octave of her voice, taking in each minor detail of her face as she turned away from him, wondering if it would be the last time.

'...There has to be something, right?...'

Zara's colours dissolved into the white abyss. The sky joined her. Meadows and redwoods dispersed. All that remained were Sebastian and the mountains that had forever confined him.

'...I mean, this can't be all there is...'

The last words lingered like an echo as the world disappeared.

'...Seb, you should find Alex...'

'...Should be easy enough...'

'...He went where he always goes...'

And once again, he was alone. Sebastian slowly turned, surveying the endless cavern. Then came a captivating glow, so bright that the white void faded to grey. It was in the shape of a person, possessing no eyes or ears, not even a nose. It did have one feature, however. A large mouth, grinning down at Sebastian, bearing large, perfectly formed teeth. The arms and legs were twisted, the neck long and crooked, the head perfectly round and gently swaying. Seated cross-legged, it tapped its elongated fingers to its supposed chin.

Sebastian studied the thing, inching closer to it through no will of his own. The creature drifted into a standing position, its featureless face staring down at him.

'...Memories...'

The glowing giant's voice boomed - its mouth unmoving. Vibrations rippled across the chasm, causing it to flash and fade. A pencil replaced the paintbrush, scribbling black erratic sketches.

'...A reflection of one's existence. A tapestry, woven from personal experience...'

It spoke once more, its pencil spinning like a drill into Seb's mind. Images began popping into the nothingness, filling it with images he recognized as his past. His friends, his mother, and the people of Lora flickered in and out of view, morphing into different moments of his life.

Smoke filled the ivory landscape, smothering it in blood-orange hues. The sounds of screaming structures sang out, followed by the crunching of debris, cracks of kindling, explosions of stone, and shattered glass. Sebastian turned in all directions, peering through the fog. Homes were left broken, licked by dancing flames, with a heavy flash of lightning illuminating it all. His people had vanished, replaced with an eternal fire. He closed his eyes, yet the image still burned in his mind.

'...Ever changing fragments of data, being broken down and reformed to fit one's desires...'

When Seb finally opened his eyes, he was staring at a campfire. He placed an arm around her shoulder, and she leaned into him, nestling into his body. Sebastian poked at the flames with a stick, releasing the embers. Gazing in awe, he drifted through his memories as if he were repeating them. Each moment was a drop of rain. Sebastian surveyed these droplets - every time he had laughed, cried, or screamed in anger. All were there. All of Sebatian's memory appeared and vanished in an instant.

'...You have been corrupted, child...'

The white figure's voice reverberated once more, distorting the images of Sebastian's mind, forcing them to spark around him.

'...You have many questions. They all do when facing oblivion...'

The white void began to crack, revealing its blackness beneath. The figure grew brighter, searing Seb's retinas. The voice morphed into an ear-piercing echo. Some great force knocked Sebastian off balance. Sudden weightlessness plunged him further into the eternal abyss.

'...Death was only the beginning...'

1.

Ocean of Sand

Beneath pale violet skies lay a wasteland. Storms of dust blew across sandy dunes, scathing the stones as they scattered. Little life resided here, only things that killed and things that died. Half buried and covered in sand, he slumbered - a boy trapped within his mind, falling through an abyss.

When suddenly, he landed.

Sebastian's eyes shot open. His breathing matched the beating in his blistered chest - short, quick and gasping. He looked to his left, and then his right, before spinning his head in every possible direction.

An ocean of sand surrounded him.

Sebastian fell back into the groove he had made for himself, allowing the salty earth to wrap around his burning skin. Slowly, his eyelids unravelled as he directed his gaze towards the sky, where a second sun loomed closer than the first. The surreal sight captivated him, a spectacle he had never witnessed. But then, how could he have? He had never ventured beyond the confines of the village. Nobody had.

He was the first.

A smile swept across his face, cracking crusted lips. A tongue, like sandpaper, tried its best to elicit a moment of moisture as it swabbed an arid mouth.

Fingers grasped at the coarse sand and dug deep to rest upon the cooler granules beneath. The sensation of planting one's hand in a freshly poured bowl of sugar washed over the boy. He wondered why it had evoked that thought. An answer flew to him in the form of a memory, his smile stretching to a grin. Sebastian was helping his mother with her baking.

A pulse rippled across his head.

Sebastian opened his eyes. His mother was no longer with him. None of them were. He struggled to push himself upright, only to crumble back to the ground. Sebastian's joints ached, his muscles seized, and every gulp of air brought fragments of grit that stung like salt - not sugar.

Time drifted. He watched the scattering sands of the hourglass, his face half-buried. Sebastian tried piecing together the tapestry in his head - how it had all led to this moment. He remembered fire, some incredible light, and then he was here. His head throbbed once more as he clamped a hand against his dome, squeezing back against the pressure. The pain subsided and he let out a relieved yet raspy breath.

His gaze drifted back to the sky. His mind drifted someplace else.

Back to Lora. He could almost feel the cool breeze as he dreamt of home. The grass, still wet from a night's rain, beads of dew glistening in the morning's light, white tufts of cloud drifting high above, scraping against the mountains in the distance. The same mountains that had always surrounded him. They had warned him of what was waiting beyond the mountains; his mother and the rest of the village folk. Even his friends.

Seb's heart swelled and his eyes opened once more.

His friends. Zara and... *Alex.* Sebastian's body seized, his hands tightening into fists.

'No...' he uttered, striking against the ever-moving ground beneath him. Using what remaining strength he had to reach out and grab at the sand, Seb dragged his lifeless body. Where? He didn't know.

'I will find you,' he said, wincing as he pushed himself over the dusty dunes, clawing at the fragments, squeezing them with enough pressure to create diamonds. Every inch was a mile. As more time passed, a medallion haze blanketed the violet sky descending into a dust storm. Sebastian forced his eyes shut, pulling his battered body, his skin scathing against the coarse sand. He reached his hand forward and it fell limp. He tried squeezing his fingers, but they no longer listened.

'Move,' he told them, his body too exhausted to even tremble.

The sand began washing over him.

The howling wind began to snarl and soon became a vicious growl. Sebastian lifted his head, sensing shadows lurking within the haze. They grunted and hissed as they circled him, growing closer.

Remaining perfectly still, Seb's eyes darted to each of the figures. Suddenly, one sprang forward from the swirling dust and wind, its face mere inches from Sebastian's. The creature had pink, feverish eyes that oozed mustard pus. Its skin was cracked and crusted leather, yet remnants of black fur remained. Most of its frail, disjointed body was a mess of open sores. Frenzied eyes gazed upon him, accompanied by a throaty growl.

Swiftly, Sebastian scooped up a handful of sand and hurled it in the creature's face. The beast howled and threw itself upon the ground, writhing in the dust. Gathering his remaining strength, Sebastian attempted to turn around, only to discover more creatures watching him with eager perplexity. The mangled wolf circled back to meet Sebastian's gaze. It was bigger than its brethren. Less diseased. Its flesh; dark, sunken charcoal. The others shuffled back when it approached. It arched its prominent spine, reared its neck, bared its teeth and finally lunged. Sebastian's eyes dropped to the sand, and his arm raised feebly to protect his face. His fist tightened, and a numbing stiffness spread across his body.

His heart froze.

A curdling cry echoed across the sandy dunes, accompanied only by the mournful wind. Sebastian's gaze slowly lifted, revealing the creature lying in a puddle, the sand surrounding them forming into fresh clay. Like a dog refusing to take a bath, the beast slowly rose, dripping wet. It turned and roared at an unseen presence hiding in the haze. Sebastian shifted his focus, squinting to discern a silhouette marching through the storm. A blast of water shot through the velvet wind, striking one of the beasts. It flew back with a yelp, drenched and trembling. Another torrent followed, crashing into the pack leader once more. It picked itself up and whimpered at the violet sky before vanishing into the moaning desert.

Sebastian remained a passive observer, watching one of the many puddles as it was swallowed by thirsty dirt. His eyes drifted to the stranger wrapped in rags, approaching through the sand and dust. They were no more than a shadow - a mirage sent to mock him. The flaxen desert transformed into static grey before fading to white.

Sebastian awoke, blinking away his blurred surroundings. The rough sand nesting in his clothes rubbed against his cracked skin. Jostling on a rickety bed, swiping grit from the sheets beneath, Seb heard the sound of children playing, people shouting over one another and the hammering of construction outside.

At that moment, he was back home.

'Thank the gods, you're awake!' called out a voice from the corner of the room.

Sebastian sat up to find a girl standing in the open doorway.

'They told me they'd charge extra if you died in here,' she said with a smile as she stepped through.

'Where am I?' Sebastian asked, each word was a knife creeping up his throat.

'You don't sound too good,' she said, her smile fading as she nodded towards the nightstand. 'There's water if you need it.'

Sebastian turned to find a pitcher of liquid glistening in the light of the sun. Without hesitation, he grasped hold of it with both hands and guzzled the lot. The pitcher met the table with a resounding thud as he gasped for air.

'You're a thirsty one.' She laughed. 'Maybe I should have hit you with that blast back in the wastes.'

'That... was you?' Sebastian asked, still trying to control his breath.

'The great Ariana,' she said in a triumphantly forced tone, placing both hands on her hips. 'At your service.'

'My hero.' Seb laughed before coughing profusely, grabbing hold of his throat.

'Here, have another drink.' Ariana gestured at the pitcher, quickly waving her hand.

Seb watched as the empty pitcher refilled itself with water. He jumped back, falling from the bed and banging his head against an already broken cabinet.

'Watch out!' Ariana said, rushing over. 'Just because you're awake doesn't mean you still can't die somehow.' She checked his head. 'I still need to get my deposit back for the room, what you do after that is up to you.'

'Thanks. Appreciate it.' Seb winced, stroking a forming lump. 'How did you do that with the water?'

'Seriously?' She stepped back, tilting her head. 'Please tell me you've seen a *User* before.'

'Don't see much where I'm from. But I've seen my share of magic. What's the trick, fake glass? Hidden spout under the drawers?'

'It's not a trick, idiot. And it's not magic either. It's... hard to explain.' The girl folded her arms and placed a finger on her chin for a moment. 'Nope, not gonna get into it with you right now. Just get over it, okay?'

'O...kay?' Seb turned his attention back to the pitcher, picking up the glass and inspecting it.

'Calm down, it's not going to kill you,' she told him with a sigh, turning to find a chair. She blew the dust off the surface and sat down. 'Go ahead, drink.'

Sebastian sniffed the rim of the glass and proceeded to take a swig. He sloshed the liquid around in his mouth before swallowing. 'It's good,' he said, still examining the glass.

'Thanks,' Ariana said with a cheery smile. 'I made it myself.'

Sebastian gazed upon this stranger who'd saved his life. She was tall. Taller than he was, anyhow.

'You're lucky I happened upon you when I did,' she said, ignoring him as he stared. 'You were so dehydrated, I thought you were another corpse at first.' She laughed again, stretching a faint but noticeable scar across her left cheek. As she turned, he saw that her clothes were different from what he was used to back home. They were frayed and well-worn, with all traces of vibrancy and colour long since faded. Once-blue denim shorts and a white mid-drift shirt revealed her brown skin beneath, partially covered by a green jacket that had more zips than Sebastian thought it needed.

'Someone up there must like you.'

'Yeah. Lucky. That's me.' Seb winced, pushing himself up off the floor.

Ariana's most striking feature was her brunette hair. The sides were almost shaved, showing her dark scalp beneath. The fringe couldn't decide whether it wanted to be wavy or curled, and some of the locks tried their best to hide her emerald eyes from him. The rest of her wonderfully bizarre mane was long, pulled back into a ponytail, with a purple band tying it all together.

She wiped a curl from her face and looked questioningly at Seb.

His eyes immediately darted to the other side of the room. That's when he noticed a window. He got up and made his way over. 'What is this place?' he asked, peering outside.

'You're in a crummy hotel that charges too much.' Ariana sighed, surveying the chipped walls layered with cobwebs. 'They know the people here are desperate, so why not take advantage?' She shook her head and turned back to Seb. 'As for the town, I couldn't tell you. It doesn't have a name.'

'No name, huh?' Sebastian pressed his face to the glass, watching the tin huts and other buildings made from discarded scraps of metal. The desert surrounded the village for miles with no other landmarks in sight. He saw villagers fortifying walls and digging in the sand. Children were playing with rocks and anything else they could find.

'It's a place for people to disappear,' Ariana continued, moving towards Seb and peering out with him. 'Why name something when you're trying to convince the world it doesn't exist? The folks out there have done well to stay undetected for now. But it won't last.' She turned to Sebastian and nudged his side. 'So, what're you hiding from?'

A pulse rippled across his skull.

'I'm not hiding from anything.' Seb pressed a hand upon the glass and pushed himself back. Turning around, he winced and stumbled towards the mattress.

'Then what were you doing out in the wastes?'

'Your guess is as good as mine.' Seb shook his head, lying back on the bed. 'Last thing I remember is…' *His head throbbed once more.* 'My home. It was on fire.'

'I'm sorry,' Ariana said with a sigh. 'I haven't heard of an attack for some time. I thought they had finally stopped.'

'Wait. You know who did this?' Seb asked, watching as she circled the room.

'Yeah, I do.' She turned and leaned in close to him. 'The same people who came to my home. And all of theirs out there too.'

'All these people?' Sebastian echoed, standing and moving past her. 'Tell me who it was.'

'*Blackout*,' she said, shuddering at the name. Ariana took a deep breath and drifted towards the bed. 'They're a corrupt bunch of scumbag pirates, spreading fear like they get off on it or something.' She pounded the mattress with a shaking fist and sat down, tapping the floorboards with her heel. 'If anyone even speaks out against them - they're dead. And Blackout won't stop there. They'll burn down an entire city, just so nobody else gets the same idea.'

'That can't be right. There was something else.' Sebastian rubbed his temples, taking one last look out of the window.

'It's okay. You're still processing it all. I've been there,' she said, staring at the cracks in the floorboards. 'I was just a girl when they came to my home. I still remember that shadow as it fell over my village.' She wiped her face and smiled. 'On that day, I vowed to do something about it. Just because they own the skies, it doesn't give 'em the right to look down on the rest of us.' Ariana jumped from the bed, staring at Seb with large eyes. 'Wanna help? I mean, you do kind of owe me one.'

Sebastian froze. 'I'm sorry. I can't help you. I can't help anyone.'

The girl shrugged. 'That's some opinion you've built up about yourself. At the very least, you can carry my stuff while *I* free the world.'

'You wouldn't want me to come with you if that's the case. I have a hard enough time dragging my own stuff around,' Seb told her, shaking his head with a slight grin forming. 'Even my friends would-' Seb's words caught in his throat. He turned and grabbed hold of her shoulders. 'My friends! Did you see anyone else in that desert?'

'Hey, take it easy.' She slapped his hands away. 'You were the only person out there.'

Sebastian began pacing restlessly around the tiny room. 'I've got to find them. They're out there somewhere.'

'Who?'

'Everyone!' Seb spun towards her - his face redder than it was when she had found him. 'The people from my village. My mother. My friends. Zara…' He let out a long breath and stared at the many cracks in the floorboards. 'Maybe they ended up like me, lost somewhere past the mountains.'

'Hate to break it to you, stranger. But we're pretty far from any mountains.'

'I don't care.' He shook his head, backing up against the wall. 'I'll find them. They're probably lost, or hurt, or even…'

'Hey, calm down.' Ariana put her hands on his and sat Seb back down on the bed. 'I'm searching for someone too. I'll be leaving this place once I find him. You should come with us.'

'I told you, I-'

'Listen. If you don't find your people here, you'll have to travel alone through the wastes again. And I don't think I have to remind you how dumb of an idea that is.'

Sebastian scrunched his eyes and took a deep breath.

'Okay,' he told her with a reluctant nod. 'I'll join you.'

'Good!' Ariana said, jumping towards the door. 'Now get ready, we've got a big day ahead of us.'

She disappeared out of the room, leaving Sebastian sitting on the rickety bed staring towards the window. The sounds of children laughing, along with clanging metal, filled the air. He turned to face the glass pitcher. Beads of condensation slid from the freshly cool water within. He took another sip of the glass and held it to the light.

2.

Oasis

Sebastian shielded his eyes as the main doors swung open. The sun's rays bounced off the white sand, almost blinding him. He stepped back within the doorway so his eyes could adjust.

Ariana was still haggling with the woman at the reception desk of the hotel and wasn't getting anywhere. 'Look at him, he's very much alive! Why are you charging me this much?' Her voice echoed through the halls.

Seb took the free time to get a feel for this village hidden in the sands. He walked around for a time, and before he knew it, he had circled the entire place. It was different from his home. Barriers made from large sheets of broken steel surrounded the community, even the buildings. Sebastian noticed some villagers watching him from their tin huts. They hid behind sheets, peeking through the windows. Sebastian smiled wearily and gave a half-wave, only for the curtains to snap shut.

'Hey, you!' Ariana called, skipping towards him. 'Enjoying the sights?'

'Yeah...' Sebastian turned, scoping the area. 'Very rustic.'

'It's all made from parts of discarded Blackout air carriers. It's crazy these folk are hiding from those idiots in their own machines.'

'Air carriers?' Seb blinked, looking around at the many scraps of metal that filled the village, wondering what she had meant.

'You know, after all this. I forgot to ask your name.'

'I'm... Sebastian Travis. But my friends call me Seb.'

'Well, Seb. Nice to make your acquaintance,' she said, offering her hand.

'You too, Ariana. So, what's the plan?'

20

'Gathering intelligence. I spoke to someone last night who froze when I mentioned who we're looking for. Means we're on the right track.'

'And who *are* we looking for?'

'He goes by the name Darius Blake. He's a legend where I come from. I've heard stories of him going toe-to-toe with Blackout single-handedly. Honestly, I'm kind of nervous.'

A small boy ran past the two of them, laughing. Ariana called him over and asked where to find the hero. He smiled and pointed towards a dusty old saloon. Ariana thanked him and patted the boy on the head, only for an older woman to run out of the house and yell at the boy in a foreign language. She grabbed him by the arm and dragged him away, all the while glaring at Ariana and Sebastian.

'Friendly folk,' Sebastian said, folding his arms.

'It's not their fault,' Ariana told him, watching the mother and her boy scurry off. 'They're just scared.'

'Yeah, I guess. But there's no reason to fear us, right?'

Ariana didn't answer. She took a moment to watch the young boy and his guardian wander back to their hut. 'Come on, let's check out that pub.' Ariana perked up, patting him hard on the shoulder. 'Darius Blake is inside. I can't wait!'

Ariana rushed ahead, making her way towards the tap house. Sebastian tried to keep up, his aching muscles and burnt skin rubbing against his tattered clothes. When he had finally joined her, she was frozen - gazing at the saloon doors. The weathered sign above had the word "Oasis" scrawled upon it.

'You ready?' she asked with a gulp.

Sebastian stood motionless for a moment, looking up at the sign. He turned to Ariana and shrugged.

The faint sounds of laughter and elated yelling turned into a chorus of merriment when the doors swung open. Sebastian and Ariana found that inside this dusty cabin, camped within a village without a name, were people leading a cheerful existence - although a highly inebriated one. A roaring fire burned at the end of the tavern. In front was a live band playing instruments Seb had never seen or heard. A crowd surrounded the musicians, spinning around in circles and clapping their hands. Others sat at red velvet padded booths, talking loudly over one another and drinking wildly.

'Now this is my kind of place!' Ariana grinned wickedly as she eagerly looked around.

Sebastian nodded wearily, faking a smile.

'Another round, Keeper!' yelled an intoxicated gentleman, barging past the two of them.

'Grab a seat,' Ariana told Sebastian. 'I'm going to grill this barkeep.' Soon she had disappeared into the crowd surrounding the bar.

'Where do I...' Seb began to ask, looking around for an empty seat, before realising she had already gone. He made his way through the crowd of proudly drunk patrons, trying his best not to get ale spilt on him.

Sebastian spotted an almost empty booth with a large man sitting alone. He drank quietly with his eyes closed and a stern look upon his face. Seb made a final scan of the pub before realising these were the only seats available and sat opposite the shady character.

The music stopped. The laughter and shouting began to subside, falling into complete silence. The only voice heard was Ariana in the distance, who seemed unaware of the change.

'Listen, Bub. I've travelled a long way to get here! And I'm not leaving without...' She trailed off, noticing the change of atmosphere also.

Sebastian surveyed the tavern and saw many wary faces staring back at him. But not only at him. They were also cautiously watching the shaggy-haired giant sitting across the table, who was now staring directly back at Seb. The moment their eyes met, Sebastian instantly threw his gaze down towards the table, before slowly raising them again - too afraid to look away. The older man smirked and shook his head, turning his attention to his half-empty pint. He drank the rest down and wiped the foam from a short, greying beard.

'Another drink over here, Keeper,' he said, piercing through the silence.

'Right, you are. Will be there shortly,' the barkeep calmly answered over the still crowd.

The band began playing once more. The patrons, forgetting the stranger, turned back and continued dancing. Sebastian stayed silent, nervously fidgeting in his seat, watching as the mountain of a man opposite grew thirsty.

'One pint of the strong stuff, as requested,' Ariana sang out, crashing onto the seat beside Sebastian, clumsily slamming a tray with three large glasses of dark brown ale on the table - spilling foam over Sebastian and his new acquaintance. 'I got one for us too. They smell horrific!'

Sebastian's eyes widened when he saw the suds of foam land on the stranger's crimson cape, quickly averting his gaze to Ariana, giving her a worried look.

'Thanks, little lady,' the man said, grabbing a glass and taking a long sip.

'No problem, Darius.' She smiled, winking playfully at him.

'Didn't know we were on a first-name basis,' he spoke sternly, placing down his ale and lighting a cigarette.

'Would you prefer, Master Blake? Besides I thought we'd skip the pleasantries and get right down to business.'

'Is she for real?' Darius leaned in close to Sebastian, pointing a thumb towards her. But at this point, Seb had retreated into himself, unable to answer.

'Look, I don't mean to sound rude. I'm just a huge fan and have been on the road for a long time searching for you.'

'So, you want an autograph or something?'

'No, I don't want an autograph!' Ariana stood up and slammed her fist on the table, then quickly sat down, cheeks turning red as she breathed deeply. 'I mean... no, thank you. Please Darius, I just want to join your cause. Ever since I was a little girl, I've dreamt of taking down Blackout alongside the resistance. I want a chance to prove myself.' She then took a hard breath and nervously gulped down her ale, retching at the taste.

Darius leaned back in his chair silently, as though he were deciding something. Seb and Ariana leaned in awaiting his answer, only to shoot back in their seats when he began bellowing with laughter, slapping his knees and thumping upon the table.

Sebastian watched him confused. Ariana, however, watched with anger.

'What's so funny?' she asked, eyes narrowing.

'I'm sorry,' Darius uttered, trying to stop himself. 'It's just, that tickled me. How long have you been rehearsing that speech?'

'I'm serious,' Ariana said, leaning closer. 'For years, I've trained for this moment. I'm going to kill every last one of those Blackout goons. And I'm going to do it with or without your help.'

'You're a tough one,' Darius said, leaning in to copy her, stubbing out his cigarette on the table.

'Damn right, I am!'

'Well, we could have used you for those years you were training. But I'm taking more of a back seat approach nowadays.'

Sebastian took a small sip from his drink, before discreetly spitting it back into the glass.

'So, what are you saying?' Ariana asked. 'Are you a recruiter now? Or are you...' She looked around wearily and leaned in once more. 'Deep undercover?'

Darius groaned and wiped a hand over his face. 'I'm saying I'm retired.'

'You're what?' she bellowed, jumping back in her seat once more. Correcting herself and performing a twitchy smile when she realised the patrons were starting to turn around and look at her. When the prying eyes were no longer on her, she leaned in and whispered. 'So, you're just giving up?'

'Watch that tongue, missy. Look around you. This whole blight-ridden planet has given up. I threw in everything I had to try and stop that from happening. And what was it for?' Darius gulped down his pint and slammed it hard upon the table. 'Nothing changed, except a whole lot of good people dying. So, I'm out.' He got up and made his way out of the booth. 'Thanks for the drink. Now run home, girl. You're too old to be playing hero.'

Sebastian whistled and turned towards Ariana. 'So... what now?' Seb asked. He waited for an answer from her, but she stared into her drink, circling the rim with her finger. 'Ariana?'

'I don't know,' she uttered, staring off into space.

'We'll find someone to help us,' Seb said, grabbing Ariana's drink from her and sliding it across the table. 'If not here, then someplace else.'

'Are you even listening to yourself? What's the point of all this wishy-washy crap when an actual living legend just told us he's given up all hope.' She slammed her head against the table and groaned miserably onto the surface. 'Nana was right.'

Sebastian closed his eyes, leaned his head back against the seat, and inhaled slowly. 'Ariana? How long have you been searching for this oaf you call a hero?'

'Too long,' she answered, her voice muffled by the table.

'And now that you've found him and realised he's not exactly what you imagined. You're just going to quit without a second thought.'

'Yep. That's about it.'

'Wow! See, I thought you were the real deal. Ever since waking up this morning, you've been adamant about stopping Black Ship.'

'Black-*out*,' she corrected, lifting her head.

'Right, whatever. And after one minor setback, you're just giving up? I'm alive right now because of you. But if you're going to quit now, you might as well have left me in that desert.' Sebastian finally exhaled and was shocked to realise the words that had been spilling out of his mouth. He looked at Ariana, her face awash with guilt. 'I'm sorry, I didn't mean to-'

'No, you're right,' she interrupted. '*I'm* sorry. I shouldn't have let that guy get to me. I just couldn't believe that *he* was what I'd been searching for all this time.' She smiled and took Sebastian's hand. 'Maybe you're the hero I came here to find.'

Sebastian watched her hand upon his.

She laughed. 'Come on, let's get out of this dump.' Ariana got up and glided through the crowd with grace, holding onto Sebastian, while he clumsily barged into drunken patrons. She stopped at the door, turning to see Darius sitting at the bar with yet another pint.

'Let's just go,' Seb pleaded softly, 'forget about it.'

'Give me one second.' She faintly smiled before making her way over to the *hero*, her smile fading and becoming a scowl. 'I would like to say something,' she announced.

'What now?' he slurred, still paying full attention to his drink.

'You told me to look around earlier. Well, I have. All my life I've witnessed atrocity after bleeding atrocity. I've seen cities, homes and families torn to shreds. I've seen a world destroyed through fear and manipulation, where even the brave are too afraid to speak out for what's right.' Ariana's speech grew louder with each passing word. Before long, the music stopped playing yet again. Everyone in the tavern turned and watched her. When she noticed this, she stopped herself briefly and spoke the next words softly. 'But the worst thing I've seen in my life... was the great Darius Blake. And realising he was as much of a coward as everyone else.'

The pub fell silent. All eyes were on Darius as he glared back at Ariana. Seb crept over and put his hand on her shoulder, gesturing for her to leave. Ariana started backing away, her eyes fixed upon the aforementioned hero.

A low rumble shook the bar.

Ariana lost her footing and fell backwards. Seb caught the girl in his arms and steadied her. The tavern began to tremble and creak, shaking glasses from their surfaces and forcing them to smash upon the floor. The patrons began murmuring and trying to keep their balance. Sebastian and Ariana did the same. Darius, however, simply sighed and finished his pint.

'What's going on?' Sebastian asked Ariana.

She gave him no answer.

The sunlight vanished, replaced by an eerie darkness that sent shivers down the spines of onlookers. Townsfolk peeked outside, only to recoil in horror, their screams mingling with the rising panic. Ariana tightened her grip on Seb, her body trembling against his. He could feel the tension in the air, a palpable fear gripping the hearts of those within the tavern.

'Everyone shut up and calm down!' Darius roared, commanding the attention of the distressed crowd. 'Panicking just makes these fools jumpy. The best thing to do is sit down and drink. They'll be here soon.' He then turned to Seb and Ariana. 'You too, kids.'

'What's going on?' Sebastian begged for an answer.

'Blackout.' Darius sighed as he reached into his jacket pocket for a cigarette. 'Another drink over here, keeper.'

3.

Blackout

The tavern continued to tremble, intensifying the sense of unease that permeated the air. Seb rushed to the window, his eyes widening at the sight that unfolded before him. An enormous structure, crimson and metallic, loomed ominously in the dusty skies, effectively blotting out both suns. It hung motionless, casting a shadow over the village. A collective gasp escaped the lips of those within the tavern.

'Please, no,' Ariana muttered to herself, hiding her face in Sebastian's chest. Others in the tavern began wallowing and cursing, all watching the floating object as its shadow loomed. 'Not again.'

A solitary winged vehicle, propelled by dancing flames, detached itself from the colossal object and descended gracefully like a bird to the sandy ground below. Sebastian took Ariana's hand and guided her towards the back of the tap house, joining the huddle of patrons. Amidst the gathering tension, he glanced over at Darius, who remained seated at the bar, calmly sipping his drink.

For a moment, all was silent.

A metallic screech ripped through the air, followed by an onslaught of footsteps. Sebastian cautiously peered through a window, witnessing individuals clad in menacing black armour. They brandished sophisticated metal pipes, ruthlessly breaking down doors and invading the huts with brute force. The villagers' screams echoed in the air as chaos unfolded. Suddenly, the saloon doors swung open, revealing a swarm of darkness that enveloped the entrance to the pub.

The invaders' faces were concealed by iron masks, each adorned with crude and sinister drawings. These macabre sketches varied from crossed-out eyes and menacing grins to scornful frowns. Some masks even bore depictions of deranged animals and monstrous creatures. Whatever image they portrayed, all were painted blood red - at least, Sebastian hoped it was paint.

As they entered, the invaders assumed a disciplined formation. The front row of masked men knelt, making way for their comrades standing behind. In perfect unison, they raised their ornate pipes, pointing them forward. The atmosphere became thick with the hushed panic of the onlooking crowd.

The unit moved to create an opening in the centre. That's when *he* strolled in, taller than the rest of them. His metallic suit, glistening in a resplendent gold hue, seemed to defy the shadow cast over the town. The commanding intruder confidently strode to the forefront of the line, letting his blue cape billow elegantly behind. He paused, removing his helmet to reveal long, flowing blonde hair that cascaded down his shoulders.

'Good morning, nomads!' he elegantly bellowed.

The Saloon remained silent.

'Please, no need to be hospitable.' The shiny knight sneered, surveying the room.

Sebastian heard the hushed murmurs of the people around him.

'Now, here I was. Hunting a rat in this accursed wasteland, only to find its entire nest. Hiding in our very own dismantled air carriers, no less. Just as rats are known to do.'

The crudely-masked squad suddenly pumped their weapons, causing many clicks to fill the room. The patrons cowered in their booths. Ariana pulled Seb to the ground with the crowd. Then came a laugh. An unhinged cackle. Seb looked up to see the golden man shaking with a twitchy grin as he looked upon the fearful patrons.

'But... your empire is nothing, if not merciful.' The man breathed and straightened himself, resuming diplomacy. 'Although this unauthorised living area was erected without our knowledge, we are willing to let it go on existing if it so pleases. However, I was originally here for a specific purpose. The aforementioned *rat* problem.' His twisted smile grew back. 'Give us the person we are looking for, and we shall leave you all unharmed. All but one, that is.'

Silence filled the bar once more. The people began to turn to one another with questioning eyes, shaking their heads and shrugging. More than a few gazed at Darius, still sitting quietly at the bar.

'We'll give you nothin', Blackout scum!' a drunken patron roared, standing from his seat. 'You can't just come 'ere and tell us-'

A loud pop sounded from one of the guard's pipes. The man dropped to his knees, collapsing on the dusty floorboards. Shocked gasps filled the tavern as a dark liquid seeped out from under him. The pop became a chime, before fading into a high-pitched whistle. Sebastian shuddered, staring at the face of the man and then towards the masked guard - a line of white smoke still emanating from his weapon. The piercing hiss dragged on. Sebastian turned to see a screaming crowd of people. He couldn't hear them - only that monotonous tone burning into his brain. Then, as if she were pulling him back from a different place, Ariana tightened her grip on Sebastian's arm and held him close to her.

'How unfortunate.' The regal man sighed once the commotion had subsided. 'But let that be a lesson to the rest of you. We will...' He trailed off from his speech, as Darius stood up from his stall and faced him. 'Excuse me, Sir. I'm trying to-' The man froze, his face etched in fear. 'Oh, my Lord.'

'Brandon.' Darius sighed. 'It's been a while.'

'Darius?' The golden knight squealed, jumping back. 'You're alive?'

'As are you. Spoiling my ale, just like the old days.' Darius finished his pint and pointed at the empty glass for the barkeeper to refill it. 'Now get to the point of why you're here. Without reciting that rehearsed crap, if you can help it.'

Brandon's pale face began to turn a bright red, his golden armour rattling as he shook within it. 'You insolent...' He seethed through clenched teeth.

The masked guards behind him turned their weapons towards Darius now, but Brandon slowly lowered his hand.

'My dear friend.' He smiled warmly with open arms. 'We are looking for a fugitive.'

'Well, here I am,' Darius said, standing to attention. 'Just leave the rest of these folk out of it.' He lowered his head and put out his arms in surrender.

Brandon looked puzzled for a moment, before breaking into laughter. 'Oh, Darius. You think we're here searching for *you*?'

Darius slowly raised his head and frowned.

'Honestly, I thought you died many years ago,' Brandon continued, looking Darius up and down. 'We all did, sadly. However, seeing you now, I believe that death would have been the kinder fate.' The shiny man patted Darius hard on the shoulder. 'I mean, look what you've become! The famous Darius Blake of legend, hiding away in some hole out in the wastes with the rest of the wretched, forgotten things.' Brandon stopped himself and scanned the pub once more. 'I should detain you, Blake. But for old times' sake, I'll pretend I didn't see you. Besides... I believe that life spent here is punishment enough.'

Darius gritted his teeth. 'So, if not me, then who?'

'A boy,' Brandon answered casually, picking up a half-empty pint of ale and sniffing the rim. 'He should be close to adulthood by now, but he is still merely a child. His last known location was hidden somewhere within the desert. So, here we are.'

Sebastian froze. Ariana slowly ushered him back through the crowd, giving him a questionable look.

'I see.' Darius sighed, turning in their direction. 'What's so special about some kid? Must be mighty important for you lot to haul that floating eyesore.'

'You will not speak ill of the Crimson Cloud, Blake.' Brandon snapped, spinning around and smashing the glass to the floor. 'And the child's importance is of no concern of yours. However, if he is here, it would be in your best interest to reveal him.'

'Would it now?' Darius sneered, finishing his pint. 'Keeper,' he called out, tapping his glass three times. The bartender nodded, ducking under the bar. Pots and mugs spilt onto the floor, clanging and smashing as he rummaged behind the counter.

'I'm growing impatient, old friend,' Brandon growled, scratching his head.

'Never one for waiting, were you?' Darius laughed. 'And here you are, still rushing head first into danger before your allies are even prepared.'

'What are you implying?'

'One carrier came down from the Crimson. Yours. I'm sure many more are prepping themselves now to descend. But you couldn't wait, could you, Bran?'

The barkeep struggled as he lifted a heavy object upon the bar, covered by an old sheet. Darius grabbed hold of Brandon with one hand and lifted the large item with his other.

'It... can't be,' Brandon squealed.

'You remember Xerxes? It's been a while since she's seen some action.'

The sheet fell to the ground, sending dust to scatter and dance in the light. Sebastian and Ariana pushed to the front of the crowd to see a sword almost the size of a person. Darius held its hilt with ease and pressed the dull blade against Brandon's neck, cautiously backing away from his guards.

'I suggest you lads put down your toys. That's unless you want to see how good of a meat shield your boss is?'

The guards flinched and turned their heads to look at one another, but all held their aim.

'Well, I'll be,' Darius said with a smirk to a squirming Brandon. 'I think they actually *want* to see that. I've forgotten how popular you are.'

'What are you idiots doing? Lower your guns this instant!' Brandon yelped. His men hesitated, but slowly dropped their aim. 'You won't get away with this, Blake! I'll make you wish you died many times over by the time I'm finished with-' Before Brandon could finish. Darius tapped him on the head with the hilt of his blade.

'That's enough of that.' Darius sighed, as Brandon slumped forward. 'Hey, kid. We best be making tracks,' he called out to Sebastian. 'You too, missy.'

Sebastian hesitated, but Ariana pushed him through the pub. As they joined Darius, one of the Blackmasks spotted Sebastian and raised his weapon. 'Don't move!' The man yelled through his muffled mask, the rest of the unit raised their guns and aimed them at Seb.

'Easy now,' Darius cautioned, tightening his grip on their captain. 'Your last order was to lower your guns.'

The guards hesitated. But soon enough, they looked at each other and shrugged, dropping their weapons to the floor.

'And if you hurt anyone else in this town, I'll gut him like one of the rats he loves so much.' With careful steps, he made his way past the guards. 'Are you two gonna take all day?' he yelled back.

Seb and Ariana glanced at one another before following the retired hero out into the open.

Sebastian and Ariana burst through the saloon doors, stumbling in the half-light as the sun crept from the cover of an incredible fortress hanging in the sky. Seb threw up his arms and shielded himself from the sudden gleam. The doors behind continued to swing back and forth, creating a rhythmic clap that spread across the dust-ridden town. Sebastian's eyes adjusted, locking onto a structure floating gently in the air, large enough to hold an entire village. It loomed, revealing its underbelly with a network of pipes and cables meshed and tangled together. It sat comfortably atop inflated sacks, reflecting the light as if it were made from cured leather. The balloons were wrapped tightly within thick black ropes, reminding him of the fishing nets they used to hang off their boats back home.

'First time, huh?'

Sebastian's head snapped back to the dusty earth. Darius stared behind his shoulder, still carrying that golden knight. He grabbed Sebastian by the scruff of his shirt and Ariana by the arm, her eyes still locked upon the floating city.

'I get that it's impressive, but the further we are from that thing, the better,' Darius said, turning back to where the metal bird rested. 'Luckily there's a flight leaving any minute.'

Seb could hardly register the words coming from the warrior's mouth. The sounds echoed and drifted as his eyes fell upon the villagers kneeling in the sand in front of the winged vehicle. Some were crying, the children especially. Others seemed expressionless like they were used to this treatment. Surrounding them were more armed guards, tying their hands and pushing them into the dirt. Sebastian shook his head before his eyes landed on the young boy from before. The one who pointed him and Ariana to the

Oasis, his face wet with tears. Seb scowled, tightening his fists. His gaze drifted to the older woman next to the boy. The one who had dragged him away. She stared back, giving Sebastian the same look as before. One of fear - of hatred. A guard barked orders at her and shoved the woman forward into the sand. The kid screamed and threw himself over the woman, only to have the Blackmask raise his weapon on the child.

'Stop!' Sebastian yelled, stepping out into the clearing.

The guard slowly lifted his head, revealing the face of a cobra upon his mask. The other troops turned towards Sebastian, as did many of the villagers. He stepped back and heard a gruff exhale from behind cover.

'Not one for the stealth approach, are ya?' Darius brushed past Sebastian, shoving him behind the hut.

Ariana grabbed hold of Seb's shoulders, pulling him back further. They both watched as Darius shook Brandon off his shoulder and stepped into the clearing.

The guards yelled to one another, readying their aim. Snake-face stepped over the old woman and withdrew two curved blades from behind his back. In an instant, he was sprinting with the daggers swinging wildly in each hand. Darius reached behind his shoulder where the steel slab rested and pulled it out with ease. He swung down at the snake the moment he was within range.

Dust scattered across the trembling ground.

Sebastian could almost taste the salt of the spreading cloud as he squinted at the dancing silhouettes. One, small and quick. The other, large and slow. The metal huts shook with each mammoth strike from Xerxes. The dust cleared. Darius stood with an unmoving stance. Crouched slightly, hunched forward, arm bent with his elbow stretched back, the point of his blade tilting slightly above his opponent.

Snake-face's attack had left him less composed. His chest expanded and deflated rapidly, one blade pointed forward with a trembling hand. The other dagger was missing, and Snake-face's right arm hung limp. With a final scream, he charged towards Darius with the remaining outstretched blade. His scream heightened in pitch as the metal slab swung up against his side. The cobra flew several yards and smashed through one of the huts, with the rusted roof collapsing upon him.

Darius stopped swinging, stumbling backwards. He placed a gloved hand on his head to steady himself, swaying for a moment before wiping his brow. Turning his attention to the remaining guards, who fumbled to turn their guns upon him. The shots popped and echoed across the sand-covered canyons.

'I can't believe it,' Ariana said, shifting forward, finally taking her eyes away from the Crimson Capital.

Seb reluctantly opened one eye to find that Darius was still moving towards the guards unfettered, his sword's wide blade acting as a shield. Bullets pinged against it, ricocheting into the sand. When the Blackmasks began to reload, he moved on quick feet and leapt over the villagers, swinging Xerxes in a lifting arc and sending one of them hurtling through the air. The other trooper dropped his rifle and took out a knife, only to be kicked with a giant boot and slammed down to the ground with a mighty fist.

'Now *that's* the famous Darius Blake I heard about!' Ariana screamed, jumping past Seb and cheering the old hero on as he stepped into the metal bird.

Sebastian smiled shyly, watching the townsfolk free themselves and run to find shelter.

But then, a glimmer appeared in the blackest corner of his sight.

'Where am I? What just...' Brandon groaned, slowly rising with a metal glove placed on his forehead.

'Erm... Guys?' Seb poked Ariana and pointed towards the golden knight.

'What are you doing with my ship?' Brandon screamed, pointing a metal glove at the retired hero. 'Guards? Guards! Shoot him! Kill Blake!'

Soon after Brandon gave the order, his men burst out of the saloon and readied their aim. Sebastian turned away and cried out. But instead of hearing a barrage of bullets, it was the sounds of a flowing wave. He turned back towards the Oasis to see a giant pillar of clear liquid form. Like a translucent swinging club, it careened into the saloon, pounding the masked guards hard against the wooden shack. Her arms lifted elegantly, spinning on her heels as the water streamed from the air around her. Ariana's eyes focused on the Blackmasks. Seb fell back as he gazed upon her, his eyes wide and glistening. Finally, she dropped to one knee, inhaled deeply and exhaled, struggling to push herself up. Seb rushed to Ariana's side, threw her arm over his shoulder and dragged her back behind the hut.

Darius emerged from the metal dove, holding on to two unconscious troops by their belts and throwing them to the ground with their comrades.

'Bin's emptied,' he yelled. 'Now let's get this girl flying, shall we?' He froze when he realised Brandon was conscious.

'Fools...' The golden knight said with a faint breath. 'I'm surrounded by complete and utter fools!' He reached to his side and pulled a gun from its holster. It was different from the other rifles. Golden - like his armour, and a little cumbersome as he held this weapon in one hand. Brandon pointed the weapon at Darius and roared furiously, pulling the trigger.

A loud shot rang out.

Darius rolled forward, pulling out his sword and swinging it at the ground. Dust scattered once more. Brandon laughed maniacally as he fired wildly into the cloud. The large cylinder in the centre rotated with every pull of the trigger, sending his arm flying back. After firing five times, he waited. His large revolver gently waved as the smoke cleared, his eyes darting across the battlefield.

Seb placed Ariana down and peered out towards the lifting cloud. The villagers had all but vanished along with Darius. He could hear Brandon's panicked breaths. He looked back. The golden knight's arm trembled, and he holstered his weapon.

'It's a shame. After all these years I seem to have forgotten your abilities, Blake.'

Standing behind him was Darius, his sword outstretched, inches from Brandon's neck. 'There's much you've forgotten, Bran,' Darius said. 'Now call off your men. It's over.'

Brandon pulled his head up to the sky and cackled. 'Look around you. The Crimson Cloud has this pitiful nest of yours surrounded. You can't escape us.'

'Tell me that again when you wake.'

'Wait, what...' Brandon began to ask as Darius knocked him out with the heel of his boot. He sighed, picking Brandon up with his free arm and hoisting the unconscious man onto his back. Darius looked up to the sky and Sebastian did the same. More mechanical birds were descending from the flying kingdom way up high.

'You kids still alive?' Darius yelled.

Seb stepped out from cover with Ariana draped over his shoulders.

'Times a factor. Let's get moving,' The old hero said, placing the sword on his back and heading towards the ship.

The saloon doors burst open and out came a cheering crowd. Many had freshly filled mugs and were lifting them into the air, spilling ale over one another. The musicians stepped out and performed their songs from before. This time with more passion, dancing with the crowd as they played.

As Seb joined Darius, he smiled. The villagers had emerged from where they were hiding and hugged one another. This time it was the elders' time to cry. They surrounded Darius and feebly pulled at his jacket and cape, calling out to him in an unrecognisable language. He replied over his shoulder in their native tongue, his voice heavier than before.

Ariana stopped before the cruiser and turned to Darius. 'We're not really gonna fly that thing, are we?'

'Congratulations, princess. You're a part of this now. Just like you've always wanted,' he replied, gently pushing her up the ramp.

Seb began to follow but was grabbed by the arm. He turned around to find the old woman from before staring hard at him. Her face softened, and she smiled, wrapping her arms around Sebastian. She spoke some words he didn't know before falling back into the crowd.

'*Libera dieses rebenka min sveta.*'

Sebastian joined the others on the ship. Brandon was slumped upon the floor, Ariana was noticeably exhausted but holding steady, and Darius was sitting at the front messing with the many dials and buttons blinking before him.

'Okay, what are we dealing with here?' Darius asked himself, scratching at his beard.

The flying ships landed outside. All of the villagers fled back into their homes, as did the Oasis patrons. Replacing them was a swarm of masked thugs escaping from the birds. Their rigid formations and uniform structure from before had all but been abandoned.

'Any time now, big guy,' Ariana said, finally able to stand.

'Just give me one... more... second.' Darius gritted his teeth and pulled at the levers.

'Disembark this vessel immediately.' A guard ordered from outside.

'Now which was it?' Darius asked himself with a low breath, fiddling with the dials. 'Yeah, that's the one!' He grinned, as the flames burst from beneath their ship.

In moments, they were flying. Sebastian braced himself as the machine rumbled beneath him.

'It's gonna get a bit bumpy from here on,' Darius yelled as the metal bird rocketed through the sky.

4.

Mechanical Wings

He could see it all. The oasis pub, the tinned huts, the crowd of villagers and the black mass of the masked army. All shrank from view and were covered by a dusty wind. It was just moments ago that Sebastian was there with them. Now he was gazing upon it all, miles above, with nothing but air between.

He pushed away from the vibrating glass, stumbling and falling backwards. Arms wrapped around his chest, steadying him. It was Ariana. Her lips quivered into a smile. She held him tightly, her body trembling more than the ship.

'Are you alright?' he asked, placing a hand on her stiffened shoulder. When he didn't get an answer, he asked again. 'Ariana?'

'I'll be fine,' she said sharply. 'I hate flying. That's all.'

'It is a little overwhelming. But have you seen that view?'

'I've seen it,' she answered quickly and quietly, 'It's the part I hate the most. It's how *they* see the world. Looking down at the rest of us. Our problems. Small and insignificant. Why would I want to see the world the way they do?'

Seb breathed in, his eyes scanning the interior of the ship. It was small and lined with many seats. Girders and support beams jutted from the heavily padded, curved walls. Darius was still at the controls, focused on steering the flying ship. On the other end was Brandon, the golden knight of Blackout, who was now their captive, slumped peacefully in the corner.

Sebastian leaned back against Ariana's chest, wondering if he had died in that desert. It would explain everything that had happened since. Perhaps this was all a mirage putting his mind at ease while the sand gradually swallowed him. 'Get up,' he told her, grabbing Ariana's hand and bringing her to the window. 'Stop looking at it through their eyes. See it through mine.'

Ariana peered closer, pressing her face to the glass. The medallion wind took a moment to clear. When it did, the two were met with a fuchsia sky.

'There was little for me to do back home. Nothing much that I wanted to do, anyway.' Seb said, noticing some large-winged creatures in the distance, too far to make out clearly. 'I would spend my days watching the birds. How they would just up and fly at a moment's notice. One flap of their wings and they'd be off in the sky with all of their problems left on the ground.' He shook his head and laughed to himself. 'It's stupid, really. But some part of me was jealous. There I was, trapped in that village, watching these creatures with the ability to take off into the clouds and go anywhere. To explore the world. And yet, they stayed.'

'Leaving home is hard,' Ariana said, watching her reflection in the glass, staring deep into her own eyes as if she were searching for something. 'It's leaving behind comfort, familiarity, friends and family. Even the people you didn't think you'd ever miss. It all goes. And you find yourself somewhere new, trying to search for it all again.' Ariana touched the window, running her fingers along the glass. 'Home isn't just a place. It's memories, experiences, and everything that's made you who you are. It's hard to leave something like that behind. And when you finally do. It becomes impossible to return.'

'Do you think you'll ever go back?'

'There's not much left for me to go back to. And even if there was, the further I got from home, the more I changed. Even if it was exactly as I remembered, I wouldn't recognise it.' She sighed and turned away for a moment, catching Seb's longing expression as he continued peering out.

'Still, I hope you get to return someday,' he said.

'Thanks, but let's focus on getting you home first.'

'Appreciate it.' Sebastian sighed and weakly thumped a fist against the window. 'They're out there somewhere. Just waiting to be rescued, like how you saved me.'

'Which you still owe me for, just so you know.' Ariana turned to him with a wink. 'But if we find your people along the way, I guess I wouldn't mind the detour.'

Sebastian grinned and opened his fist, pressing his palm upon the glass. 'Well, now we have these wings. I can explore the entire world if I need to. I don't have to envy those birds anymore. And you don't have to be scared of the cloud people.'

'I'm not scared, idiot,' she said, pushing him away. 'But I have to admit, your way of looking at the world is better than theirs.' Her lips creased into a small smile.

The tufts of white wisps soon passed, revealing another structure in the sky, shrouded by dust. However, Seb could still make out the large red sacks it sat upon, spinning blades from the turbines that reminded him of the windmills back home. The Crimson Cloud. That's what Brandon had named it. From this new vantage point, Seb could see it all. There were homes, grand buildings, lush fields and forests stretching across the surface. Even a lake that led to a waterfall descending to the towns below. It was a real city. A kingdom in the sky. Sebastian grinned wildly as he pressed his face against the glass, shifting across the window to find a better view, trying to take in every detail.

'I've never seen it from above,' Ariana said, peering closer. 'It's pretty.' she sniffed, turning away from the window.

'Hate to break up the heart to heart. But we've got company,' Darius yelled from the cockpit.

Shadows appeared in the clouds, looming ever closer. The ship turned sideways, and Sebastian's face smacked against the glass once more. He fell back, finally finding his footing. He looked over at a shaken Ariana, and she nodded back at him. Darius weaved in and out between soot-filled clouds like a needle through wool.

'Don't just stand there, kid. Do something!' Darius roared over his shoulder.

Seb stood there, doing nothing. His eyes moved between the many flashing buttons and sturdy levers that surrounded the ship.

'That's one problem sorted.' Ariana chimed in, pulling a pair of handcuffs out of some drawers. She skipped towards the knocked-out Brandon and tied his wrists together. 'Not so big now, are we?' she said triumphantly at him, before giving a thumbs up to Seb.

The ship trembled, knocking Seb and Ariana to the floor.

'Damn, we're hit,' Darius called out, 'Everyone alright?'

'Don't worry,' Ariana called out, 'We'll be-'

A sudden crash violently jolted the bird, tossing Seb and Ariana against a side panel. Through the glass, they witnessed another ship closing in, intent on ramming them. Acting quickly, Seb seized Ariana by the waist and propelled her to safety just as the panel cracked and tore open. Caught in a fierce gust, Sebastian clung loosely to the jagged edges of broken metal, witnessing the impending collision of the Blackout cruiser. Tears streamed from his burning eyes, and in that moment, he wondered if he, too, would soon be swept away into the vast sky.

'I hate you...' a voice spoke out. Low and muffled by the howling wind.

Sebastian raised his head, his eyes meeting Ariana's silhouette in the tumultuous hurricane that engulfed them. The wind tugged at her ponytail, and tore at her jacket, yet she persisted. With a circling motion, her hands initiated a rhythmic dance that extended to her arms and soon enveloped her entire body. Each repetition of the movement echoed through the storm, her declaration growing louder than the tempest itself. 'I hate you all!'

A celestial pool materialized from the heavens and cascaded over the wings of the opposing bird, disrupting its balance. Sebastian watched in awe as water defied gravity, streaming through the air and consigning the enemy ship to the depths of the sandy ocean. Amidst the spectacle, he felt Ariana's hand clutching onto him. With a strained groan, she pulled Sebastian inside the battered ship and pushed him into a seat.

'You're not getting away from me that easily,' she told Seb, pulling a harness over him.

'What the hell was that?' Darius yelled.

'That was my training finally paying off.' Ariana cooed before falling hard on the seat next to Sebastian. 'Now let's get this puppy out of here.

'I'd love to, princess. But-'

The wounded bird emitted a loud chirping sound, accompanied by a flashing red light. Soon, the ship started its descent, gracefully drifting out of the sky.

'Is something wrong?' Sebastian asked.

'Your boyfriend's real perceptive. 'Darius told Ariana, fiddling with dials and pulling many levers.

'He's not my-' An explosion from outside knocked them to the ground. One of the wings burst into flames. The bird shrieked, shuddering, falling. 'What do we do?' Ariana asked, holding onto the chair in front of her.

'Best make peace with any gods you pray to,' Darius said through clenched teeth, trying his best to hold the ship steady. 'Though none of 'em can help us now.'

'Maybe none *you* pray to, Blake.' A voice came from behind them. The three turned to find an oddly relaxed Brandon, leaning up against the back of the bird, free from his bonds.

'I almost forgot you were here.' Darius laughed. 'Not such a bad day after all.'

'I hate being the one to ruin your grand plans, Blake. But I have a way out of this mess.'

'Oh, please, do tell.'

'The craft behind us. They know we're going down and have no intention of getting close enough to ram us.'

'So insightful. Are you two friends?' Darius asked Sebastian.

Brandon sighed. 'Give me the transmitter. I'll order them to let us board.'

The three looked uneasily at each other.

'And why would you help us?' Ariana asked.

'Help you?' Brandon laughed. 'I'm helping myself. If you rats don't want to die, you'll help yourselves as well.'

'Forget it. we can't trust him.' Darius said.

'You'd rather put your faith in falling with this burning wreck?' Brandon asked with a smirk.

'Every time,' Darius answered gruffly, furrowing his brow.

'Will you just hand him the thing already!' Sebastian yelled. 'Who cares, we're all gonna die anyway. Give him what he wants.'

Darius looked over at Ariana, who simply shrugged in return. 'Fine...' he threw the communicator over to Brandon. 'Make it quick. We're eating sand real soon.'

Brandon caught the device, brushing gilded hair away from the side of his face and pressing the communicator against his ear. He then winked at Ariana, who met him with a scowl. 'This is your captain, Brandon Frost. My confirmation number is zero-five-eight-two-six. I have apprehended the targets. However, my ship has sustained major damage. Requesting immediate extraction.' Brandon dropped the device and gave a bow as the other bird swooped in alongside them, extending a short runway that linked the two. 'Now, if you would ever so kindly escort me.' He turned, gesturing towards the opening.

Ariana jumped up and freed Seb from his seat. They both ran past Brandon and onto the other ship, leaving Darius with the controls.

'You're not joining us?' Brandon asked Darius.

'You know the instant I let go, this thing will throw itself out of the sky.'

'Oh. That's true...' Brandon's unhinged cackle burst from his lungs. 'What a shame. Still, it was great seeing you again, Blake.' Brandon stepped onto the platform and shouted back. 'And... I'm sorry about *Ethan*.'

Darius let out a furious roar, abandoning the controls and leaping towards the golden knight. But it was too late. The bird broke free from the platform and hurtled towards the sands below.

Brandon watched on, as the ship fell upon the dunes, exploding into a symphony of fire. 'Goodbye, old friend.'

The interior of this new ship was identical to the last. Inside were two masked guards; one was at the helm, flying the cruiser. The other was sitting opposite with rifle in hand, his face paint depicted fierce red eyes and a screaming mouth. Sebastian stole a glance at Ariana, whose unwavering gaze remained fixed on the smouldering wreckage strewn across the distant sands growing ever more distant.

'He can't be...' Ariana breathed. 'He's not,' she repeated. 'He can't be.'

'Dead?' Brandon asked, stepping in from outside. 'We can swoop down to make sure if you'd like. I know I would feel better knowing for certain this time.'

'You said you'd help us!'

'I said I would help *myself*. And look at that. Here I am.'

Sebastian took Ariana's hand and pulled her beside him. 'So, what happens now?' he asked, turning towards the gilded knight.

Brandon leaned forward and squinted at Seb, trying to get a view of him from all angles. Seb leaned back in his seat, eyebrows raising.

'We've received orders to return to the capital, sir,' Called the Blackmask from the cockpit.

'Hold your position, soldier,' Brandon spoke sternly, never taking his eyes off Sebastian.

'Sir, are orders are to-'

'I give the orders here, cretin!' He spun violently and reached a hand towards the pilot, tightly squeezing his claw-like glove. His face was wet with sweat, eyes twitching.

Seb pushed further into his chair, wishing it could go back even deeper, realising the other Blackmask leaning back also.

Brandon turned back to face Seb and the expression waned with a heavy breath. 'So, you're the boy, are you?'

Seb sat motionless, watching the cold, distant eyes. Completely different from the ones just moments before.

'Tell me your name. Where do you call home?'

'He ain't gonna tell you nothing, Blackout scum!' Ariana spat.

'That is a shame. I do like sharing stories.'

'If you're so fond of sharing. What happened to my home?' Sebastian asked, leaning forward.

'I'm afraid I can't help you if you don't reveal your identity, boy.'

'Don't fall for his-' Ariana tried to warn him.

'I'm Sebastian Travis, from Lora. The village hidden within the mountains.'

'Tricks…' Ariana finished, shaking her head. 'Idiot.'

'From Lora, you say?' The golden knight leaned in slowly, his eyes growing as wide and gleaming as his armour. 'Incredible.' He stared in wonder, prodding Seb's head with his glimmering claw. 'It really is you.'

'Tell me what you did to the others. My people. Please, I need to find them.'

'The others?' This time it was Brandon's turn to lean back.

'Captain Hawks, Sir.' The pilot spoke, cutting him off. 'We seem to have some extra weight on the exterior of the ship.'

'Probably some debris,' he said, with a shrug and a wave. 'Just kick it off, will you?'

'Sir,' said the helmsman with the screaming mask as he brushed past them and opened the hatch. 'What is that?' he asked, before being flung from the ship.

'Thanks for getting the door for me.' A familiar voice came from the opening, as large grey gloves gripped hold of the edge. The three turned suddenly, each of their expressions changing drastically.

'Darius!' Ariana squealed, leaping towards the retired hero and throwing her arms around him, almost knocking him back out of the opening.

'Easy there, girly,' he said, patting her on the head.

'Blake,' Brandon said with a sigh, 'You're alive... again.'

Darius moved Ariana aside and stomped towards the golden knight.

'I'm getting awful tired of you trying to kill me,' Darius told him.

'Listen, friend,' Brandon urged, putting up his hands in a reassuring manner. 'There's no need for any vio-'

Darius seized him by the throat, forcefully driving him to the floor. The grip tightened, the pressure causing Brandon's face to shift to a shade of purple, his eyes bulging from their sockets.

'Orders, captain?' The pilot asked, only to hear strained gargles.

'What's that?' Darius asked Brandon, putting an ear close to his pink face. 'I think he said to land.'

'Right. Sure thing, Captain.' the pilot laughed uneasily.

The ship descended, returning to the desert. Darius released his grip, leaving Brandon to wheeze uncontrollably on the floor.

'Yeah! Take that, Blackout scum,' Ariana yelled.

'Get up.' Darius told the purple-faced Brandon.

The proud knight complied, as did the pilot. Seb observed them, finally discerning the image on the other guard's mask: a crude crying face with teardrops shaped like bullets.

'Now get out.'

The two stepped out onto the sand. They exchanged glances before surveying the vast desert. There was no sign of life for miles. The pilot dropped to his knees and began to sob, the sound muffled by his mask.

'Now Blake, I know we've had our differences, however-'

'You took everything from me,' Darius told Brandon, reaching for the greatsword on his back.

'You can't!' Seb yelled, jumping off the ship and running between them, holding out his arms to form a barrier between the two.

'And you're going to stop me?' Darius growled.

'He was about to tell me about my people.' Sebastian said pitifully. He turned to face Brandon and lowered his gaze to the sand. 'I need to know where my friends are. My family.'

Darius held his gaze for a moment, before lowering Xerxes to the ground with a groan. 'Listen, kid...' he said, dropping down to one knee and placing a hand on Sebastian's shoulder. 'These guys, they're gonna tell you no more than I will. Your friends are dead - or good as. The people Blackout takes can only be saved with a bullet.'

'You're wrong.' Sebastian uttered, stepping backwards. 'They're still out there somewhere. I know it.'

Darius lifted his blade once more. 'Stand aside.'

With wide eyes, Seb gazed at the nasty end of the giant's knife, before finally nodding his head and hopping back to the ship.

'That's better. Remember this, kid...' He raised Xerxes high above his head, glaring down at Brandon's frightened face. 'Hoping will get you killed. It'll get the people around you killed. When it does, all you can do is turn the knife back around.'

'Wait!' Brandon wailed, 'I know where they are. Your people!'

Darius stopped the mammoth swing just in time, holding his grip on the guillotine. He looked down at the pleading knight, then back to Sebastian.

Seb met his gaze and dropped to his knees. 'Please...' he begged, clawing at the sand with trembling mitts, allowing it to escape through his fingers. Sebastian looked back up with a sniff, meeting Darius' stare.

The retired hero reluctantly nodded back at Seb.

Seb pushed himself off the cruiser. 'Where?'

'I can't tell you *now*. It'll be here soon - the Crimson Cloud.'

'Then come with us. They won't be able to catch us with our bird.'

'*My* bird.' Brandon grumbled under his breath.

'That won't be an option,' Darius said, stepping towards the air carrier. 'Checked the fuel gauge when we landed. We won't be flying far unless we get some juice in this piece of scrap metal.'

'Then we'll find some fruit and Ariana will do that water trick and we'll have juice.'

'Not that kind of juice, Seb,' Ariana called out from the ship.'

'And I'm still unsure where the blight you crawled out from, but around these parts, fruit isn't exactly growing from the trees.' Darius told Sebastian, scooping up a handful of sand and letting it fall back to the ground.

'Then we'll walk. I don't care what it takes. I'm not-'

'You don't get it, kid. We can't take him with us!'

'Why not?'

'Because he's tagged.' Darius turned and stared down at the Blackmask and golden knight, still quivering on their knees. 'They all are. Blackout has a tracker on everyone that works for them. Even members of their family.' He shook his head and pulled a cigarette from his jacket. 'If we take Brandon we'll be swarming with these masked bugs before daybreak.'

'You can't just tell me?' Sebastian dropped to his knees and grabbed Brandon by the shoulders.

'It would take all day trying to explain it,' Brandon answered, laughing to himself. 'And a lifetime to understand.'

'I don't trust him,' Ariana said, leaning out of the ship. 'Let's just kill these Blackout creeps and get out of here. I'm hungry.'

'Food does sound good,' Darius said, picking up his sword.

'Platto!' Brandon yelled. 'I'll tell the others back on the cloud that you escaped and then I'll meet you at Platto. From there, I'll lead you back to your people. Your home.'

'You got some nerve even naming that place.' Darius raised Xerxes high above his head.

'Wait!' Ariana called, jumping from the ship. 'Whatever you decide to do with this creep, we're going to Platto. Seb needs to find his people. That will be the best place to start.' She shrugged and turned towards tall shadows looming on the horizon. 'And maybe you'll find something too.'

Darius gazed along with her, his mammoth sword finally growing heavy as he dropped it to the sand. 'You're lucky I'm a sucker for some intrigue,' he said, turning to Brandon. 'I'll let you live. For now.' Darius returned his sword to the resting place on his back. 'But I'll need more than the kid's people. I want to know your game in all of this - why Blackout is involved with some lost brat.

'Oh, thank you, thank you, thank you,' Brandon said, bowing down to kiss Darius' boots.

Darius backed away, gesturing for Sebastian to return to the ship. 'And if I don't find you in Platto, you better hope I *don't* find you.'

They had landed somewhere new, a place where the sand gave way to fields of scorched earth and rocky hills. Hidden within the cracked cliffs lay a black forest. They disembarked the ship and silently set up camp. Darius dismantled the metal bird and used the exterior for shelter. Ariana danced, conjuring water from the ether, filling makeshift containers for the journey. Sebastian sat upon the black dirt, watching her. He was unable to focus clearly. His vision blurred and fell upon the black brittle trees surrounding him. They were like sculpted, frozen ash, too afraid to blow away into the next life. Sebastian clawed at the dead soil and squeezed it into a pitiful clump.

'What are you doing?' Darius asked.

Seb didn't answer. His hearing had not returned. His sight and touch were still coming to terms with this new world. Maybe his other senses were too afraid to return after-

'Hey, kid,' Darius said, nudging Sebastian with his foot.

'What?' Seb asked, returning to his false reality.

'I don't care how special you are. We all work.'

'Leave me alone.' Seb answered, wilting to the ground.

'Leave *you* alone?' Darius asked, stepping back. 'Leave *you* alone! If you had just left *me* alone, none of this would have happened!' He picked Sebastian up by the collar and shoved him against the metal shelter.

'I'm... going to go somewhere,' Ariana said aloud, no longer feeling inclined to dance. 'Food!' She exclaimed, 'I'll kill us some food.'

Darius waited as Ariana drifted into the woods, all the while glaring menacingly at Sebastian. Once she was gone, he finally spoke. 'Do you know how many lives back there were ruined because of you?'

An invisible force struck Sebastian. His lungs tightened and constricted. He thought back to all those men, women and even children in the hidden village. Seb started trembling when the image of the drunken patron who bled out at the Oasis flashed in his mind. He then thought of what would happen to all of those poor souls.

'I'll be surprised if that place is still standing,' Darius continued, pacing over the decayed soil. 'It was the only home I knew since giving up on the mercenary life. Now it's gone, and I'm back to fighting for some lost cause.' Darius dropped Seb to the floor and walked away, removing his giant knife from the holster on his back. He sat on the ground and rested it upon his crossed legs. 'I should have stayed there to help them,' Darius slowly turned to look at Sebastian, 'but instead, I forfeited all their lives for some brat who can't even pull his weight around camp.'

'I'm sorry...' Sebastian uttered, trembling gently, eyes fixated on the dirt beneath him.

'It was my decision.' Darius sighed, sheathing his blade into the earth and using it to pull himself off the floor, 'I might as well have tied the noose around their necks myself.'

'Darius... I...'

'Get some wood for burning. We'll speak no more of this.'

Sebastian shot up and ran into the ashen woods. He frantically collected the black sticks that almost crumbled to dust in his hands. Seb wiped his face of all the tears that were flowing uncontrollably, covering himself in soot. His weak moans of anguish echoed all around him as he ran further into the forest devoid of life. Sebastian collapsed, curled himself into a ball and allowed his fractured mind to escape its torment, bleeding back into the white abyss that brought him here.

5.

Black Void

When he opened his eyes, Sebastian was no longer surrounded by the ashen trees and brittle dirt. Instead, he gazed upon pillowy, empty nothing. He lifted a hand in front of his face and watched as it squeezed into a fist and pounded at the non-existent ground. Like the ghostly reverb of a hollow drum, an echoing thump bounced around the white void, changing pitch as it returned. With the sound came particles exploding into the ether around him. Colourful wisps of paint planted themselves into the canvas and sprouted into tall thick trees, expanding and multiplying in mere moments. Sebastian jumped to his feet as vines slithered along the ground. Thorny bushes grew, brown bogs formed, and a plethora of insects along with them. Then the mist drifted in, hiding it all.

The painting was complete, and Sebastian knew where he was. It was *Moth Forest*, named after its most prominent residents. If there was one place Sebastian hadn't missed, it was here. Seb couldn't yawn in this foul forest without swallowing a bug or two. Worst of all, he could hardly see his own feet through the fog. He never knew if he was walking into a hive, a nest, or even a lake filled with leeches. Because of this, he would always take it slow when coming here - or better yet, avoid the place entirely. He inched deeper into the mist, swatting away any insect that dared make him flinch.

'...You have to give me more time...'

The light distorted. The thick paint dried and cracked, peeling as the words drifted through the fog. Sebastian slowly turned and looked ahead. The crevices of each shadow appeared to be staring with their many faces.

'...There is no way I can prepare for something this big on such short notice...'

The voice spoke once more. The colours of the forest began to fade. Seb's neck snapped straight. He pushed further into the fog, sweeping a vine from view. His eyes lit up.

'...If there is no other choice, then I will do my duty...'

He could see so clearly as if the mist had vanished. Some radiant light engulfed the clearing and within the whiteness knelt a boy. It was Alex. His blonde hair sparked gold from the intense light as he knelt before a transcending glow, fist over his chest and head bowed. It was more than light. It was energy - limitless, unrelenting power. It surpassed Sebastian's eyes and drilled straight into his skull. He screamed and fell backwards, clambering as he fled through the forest.

'...Who's there?...'

Alex's roar echoed through the trees as Sebastian leapt blindly through the bogs and bushes. Thorns tore into his clothes, scathing his skin. He kept running, never stopping to turn back. Moth Forest began to disintegrate. The vines reached and wrapped around his legs, the mist began to rise, and finally, he collided with a mighty oak. His head stung. A chime resonated that seemed to stop time altogether. The forest fell into dust before dispersing entirely. A shadow loomed above him. It sighed and simply said.

'...Seb...'

Sebastian reached up to touch the shadow, but it soon faded along with the forest, leaving him engulfed in the empty chasm. Seb floated for some time. Chaotic energy filtered through like a storm on the horizon and with it came seismic words.

'...*A world wrapped within the darkness. Is it everything you ever dreamed?*'

The grinning creature had appeared before Sebastian, staring with two newly formed bulbous eyes to match its unsettlingly wide mouth. Black pupils darted around the void, seemingly seeing everything within the nothingness. Sebastian recoiled at the otherworldly creature, and without thinking, his thoughts spilt out of his mouth.

'What are you?' he asked.

'...I am the light that eradicates the bile, the blackness that sleeps within you...'

'I don't understand.' Seb drifted backwards as a sharp pain pulsed through his mind. He opened his eyes, fearing his vision would never return. All around him was a lifeless white fog. He reached out and saw his arm cut right through it. 'Just... mist?' Sebastian breathlessly laughed to himself, thankful his sight hadn't failed him. Less thankful when he remembered he was still in Moth Forest.

'You're awake, then,' came a familiar voice from above the haze.

Sebastian tried picking himself up, but the weight of his head brought him back to the ground with a thud.

'Easy there, Seb. You need to stay put. That's a nasty bump you've gone and gotten yourself.'

'Alex, what happened?'

'What happened was you running around like a lunatic. You're lucky that it was just a tree that stopped you,' he said, his lips creasing into a smirk.

'No. I mean, what were you doing out here? What was that light?'

'Light? I don't know what you're... you must mean the fireflies that migrated here. There's a whole nest of them further south.'

'But that glow. It was incredible. You were talking to it.'

'Seb, you have to rest. You're not making any sense.'

Sebastian's head was spinning. He could hear his words coming out as a jumbled mess. Listening to himself, he sounded delirious - insane, even. But that's what Sebastian saw. He was positive. It had only been moments since he had fallen and yet it felt like days had passed. It was as if he had been someplace else. A place past the mountains.

They sat for a time, with Alex telling a tale of how he came close to snagging a deer. All the while, Sebastian fought off the insects nesting in his clothes. Soon he was able to stand. Alex put Sebastian's arm over his shoulder and began dragging him out of the cursed forest with ease.

'What is it with Moth Forest, Alex?' Sebastian groaned. 'Why spend all your time here?'

'I thought I told you not to call it that,' Alex said with a faint chuckle. 'It's just a good place to clear my head.'

'Well, your head must be empty at this point.'

'Look, Seb, I know you hate this place. Everyone back home does.' Alex took a moment to collect his thoughts, scanning the misty wilderness with a careful eye. 'Maybe that's why I like it. This energy. All this life. Don't you think it's astounding that this world can create anything so perfect?'

'You really *are* crazy.' Sebastian joked, swatting another bug off his neck. 'All this life and energy can be wiped off the face of the planet for all I care.'

'Careful what you wish for, Seb. For all we know, this place is the last of its kind. It too will be gone one day, and all the life along with it.' Alex uttered. His tone as serious as usual.

They said no more for the rest of the journey. Soon, the two emerged into the clearing. The campsite was just a stone's throw away and never had it looked so good. Sebastian breathed a sigh of relief before his eyes fell upon the red-headed girl reading by one of the tents.

'You reckon you can walk the rest of the way?' Alex asked.

'Yeah, I think I'm okay,' Sebastian replied. 'Why? You're not heading back in there, are you?'

'I still have to fetch us some dinner, but we can always go hungry tonight, if you prefer.'

Sebastian's stomach made a loud gurgling sound. 'Maybe you could scout around for something, if you want.'

'Besides, you wouldn't want me carrying you back to camp like some lost kid. What would Zara think?' Alex patted Seb hard on the shoulder and started making his way back through the fog.

'Wait, what's that supposed to mean?'

'Figure it out yourself for a change,' Alex's voice called as he descended back into the smoke.

Sebastian continued to stare into the mist long after Alex had disappeared. He brushed himself off, finally turning away from Moth Forest. Sebastian smiled as the open valley embraced him with a warm breeze. The grass was still wet from the night's rain, reflecting the light that caused the meadows, hills, and rivers to glow. His grin grew wider as he spun on his heels. Taking a deep breath, Sebastian closed his eyes. When they opened, his smile was gone. He was staring at those mountains again and the abyssal whiteness lying beyond. Seb sighed and drifted back towards the campsite. Zara was sitting on one of the logs, reading a book. Sebastian collapsed by her side.

'Took you long enough,' she said, keeping her eyes on the page.

'I had some trouble,' he replied, his face in the dirt.

'Did you find Alex?' Her eyes briefly glanced over him.

'Sort of, he was acting like the nature freak again. I swear it's getting worse. I overheard him talking to some fireflies this time.'

'What was he saying to them?' she asked, putting her book down.

'I don't know. Something about needing more time. And he mentioned doing his duty, I think.' Sebastian rubbed his sore head, trying to remember clearly.

'He has been acting strange lately,' she said, her eyes falling to the ground.

'It's Alex. He's always acting strange.'

'You know what I mean, Seb. Honestly, I'm getting worried. There's something he's been hiding from us and I'm starting to think-'

'He'll be okay, Zara. It's just a dumb phase he's going through. He's gonna be back to his old self before we know it.' Sebastian said, getting up off the ground and giving her the most reassuring grin that he could muster.

'Maybe you're right...' She laughed. 'Thanks, Seb. You always know what to say.'

'Let's just forget about it and get the fire started.' He sat down on the log they'd arranged by the fire and gingerly placed his arm around her shoulder. Zara instantly nestled herself into his body and rested her head on his chest.

'So, Sebastian... where's the firewood?' she asked, turning to him, her movement slowing and stopping completely as if she had frozen.

Sebastian leaned in and waved his hand over her face. 'Zara, are you...'

'...You have not experienced loss. There is no such occurrence...'

The ground trembled as the creature spoke, drifting into the campsite as everything else drifted away. Zara's shoulders began to crack and dissolve, becoming a puff of colourful smoke. He fell back as she faded, swiping at the air to reach her. She was gone, along with the campsite and surrounding fields. All that remained was Sebastian and the glowing entity. The white creature made steps towards him. Its limbs made stiff disjointed movements as if encased in hardening cement.

'...Just a twisted ego, telling you that you once owned a thing...'

Sebastian crawled away, distancing himself from the creature. With each new word that formed from the glowing thing's mouth, the void stretched and bent in on itself, sending shock waves up Seb's spine.

'...Something you can control...'

The white being gained momentum, breaking into a frenzied sprint. Sebastian got up and ran. The void vibrated and began breaking around him. He could hear the glowing one's voice grow louder, as it closed the distance between them.

'...It is all just a myth...'

It grew closer…

'...A brittle construct based on illusions of fear and power…'

And closer…

'...Two ideological ideas that cling to a primal lust for survival...'

Sebastian could feel himself slowing down, unsure if he was ever moving at all. He felt the cold breath of the entity on the nape of his neck. He closed his eyes, bracing himself.

'...You don't know loss...'

And then, it was gone. Seb cautiously opened his eyes, discovering that the void of light had become submerged into complete and utter shadow. Black and oily, a bubbling gooey substance enveloped the realm. Sebastian began to walk within the darkness, desperate to find a way back.

'...But it knows you...'

Something had caught his leg. He looked down to see that the black bile he walked upon began creeping up his ankle. He shook it off, following a flickering light in the distance. It was their campfire. It had been burning for some time.

Zara had convinced Sebastian to return to Moth Forest so he could scavenge some twigs and branches. When he returned with what he had found, she sighed and began chopping at one of the logs she had collected earlier with her axe. Before long, they had a roaring fire, and just in time for the sun to start setting. All they had to do was wait for Alex to arrive with dinner.

But he didn't return.

It had been hours since Sebastian had last seen him, and the night had been at its darkest for some time. Something had to be wrong. They both knew, but neither of them dared say anything, hoping that he would join them eventually and fearing that he wouldn't show up at all. The hunger soon began to play with Sebastian's mind. The glow of the fire reminded him of that light - the unnatural glow Alex spoke with.

It was all so wrong.

'Where is he?' Zara asked, finally breaking the silence.

Seb didn't answer. He figured she wasn't truly asking him. Any response he could give wouldn't satisfy her, anyhow.

More time passed, and the foundations of the fire had become a blanket of embers. The flames were beginning to grow faint, fighting against the harsh winds.

'It's dying...' Zara spoke in a tone as sombre as her words.

Sebastian leaned over to pick up some branches and threw them in the glowing pyre. His face began to crack from the heat of the fire, his eyes ached from the smoke. But he didn't avert his gaze. The faint glow reminded him of what had happened in the forest. Sebastian tried fighting back against these dark thoughts, but it only made them grow and fester.

Finally, Zara turned around and looked out towards the forest. 'What are we going to do? I can't just sit here anymore.'

'I knew I should've gone back with him,' Sebastian muttered to himself, poking at the fire with a stick.

'We have to look for him. He could've gotten lost or...' Zara trailed off and pushed herself to her feet. After scanning the black woods, she began pacing restlessly between the fire and her tent.

Sebastian looked up at her. Half of Zara's face was illuminated by the fire's glow. Her constant cheerful smile was gone, her rose-coloured lips had become pale and lifeless. Zara's vibrant flowing red hair was tangled. Even her eyes which had always burned with hope were now as dim as the fire they reflected.

'Stay here,' he told her with a groan, standing and turning towards the forest.

'Where do you think you're going?' Zara snapped at him, her voice trembling.

'Where do you think? I'm going to find Alex. I'm sick of waiting around.' Sebastian took a few steps into the darkness when he heard something scurry behind him. Small arms wrapped tightly around his chest.

'Please stay...' Zara begged, her tears soaking the back of his shirt. 'Don't leave me alone out here.'

Sebastian stood silently for a moment before turning and embracing her. He felt her shudder in his arms and pulled her closer. Zara slowly fluttered her eyelids, illuminating the blues in her iris all the more as she moved her face closer to his. Sebastian leaned back, before edging his lips towards hers.

'...All you've ever had was the dirt you stand on...'

Zara unravelled the moment their lips touched. He held her shoulders tight pulling her towards him as she crumbled to dust and scattered throughout the darkness. His hands curled into claws and shook violently as he watched her drift away.

65

'...My dirt...'

The muck gripped at his ankle as if it had become alive and desperate. He pulled his foot loose and noticed the other being swallowed. Sebastian broke free and ran through the black void, or tried to, at least. Sebastian's pace slowed but was still enough to escape the oily abyss. In the distance was another light. It was only a flicker, but it gave him hope. He rushed towards it, reaching out his arm.

'...Give it back to me...'

As the light grew brighter, it became a glimpse of his old life. He could see them - Zara, Alex and himself. The sun shone over the valley, and even Moth Forest looked vibrant from where the three had camped. White tufts of clouds drifted high over their heads and elegantly scraped across the mountains in the distance. Red robins glided with the wind towards the village. Seb and his friends followed them home. Back to their dull, unimportant lives. Past the foothills and cobblestone paths, they travelled. Zara and Sebastian told jokes and shared rumours. Alex walked ahead of them, silent as usual.

'...Still, you could have helped out this once...'

'Zara!' he called out, still running, eyes closed, tears escaping. No matter how much he pushed himself further, he couldn't catch up to them. The world he glimpsed was one without sound. There were no trickles made by the river's stream or the chirping of the birds above. He could see his own lips moving, but his words were silent. The only voice was hers.

'...I've watched you gaze at those mountains for years now...'

'Where are you?'

'...Don't you ever get bored of it?'

'I promise I'll find you again.'

'...Maybe one day, we can all leave together...'

'Together...' Sebastian repeated her last word, slowing to a stop. He dropped to his knees, allowing the black ooze to finally take hold of his legs. The ghosts of his past continued walking, leaving him alone in the darkness. 'We... were meant to leave together.' Seb reached up to find colourful smoke filling the black sky. The vibrant cloud began to form into her. The bile had reached his stomach now, climbing higher. Sebastian simply stared at her. She turned to him with a smile and held out her hand.

The bile was climbing up his chin, creeping towards his mouth. He had stopped struggling. His last moments were spent looking into those cerulean eyes. Sebastian breathed deeply and gave the most reassuring grin he could muster. 'Don't worry, Zara. I'll find you,' he told her, as the inky liquid filled his lungs, pulling him back through the void. Sebastian hoped that this time it would send him home.

6.

Ariana's Dance

Sebastian sensed himself drifting back from the void. He was greeted by the cool breeze nipping at his skin, merging with the warmth of a crackling fire close by. Seb opened his eyes and saw Ariana sitting alone with the flames. She was staring at the warm glow, lost in thought and scratching pitifully at the dead dirt beneath her, rubbing the black soil between her fingertips. She ran one of those fingers elegantly across her cheek, along her scar. Shaking her head as she threw another ashen stick into the pyre.

'You're awake,' she said, still watching the fire.

'I guess so,' he said, checking his hands for any signs of black bile.

'You must be cold.'

'It is nippy.' Seb removed the sheet that covered him. 'It almost feels like...' Sebastian looked down to find he wasn't wearing any clothes. He made a high-pitched yelp and covered himself with the quilt. 'Ariana?'

'Seb?'

'Why am I naked?'

She burst into laughter at the question, turning towards him with a sly grin. 'Your clothes were filthier than the ground we're sleeping on.' She pointed at a metal pipe from the ship lodged between two brittle trees where his tattered clothes were hanging. 'I thought I might as well clean your gear while I cooked dinner, but don't think for a second that this makes me your personal maid.'

'I didn't. I mean, I don't. But does that mean... did you undress me?'

'Would you have preferred if Darius did the honours?'

'No!' Sebastian said, falling backwards, managing somehow to maintain his cover.

'Don't worry, Seb. I didn't see anything.'

'Oh. Well, that's good.'

'Nothing I haven't seen before, at least.'

Sebastian felt the heat of embarrassment wash over his cheeks as he glanced over at his clothes drifting in the breeze. 'Are they dry yet?' he asked.

'Not gonna be ready 'til morning, I'm afraid.'

Sebastian sighed and made his way towards the fire, wrapping the cover around himself. He sat by her side and warmed his hands by the flames. 'So, where's Darius?'

'He wanted to be left alone, figured as much after what happened.'

'Yeah.' Sebastian sighed pitifully, looking up at the pale white moon that hung heavy in the night sky. His eyes lit up, mesmerised by what hung before him. 'Two moons?' he asked, gazing as if caught in a trance.

'You really aren't from around here, are you?' Ariana shook her head. 'The larger one is Etheria. Endura's trapped in its orbit, so we're always facing one another. People on the other side of the planet probably don't even know it exists. You really from that far out?'

'I must be,' Seb replied staring up at the giant moon, almost feeling its heat. 'You have two suns and two moons. Is there anything else I should know?'

'Two moons. One sun. Etheria is so bright that we even see it during the day.'

'Then what's Endura?'

Ariana rolled her eyes with a playful groan. 'Dummy, you're sitting on it. Seriously, how have you made it this far through life without knowing the name of the planet?

'We called it Lora. As far as anyone back home was concerned, the world was no wider than the village itself. Nobody thought anything existed past the mountains. Or rather, nobody cared enough to find out.'

'Well, you found out.'

'Not by choice.'

'Like anything we do is by choice.'

'It's funny, but it feels like I've lived more since waking in the wastes than in all my years back in Lora. Life was dull. You would go to school, get older and work in the town or farms, get older still and retire. Everything had been planned out.' Sebastian looked up at the night sky and exhaled. 'Not knowing where I'm going to wake up tomorrow is scary. But still, I've never felt more free.' Seb closed his eyes and smiled to himself. The air was thick, yet calming. He breathed deeply and heard cracking branches beneath the flames calling out across the still trees.

'So, who's Zara?' Ariana asked, turning towards him with a wink.

Sebastian's eyes snapped open at the sound of her name. 'How did you-'

'You were calling out to her in your sleep. She sounded mighty important.'

'She's a friend,' he answered quickly, shifting away from her.

'You two must have been close,' Ariana said, turning her attention back to the fire.

'We were... I mean, we are,' he said, staring back at the larger moon of Etheria.

'You think she's still alive?'

'I know she is. She has to be.'

'So, you don't know for sure?'

'She's alive,' Sebastian snapped, turning away from her, arms folded.

Ariana fell silent and placed another branch in the fire, then resumed fidgeting with the soil beneath her.

'Look, I don't know.' Seb breathed, turning back to face her. 'Even if she is out there somewhere. Who's to say I'll ever find her, or anyone else from back home.' He wiped a bitter tear from his cheek and clawed at the dirt with her.

'I lost someone too,' Ariana said.

Seb stopped playing with the decayed earth. 'I figured as much. You said you lost your home too.'

'It wasn't lost. It was taken. Besides, what I'm talking about happened later. I lost someone like your Zara.'

'What happened?'

'He saved my life, and ended up getting himself killed in the process,' Ariana said, her voice breaking slightly. She leaned into his chest and wrapped her arms around his shoulders, shuddering against him. 'He was such an idiot,' she said, almost laughing. 'Sacrificing himself, like he was doing *me* the favour.'

Seb cloaked the blanket around the girl, feeling her tears on his neck. And without realising, his eyes began to well up also. It felt good. Like all of the hate and pain inside him was finally being washed away. They sat and wept together, holding each other in a warm embrace. When their tears ran dry, Ariana started giggling to herself.

'What's so funny?' Seb asked, still sniffing.

'You know you're still naked under this blanket, right?'

Sebastian looked down, realising the blanket wrapped itself around them both. His face turned red as he felt the blood escaping where her hands were placed and rushing towards his cheeks. 'I do now!'

'How about I close my eyes and get up, so you can keep your... *dignity.*' Ariana said, trying her hardest not to burst into laughter. She closed her eyes but still held the grin on her face.

Sebastian waited for her to stand, then immediately wrapped himself up tightly within the blanket.

'Everybody decent?' Ariana asked, covering her hands over her face.

'Well, I know I am, at least.'

'Ha, ha,' she said, removing her hands and sitting back beside him. She smiled and nestled herself into him. Seb smiled back, placing his arm around her shoulder.

'Ariana...' Seb breathed, shifting his body awkwardly. 'I want to thank you for saving me out in that desert. If you hadn't come along-'

'Don't mention it,' she said, sitting poised but still managing a shrug.

Sebastian could see her cheeks redden a little. 'I'm serious. I wouldn't be alive without you.'

'And I'm serious too, shut up about it,' she snapped playfully at him, jabbing Seb with her finger.

They both laughed, shoving each other into the dirt. Eventually, Ariana gave her arm a quick swirl, and a ball of water fell from the sky, splashing onto Seb's head.

'Okay, you have to tell me how you do that,' Seb pouted, shaking himself off.

'You really want to know?'

'I really do.'

'Then I guess class is in session,' she said, narrowing her eyes. Ariana stood up and began circling the fire, keeping her eyes fixed on Sebastian. 'The art of water stirring isn't magic. Although, I guess that depends on who you ask.' She began swaying with the breeze, looking into the sky. 'It's the process of changing the very atoms around us and bending them to our will.'

'What are atoms?' Sebastian asked, tilting his head.

'Seriously?' Ariana dropped her arms. 'You really are clueless. They're the tiny molecules that make up everything. Even your body is filled with billions of the tiny buggers.'

'Gross,' he said, wiping his arms over himself. 'How do we get rid of them?'

'You don't get rid of them,' Ariana said with a smile, shaking her head. You *are* them.' Ariana pointed towards the fire. 'These flames.' She spread her arms out. 'All these trees and the soil beneath them.' She spun around on her heels. 'Everything on the planet, even the air we breathe, is created by these particles.'

'And... you control them?' Seb asked, leaning back, eyes wide.

'I *use* them,' she corrected, 'hence the term, User. That's what we call ourselves.'

'There are more of you?'

'Loads more.' She laughed. 'Some can summon fire instead of water, others can form stone and even metals from out of the ground. There's even a few who can harness the power of lightning and use it to eradicate their foes.'

'People do that?'

'Or they power their homes with it, so they don't have to pay the electric bill,' she shrugged, scratching the shaved sides of her head.

'Well, sign me up! How do I become a User?' Sebastian asked, jumping to his feet, forgetting about the blanket yet again. It fell to the ground, forcing Ariana to stifle a cough and look away.

'I think your clothes are probably dry now,' she told him.

After Sebastian had gotten dressed, he saw that Ariana was still sitting by the fire, she yawned into a fist and grabbed more branches to feed the hungry flames. The sun had started to rise on the horizon, turning the black sky a pinkish hue. As Seb watched the smaller moon disappear into the light of a new day, he thought that they could probably do with some sleep. But he was too eager to learn more about Ariana's abilities, and he couldn't help but keep asking her questions.

'Can you teach me some magic? I've always wanted to shoot lasers from my hands.'

'Not without giving you years of training,' Ariana sighed. 'And stop calling it magic!'

'Okay, okay. So, how does it actually work?'

'I'll show you,' Ariana answered, giving him her hand.

He squeezed it tightly and pulled her from the log, Ariana nodded at him and once again, she circled the fire.

'Atoms can be manipulated. Changed into anything of one's choosing; however, what one chooses can take a lifetime to learn.' Ariana began to dance rhythmically as streams of a transparent liquid filled the air. 'I chose water.'

The flowing liquid swam elegantly across the campsite, surrounding the two of them. Seb turned slowly, in awe of the orbs of liquid. He held out a hand, letting it brush through one of the streams, feeling the cold, fresh chill as his arm became submerged.

'This is incredible,' he said, gazing towards her.

Ariana smiled back, but Seb could see how hard she was concentrating. Ariana bit her lip with some force, and beads of sweat trickled down her brow. Her glistening eyes stared hard at the air around her as if solving a complex puzzle. Sebastian leaned close to her and wrapped his arms around Ariana's body. She stopped, and the floating pools of water fell to the ground with a splash.

'You should get some sleep.'

'Thanks,' Ariana said with a faint laugh, feebly hugging him back.

Her body wilted as she leaned into him, almost collapsing, but Sebastian managed to catch her, helping to walk her back to the broken scrap of debris that was her tent. She got in and grabbed his hand before he could leave.

'Goodnight, Sebastian, I had a really good time with you tonight.'

'Goodnight, Ariana.' He grinned back.

'Man, I needed that!' a gruff voice boomed, shaking the trees.

Sebastian and Ariana turned to see Darius emerging from the metal hut that he had made for himself. He stretched, clearing his throat and spitting out what had come up. He then proceeded to the fire and warmed his hands before unzipping his fly to excrete his own waters upon the campsite. Seb and Ariana slowly looked back at each other as Darius began whistling a tune.

'Oh good, you're awake,' he said, turning towards them and zipping himself up.

'Actually, we're-' Seb began to say.

'Glad you two understand the strict deadline we're under,' Darius interrupted, pacing the campsite. 'We've given 'em the slip for now, but soon enough they'll find this place. So, let's eat and get back on the road.'

Ariana sighed and gave Sebastian her hand. He held it tight, pulling her back out of the metal tent. The three then ate the broth that Ariana had made.

'Where did you get the meat from?' Seb asked, mouth still full.

'You don't want to know,' she answered with a shudder.

Sebastian put his bowl down, only to have Darius scoop it up and pour the leftovers into his own.

'So, Darius,' Ariana asked, 'want to tell us the story about you and the golden boy from Blackout?'

Darius furled his brows but continued his meal.

'Figured as much.' She sighed, taking another bite of the grey meat.

After dismantling the campsite, the three traversed through the ashen forest. When they had finally reached the clearing, Sebastian could make out giant towers in the distance. There were hundreds of them, all touching the sky, their tips hidden within silver clouds.

'What is that?' Sebastian asked, gazing up at the horizon.

'That's Platto, kid,' Darius answered with a smirk. 'That's where we're going.'

7.

Platto

The three had walked for miles through the cracked rocky terrain. Holes and canyons littered the landscape, along with the remains of buildings and roads left broken. Sebastian looked ahead towards the tall towers in the distance. It helped to focus on something other than the remnants of this forgotten world. Many creatures lurked within the wreckage of stone, steel and broken earth - watching with their many eyes. The others seemed unphased by it all, although Seb did notice Darius' hand lightly gripping the hilt of his blade for the entire journey.

'What are they? Seb asked, his eyes fixed on these scaly-skinned creatures.

'Surphites,' Ariana answered, keeping her view on the road ahead. 'If we keep our distance, they're harmless.'

'Harmless, my arse,' Darius said with a grunt, glancing at them. 'Those good-for-nothing demons will tear you limb from limb if you give 'em a chance. Best stay weary, kid.'

'And it's that kind of prejudice why we have to keep our distance.' Ariana shook her head with a sigh. 'Humanity hates the Suphites. And in turn, they hate us. It's a never-ending cycle that will always keep us separated.'

'You almost sound sweet on them lizards.'

'Don't call them that!' Ariana spun around, throwing her arms down. 'They're people. Just like us. They shouldn't be treated any less just because they're different.'

'Treated any less? Girly, you don't know what you're talking about. I've seen first-hand what those things do to people. Best stop showing them compassion. Cause they've got none for you.'

Ariana stared Darius down, her hands clenched into fists. They had all stopped. Seb turned to see the unbending glare in Darius' eyes, then towards the trembling Ariana. He stepped forward and placed a hand on her shoulder. As soon as he touched her, she turned back around and continued walking.

The heat brought with it a stagnant air, forbidding them a breeze. Sebastian was thankful to have Ariana there, not only because she was providing water for the trek, but she was also bringing some much-needed conversation.

'So, how long have you been a User?' Sebastian asked.

'About... ten years?' She replied, unsure.

'Impressive,' Darius said with a whistle, 'I knew some who had been channelling their abilities for decades, and none of 'em was half as good as you.'

'Well, what can I say, I'm a natural,' Ariana said, grinning back at Darius. But Seb noticed the smile fading as she turned back, leaving only that determined look in her eyes.

'Are there any other elite, master Users, or is it just you with that title?' Seb asked, giving her a nudge with his elbow.

'Let's see now...' Ariana mused, pressing a finger and a thumb to her chin as she puckered her lips. 'Well, there was Bella "Barrage" Doverty, a Fire User who could engulf an entire village in flames with the snap of her fingers.' She instantly clicked her own in Seb's face.

He flinched, before timidly laughing it off.

'Heard she could summon volcanoes beneath her enemies, roasting 'em like chickens. Hell hath no fury, huh?' Darius chimed as he lit a cigarette.

'And there was also Buano "The Rock" Crane, Master strategist and Earth User. There are still fortresses made from stone that he built with his own two hands. I've actually slept in one.' Ariana said, starting to skip when she remembered the memory.

'You're not wrong about the master strategist thing either.' Darius agreed, scratching at his unmanaged beard. 'The man had a real knack for battle.'

'That's right, I forgot you knew the Rock!' Ariana yelled, stopping instantly and jumping to face him.

'Knew him? Girly, we were comrades. The man practically taught me all I know.'

'He must have been an incredible teacher,' she said, smiling weakly. Ariana turned around and began walking, enthralled as Darius recounted past war stories with her.

'I don't get it. So, where are they now?' Seb asked.

Ariana stopped before looking back over her shoulder at him. 'They're dead, Sebastian.' She huffed and marched away at a quick pace, leaving Seb to trail behind.

Darius slowed down and leaned forward to match his height. 'Didn't know you were such a hit with the ladies, kid,' he said before picking up his stride.

By their next break, Ariana had forgotten about the incident and was laughing with Sebastian as if nothing had happened. She talked at length about all of the different Users with him. Seb smiled, watching as she eagerly asked Darius about his past glories, which seemed to make Darius happy for a time. The bitter silence would have been excruciating without her, as Sebastian dared not say a word to the grizzled warrior. Their brush at camp was still fresh in his mind, and judging by how Darius wouldn't even look at him, he assumed the retired hero felt the same.

The closer they got to the massive city, the more Sebastian became enamoured with the place. He could make out flying ships swooping in and out of the metallic structures. He ran past Darius and Ariana, eager to see more. He stopped when noticing vacant buildings before him. The roads were left broken, and the homes had crumbled to the ground. Pieces of the past had been left scattered throughout the desolate streets.

'Move it, kid. We ain't got all day,' Darius said as he shoved ahead.

'Is that a town?' Seb asked.

'Used to be,' Ariana answered, joining him. 'Now it's just a reminder of the cruelty that-'

Sebastian dropped his bag and rushed closer. Debris littered the soot-covered streets. Shards of glass gathered around the burnt buildings.

'Where the blight are you going, Seb?' He could hear her calling, but he didn't answer. Sebastian continued running, with fossilised wood crunching beneath his feet. Eventually, he came across a crumbled building. The exterior had all but worn away. Inside were people. Or rather, their remains. Though stained in ash, the white of their bones shone through. Someone cradling another in their arms. Sebastian dropped to his knees and held his head to the ground. Who were they? A parent sheltering their child? A teacher trying to save a student? Perhaps a stranger simply trying to help another. Whoever they were, they had failed. A hot sting filled Seb's face as salty tears swelled his eyes.

'You couldn't protect her…' he growled into the concrete. 'You couldn't do anything!' He pounded a fist into the rubble. 'What good are you?'

'Seb!' Ariana yelled as she caught up to him, 'Hasn't anyone ever told you not to enter the dead zones? These places are…' Her words caught in her throat. Seb knew she had finally seen what he had. 'Oh gods, no.'

After a few moments of silence, with only the haunting wind behind them, large footsteps grew louder with the grumblings of a retired hero.

'We shouldn't be here,' Darius said, wearily watching their surroundings, his fingers wrapped tightly around the hilt of the sword on his back. 'Mass graves such as this are no place for the living.'

'Darius.' Ariana turned towards him and swiped her hand across her neck as she gestured at Sebastian. 'This isn't the time.'

'What's wrong, kid? You ain't ever seen death before?'

'No,' Seb answered, lifting his head to gaze upon the mummified souls before him. 'Nothing like this.'

'Well, get used to it. The corpses scattered around here are as plentiful as the rocks. There's no hiding from it.'

'Can't you see this isn't what he needs to hear right now?' Ariana asked through gritted teeth.

'He's gonna have to hear it sometime, girly. I don't know where he came from to be this green. But it ain't gonna work out here. Not with me.'

'I give up. I'm heading back to the road. Meet me back there when you're ready. Okay, Seb?' She placed a hand on his shoulder.

As she left, Darius sighed and reached into his jacket for a cigarette. Lighting it, he turned to leave.

'Darius?' Seb asked, still staring at the two souls gripped together for eternity.

The bearded giant turned back and answered with a huff.

'All this. Is the same thing going to happen to your village?'

The giant sighed. 'This kind of thing happens everywhere. The sooner you accept that the sooner you'll-'

'It's all my fault,' Seb told himself, his fists shaking on the ground. 'I shouldn't have been there. It would have been better if I'd just been left scattered out there with the rocks.'

'Listen, kid.' Darius sighed and took a long drag of his cigarette. 'What happened back there wasn't your fault. I said some things at camp that I'm not proud of. Whatever fate befalls those people can't be helped now. We just have to keep moving forward.'

'What if more people get hurt?'

'More people *will* get hurt. Regardless of what you do. It's gonna happen. Your choice is to fight or hide. People will die no matter what you choose.'

'Then what does it matter?'

'It doesn't,' Darius told him, blowing out smoke as he flicked the butt into the air. It landed between Sebastian and the clutching statues. 'Nothing changes. The loudmouthed girl back there doesn't get it. But you do, at least. Your actions depend on one simple question.'

Sebastian turned to face the retired hero.

'Don't look at me. Look at them.'

Seb did as he was told, looking back at the poor unfortunate bodies as they cradled one another.

'Does it make you angry?'

Sebastian's fists tightened. 'Yeah. It does.'

'Are you going to punish those who caused this?'

Seb's eyes widened and he turned back around, catching the old warrior's eye.

'Well? Are you?' Darius asked.

'No…' Seb answered, pushing himself to his feet. 'But I'm not going to stand by and watch it happen.' He stood up and made his way back through the desolate streets. 'If I can save one person. I would have changed something.'

Darius smirked and patted the boy on the shoulder as he passed. 'Is that right? Well, I can't wait to see it. Lead the way, Hero.'

Sebastian gritted his teeth when the large mitt landed on his shoulder. He wanted to scream at the giant. But instead, he sniffed, his vision muffled through the tears.

'What I want to know is why they came for you in the first place,' Darius yelled, 'you got something you're not telling us?'

Sebastian stopped and turned around. Darius was staring at him with arms folded and a questionable look on his face.

'It's because he survived,' Ariana answered, stepping out from a dilapidated building. 'Blackout doesn't like to leave witnesses. I should know.'

'I thought you were back on the road,' Darius said.

'What? And leave you two together? I don't think so.'

'Fair point. I think it's time we took our leave. You ready, kid?'

'Yeah. Let's get out of this place.'

After almost another day, they had finally arrived - the city of Platto. Seb thought the towers were tall from a distance, but as they drew closer, the structures went on seemingly forever, soaring into the sky, their heights challenging the limits of imagination. Sebastian froze with a foolish grin etched on his face. He watched in awe, marvelling at the splendour of the metropolis before him, becoming a little light-headed and losing his footing. The metropolis was encased by sturdy steel walls, gracefully curving along its perimeter and offering only a few small entrances for the ebb and flow of its inhabitants. The sight was nothing short of mesmerizing, leaving Sebastian in a state of enchantment as he contemplated the mysteries concealed within the city's confines.

'You coming in or what?' Ariana yelled, waving her arms near the entrance.

Seb broke free from his thoughts and stepped closer. His feet became bricks as he nervously tried to place one in front of the other.

'Come on, you idiot,' Ariana said, pulling him into the city of Platto.

It was an orchestra of disruption. Market stall traders screamed over one another as poorly-clothed folk stole from their stalls. Some were begging for money and food as the rest of the populace rushed past them. Sebastian couldn't even see the towers anymore, lost in the polluted air, graffiti and flashing lights. The Blackmasks asserted their presence across the cityscape, their disciplined march weaving through bustling bazaars and forming a vigilant presence outside the more pristine, towering structures painted in stark white - a challenge to the defiant graffiti artists of Platto. Amidst their duties, some Blackmasks engaged in harassing the locals and interrupting a group preaching their religion in the street. Seb navigated through the dense crowd to investigate further, discovering that these devout figures were no ordinary individuals. Towering above the ordinary citizens, they bore animal-like faces, their elongated arms nearly brushing against the ground.

'Do not turn away from the light!' One wailed as it was forced to its knees, sounding no different from any ordinary man. 'For he will sculpt a new world from the blackness in which we sleep!'

A Blackout trooper swung around, brandishing their rifle and urging the crowd to disperse. Sebastian needed no more convincing, but as he turned, he realized he had lost sight of Ariana and Darius in the chaotic swarm. The clamour of yelling and the incessant noise melded into a piercing tone, while the neon lights intensified, momentarily blinding him. The frenzied movement of the crowd gradually slowed, coming to a complete standstill. A shrill chime reverberated in his ears, and Sebastian clutched at his chest, struggling for a breath that eluded his gasping lungs. He looked up to see a figure in a hooded white robe navigating the motionless crowd towards him. The stranger's face remained hidden, revealing only their mouth. Though their lips moved, Sebastian was too distant to discern the words being spoken.

'...You can't save her...'

Words appeared in his head like a thought. Sebastian's eyes widened. He had heard that voice before.

'Alex...' Sebastian uttered, reaching towards the robed figure.

Movement flooded back into the crowd. Sebastian was shoved and landed in a puddle. A hand reached out to him from the sea of people, pulling him back to the surface.

'You never forget your first time in Platto,' Ariana said, dusting him off. 'You okay?'

Sebastian turned his head in every direction. But the stranger was gone. He scanned the rabble around him before his frantic eyes found hers, then Ariana's reassuring smile.

'Sorry, I'm not good with crowds,' he answered, faking a laugh and rubbing the back of his neck.

Ariana rolled her eyes and swiftly manoeuvred him through the bustling market plaza. The sights and scents, both captivating and unsettling, competed for Sebastian's attention, yet he remained fixated on the girl leading him through the chaos. It conjured memories of home, remembering how Zara would take his hand and guide him through crowded streets. Ignoring the throng of strangers surrounding him. Sebastian kept his gaze fixed on Ariana's ponytail, bobbing rhythmically as she navigated the turmoil.

Amid the swarm, there emerged an open space. At its centre stood Darius, unaffected by the tide of bodies swarming around him. Like an island amid waves, Darius maintained an aura that deterred anyone from venturing too close, let alone attempting to push past him.

'It's been a while,' Darius said, slowly scanning the area. 'Things have… changed.'

'It's been like this since I can remember,' Ariana told him, reaching up to pat him on the shoulder.

Darius remained silent, his watchful eyes scanning the unfamiliar surroundings. It was evident to Sebastian that the retired hero was just as much a stranger to this place as he was. Sensing the need to navigate away from the bustling crowds, Ariana let out a sigh and took both of them by the arm, guiding them through the labyrinthine alleys.

'Follow me, boys. I know the best place to get some eats around here.' She beckoned them through the nooks and squares, past the housing districts and factories. Before finally stopping at a small cottage, it looked uncanny from the ones back in Lora.

'It can't be,' Darius uttered, looking back at Ariana. 'How did you…'

She shrugged and smiled back at him. Darius grinned like a child and began running towards the small cobblestone home.

'What is this place?' Seb asked her.

'You'll see.' She turned and winked at him, skipping after Darius.

Sebastian hesitated but quickened his pace to catch up with them. As they approached the door, it swung open, revealing an old woman who greeted Ariana with a warm hug, lifting her off the ground. Once the embrace concluded, the elderly woman turned her attention to Darius, offering a kind smile before delivering a slap to his face.

'Where the blight have you been?' she asked, before squeezing the life out of the brute. 'I thought I'd never get to smack that mug again.'

'It's good to see you, V.' Darius looked pained but hugged her back.

'I just knew Ariana would find you,' she told him, squeezing tighter. 'I didn't think she'd actually manage to bring you back though. The girl must be more stubborn than you are.'

'Why didn't you say anything?' Darius asked, turning to Ariana. 'If I knew Viola had sent you, it probably wouldn't have taken much convincing to bring me home.'

'Home?' Seb asked, scratching his head.

'I made the girl promise not to mention me,' the old woman answered, giving him a wink and a jab with her bony elbow. 'Guilt and obligation shouldn't be what drives you. Nor should they be what render you immobile.'

'Forgive me, Viola.' Darius dropped to one knee and bowed his head. 'After everything that happened, I had to leave. I just couldn't bear the thought of-'

'There's nought to forgive, you old fool,' Viola said, throwing her arms around him.

It was funny to see the giant bend so low to embrace this tiny woman. But Seb stopped smirking when he saw a single tear creeping along Darius' cheek.

The old woman opened her eyes and noticed Sebastian staring at the pair. 'Who's your friend?' she asked Darius.

He grunted in response and stepped into the cottage.

'This is Sebastian,' Ariana answered for Darius, grabbing Seb by the arm and bringing him closer. 'Seb, this is Nana Viola.'

'Nice to meet you,' Sebastian said, smiling kindly and extending his hand.

The woman batted his arm away and hugged him hard instead, squeezing the air from his lungs and crunching his bones. 'A bit on the frail side. But I sense *husband* material,' she said with a wry smile and winked wickedly at Ariana.

'Nana,' Ariana huffed, shaking her head.

'Honestly, youth these days. You never know when you've truly found something special, even when it's right in front of you.' Viola seized both of their hands and joined them together.

Sebastian and Ariana, somewhat reluctantly, clasped each other's palms, exchanging hesitant glances. As they averted their eyes, they discovered that Viola had ceased her efforts to unite their hands. Ariana swiftly withdrew hers with a nervous laugh, leaving Sebastian holding his hand out.

'Come. You must be tired,' The old woman said, pulling them both inside.

Stepping into the cottage, Sebastian was immediately embraced by the warmth emanating from a crackling fire in the next room. The interior was surprisingly spacious, despite the appearance from outside. The main living area was adorned with furs and dotted with inviting sofas and chairs. As Sebastian took in the cosy atmosphere, he spotted Darius in a corner, engrossed in a collection of photographs arranged along the walls and mantels.

Sebastian approached, captivated by the glimpses of a younger Darius captured in the photographs, surrounded by people who once filled this room with joy. The images hinted at a happier era in the old hero's life. Darius paused at one particular frame, his fingers delicately tracing the contours of the image before placing it back face-down on the mantle. When Darius turned around, Seb's attention instantly darted towards the flames. He could feel Darius' piercing glare burning into him more than if he were to jump into the fire. Sebastian held his position and waited patiently as the brute left the room.

Once he was alone, Sebastian turned his attention back to the photos covering the wall. He crept closer, looking around to see if he was in the clear. He reached up to the frame that Darius placed facing down and he lifted it, revealing the image within.

'Memories,' A frail voice said, inches behind him.

Startled, Seb threw the picture into the air, and as it descended, he turned to find the old woman wearing a melancholic smile. His eyes followed the frame's fall, and just as it seemed destined to shatter, Nana Viola smoothly extended her hand overhead, catching it with ease. Her gaze remained fixed on Seb as she gracefully moved past him, delicately restoring the picture to its resting place.

'A reflection of one's existence. A tapestry, woven from personal experience.'

'What are you talking about?' Sebastian asked, stepping away from the unsettling woman.

'Ever-changing fragments of data being broken down and reformed to fit one's desires.' Viola turned back to Seb, yet her light brown eyes had become a lifeless white. White like a void Sebastian couldn't scrub from his mind. She raised a trembling finger and placed it swiftly on his forehead.

'Listen, lady. You're starting to scare me.' Seb told her, pushing her hand away.

'Oh!' Viola croaked, quickly shaking her head. She blinked at Sebastian, her eyes returning to their rightful hazel hue. The elderly woman then looked around, bewildered.

'Are you okay?' he asked her.

'Yes, yes. I'm fine. I don't know what came over me just now.'

'Those words. It was like you were there. Did you-'

'Nana, I'm hungry,' Ariana yelled, bursting into the room. 'What's for eats?'

They both turned around, staring wide-eyed at the girl. Viola stepped away from Seb and laughed innocently.

'With all this excitement, I must have forgotten my manners,' the old woman said, bowing elegantly at Ariana.

Ariana curtsied in return, with a cheesy grin on her face.

'Wait,' Seb interrupted, 'Viola, you have to tell me what you were-'

'The girl is hungry. There will be time to discuss such things later. But for now, you need to rest.' The elderly woman ambled towards the kitchen, creating a cacophony with pots and pans clanging around. Seb and Ariana found themselves seated by the fire. Although Sebastian wasn't happy about being left with his questions unanswered but soon perked up when he laid eyes on the feast presented before them. A plump, perfectly cooked bird took centre stage on the table, flanked by a medley of roasted potatoes, a vibrant array of steamed vegetables, and a jug of rich, bubbling brown gravy standing nearby.

'This looks great! I don't know where to start,' Seb said to Viola as she placed his plate in front of him.

'My advice is to start soon. Before these two leave you with the bones.'

Sebastian beamed as he filled his plate, liberally dousing the contents with a generous amount of gravy. He devoured every last morsel, licking the plate clean and wearing his satisfaction on his gravy-streaked face. When he finally lowered the dish, he found himself met with the gaze of Ariana, Darius, and Viola, all wearing a mix of amusement and disbelief.

'That was incredible!' Sebastian yelled, grabbing a glass of juice and guzzling it down. 'I haven't eaten anything this good in years.'

'You two bring this one back with you more often.' Viola chuckled, taking Seb's plate.

'I'll make sure he doesn't disappear.' Ariana smiled at him from across the table.

Darius grunted and poured himself another glass of wine.

After their meal, Viola graciously prepared rooms for the trio. Sebastian ascended the spiral staircase, discovering that the seemingly modest cottage had more rooms than he would have guessed. The bed in his room was perhaps the cosiest Sebastian had ever experienced, yet he resisted the urge to sleep. The words that came out of the mysterious woman's mouth were still lingering in his mind. Just hearing it all again made him feel like he was back in that lifeless void. Sebastian fought against the pull of slumber. However, with the mountain of food resting in his stomach and the lack of sleep from the previous night, Sebastian's eyes grew heavy, drifting into a realm where dreams and nightmares entwined.

8.

Lora

The bridge groaned its familiar creak as Sebastian and Zara strolled across its sturdy planks. Fish leapt from the water, creating ripples as they splashed upon returning. Villagers engaged in various activities - some were casting fishing lines into the radiant lake surrounding Lora, while others swam in the refreshing waters. Sebastian always got a good feeling when returning home like this. It's just what he needed; to see their community through the eyes of an outsider. Although they had been away for just one night, it felt like days since he had last set eyes on the place. Sebastian dropped his bag and ambled towards the edge of the creek beneath the bridge.

'Don't rest yet, Seb,' Zara yelled above him. 'Let's get some food first.'

'...But this place. It's the last time we three will be together...'

The brief whisper vanished almost as quickly as it had emerged. He weighed the pros and cons of hunger versus more walking in his mind and decided that he could do with a cooked meal. Sebastian rose, grappling with the weight of his backpack, and once again, they set out on another arduous journey.

The market plaza was alive with activity. Vendors competed for attention with their boisterous calls, energetic children dashed through the cobblestone streets, and myriad conversations happened all at once. Amidst the bustling symphony, Sebastian often found himself feeling out of place, drifting through the chorus of villagers without making a sound. He weaved through the vibrant tapestry of the crowds, sidestepping the occasional shove and growing increasingly irritated by the overwhelming noise that surrounded him.

Zara seized his hand, guiding him gracefully through the sea of people. As they passed, the village folk would turn with smiles, calling out her name. Sebastian, on the other hand, stumbled through the throng, bumping into villagers and apologising half-heartedly. Once they managed to escape the market, Zara released his hand and skipped over to Avalon Fountain, Lora's centrepiece. Every district of the village interconnected at the marble fountain. Crowning it was a statue of a bald, slender man with large, piercing eyes that gave the illusion that he was always watching. Sebastian stopped and squinted up at the white visage, as he often did.

'...I do miss apples...'

Sebastian skidded back, raising his arms in a defensive stance. He took a moment to steady his breath, shaking his head with a nervous laugh. The bump on his head from Moth Forest must have affected him more than he realised. But still, he couldn't tear his gaze away from the pristine face in the marble. Stepping closer, Sebastian squinted against the sun's glare, only to become momentarily blinded. Shielding his eyes, he traced the source of the reflection to Union Tower.

'...I remember picking them from the trees and biting into them....'

The tower loomed above, a stark contrast to the traditional stone and mortar structures that surrounded it. Crafted from steel and adorned with glass, it boasted an oval shape, standing tall and imposing. Intricate patterns of black and white panels decorated its surface, resembling a massive chessboard in the sky. Sebastian had never ventured inside the tower, nor contemplated its purpose until that moment. It had always been a fixture of Lora, like Avalon Fountain and the enigmatic figure perched atop it. Always present. Always watching.

'...That taste became foul as they withered and rotted from the barren land...'

A low, rumbling voice resonated in Sebastian's ears, but its source remained unknown. Shaking his head to dispel the peculiar sound, he turned his attention to Zara. She was gracefully scooping water from the fountain and delicately splashing it on her face. Sebastian sat down beside her and dropped his bag.

'You not washing, Seb?' she asked, reaching her hands in again.

'I'll clean when I get home. Who knows what's in that water.'

'Thanks for the warning.' Zara laughed, burying her head in wet hands. 'You could do with a wash. You're covered with dirt.'

Gazing into the waters, Sebastian sought his reflection amidst the ripples. His round face had become speckled with muck. Seb's short wavy black hair had turned an ashen grey, littered with dust and cobwebs from his ordeal in Moth Forest and tattered clothes clung to his frail frame. Despite the wear and tear, Sebastian met his own hazel eyes and managed a smile.

'I reckon it's a pretty good look for me. Don't you think?' He turned, giving Zara a wink.

She shook her head and splashed him with water. His reflection rippled away. 'That's much better,' she said.

Sebastian pouted before retaliating with a playful splash. In no time, the two found themselves in an all-out water fight, drawing laughter from onlookers. Village children, undeterred by their mothers' shouts, jumped into the fountain to join the gleeful chaos, their fathers watching with indulgent smiles, shaking their heads at the youthful antics. As the battle subsided, Sebastian and Zara stood sniggering and ringing out their drenched clothes.

'Guess I don't need to wash now,' Seb said, still laughing.

'I'm sure you'll find some way to muddy yourself up before long.'

'Yep, then it's back here for round two. And I won't go easy on you next time.'

'Easy going is all you've got, Seb. I practically live in this fountain. I'll beat you every time.'

'You do spend a lot of time here, don't you?'

'Of course, I do. It's good luck. They say the waters of this fountain are a source of protection.'

'You don't believe in all that stuff, do you?' Sebastian turned away from her as he tipped water from his shoe.

'It's worked for me so far.' She shrugged. 'That's good enough, I guess.'

'Where in Lora have you guys been?' A voice came from the market. The two turned to see Alex, shaking his fist at them. Sharing an awkward glance, they burst into laughter as he walked over. 'What do you two get up to when I'm not around?' Alex asked, looking them up and down.

'We just had a... fountain fight,' Seb answered, averting his eyes and rubbing the back of his neck.

'I won!' Zara squealed.

'That's great news.' Alex smirked, patting Zara on the head as he rolled his eyes. 'Now, can we get some food already?'

'...The fruit we eat has become artificial. It looks the same. Even tastes the same. But there is something about it. Some intangible thing I can't seem to grasp...'

For the remainder of their day in Lora, the trio wandered around the village, eventually finding themselves at their usual hangout spot by the creek under the bridge.

'Looks like it's time to turn in,' Alex said, watching the sun inch behind the mountains.

'What's the hurry? It's not even late,' Seb asked.

'I reckon we're going to need all of our energy for tomorrow. Especially you, Seb.' He glanced over at Sebastian, sprawled across the ground, half asleep.

'What's happening tomorrow?' Seb yawned.

'Honestly, Seb.' Zara shook her head. 'Classes start back up again in the morning.'

'Already? I thought we had two weeks of vacation.'

'We did.' Alex sighed. 'That was a fortnight ago.'

'Well, that's ruined a perfectly good day.' Seb sat up with a stretch. 'Wish it could have lasted longer.'

'Yeah... I wish it could have too,' Alex whispered to himself, watching the last inch of sun creep behind the mountain, shrouding them in shadow.

'...It angers me. It compels me to want the real thing...'

'Well, there's no use crying about it, boys. Who knows, the change might be good for us.' Zara said, patting Alex on the back before skipping towards the top of the bridge, humming to herself.

Sebastian got up with a groan and began to follow.

'Sebastian,' Alex uttered.

Seb stopped and turned to face him. Alex's face was grim - his expression was like that most days. And yet, something about his demeanour seemed different. He stood rigid, still watching where the sun should have been past the mountains.

'What you said before. You were right.' Alex sighed, turning his attention to the lush fields, the serene lakes, and then back to the looming mountains, all growing darker as the seconds passed. 'The outside world may not be perfect, but it has to be better than this.' His eyes glistened, and he turned away.

'What are you talking about?' Sebastian asked, inching closer.

'How could I even explain it to you?' Alex laughed bitterly. 'On some level, you've always known. You've managed to see past it all along.'

'Alex, please. This isn't funny.' Zara yelled, running up beside Sebastian.

Seb tried to say something, anything, but words wouldn't form. Moments creaked by with no sound except the fresh breeze of another dreary, unimportant night in the village.

'I didn't mean for it to end like this. But what does it matter? The outcome will be the same.' Alex breathed, backing away.

'Let's just go,' Seb told Zara. 'It's late, we don't have time for one of his tantrums. Come on, I'll walk you home.'

Zara took a deep breath and nodded.

Sebastian took one last look at Alex. 'Guess we'll see you tomorrow.'

He got no answer.

'...There's something about you too. Something I can't put my finger on...'

They were silent the entire walk home. When they arrived at her home, Zara stopped.

'You okay?' Sebastian asked.

'I don't know,' she answered, staring up at the sky.

Seb sighed, leaning against a wall. 'Alex will be alright. The stress of classes must be getting to him. That's gotta be it.'

Zara turned to face him, and he grinned back at her. She smiled and shook her head. 'Seb, you know I can tell when you're lying to me, right?'

Sebastian's eyes widened.

'And that cheesy face you pull can't fool anyone.'

His grin softened.

She moved closer, placing her arms around him, and whispered into his ear. 'It's okay. You don't need to be strong for me. I'm just happy you're here.'

Sebastian froze as she kissed him on the cheek.

She looked at Seb once more, his eyes wide - motionless as a statue. She laughed again before opening her door. 'Goodnight, Sebastian.'

'Good... night,' Sebastian uttered some words a few moments later, realising she had already closed the door behind her. He shook his head and wiped a hand over his face. 'Stupid...' he told himself, touching the cheek Zara had kissed. He then smiled and made his way home.

Except, he wasn't home. The wide streets grew wider still. Cottages detached from the cobblestone path and drifted into the air, disappearing as the sky disintegrated into empty white. Sebastian kept walking, taking the route he usually would back to his cottage. He turned a handle that wasn't there and stepped through a non-existent door.

Before him was that entity; the being made of light. It stood motionless, staring at him from across the void. Sebastian stared back vacantly and started to grin once more.

'...Seb. Wake up...'

He shot up in a cold sweat. Eyes wide and darting across the room. He was back in Viola's cottage and Ariana was leaning over him.

'Bad dream?' she asked, mustering a smile.

'You could... say that,' Seb replied through heavy breaths.

'It's okay. I get them too.' She paused and leaned back, giving him some space. 'I know it ain't saying much, but... you'll get used to them.'

'Funny. That's what I'm afraid of.'

'When you're ready, come down. Nana is sorting out breakfast.'

'Sounds good. I'll be there soon.'

'Okay.' Ariana sighed and left the room, closing the door behind her, leaving Seb to stare down at his hands briefly before pulling off the sheets.

9.

Memories of a Mercenary

Sebastian stepped into the living room, still yawning from his restless night. He found Ariana and Darius already eating at the table. Seb sat down, rubbing his eyes, and was greeted by the enticing aroma of the banquet before him. A harvest of bread, both soft and toasted, graced the table, with a stick of butter at their side. Eggs, cooked in all possible ways Seb had known and even some ways that he hadn't, adorned the plates. Viola must have raided a farm to prepare a feast such as this.

'I trust you slept well,' Viola said as she danced out of the kitchen with a pitcher of orange juice.

'Yes, thank you,' Seb lied, averting his eyes. The bed was very comfy.'

'Flattery will get you everywhere with me, my dear,' she cooed, filling his glass, before gliding around the table to attend to her other diners. Darius sipped at his drink, which looked too red and smelt too ripe to be orange juice.

After the meal, Darius placed an old map of Platto on the table. 'That idiot Brandon told us that he would be somewhere in the city.'

'Did he say where he would meet us?' Sebastian asked, 'This place is kind of big.'

Darius' smile turned into a scowl as he turned towards the boy. 'He didn't.'

'That's where Nana and I come in,' Ariana said in a sly tone.

'You know where to find him?' Darius asked.

'I found the two of you easy enough. And while you boys were sleeping, we took the initiative to scour the city for info. Ariana leapt onto the table and began dancing across the map, a melody humming from her lips. She ended with a twirl and tapped her toes on a spot in the western region of Platto. Sebastian and Darius leaned in.

'The Gallows...' Darius said with a sigh. 'Should've known he'd choose that place.'

'Gallows?' Ariana asked, kneeling to match his eye level. 'That's the entertainment district. Nothing but a place for people to forget their troubles and lose their money.'

'It might be now. But the last time I was here, the only people being entertained were Blackout. The Gallows was a place they held their executions.' Darius poured his wine over that part of the map. 'The place is stained with blood.'

Ariana backed away as the red liquid seeped towards her. She jumped off the table and reached for a cloth. 'I had no idea,' she whispered, wiping up the spill.

'When do we leave?' Sebastian asked.

'*We?*' Darius repeated. '*You're* not going anywhere.'

'But... that Brandon guy. He said he'd tell me why I'm here, why they're after me.'

'They *are* after you, kid.' Darius kicked out his chair and picked up his gear. 'If you tag along, we might as well march you right to 'em with a pretty pink bow wrapped around that thick skull of yours.'

'But I need to-'

'Darius is right, Seb,' Ariana said, sitting down beside him and placing an arm around his shoulder. 'You'll be safe here. Me and the big guy can look after ourselves. But you're not cut out for this sort of thing.'

Sebastian lowered his eyes and pushed himself away from the table. 'I get it. I'd probably just get in your way.'

'Looks like he's finally learning his place,' Darius said with a laugh. His chuckling soon tapered off when he met Ariana's cold glare. He shrugged and wandered out of the room.

'Don't listen to him,' Ariana placed her hand on his. 'We would take you along if they weren't all gunning for you, but that's just how it is. Take the time to relax a bit. You look like you got no sleep at all last night.'

Sebastian looked up at her and smiled. 'You're right,' he said, giving her a nudge. 'I'm just worried about you guys. Who knows what kind of trouble you'll get into without me there to protect you.'

'Yeah, right,' Ariana laughed. 'We're nothing without you, Seb.'

Before long, both Ariana and Darius were ready to leave.

'Be careful,' Seb told them.

'When are we ever?' Ariana said with a wink and gave him a quick hug.

'You better come home this time,' Viola told Darius.

'I promise,' the brute said, 'I'm done running.'

The two left, leaving Sebastian alone with the old woman. Viola stared out of the open doorway long after Ariana and Darius had disappeared from view. She exhaled deeply and closed the door, only noticing Seb once she had turned around. 'Sorry, child. I rarely have company when my kids go on a mission.'

'It's okay, I'm not exactly the "mission going" type,' Seb smiled shyly at her.

'You hungry?'

'We've just had breakfast.'

'And it's almost time for lunch. Sit down and I'll make you something.'

After being forced to another meal, Sebastian hibernated on the feathery sofa in the main room. Viola was sitting across from him, knitting what looked like a rug from a big ball of twine. 'You survived,' she said with a comforting smile. 'Not many can withstand two of my meals and live to tell the tale.'

'I can think of worse ways to go,' Sebastian said, rubbing his swollen stomach.

'As can I, child.'

He looked past Viola, towards the photos of Darius and his old comrades.

'So, how do you know the big guy?'

'You know, it's been so long since we first met, I'm not sure I still remember,' the old woman looked back at the pictures on the wall. 'We were allies once upon a time, back when there was still a reason to fight.'

'Why did you stop?'

'This world is unbalanced, child,' she said, her tone filled with both wisdom and sorrow. 'Something has been ripped away. Endura aches to have it back. Until that time comes, it will forever lie in waiting.' Viola turned back to face Seb, her voice sharpening. 'Tell me, how much do you truly know of the Blight?'

'Not much, really,' he said, throwing a hand behind his neck. 'I mean, I've heard Darius and Ariana mention it.'

'The girl did say you were clueless about our history.' Viola laughed, lifting her head. 'But it is not like there is much known of that dark day.'

'So, what is it?'

'It is a blackness.' Viola shuddered. 'It swept across Endura like a dust storm, stealing fertility from its soil and filling her oceans with an alien oil that only fuels destruction and pollutes the very air we breathe.' Viola sighed and stepped towards a window overlooking the street outside, watching the people as they went about their lives. 'There is nothing natural about this place. Things aren't as they should be.'

'Everyone back home believed as much. I hoped they were wrong. Even planned to find out for myself one day. I should have listened.'

'You were right to find the truth for yourself, child. Taking the words of others as fact is partly why we're still suffering. Many believe the Blight to be a thing of myth. A silly tale thought up by the Church of Unification to make their next life in Etheria sound all the sweeter.' She shook her head and laughed to herself, turning back to Seb. 'But the Blight is as real as you or I. That's what this old coot thinks, anyhow. These tired feet have stepped upon the shores of the Oil Ocean. These milky eyes have stared across that black sea. And these worn-out lungs have inhaled the poisonous air those waters spew. The Blight is a cancer that eats away at this world. But still, most will bury their heads in the sand and pretend it doesn't exist. If that brings them comfort, who am I to take that from them? But my children and I wanted a better world. The Blight isn't some myth to be forgotten. It's a problem that needs fixing. And we were foolhardy enough to be the ones to do it. Or try to, at the very least.'

'How can the Blight be fixed?'

'Anything can be fixed.' Viola smiled. 'All it takes is elbow grease, a can-do attitude and a little know-how. And if there's one group with the *know* and the *how*, it's them.'

'Blackout? If they know how to stop the Blight, then why aren't they doing anything?'

Viola wandered towards the wall of photographs, Sebastian instantly shot up, forgetting his cramps, and followed her. She picked up a picture and handed it to him. Seb looked upon the faces of many men and women, even a younger Viola, all standing proudly and smiling for the photograph.

'It was a war of ideologies. Good, evil and all of that nonsense. There weren't many on our side. Just a few good people who believed in a future for this world.'

Sebastian took the time to look at each of their faces, stopping when he found Darius, whose smile was bigger and brighter than everyone else's.

'We were fighting an Empire. It didn't matter how strong we were. Their power had been rooted into Endura for centuries.' Viola took a long look at the photos filling her wall. 'As the people on our side vanished from view, we knew that it would soon come to an end for us.'

'I'm sorry,' Seb said, handing back the picture.

Viola smiled sadly and gave it one last look. Her tired eyes traced over the faces of her departed friends, Viola's fingers brushing against them all before placing the photo back in its rightful place. 'It feels like only yesterday.' She picked up the picture that Darius had placed face down and handed it to Sebastian.

He could make out Darius putting his arm around a dark-haired boy who looked around Seb's age. The boy seemed to be annoyed that he had to be in the photo, but Sebastian could tell that the kid was trying his best to hide a huge grin.

'That's Dillon. He was always so full of life. I just wish that he would have let me take more photos of him.'

'Who's Dillon?'

Viola looked back at Seb, raising her bushy white eyebrows. She shook her head feebly, with tears forming as she spoke once more. 'Dillon was Darius' son.'

Sebastian's eyes darted back to the boy in the photo. His face was the spitting image of the giant's. Seb handed back the portrait and stepped away from the wall. 'I had no idea,' he said quietly to himself, trying to grow further from the wall of memories. He then noticed another group photo. But this one was torn where someone's face should have been.

'Viola, what happened here?' he asked, picking up the frame.

'Someone whose mug I never want to see again,' she said, snatching the frame from Seb.

He looked around the room, noticing more photographs of the mystery man ripped from the memories, even one of him and Darius with their arms around one another's shoulders.

'These pictures tell a lie.' Viola said pitifully. 'All these smiles were painted on for a portrait. In reality, we were broken. My children fought and died because it was better than living life as a prisoner, controlled by Blackout and their Blight.'

'If the world is really dying, why would Blackout want to stop anyone from saving it?' Seb asked, watching all of the faces in the frame.

'I couldn't tell you,' Viola answered with a shrug. 'All I know is that my children were ready to sacrifice everything for the answer. Until one day, they did.'

Sebastian said nothing. He simply drifted back to the sofa. Terrible thoughts swirled in his mind, making him more worried about Darius and Ariana than he already was. His eyes, heavy with fatigue, betrayed him. Unbeknownst to Seb, the boundaries between wakefulness and slumber blurred, and the worries that had plagued him faded into the background. The warmth, the crackling sounds, and the flickering dance of flames became a lullaby.

When Seb awoke, he could feel pressure on his forehead. His eyes opened to see Viola's long crooked finger pressing down on his temple. 'What are you doing?' Seb yelled, almost falling from the sofa. Viola didn't reply. Her mouth hung open and her eyes had become white and lifeless yet again. Seb crept closer and waved a hand over her face.

'You have been corrupted, my child.' the old woman spoke with a voice that didn't seem like her own.

'Viola, what's happening?' Seb asked, shaking the old woman.

'You have many questions. They all do when facing oblivion.'

Viola's crooked finger snapped back onto Sebastian's head as she screamed in anguish.

'What are you doing?' Seb begged, trying to push her hand away. But she stayed connected to him with a strength he could not fathom.

'Death... was only... the beginning,' Viola uttered before falling to the floor.

Sebastian reached for her hand and felt for a pulse. Thankfully, she was still alive. He picked up the frail woman and laid her on the sofa.

As the day gave way to evening, Sebastian sat longing for Ariana and Darius to return, waiting for Viola to awaken, yearning for an end to his torment. The minutes crawled by as Seb sat by the window for a time, the looming darkness only making him more agitated. To distract his festering thoughts from growing, he decided to explore the cottage. Even though it looked small from the outside, Seb found a staircase that went up many flights. He crept up the steps, finding room after room until he finally stopped at a door that had Ariana's name scrawled upon it. He turned the handle and stepped inside.

The bedroom looked no different from the one he had slept in the previous night. A modest desk nestled against one wall cradled worn notebooks, their pages filled with intricate sketches and notes. A weathered tapestry, draped across a corner, depicted scenes from a bygone era. Seb squinted, tilting his head as he read the titles of the books; Users through the Ages, Water and Will, Coping without Hoping, and the list went on. Sebastian picked one at random and blew the dust off.

'That girl.' a frail voice spoke from the doorway.

Sebastian yelped and dropped the book, turning to find Viola smiling sweetly at Ariana's collection.

'She always loved her books. Weeks went by where I would hardly see her. Always studying and practising up here.'

'Can you stop sneaking up on me?' Sebastian asked, feeling his heart racing.

'You say I'm sneaking when *you're* the one going through Ariana's things,' Viola said with a wink that was all too familiar.

'I was just curious,' Seb answered, rubbing the back of his neck as he looked away from the old woman. 'I guess I just wanted to know what she liked.'

'And why would that be?' Viola asked, her grin widening.

'No reason,' Seb answered, facing away.

Viola laughed and made her way to the bed, letting out a sigh as she sat down.

'There's nothing that girl wants more than to see Blackout suffer. Do that for her, and she'll be yours forever.'

'I think you've got the wrong idea about us,' Seb said, holding out his hands. 'We're just friends.'

'That's how it always starts.'

'Look, Ariana saved my life. More than once, actually. I just want to repay her somehow. That's all.'

'Yes, she told me of your situation, child. To be plucked from your home and discarded in a land you do not know. You must have been scared.'

'I am. I mean, I was.' Sebastian walked to the desk and sat down with a sigh. 'I'm trying not to be.'

'She was much the same when I first found her. It was a few years back. The girl had travelled far to get here. She was strong-willed, even then. And her magic was impressive for one so young. She was like a child of the ash.'

'Child of the what now?' Sebastian asked, lifting his head.

'Ash,' the old woman repeated. 'They are said to be the first beings who ventured into the world after the Blight. It is just a fable, but some believe-.'

'Right. So, Ariana, how did you two meet?' Seb interrupted, trying to get back on the subject.

'Oh, right. Well, she had been on the run all her life. By that time, it was just me, alone with memories of better days. So, I took the girl in.'

'Who was she on the run from?'

'The same as you, child. Thankfully they gave up their chase soon after. She hopes the same will happen for you. But her hatred for them only kept growing. That's when I told her of Darius and how to find him.' Viola looked around the girl's room. 'I hoped that maybe when they found each other, they could truly find themselves. Now I fear that I've sent my children back into a war they can't win.'

'She told me that they burned down her home,' Seb said, flipping through the pages of an old tome.

'And that is all she will ever say. Unlike this old gal, Ariana doesn't think so fondly of the past. She's always looking forward.'

'She's probably right to do that. Maybe I'd be better off forgetting about my past.'

'But do you think you could ever forget *Zara*?' Viola asked with a wicked smile.

'Of course, I couldn't,' he answered. 'It's just that, maybe-' Sebastian froze mid-sentence. He slowly turned towards the old woman and backed out of his seat. 'How do you know about Zara?'

'Ariana told me about her,' Viola answered, looking away from him.

'Well, that's all very well and good. But tell me, how do you know about that white void?'

Viola stiffened when he asked her. She looked up at him with fear in her pitying brown eyes. 'That was real?' I was hoping I was going senile.'

'You saw it too, didn't you?' Seb stepped closer. 'The thing that brought me here.'

'All white, all-knowing, all-powerful. Whatever it is, it seems very interested in you, child.'

Sebastian's mind flashed back to the white realm of wakeful sleep. He grabbed hold of his head, wincing and shaking slightly. 'But it was just a dream. How could you have seen it? You were repeating what it told me, word for word.'

'I can't say for sure what that place is. But I can take you back there if you want?'

Seb let go of his head and stared at Viola. 'Why would I ever want to go back?'

'To find answers,' Viola told him, standing from the bed. 'This isn't a place in your dreams, child. It is a place you visit.'

'What are you talking about?'

'This realm, the void, as you call it, works much like one's subconscious does. However, yours has a tangible location. It exists outside of your mind. And stranger still, it harbours another entity within its walls.'

'How do you know all of this?'

'I am an Echo User.' She declared proudly, planting her hands on both hips.

'And... that is?'

'Child, it is so many things,' she told him with a sinister cackle. 'I can manipulate people's thoughts or make them see things that aren't real. Although it has been many years since I've performed, I believe I can walk through your memories and discover truths that even you do not know.'

'You'll be able to go to the void?'

'Not without you, child,' Viola told him, 'We would have to make the journey together.'

Sebastian's eyes widened. The hairs on his neck flared up and a wave of nausea swept through him. He swallowed down the bile creeping up his throat and forcefully nodded his head. 'If it means I get some answers. I'll go back.'

'You are brave, young one. Truth be told, I am not all that fond of going there myself. But when you get to be my age, you find that discovering something new doesn't come around too often.' The old woman clapped her hands and laughed like a little girl. 'Now what are we standing around wasting time for? Let's get started.'

10.

The Gallows

Under Viola's instructions, Sebastian reclined on a plush rug, with the glow of the dwindling fire casting shadows across the room. Viola positioned herself cross-legged near Sebastian's head, a soft hum emanating from her lips as she uttered incomprehensible words. Her fingertips delicately encircled his temples, applying pressure.

'Are you ready, child?'

'Let's get it over with.'

'Very well.'

Viola's voice boomed as she spoke her foreign words. They pierced into Seb's ears and chimed through his trembling body. He let out a scream as the pain pulsated within him and felt the heat of the growing flames. The room became intensely bright, burning his eyes. Sebastian forced them closed when he felt the ground shake beneath him. The vibrations moved Sebastian across the floor, along with much of the furniture. Photos fell from the walls, and even the sofa began shaking.

'What's happening?' Seb yelled, his voice a whisper in the chasm around him.

'I'm not doing this,' Viola answered in a weary scream.

Seb opened his eyes and looked up at her, watching her eyes as they scanned the dismantling room. He jumped to his feet and pulled her up, making his way to the front door. The ground still trembled as they left the cottage. Sebastian looked around to see other city folk gazing up into the darkening sky. Seb's eyes followed theirs, falling onto the shadow that covered the city of Platto.

The Crimson Capital drifted high over everything. Seb couldn't see it clearly back in the desert what with all the dust clouds littering the sky, but now, even in the dwindling twilight, he could examine the Crimson for all its glory. The flying fortress consisted of dark metals and red fabrics covering giant balloons being held aloft by large, swirling blades and enormous flames sputtering across the sky, creating dark looming clouds.

Viola pulled Sebastian inside before he could see more, slamming the door and bolting it shut. 'Now I see why Darius is such a big fan of yours,' Viola said, pressing herself against the window.

'You think that's here for me?'

'Well, it's the first time I've seen the Cloud fly over my home. And, sonny, I've been living here a long time.'

'We've gotta warn the others.' Sebastian moved past her, his clumsy fingers toying with the locks on the door.

'I'm sure they're already aware,' she yelled over the loud rumbles.

'This is Brandon's doing,' Seb growled, pulling at the latches and bolts. 'He must have tricked them. Maybe they're trapped or-'

'Child!' Viola screamed, louder than the earthquake outside.

Sebastian stopped with the locks and looked towards her.

'Those two knew the risks when they went to find that cursed fool, Brandon. Darius especially.'

'Yeah, but-'

'And their goal is to find out what makes a boy like you so special. They're willing to risk it all because they know those people flying up there in their fancy floating kingdom, they *fear* you.'

Sebastian slid to the floor and gazed back at the Crimson Capital through the window.

'They... fear me?'

'You think they would bring the fleet for someone they don't fret?' Viola smiled sadly at the boy.

'This is madness,' he uttered, holding his head in his hands. Tears began to fall down his cheeks as Sebastian banged the back of his head against the door.

Viola rushed to his side and pulled his hands away with a warrior's strength. 'Hush, child,' she said as she cradled Sebastian, stroking his hair. 'Your fate is a cruel one. But you must be brave now. Miracles like you don't come around often.'

'I'm no miracle,' Seb told her, pushing her hand away. 'I'm a curse. Everyone I get close to ends up getting hurt.' His voice started to strain as he went on. 'I couldn't protect any of them.'

'You haven't done anything to harm a soul,' Viola said sweetly, 'It was all *them*, they're the ones who hurt, who kill, who rule through fear - Because they're the ones who are truly scared. We just never knew what they were afraid of, until now.'

'You think so?' he asked, looking up at her.

'I do.' The old woman smiled. 'I've seen the light inside you, child.'

The boy wiped salty tears from his face and met her smile with his signature grin. 'Well, then. Let's get the Blackout scum outta this city!' Sebastian marched through the cottage with determination, collecting what he needed for the mission ahead.

'Where do you think you're going?' Viola asked him as he was rummaging through Darius' things.

'I'm going to find Darius and Ariana,' Seb told her, reaching for a long dagger in its holster. 'I'm done running.'

'You can't be serious.'

'You said it yourself, V,' Seb said, attaching the holster to his belt. 'They're scared of me. So, I'm gonna chase them off.'

'I didn't say you could fight off an entire army with just a blade, you daft sod!' Viola shouted, jumping up and down. 'They're scared of the secrets you hold, the hidden memories you repress.'

Sebastian moved past her, tearing off the stained map of the industrial area - the place Darius had called the gallows. 'I don't care what they're scared of. If Ariana's in trouble, then I'm going to help her. And Darius too, I guess.' Sebastian made his way towards the door when he noticed Viola had blocked his path.

'Don't do this,' she begged him, placing her hands on his shoulders. 'We must perform the ritual of echo. It's the only way we can know what makes a boy like you glow so brightly. Isn't that what you wanted?' Viola's plea became a shrill scream of desperation as she sobbed over her words. 'If you leave now, we may never know what power lies within you. And my Ariana and Darius would have been lost for nothing! Like all the others.'

Sebastian froze for a moment before turning to meet her gaze. 'You won't lose them. I'll make sure of that,' he told Viola, wrapping his arms around her.

'You know nothing,' she hissed, tearing herself away from him. 'If you did, you'd know they are as good as dead by now.'

Sebastian stepped past Viola and made his way towards the door, unlocking the last bolt before facing her again. 'I'm sorry for what happened to your family. But you can't keep living in the past. Things are happening *now* that need to be fixed.' Sebastian turned the handle and stepped outside, briefly checking the piece of the map and casting his gaze to the west. He glanced back and saw Nana Viola staring at him from the door, giving him the same look that she gave Darius and Ariana. The look that said; *we may never see each other again.*

'I'm done with chasing the past,' Seb told himself, as he ran from the old woman's haunting stare. Sebastian broke into a sprint, trying to keep up with the blood-red cloud gliding above him.

A hush had fallen over the Platto. Heads raised to the blood-red cloud looming overhead as Seb swept past them, threading through the alleys as if he knew them. He glanced at the piece of map in his hand, as stained red as the place it represented - the Gallows.

Sebastian slowed to a stop as he approached the entertainment district, joining the mass of residents that pushed and shoved before a blockade of Blackout soldiers, maintaining formation around the perimeter. Pressing to get a closer look, Seb witnessed a Blackmask forcefully shove a citizen to the ground. The fallen man became surrounded by other guards who subjected him to a brutal assault with the butt of their rifles.

Sebastian should have kept moving. He could have used this distraction to slip through the blockade or find an alternate route, yet a surge of anger welled within him from a place he couldn't quite fathom. Clenching his fists, he forcefully moved through the swelling crowd, pushing aside the Platto citizens as he neared the masked adversaries. Sebastian drew his dagger, keeping it concealed at his side.

A sudden cascade of water sent the group of Blackmasks hurtling into the midst of the crowd. Seb blinked dumbly before sheathing his blade and pulling the battered man into the crowd. A whistle from above caught Sebastian's attention, and as he looked up, he spotted Ariana standing on a rooftop shaking her head at him. Sebastian responded with a shrug and a smile, making his way towards her.

'What are you doing here?' she hissed, pulling him onto the rooftop.

'Saving your butt,' Seb answered. 'Where's Darius?'

'He's refusing to leave until Brandon shows himself.'

Ariana pointed at the square in the district, encircled by Blackout guards. In the centre stood Darius, wielding his sword, Xerxes. Together, they carved through a horde of Blackmasks, whose agonised cries served as a haunting reminder that there were people beneath those ominous masks. A wave of nausea swept over Seb, prompting him to avert his gaze, the taste of bile rising in his throat.

'You don't belong here, Seb,' Ariana said, placing a hand on his shoulder.

'Does he think he can take them all?'

'He's been doing alright so far.'

'We have to do something.'

'I *am* doing something,' she said, dancing over the rooftop, sending a flood around the massive warrior. It flowed past the island that was Darius, washing the filth away.

'I can help too,' Sebastian said, taking out his knife.

'You can help by getting out of here. We've got this, Seb.'

'Stop treating me like I'm useless,' he yelled, spinning to face her.

'You're just getting in the way!'

'They're here for *me*, not you. Take Darius and run. I'm not gonna stand by and-' Before Sebastian could finish, a jet of liquid smashed through him, slamming him across the rooftop.

'I'm sorry, Sebastian,' she said, jumping from the roof.

As he rose to his feet, Seb gripped his knife, his eyes fixed on the open area where Darius was fighting. Ariana had since joined him, spinning through the air from the rooftop, descending on jets of water from her palms. She leapt the last few feet, delivering kicks and strikes before landing, then blasting a pressure of water to knock down the masked unit around her.

Darius swung his sword around her, creating a whirlwind of steel that cut through the opposition. Ariana flipped over the giant, cartwheeling through the air with well-timed spears of liquid knocking into the army.

Darius broke away from her, carving through the ranks with his sword slashing through the air like a lethal gust.

The echoes of frenzied grunts rang through the night. Sebastian winced, stroking at his scrapes as he watched Ariana send violent streams to knock the Blackmasks upon the hard ground, now knowing how painful it was.

Darius charged at them with his incredibly heavy-looking blade, pointing it forward like a lance. It swept across the battlefield like it had its own will, and Darius was merely holding onto it. Ariana directed the liquid in intricate patterns, creating ethereal tendrils that danced around her. As the Blackmasks closed in, she manipulated the water to create translucent whips that lashed out, striking all foes surrounding her and encasing them within watery restraints.

Sebastian managed a smile as he peered closer at the two. He almost felt compelled to cheer them on. He had already seen Darius fight, but to see Ariana like this was something else entirely. His growing grin fell as a figure emerged in the corner of his eyes, almost as if they had stepped out from the shadows. Clad in a hooded white robe, the mysterious individual lingered high on a distant rooftop, watching the skirmish below with an almost detached interest.

Seb's attention wavered between the skirmish and the hooded figure, a sense of unease settling in his gut. It was the same stranger as before, the person who had stilled the crowd and whispered from afar. Seb pushed his thoughts aside, focusing on the immediate threat. As he turned, he realised that Darius and Ariana's movements had dulled, the surrounding enemies moving closer.

With a frustrated groan, Sebastian ran to the end of the rooftop and leapt to the next. He continued along the brittle buildings, the rhythmic panting of the combatants echoing through the narrow alleyways. Seb leapt across a wide gap, landing with a roll that sliced his leg with the concealed blade strapped to him. Despite the sharp pain, he pressed on, groaning and using both hands to stem the bleeding.

'Great job, Seb. Your friends are fighting an army, and *you* manage to cut yourself.' Sebastian quickly improvised a makeshift bandage from a torn piece of his jeans, tying it tightly around the bleeding wound on his leg. The fabric soaked through almost immediately, but he couldn't afford to dwell on the pain. Rising to his feet, he surveyed the scene below. The situation had escalated. Ariana and Darius found themselves encircled, standing back-to-back as they fought. The ground was littered with the fallen bodies of Blackout guards, but many more had taken their place. The Blackmasks advanced with eerie determination, wielding an assortment of crude weapons. Strangely, they seemed reluctant to use their guns. Darius stood steadfast, employing his massive sword as both a weapon and a shield. Meanwhile, Ariana summoned just enough water to barely hold the encroaching forces at bay.

Sebastian hobbled towards a rooftop's edge, a roar escaping his lips as he made the precarious leap across the gap. Landing grimly, he positioned himself at the end of the row of buildings, overlooking the chaotic scene below. The citizens of Platto had been cheering as Darius and Ariana fought on, some even began breaking through the barrier and attacking the distracted soldiers. Seb knew he couldn't remain a spectator any longer, yet the next gap between buildings was far too wide to leap. He spun around, scanning the rooftop for anything he could use. His gaze landed on a loose cable dangling from a neon sign above. Without hesitation, he reached up and grabbed hold of it. Walking back to create enough space, Sebastian gripped the rope and leaned back, testing its weight and flexibility.

'...You can't save anyone...'

Sebastian showed teeth as he sprinted forward towards the building's edge, launching himself into the air. He swung high above the gap between buildings. As the cable's arc slowed, Sebastian released his grip, feeling the rush of wind around him. Arms flailing and legs kicking, he descended to the rooftop below. The anticipation of impact surged through him, and in that critical moment, Sebastian closed his eyes and reached out. His hands clutched onto something, his body swinging before colliding with steel and concrete. He pulled himself up onto the roof, rolling onto his front. Deep, quick breaths escaped him as he glanced back at the last building he had just left. The distance seemed more significant now, and the cable he had used to swing over appeared shorter than it originally seemed.

Suddenly, a clap rang across the air, followed by another. The sound emanating from a singular pair of metallic gloves. Sebastian limped over to find Darius and Ariana leaning against each other on the verge of collapse. The citizens, too, halted in their tracks upon hearing the applause. The guards encircled the weary duo and arranged themselves to create a path leading towards the entrance of a nearby pub. In the doorway stood a man, his mocking applause persisting. His armour glinted in the sunlight, and his long blonde hair danced with the wind.

It was Brandon Frost.

'Marvellous show of strength and vigour,' the golden knight bellowed with a callous sneer.

Ariana and Darius gazed uneasily at one another.

'Finally decided to... show up, huh?' Darius breathlessly jeered.

'I've been watching from my drinking establishment this entire time,' Brandon answered, 'I do love a spot of entertainment with my ale.'

'Your men are dead!' Ariana called out, waving a limp arm. 'Don't you care?'

'They served their purpose. I'm sure you've exhausted enough energy to now act like dignified folk. So then, their deaths were not in vain, and they shall be remembered.' Brandon wiped away a fake tear. 'Now tell me, where is the boy?

'I thought you came here to answer *our* questions,' Darius told him. 'Now has that changed? Because I've been conserving a bit of energy just for you.'

Brandon scowled and shook his head. 'Very well. Follow me.' He gave a signal for them to follow, and the two cautiously began to make their way towards the pub.

While Brandon was talking, Sebastian cautiously made his way across the rooftop, mindful not to attract any unwarranted attention. Upon reaching the tavern roof, he glanced at the neon letters above the main doors, spelling out "Gallows Pub". Determined, Seb clenched his fists and entered through a nearby window.

11.

Ender Knights

Sebastian pushed the rest of his body through the small window and landed clumsily on the wooden floor. He lay still, trembling from the fear of being caught, or possibly from the ground shaking beneath his feet. It was an old dusty room with an uncomfortable-looking bed and a desk with some books sprawled across its surface. Seb rolled onto his front and crawled towards the door, opening it slightly. He saw a flight of stairs that descended to the pub but not much else. The Crimson Capital still rumbled in the sky, causing everything that wasn't bolted down to shake uncontrollably.

Beneath his feet was a frantic rattling. He pulled up the thick carpet and found a trembling hatch in the floorboards. Seb lifted the palpitating door that mirrored his heartbeat and peered inside. Cobwebs and debris glistened within the darkness, and muffled voices escaped from below. Sebastian leaned closer into the shadows trying to make out what was being said. The trembling suddenly stopped, becoming an earthquake that shook the room, throwing Sebastian forward into the dark pit. He landed on soot-covered floorboards and broken glass. The pain shot through his forearms, knees, and stomach as Seb felt the hot sting of blood seeping from the cuts. He wanted to scream, but before he could, a muffled voice appeared.

'What was that?'

'Looks like the capital has landed,' a clearer, more recognisable tone answered - the voice of Brandon Frost. 'Finally, I can hear myself think.'

Sebastian carefully shifted his body forward towards a beam of light, emanating from a crack in the floorboards. He peered through a hole, finally able to see Brandon sitting on one end of a table, a frosty mug of ale in one hand and a large revolver in the other, with a gang of those Blackmask thugs standing solemnly behind him.

'That noise was starting to wear my patience. I even forgot to offer you both a drink. Now then, what's your *poison*?'

Seb's eyes moved along the table to where Brandon's attention lay. Relief washed over him when he saw an uncomfortable-looking Darius and Ariana sitting across from the golden knight.

'We're not thirsty,' Ariana answered, refusing to make eye contact.

'I'll have the most expensive swill you got,' Darius said with a sly smirk forming. 'And seeing as this is your round, the girl will have the same.'

Brandon spun his revolver around his fingers before placing it on the table. He mused at the thought and started to laugh like it was the funniest thing he had ever heard. 'That doesn't sound half-bad,' he bellowed, pouring his ale on the floor. 'This filth should be reserved for the rats outside.' A waiter came to the table with a sparkling blue bottle, uncorked it and poured the contents into three pristine glasses. 'Only the best for men such as us. Wouldn't you agree, Blake?' Brandon asked, lifting his glass and twirling it in his hand to reflect the light.

'Men such as us.' Darius growled, snatching his glass from the waiter and pouring it down his throat. 'We are no longer men, Bran. Just ghosts waiting for the rest of the world to join us.' Darius threw the glass over his shoulder, grabbed hold of the blue bottle and took a huge gulp. 'That ridiculous outfit you wear doesn't distract from what you did. Still, it's protected you thus far. Being Blackout's lapdog doesn't seem to be hurting too much either.'

'The things I've done to lead me to this table are no concern of yours.' Brandon's eyes darted to his glass as he took a long sip.

'And what a fine table it is. You could hardly believe that this was the place where it all happened. Tell me, Bran. Do you remember the faces of those you've sacrificed for your fancy suit and tables?'

'They…' Brandon's drink spilt upon his breastplate. He slammed it upon the table. 'They were extremist fools, Blake! They had no clue of the powers they were meddling with, and they were punished accordingly.'

'Even Dillon?' Darius uttered, staring longingly at the table.

'Darius, I…' Brandon leaned back and shook his head. 'I can't be held responsible for what happens to criminals.'

'You are responsible. You alone.' Darius rose from his seat.

'Now, Now, old friend.' Brandon picked up the revolver and swivelled it in his hand.

'You think I'm scared?' Darius asked, grabbing the empty bottle by the neck and smashing it upon the table. 'We'll see how powerful that peashooter of yours is when it's in the hands of a dead man.'

'Whoa there, big guy,' Ariana said, standing up and placing a hand on the retired hero's shoulder. She sat him back down and looked nervously at the guards surrounding her, then at Brandon, then at her glass. She gulped down the liquid and wiped her mouth with the back of her hand, smiling briefly at the taste. Her eyes darted back to Brandon, no longer filled with fear. Instead, they burned with the same determination Sebastian would always see within her. 'Listen up, Brandon,' Ariana perked up. 'We could sit here and hurl idle threats at each other all day, or even go back to killing each other. As long as we get some more of that drink, I'm up for whatever. But we came here to discuss Sebastian, and why you're after him.'

'Sebastian?' Brandon asked, dropping his revolver to land clumsily on the table.

'Yes, Sebastian,' Darius chimed in. 'Short kid? Doesn't take direction well? Has a face like he's lost his favourite cuddly toy?'

Seb pouted at these descriptions.

'*Sebastian*. Oh, yes! That's his name, isn't it?' Brandon's open mouth quickly grew into a vicious grin, revealing shiny white teeth. 'Where do I even start with that boy?'

'What's so funny, chuckles?' Ariana asked, raising an eyebrow.

'It's just *semantics*,' The gold knight answered, collecting himself. 'But you are indeed correct. This *boy*. Sebastian, was it? He's been a person of great interest for some time.'

'Why?' Ariana asked, leaning forward and staring down the Blackout knight.

'You wouldn't believe me if I told you.'

'Try me.'

'Very well.' Brandon sighed and stood from his chair. 'The boy is different to you or I. Special, some might say. Others would call him dangerous.' Brandon turned to face them, allowing all traces of his twisted smile to fade, showing very human and sincere eyes. 'He has eluded Blackout for many years. Hiding away in a village shrouded by mountains. And now, he travels with the two of you.' Brandon extended his open palm towards them. 'We simply must find him. The details of this I cannot announce so freely, but the fate of-' Brandon stopped himself, tensing slightly as the hand furled into a fist. 'The fate of *our* world depends on it.'

Sebastian's mouth dropped, almost hitting the shattered glass littering the floorboards.

Ariana and Darius gave each other a worried look. When they turned back, huge grins appeared on both of their faces. They sniggered in their throats before breaking into laughter. The girl couldn't help but hold her sides as she giggled to herself, and the giant pounded hard on the table with fists that made more noise than the floating city up above had previously.

Brandon watched on with shocked irritation. 'The boy's a time bomb. If you don't hand him over to us, there will be no telling when he'll detonate.'

'The only thing that kid will *explode* into, are tears,' Darius said, trying to stop his pained laugh as he pointed towards Ariana. 'And I thought this one was the Water User!'

Sebastian scowled at Darius, wiping a tear from his cheek.

'Be that as it may, the boy is a menace to the society we are trying our utmost to protect. The people are not safe with him walking the streets.'

'Yeah, because you're so concerned with the well-being of the people,' Ariana squinted back at Brandon. 'Didn't I see your soldier drones trying to beat a man to death earlier?'

'If they did, then he must have been asking too many questions. You should be careful not to do the same,' Brandon answered, narrowing his eyes back at the girl.

'Well, maybe if you start telling us what the blight we're doing here, we wouldn't be raising our hands for teacher!' Ariana shot up, pounding her fist on the table, causing Brandon and even Darius to flinch.

A bell rang as the main doors swung open, Sebastian heard their footsteps but did not see who it was from his current position in the rafters. But what he could see was Ariana's and Darius' faces as they turned pale. Their eyes fixed towards the entrance.

Ariana looked up to the ceiling with her eyes scrunched tight, mouthing incomprehensible words like a prayer and holding her cheek - her scar.

'Well then,' Brandon said with a crooked smile, placing his gun on the table 'The gang's all here.'

Sebastian wished for someone to say something, anything. Instead, silence filled the room. He had to see what had made Darius and Ariana so afraid, he moved across the broken glass - the shards slicing further into his flesh, forcing him to wince and bite his lower lip in fear of crying out in pain.

'I'm glad you could join us,' Brandon finally said, his voice growing more authoritative as he stood to attention and saluted. The Blackmasks behind followed suit.

'At ease, soldier.' A calm voice spoke from outside Sebastian's peripheral.

Brandon and his men let down their guard.

Darius turned back to the table, almost quivering as the footsteps grew closer.

'We meet again, Darius Blake,' the composed man spoke again. His voice was rough yet profound. He stepped close enough for Seb to catch a glimpse of his back. The man was of average height, slender and wearing pristine jet-black armour, with a thinly curved blade resting at his hip. He had silver hair tied into a short ponytail that fell just below his shoulders.

'So, I guess Brandon isn't a complete liar. You wouldn't have come if things weren't serious, Vincent Vale.'

'I'm afraid it is quite serious. Although I must admit that even I can see the humour in all of this. It has been many years since I've taken it upon myself to tend to the affairs of our organisation. And somehow, after all this time, you've returned yourself.' Vincent didn't sound bitter or vindictive as he turned to Brandon. 'Just like old times, ey?'

'What you doin' wastin' words on these losers, Vincey?' A girl's voice tore through the room like the shattered glass through Sebastian's skin, causing him to wince just as much. 'I say we torture 'em. Make 'em bleed 'til they give 'im up.'

'Patience, Nina,' Vincent said, turning back towards the door.

Seb could see Vincent's face now. It was a canvas of wrinkles, blemishes, and battle scars. His dull, grey eyes pierced across the room as he stared back at the girl - silencing her. He took a long look around the tavern, staring into the faces of everyone there. Even Brandon looked worried when the silver-haired leader's gaze brushed past him. The man's hardened expression finally broke into a smile when he laid eyes back on the retired hero. 'Tell me, Darius. How long has it been since our paths last crossed?'

Darius answered, as if on cue. 'Sixteen years, four months, eleven days.'

'Most people don't get it down to the exact day. I must have made quite the first impression.'

'It's not you that I remember.'

'Yes, that was the day all of this misfortune started,' Vincent said, closing his eyes and leaning back against a dusty pillar, turning towards Brandon once more.

The golden knight suddenly jerked his back and turned away from Vale's piercing stare.

Sebastian began to tremble. This Vincent Vale had an aura about him - a darkness that almost seeped from his skin. Sebastian couldn't see it - but he could feel it, lapping in and out of the old warrior like waves on a shore.

'This girl, she keeps staring,' Another voice from the doorway spoke in a gruff dialect.

Vincent turned back to find Ariana. She had not moved an inch since they had walked in. Ariana's brow creased as she glared at the unseen man, trying her best not to tremble.

'I can see why, Reid,' Vincent said, staring mournfully at the girl before returning his gaze to his comrade. 'This is Ariana Lane she was once a resident of Farrow Farmstead, in the Ambulia province. That was until I ordered you to burn her village to the ground.'

Ariana shuddered before slowly turning her sights onto Vincent.

'So, that's it,' Reid said with the snap of his fingers. 'How could I forget! The girl who got away.'

Her eyes slowly traced back to the man who destroyed her home.

Sebastian couldn't take it any longer. He had to see what this monster looked like. He slid his body clockwise until he was facing the other way, allowing the embedded glass to slice into his stomach, Seb lifted his arm to his face and bit down hard into his flesh to fight the impulse to scream. Somehow, he managed the manoeuvre without making a sound. He peered back through the eyehole, now seeing the tavern doorway. Two people were standing there. Sebastian's eyes were immediately drawn towards the girl who had just begged to torture his friends. her skin was as white as the mountain peaks back home, with as many scars littering her body. They were everywhere, apart from her face. She wore knee-length boots, a skirt, a small top revealing her midriff, and an open vest jacket, all black. Her long blonde hair glided down to her slender, pale waist. Nina's piercing red eyes grew almost as large as her smile as she watched Darius and Ariana's discomfort.

Sebastian's eyes glided over to Reid, the man who had burned down Ariana's home. His skin was darker, covered in tattoos and piercings that spread across his body like a canvas. The drawings depicted people burning and demons laughing maniacally. The man was quite short with a shaved head. He didn't have eyebrows, giving his light blue eyes even more depth. He folded his huge arms and puffed out his chest, covered by a grey vest and dark jeans, grinning back at Ariana like he was enjoying the attention from her.

Brandon finally clapped his hands together. 'Lord Vale, can I just tell you personally while I have the chance how very sorry I am that you had to concern yourself with a task as arbitrary as this? The boy will be found I assure you, even if I have to torture every last-'

'That will not be necessary, Lieutenant Frost,' Vincent said, narrowing his eyes at the golden knight. 'I have already taken every precaution required to make sure our elusive friend does not escape again.'

'You dare tell our lord to trust ya?' Nina asked Brandon, folding her arms. 'After you failed to follow orders back in the wastes and tried to catch 'im yerself, like you're some big hero or somethin' in yer big shiny suit.' She stepped forward, scowling at the golden knight.

'About that, my lord.' Brandon turned to Vincent, clasping his hands. 'I felt it was my duty to be first on the ground, in case it was a trap.'

'Glory hunter, that's what you are, Frost.' Reid spat on the ground, lifting his upper lip to show teeth. 'Trying to make up for what you did. It's your fault we're all in this mess, beast killer!'

'Please, I just felt that it was my time to prove what I can-'

'There ain't nothing you can do,' Nina interrupted, stamping her heel on the floorboards. 'You're a traitor. If it weren't for you, my Leon would still be here with us today!'

'Enough.' Vincent said solemnly. The room fell silent, the Ender Knights all hesitated, staring at the ground. Vincent surveyed the area once more. 'This is not our way,' he spoke calmly, wiping a hand over his face. 'We do not fight amongst ourselves; that is not what *he* would have wanted. And what is more, we have company.' Vincent moved towards Darius and Ariana. 'I apologise on behalf of my comrades. This discussion is not becoming of your rulers.'

'You are not my ruler,' Ariana said through clenched teeth.

Darius turned to her, mouth agape. Brandon and Reid also stepped back. Nina, however, let her wicked smile appear once again.

'Dear sweet, Ariana.' Vincent smiled at her. 'I can see just by looking into those eyes of yours, how your story will end.'

She stared back at him, shaking slightly, eyes glistening.

'I've read your dossier,' Vincent continued, 'The lone survivor of a torched village while still only a child, taken in by a coven of Users, only to rise through their ranks. That is until we came looking for you. You somehow managed to escape us every time, leaving behind the people who helped you to perish in your place.'

Sebastian gasped as he looked into her tear-filled eyes, seeing only himself in that moment. He ran a bleeding hand over his face and ground his teeth.

'I believe the last time was when you were travelling with a certain... *Jason Miller,* was that the name? When one of our knights came across-'

Ariana punched Vincent in the face and pushed him back towards the door. 'Don't say his name!' The room fell deathly silent, as Ariana leaned away with fear flooding back into her like an ocean.

Vincent smiled and wiped his cheek before placing the same hand on the hilt of his Katana.

'Please, don't,' Darius begged, placing an arm around her.

'Where is the boy?' Vincent asked, all traces of kindness vanishing from his voice.

'We'll never tell you!' Ariana screamed once more, now sobbing into Darius' arms.

'Very well, then I'll-'

'No!' Seb roared from above them.

Everyone looked up to the rafters as the thick planks of wood were broken into pieces, with a bloodied Seb spilling onto the table.

Vincent watched with a raised brow at the boy. 'Is this one of your torture victims, Brandon?'

'My name is Sebastian Travis,' Seb uttered, picking himself up and meeting the Blackout lord's cool expression with his own. 'And I'm warning you. If you hurt them, I swear I'll kill you.'

Stillness filled the tavern as they watched the bleeding boy, his heavy breathing amplified by their silence. His eyes were locked on Vincent Vale. The silver-haired leader squinted back as if he were evaluating Sebastian.

Slow, patronising claps of metallic gloves broke the trance. 'Marvellous,' Brandon said, grinning wildly. 'It's as if fate herself has brought you back to us.'

Sebastian unsheathed the dagger and flung it across the pub. The blade glided through the air and sliced through Brandon's left cheek, sending a stream of crimson blood to paint the Blackmasks around him. Sebastian returned his attention to Vincent.

Brandon was flailing about the floor with his masked men huddled around him. Everyone could still hear the golden knight cry out. But they could not keep their eyes off the blood-covered boy.

'Impressive,' Reid said with a thumbs up.

'Is that... could it really be him?' Nina asked, her eyes widening.

Vincent said nothing. He simply smiled and bowed his head at the boy.

'You insolent wretch,' Brandon growled, rising with a face half red with blood, and half red with fury. He raised his revolver in his shaking hand.

'Careful, Brandon. We wouldn't want you firing holes into the boy before knowing it was safe to do so,' Vincent said.

'Look what he did to my face.' Brandon pointed the gun to his cheek, before quickly averting his aim.

'You provoked the child. I've told you before that your words often echo back in various forms. This time it was a knife, next could be a bullet or even a sword. If you are so fond of following fate's guiding hand, then maybe you should accept yours.'

Brandon stopped shaking as he readied his aim. 'Maybe fate means for me to kill this creature.'

'A sound theory.' Vincent chuckled. 'Or was it the boy who is destined to put an end to *you*.'

'No!' Brandon roared, his arm trembling once more, causing the revolver to shake wildly. 'I've sacrificed too much. This boy will die by my hand. Only I can be the one to-'

'You may do as you wish, Lieutenant Frost.' Vincent shrugged, turning away. 'It would be a great shame though. For finding the child and bringing him back to us unharmed. Surely, you realise the opportunities that would be awarded upon his return.'

'Well, I...'

'However, if you would rather kill the boy, then-'

'No, sir.' Brandon dropped to his knee and bowed abruptly. 'I will entrust the child to you.'

'Very well, then I-'

'You've gotta be kiddin' me!' Nina called out. 'You gonna reward this traitorous coward? After everythin' he's done, we should gut 'im like the rest of 'em!'

'Or demote him to Blackmask if he's so concerned with his ruined face,' Reid added.

'Oh yeah, I like the sound of that, have him fight and die for our amusement just like he's done to the men assigned to 'im,' Nina agreed.

'My men are my comrades, Lord Vale.' Brandon rose with a sour face. 'Their lives are as important to me as my own.' The Blackmasks behind him faced one another, tilting their heads and shrugging glumly.

By this point, Sebastian's breathing had returned to normal. He was no longer filled with the adrenaline that had fuelled him just moments prior. He looked around nervously at the people bickering, before smiling towards Darius and Ariana.

They met his expression with uneasy looks of their own.

'Well, at least my methods have yielded results,' Brandon said with a sneer, clutching at his cheek. 'What have you two been doing? Apart from hiding behind our ruler.'

'Careful how you talk to us before I melt down your gold suit and make you drink it,' Reid snapped.

'Reid's right, Frosty-boy. I'm gettin' used to seein' you covered in blood. You better hope I don't decide to make it a permanent look.' Nina licked her lips and grinned wickedly at the golden knight.

Darius looked around with an eyebrow raised before shrugging. 'Well, that's as good a distraction as any,' he said, lifting Xerxes high from his back and swinging it upon Vincent's head.

Lord Vale hadn't turned to know the attack was coming. However, his blade was unsheathed in a flash, repelling Darius' mammoth sword with ease. Vincent simply smiled, slowly turning his sights towards the retired hero. 'I commend your efforts, Master Blake. But that is the closest your blade will ever get to me,' Vincent said, rising with little effort.

'And this is... the closest you'll ever get to the kid,' Darius said through clenched teeth, kicking at Vincent.

The grey-haired warrior leapt back across the room to join his comrades.

'None of you leaves this room alive,' Reid shouted, cracking his fingers and making disjointed arm movements, producing balls of fire, growing more significant with every crunch of the man's bones.

'Well, nobody 'cept the cutie covered in blood,' Nina added, twirling her arms and producing blades made from ice to float through the air around her. 'And I'm not talking about that idiot with the gun.' She retched when mentioning Brandon.

'Girly?' Darius asked, facing Ariana.

'You got it!' she yelled, cartwheeling up onto the table with Sebastian, and dancing around him.

Darius jumped onto the table just in time for the monsoon to flood the tavern, leaving the three of them caught in a pocket of air.

'What the blight do you think you're doing here, kid?' Darius asked, grabbing Sebastian by his bloodied shirt.

'Is that your biggest concern right now?' Sebastian asked.

'The hole,' Ariana murmured as she glided around them with powerful swaying movements, erecting walls of water and pushing them out in waves.

Darius and Seb looked up to see the opening he had made in the ceiling.

'How did you break through them beams?' Darius asked, 'Even I would have trouble-'

'I'm not wasting all this energy... so you girls can compare who's strongest,' Ariana urged them through gasping breaths.

Darius nodded and hurled Sebastian up into the room above, then grabbed Ariana and jumped through the hole himself. Seb helped pull Ariana from the hole below and guided her to the window.

'Don't worry about me, kid,' Darius growled, straining to pull himself from the room below, watching as the two escaped through the small window.

'Darius, what do we do?' Seb asked, looking through the small gap in the window 'You're too big to fit through-'

The retired hero swung his sword, smashing through the wall with no resistance. He climbed out and scoped the area.

'Well, I guess that works.' Seb shook his head.

'Over there,' Darius said, pointing towards a series of metal grates running along the ground where Ariana and he were previously fighting.

'What are they?' Sebastian asked, grabbing hold of a wobbling Ariana.

'Grates to the sewer; it helped with the pools of blood that stained this place. I'm guessing they lead outside of the city,' Darius answered, grabbing Ariana and throwing her over his shoulder.

Luckily, the city folk had already broken through the barriers set by the Blackmasks and had swarmed into the industrial area. An onslaught of chaos spread throughout the area as the two factions fought. Seb and Darius weaved in and out of the many skirmishes happening around them, before breaking away towards the sewer grates.

The retired hero dropped Ariana and lifted the metal bars with a strained roar. 'Ladies... first,' Darius said through deep breaths while gesturing at Sebastian.

'I think he means you, Seb.' Ariana giggled, giving him her hand.

'Hilarious. Now can we get out of here, please?' Sebastian asked.

The doors to the Gallows' Pub blew off their hinges in a mighty explosion. A stream washed out of the tavern and onto the streets, where Platto citizens were fighting with the Blackmasks. Out stepped the three Ender Knights, dripping wet and furious. Sebastian locked eyes with Vincent as Darius helped Ariana down into the sewers. The Leader of Blackout calmly raised his katana in their direction. And without hesitation, the battling Blackmasks stopped fighting and turned towards the blood-soaked boy. Darius yelled for him to follow, but Sebastian needed another moment to look upon the face of the silver-haired leader of Blackout. He then climbed down into the dank sewers that would hopefully lead them to freedom.

12.

Carnage in the Sewage

The stench had struck his nostrils long before Sebastian realised. He was still climbing the rungs of a rusted ladder when a blast exploded topside. His grip almost crushed the rusted ladder as it swung loosely. Sebastian trembled, dropping the last few feet and landing with a splash, soaking Darius and Ariana in the murky brown sewage. The fighting continued above, scattering dust of clay from the ceiling. As they cursed and retched, Sebastian surveyed the sewers - spherical canals of stone slabs lined the waterway, green and mossy. Clay pipes spread along the walls, stretching as far as the tunnel itself, with lights fitted above.

The grate to Platto opened and a hundred angry mouths yelled as one. Darius was already up ahead with Ariana in his arms, shouting for Sebastian to keep up. He nodded in return and began to follow, only to grip hold of his stomach and feel the wet sting of blood trickling. His body burned and itched and screamed.

A sound of grinding gears and screeching metal rang out through the tunnel ahead.

Darius stopped and gazed into the distance as a steel gate began descending from the ceiling. 'Keep up the pace, kid!' he yelled behind his shoulder. 'Looks like we ain't the first ones to slip through these tunnels.'

Sebastian watched as the barrier screeched, scraping along the grimy walls as if it were screaming out to the horde chasing them. He breathed deeply and let his body go numb. He kicked one foot in front of the other and ran, almost skipping on top of the water, leaping the last few inches and sliding under the gap before the gate closed.

Darius stopped to join him, giving Sebastian his hand. Seb took it with a grin and pulled himself to his feet.

'Where did that come from?' Ariana asked.

Sebastian breathlessly shook his head, unable to answer.

Another sound was heard, a screeching hiss from up ahead. They looked up to see another gate closing.

'Bastards,' Darius said under his breath, before making another mad dash for the closing exit.

'Sebastian!' Ariana called out, reaching out for him.

Seb sighed between panted breaths and began running yet again, his feet trudging further from his friends.

Darius smirked when he made it through the gate with Ariana. His smile dropped when he saw that Sebastian had almost crawled to a stop, limping through the puddles of muck, clutching at his bleeding leg. 'Bring up that speed, kid. You ain't got time to smell the roses,' he yelled, his voice echoing across the tunnel.

Sebastian nodded, staring down at his feet as they waded through the rancid waters, his jaw tightening with each step.

'What are you doing? Start running, Seb!' Ariana cried out, trying to break free from the giant's grip. 'I swear if you give up now, I'll never forgive you. I thought you wanted to go home!'

Sebastian stopped. His eyes found hers. He saw tears glisten, sliding along that scar. Sebastian spat blood and ground his teeth. He took one deep breath and launched himself from the pool, leaving explosions in the water behind. His pain became his energy, sending an overpowering force throughout his body as he pushed his feet further with a strength his body didn't understand. He reached out a hand to touch Ariana, just inches away.

What followed was a clang that bounced across the walls, echoing through the sewers. Sebastian broke free from the murky pool and sat up, stroking the lump forming on his head. Before him, Darius frowned, turning away. Ariana shook her head and covered her mouth. The gate had closed, separating them. It was sturdy - several inches thick, with bars wide enough apart to reach an arm through, but not his body. Sebastian leapt up and pried at the bars, trying to bend them.

'That's... not gonna work, kid,' Darius uttered.

'Sebastian,' Ariana whimpered, putting her arm between the bars to stroke his face.

'Ari...' Seb choked, falling to his knees. 'C'mon Darius, can't you do something? Smash through the gate with your sword. Pull the bars apart.'

'Kid, I really can't. This is reinforced steel,' he said, knocking against the solid bars. 'Only an Earth User could break this. And it would take a skilled one at that.'

The sounds of Blackout troops echoed through the sewer. They cackled and hooted, finding pleasure in the hunt.

Seb turned towards the claps and splashes of boots in the water, using the distraction to hide his face. 'You guys should get going. They'll be here soon.'

'We're not leaving you,' Ariana said, grabbing hold of Seb's wrist through the bar.

'Yes. You are.' Seb smiled, pulling away from her. 'No point in all of us getting captured. Besides, I still have a few questions to ask them.'

'Don't you dare…' Ariana growled, grabbing the bars tighter. 'Don't tell me to run. I won't do it.'

'Who said anything about running? Think of it as a tactical retreat. Once I've got my answers, I'll find you. I swear it.'

'Girly, he's right,' Darius told her, placing a hand on Ariana's shoulder. 'If we don't leave now-'

'I'm not going anywhere.' She slid to her knees, resting her head on the gate. 'If you want to get captured, then that's fine. Get captured! Just know that I'm staying with you.'

A violent shriek of rusty metal sang through the tunnel as the gate behind Sebastian began to rise. He looked back briefly and swallowed, kneeling beside Ariana and lifting her chin. 'Look at me. It's going to be okay.'

'No. It won't,' she said, wiping tears from her face with the back of her wrist.

'You have to get away from here.' He grinned, wiping a tear she'd missed with his thumb. 'I'm the one they want. Which means you have to keep fighting.'

Ariana stood up and glared scornfully at him. 'I'll kill… every last one of them,' she said, wiping the tears away with the back of her wrist.

'I know you will.' Seb forced a smile.

She smiled back.

'Darius,' Seb said, nodding at the brute. 'Make sure she gets out okay.'

The retired hero nodded in return, hitting Ariana soundly on the back of the neck. Her eyes grew wide and then closed. She slumped forward with Darius catching her before hitting the water.

'You didn't have to knock her out,' Seb said, shaking his head.

'We both know she wasn't going to leave willingly. Relax, she'll be fine in an hour or so.

'She'd better be.'

'What about you, kid? Think you'll be okay facing Blackout solo?'

'I think I'll manage.'

'These people, they got something special for you. From what little Brandon said, you're the piece they've been searching for.' Darius used his free arm to remove Xerxes from his back. 'Looking at you, I wouldn't believe it. But Vincent Vale showing up means something.' He pushed the slab of steel through the bars, pointing it at Seb. 'A wiser man would smash that piece before they had a chance to use it.'

Sebastian stared motionless at the blade.

'You're just lucky my swinging arm's gotten tired,' Darius said with a smirk, sheathing his sword.

The screech of rusted iron appeared once more up ahead.

'Sounds like that's your cue,' Seb told him.

'What? No heartfelt goodbye?' Darius smirked, turning towards the exit.

Seb shook his head and gave the giant a cheesy grin. 'I couldn't think of anything nice to say to you if I tried.'

Darius looked back at Sebastian. 'I wish I could say the same. But what you did back there. How you came back for us. Well, you're okay by me, Seb.' He turned, sprinting down the tunnel and past the next closing gate, disappearing out of sight.

Sebastian smiled, finally allowing tears to form. 'They'll be okay,' he whispered to himself.

Seb's smile faded when he heard the gate behind him finish rising with a pained crunch. Blackout guards swarmed the tunnel. Some pointed rifles and others had vicious-looking blades at the ready. Sebastian's hand still reached out through the gate. He heard footsteps surround him and he began to laugh.

'Target acquired.' A guard's muffled voice called out through his mask. 'Surrender yourself, or we will be forced to-'

Sebastian grinned cruelly, letting his laugh grow louder. He slowly twisted to meet the horde with a cold glare. He stepped forward and the lights from the tunnel began to flicker. One by one the bulbs burst, shattering glass and creating darkness, trapping everyone within. Seb could see so clearly within the blackness. He sensed their faces twisting with panic behind the masks. The guards in the front row stepped back, tripping over their comrades standing close behind. The cries of fear echoed throughout the sewers as the Blackmasks scrambled to escape.

Sebastian waved his hand to the left and several guards were thrown against the wall. He raised that same hand as more guards flew up into the air and crashed into the ceiling, falling back to the ground, unconscious. The rest tried to escape. A slurry of screaming soldiers smashed into one another in mad haste, crushing their fallen comrades in a stampede to break free. They were blind in the darkness, unable to see the exit. Sebastian pointed out a lone guard before making a fist. The guard stopped and was lifted off the ground, struggling to break free. Seb pulled his fist back. The trooper, now crying out in anguish, was dragged closer through the air towards the blood-soaked boy. Sebastian grabbed hold of the man by the throat, grinning cruelly as he gazed into the crimson crazy smile on the guard's mask - no more than a reflection of himself. The trooper made a feeble gasping sound, clawing at Seb's hand.

A loud pop rang out through the sewer. Sebastian's hand exploded into a hail of blood and bone. He roared in pain, clutched onto his wrist, thick blood pumped black within the darkness.

'So, he finally reveals himself,' Brandon called out, blowing the smoke away from his recently fired revolver.

'Make sure you don't kill him, Frost' Reid yelled, following close behind, lighting the tunnel with balls of fire spinning on his fingertips.

Sebastian let out a thunderous growl and grabbed at the air with his one remaining hand. Brandon was lifted and flew into Reid. Seb laughed and cracked his knuckles, only for a stream of water to pry his hands to the gate behind him, before freezing into chunks of ice.

'Can't let you escape me that easily,' Nina said from behind Seb and the gate, she grabbed his head and slammed it against the bars, kissing him on the cheek.

Seb screamed as he broke free from the ice, only to be scorched by flames that ate through his skin. He submerged himself into the muck to escape the searing burns, only to have a barrage of bullets tear through him once he emerged. Seb fell back into the pool, looking up to find the face of Vincent Vale above him. The Lord of Blackout stared mournfully into Seb's eyes and raised his katana high in the air. Sebastian's eyes rolled back as he sunk into the putrid sewage. Sinking deeper into the pitch-black water, he felt himself returning to that place. The infinite nothingness that tore him from his home. The mysterious world of non-existence he had become a part of, just as it had become a part of him.

13.

Of Black and White

Sebastian gasped for breath, yet it was water that filled his lungs. He emerged from a shallow black pool, coughing up bile and wincing at the brightness. Seb stood up, surveying the changes to the void. That black, knee-deep liquid continued endlessly, serene like a pool and fresh on his skin. For the first time, Sebastian felt at peace within the nothingness. He waded through the calm waters, enjoying the stillness of it all. It gave Sebastian time to wonder how he had ended up in this realm, and when he had fallen asleep. He remembered the gallows pub, escaping Blackout with Ariana and Darius, running through the sewers, and then... nothing.

The sounds of rippling water were soon accompanied by splashing and giggling in the distance. Sebastian smiled and waded faster through the colourless water until he saw a grey shape throwing the black bile into the absent sky.

It was *Zara*. She was wearing the same clothes as she had that day. A white ruffled shirt and green shorts danced in a non-existent breeze. Sebastian stopped to watch her as if it would be the last time. The fiery-haired girl hummed sensually to herself, dipping her hands into the waters to cup some of the liquid, and splashing it over her face. Before Seb realised, she was looking at him.

'...You not washing, Seb?'

Her voice lingered in the air as it breezed past him.

'Is it really you?' he asked, reaching out for her. 'We have to leave. This place is dangerous.'

'...Thanks for the warning...'

She smiled and stepped closer to him. Sebastian grabbed her shoulder, only for his hand to pierce through her skin as an explosion of colours flew out. Seb brought his arm back with a jolt, watching as the molecules reconstructed around her. She was simply a painting. A rendition of what he remembered, almost uncanny. Yet, it was nothing like her. Sebastian knew when and where he was. It was Avalon Fountain. It would only be a few hours from this moment until...

'...You could do with a wash, you're covered in dirt...'

Sebastian gazed at her, his mind still lingering through thoughts. He peered down at the water to find himself. However, greeting him was not a reflection. It was a child. A young boy with grey skin peered back at Sebastian, an unsettling sneer on his face. Sebastian fell backwards into the black lake. As he emerged, Zara stood before him, her smile sweet and innocent.

'...That's much better...'

Seb got on his feet and looked down only to find his own face staring back at him from the black liquid. 'Why is this happening?' he asked, looking up at her. 'Being forced to live out these last days with you.' He punched down, allowing an explosion of liquid to burst into the air and freeze suspended. Sebastian reached for her once more, obliterating her body into a cloud of smoke when he touched her. His hands turned to fists as he screamed up at the dust that was his Zara. He lowered his arms, letting them wilt to his side. Sebastian looked upon his reflection once more, a pathetic excuse for a person staring back. 'I'm trying to stay strong for you. I just don't know if I can.' Seb sighed and closed his eyes as Zara's molecules drifted back to create her. After some time, she had fully formed, yet again.

'...Easy going is all you've got, Seb...'

Seb's eyes instantly darted to hers. Zara's tone was different, almost synthetic and devoid of all emotion. There was another Zara behind her, and third past that copy. He looked to his left and his right, and there she was. Hundreds of her, thousands even.

'...Easy going is all you've got, Seb...'

He tried to run, covering his ears. Anything to escape that artificial, orchestral tone. The swarm of Zara's blocked his path, appearing from the air in a cloud of rainbow mist. Some wore different clothes, some appeared younger or even older. All looked at him as if he were a stranger.

'...I'm sure you'll find some way to muddy yourself up before long....'

'...Easy going is all you've got, Seb...'

'...I practically live in this fountain, I'll beat you every time...'

'...Easy going is all you've got, Seb...'

'...They say the waters of this fountain are a source of protection...'

'...Easy going is all you've got, Seb...'

'...Seb...'

'...Seb...'

'...Seb...'

'...Seb...'

'...Seb...'

'...Seb...'

'...Seb...'

'...Seb...'

'...Seb...'

'...Seb...'

They grabbed hold of him and held Sebastian under the black waters. He scrunched his eyes and screamed bubbles. Slowly, he felt the black water beginning to evaporate around him. Complete silence followed soon after. He opened his eyes to see the many mannequins still watching him, frozen. Their silence was almost as deafening as their overlapping voices. But no sound was as ear-splitting as the voice that spoke next.

'...What is a dream, and what is reality?'

The void flickered and distorted, becoming flashes of grey. The booming voice echoed throughout the empty abyss. Sebastian turned around to see the being composed entirely of light descending from the heavens to join him.

'...It all comes down to what you perceive as true....'

The army of Zara's stiffened like figurine dolls and held out their arms to welcome their creator. Its feet touched the hallowed ground, finally free from the darkness.

'...The stories we tell ourselves, the choices we make. That is all we really are...'

As the glowing figure moved towards him, Sebastian could see that even more of the entity's features had been revealed. He could see a large nose and big ears, even the traces of hair that flowed down from its head in an incredible ray of twilight.

'...But stories are things of fiction. Choices can be swayed by another's input. If that is true, then how do we truly know ourselves?'

The being's animalistic qualities had diminished, now looking more like a person. However, its sinister grin never changed. Neither did its eyes - bulbous and moving erratically.

'...I know who I am, what I am. But tell me truly. What are you?'

Sebastian simply watched as the being approached him, growing taller with each step. Its mouth was perfectly still as if it wasn't the one talking.

'...Broken, useless, corrupted. This is your story...'

Sebastian turned and ran, pushing past the copies of Zara. They stood solid, almost impenetrable as he tried to shove them back. Sebastian was trapped within their embrace, as the entity of light towered above them all, Its voice louder than ever.

'...I've given you a different narrative. I am your new author....'

It reached down and wrapped a claw around Sebastian's body, plucking him from the ground. It held Seb close to its monstrous face and grinned wickedly at the boy, its eyes practically popping from its skull.

'...Your story is mine. Your life is forfeit....'

Sebastian squirmed in the entity's mitts. It squeezed him in its fist, releasing the black ooze from Seb's very being. It squelched from his skin and dripped down, filling up the white void until the floor had become as dark and filled with bile as when Sebastian had first arisen.

The sounds of glass shattered around him. Seb turned, watching as a rip tore open through the void, revealing machinery and electricity pulsing through the nothingness. From the hole, Zara jumped into the void and brought with her the true light from the outside world.

'Seb!' she yelled, causing all of her clones to seize up and burst into a thick rainbow haze, evaporating into the ether with distorted screams of pain.

The entity relinquished its grip with a sigh, allowing Sebastian to fall into the darkened waters. The black pool was deeper now. The hole Zara had broken through had become a vacuum that brought a storm. Sebastian broke free to the surface, gasping for breath, flailing helplessly as the violent waves pulled him under. Beneath the black waters, Sebastian didn't know if he was awake or asleep. He could have simply been dreaming when a hand wrapped around his own and pulled him to the surface.

Sebastian breathed deeply, gasping for air. Zara was holding him tenderly within her arms, stroking his hair and looking into his frantic eyes.

'I almost thought I'd never find you,' she said with a hopeful smile.

'Zara...' Seb croaked, looking up at her. 'Please, let it be you.'

He reached a hand out to touch her face, thinking she would disappear into a puff of smoke. But his fingers brushed up against her warm skin, tears glistening in her eyes.

Sebastian and Zara stayed on the white beach as the black water lapped at their heels.

'What happened to us, Seb?' she asked, looking up into the lifeless sky.

'That's something I'm still trying to figure out.' He sighed, shaking his head. 'I thought I had it all planned out. We'd leave the village, climb those mountains, and see what was waiting on the other side. But it was all some childish fantasy. A stupid dream.'

'That's one way of looking at it.' Zara shrugged, lifting her arm and waving it across the nothingness before them. 'If Lora was a dream. Then, what would you call this?'

Sebastian sat up and dug his hands into the gravel that had materialised around them. He picked up a grey stone and hurled it into the ocean. 'Viola told me that this isn't a dream. This void, whatever it is, it's real. And if it is, it means that glowing freak back there is also real.' He slowly turned to Zara. 'And it means you're real too.'

She looked at him and smiled briefly before facing away. 'You have to give up on me, Seb.'

'You know I can't do that.'

'Sebastian,' Zara said in a soured tone, as she stood up and turned her back to him. 'You have to stop searching for us. You won't like what you find.'

'I don't care.' Seb stood up and pulled her towards him. 'I'll find you no matter what it takes.'

'I should have known better than to argue with the most stubborn boy in town.' She shook her head and gently slapped his cheek. 'Just don't get upset when you realise, like always, I was right.'

'You're not always right. You told me that nothing was waiting for us past the mountains.'

'Take a look, Seb. This *is* nothing.'

Sebastian gazed with her at the brittle abyss. He tried his best to hold back tears, but they seeped out as he turned to her. 'I have all I need right here.' Slowly, with uncertainty, Sebastian lowered his head and Zara pressed her face towards his, closer and closer until their lips touched.

An explosion of colour lit the white sky. Sebastian and Zara held each other for what felt like an eternity, too afraid to let go.

'We have to stop this,' she said, pushing him away.

'Was I not doing it right?' Seb asked, rubbing the back of his neck. 'This is sort of my first time.'

'I didn't mean it like that.' Zara laughed. 'But you shouldn't be here. This place, it's changing you. You need to escape.'

'Escape from what?' Seb asked, throwing his arms down. 'As long as you're here, this place is more alive than the outside world will ever be.'

Zara was silent. She held Sebastian from behind and wrapped her arms around him. He crumbled in her embrace, turning to face her once more. Only now he could see that they weren't alone.

'Alex?' he asked, squinting at the blonde-haired boy standing in the distance. He let go of Zara and got to his feet. 'What are you doing here?'

'Sebastian. It's been a while,' Alex said calmly, folding his arms, a light smirk breaking upon his pristine cheek. 'I'm not interrupting anything, am I?'

'No…' Sebastian turned to Zara. 'We were just catching up.' He looked back and Alex was no longer there.

'A touching reunion indeed,' Alex said from behind Seb.

'Alex, don't.' Zara warned.

'We haven't got time for this,' Seb said, spinning to face him. 'Tell me where you are. Name a place and I'll be there.' He turned to Zara. 'Both of you.'

'Well, I…' Zara shuffled awkwardly.

'Does it matter what we tell you?' Alex asked, 'You've been here long enough to realise this is all in your head. I'm nothing more than a version of yourself, telling you exactly what you want to hear.'

'No, you're not,' Seb replied with a laugh. 'Only you, Alex, would ever sound so paranoid.'

Alex's eyes opened, and the faint smirk became a sneer. 'You have no idea what this place is, do you? You know nothing of Endura or even Lora for that matter. You're a sheltered, coddled infant who has no clue of the life that exists outside of their crib.' He shook his head as his colours scattered in the wind, only to rematerialise a few yards back on a freshly formed hill.

'And what do you know?' Seb asked, covering his eyes from the white sky as he stepped closer. 'You grew up in Lora, same as me.' He waved over towards Zara. 'We all did.'

'...If there is no other choice, then I will do my duty...'

Alex's voice drifted high from over the ocean.

Seb stared at the words as they faded back to white. 'It was you, wasn't it? You're the reason we're trapped here.'

'This wasn't my doing, Seb. It was yours. You were always so *special*. Everything you could have possibly wanted was at your disposal, and even then, you weren't satisfied. Well, now you've finally woken up. This is real life, Seb. It's pain. It's suffering. It's losing everyone you've ever loved. It's doing things to survive - things that make you want to kill yourself.' Alex burst into a cloud of colours and appeared before Seb in an instant, grabbing him by the collar.

'Alex, please stop! We're finally together again,' Zara pleaded with him.

155

'Isn't this what you wanted?'

'Stay out of this,' Alex said, never taking his eyes off Seb. 'I'm sure he doesn't need a girl fighting *all* his battles.'

'Don't talk to her like that,' Seb uttered, grabbing hold of Alex's arms and pushing him to the ground.

'There he is!' Alex laughed, rising to his feet. 'Finally, where has this Seb been hiding?'

'Start talking, Alex. What happened to our home?'

'You were there. Don't you remember?'

A pulse rippled across his skull. The white void cracked around him. Sebastian roared at the pain and pushed his feet off the ground, charging towards Alex.

Alex burst into a puff of smoke as Seb's knuckles made an impact.

'Very good,' Alex said, standing inches behind Zara, giving a pitiful clap. 'I could tell you put all your weight into that one.'

'Get away from her, Alex. Or I swear I'll-'

'You'll what, Seb?' Alex leaned down and grabbed Zara by the back of the neck. 'You'll kill me? Your best friend?'

'You're not my friend. Not anymore.'

'Look at you,' Alex said with a sigh, letting go of Zara and sidling up to him. 'You're broken. A fractured soul converging between fantasy and reality.'

Sebastian's head throbbed once more, sending more cracks to form in the sky. Shards broke away, bringing back the storm from before. 'I know this isn't real,' Seb answered bitterly under his breath.

'Who's to say? Maybe it's your little journey with Darius and Ariana that's all in your head. I mean, a girl conjuring magic and a big gorilla wielding a sharpened lamp post? That sounds like the fairy tale from where I'm standing.'

Sebastian dropped to one knee, pressing a hand upon his face. The black ocean had turned erratic, blowing a fierce wind. 'They're real!' Seb screamed through the growing storm.

'But how do you know, Seb?' Alex asked before flashing in front of Sebastian, whispering in his ear. 'How do you know?' He grabbed hold of Seb and threw him far into the distance with an inhuman force.

Sebastian landed in the dark waters with seaweed wrapping around his arms and legs like tendrils pulling him under. He struggled to fight back against them, all the while pleading for Zara to help him. His eyes met hers as he flailed helplessly. She simply waved at him by the shore as if to say goodbye. The black ooze wrapped around his stomach and tightened around his neck. Seb made one last attempt to scream for her. But he couldn't even find the strength to breathe. Sebastian sank into the depths, knowing that wherever he washed up, it wouldn't matter. She wouldn't be there.

14.

Phantom Pain

Tendrils wrapped around Sebastian's neck, growing tighter the more he tugged against them. With his wrists and ankles constricted, Seb sank into the jagged depths of the black ocean. A weight fell upon him, crushing Seb's entire being. The void, the empty abyss, enveloped Sebastian without mercy. He told himself not to breathe - forbidding the black bile to consume him from within. Sebastian begged for his lungs to constrict, resisting the urge to give them the sweet nectar they screamed for. His mind became numb to the pressure of the venom surrounding him. The tendrils pulled his body apart, stretching it into a twisted thing - ugly and broken.

Sebastian's heart gave out, permitting one final gasp so the dark waters could fill his lungs. Sebastian inhaled deeply, shocked to realise that cold air entered his chest instead. Not the cleanest breath he had taken, but the thrill of oxygen forced his body to repel the blackness within. He opened his eyes to find a large lightbulb swinging loosely above him. Shades of blue shone upon tables, tubes and sharp metal devices. Across from him were dull green lights jumping from black screens, displaying never-ending lines of text.

Seb lifted his head only for a strap to tighten around his neck. His arms and legs must have been pinned also. He could hardly feel them, let alone move them. It would seem that it did not matter where the waves had washed him. Sebastian was still trapped within the darkness.

'So, he finally awakens.' A croaky voice emerged from the shadows.

'Who's there?' Seb asked, lifting his head.

'Eager to meet me, are you?' the man spoke again, stepping out from the shadows. 'Can't say I blame your excitement, Subject. It's not every day, you find yourself in the presence of a genius.'

The man was incredibly short, matching Sebastian's eye level, even whilst lying flat on a table. His skin was dry and pale, almost peeling from his face. The man's small eyes sunk into his large meaty head, with a small, sharp nose sticking out just beneath, barely able to hold his perfectly round glasses. The mouth stretched across his face with thick crusted lips that creased into a grin, revealing crooked yellow teeth.

'You're with Blackout, aren't you?' Seb asked, struggling against his bonds. 'Tell me where my friends are. What have you done with them?'

'So many questions. I'm happy to have found a kindred spirit within you, Subject.' The short, stout man cackled to himself. 'I too am searching for answers. So, why not help each other? I will tell you what you want to know to the utmost of my abilities. But you will have to do the same for me.'

Sebastian gulped. 'Okay, you first. Who are you?'

'They call me, Doctor G.'

'Doctor G?' Seb repeated with a smirk as he raised his eyebrow.

'A name is forgetful in my line of work, Subject. But a letter is memorable, singular, elusive and powerful. My legacy will not only be remembered but the name shall never be forgotten. Cementing my everlasting life. Figuratively, of course.'

'Right, well, okay then,' Seb said, turning away from the self-professed Doctor G.

'And to answer your other questions. I am not with those snivelling dogs who presume claim over this world. However, they do pay well. So, I have built a certain... trust with them. From time to time, they give me new toys to play with.'

'Lucky me.' Seb sighed.

'Lucky you, indeed. But do not fret. I will be careful not to break my newest toy. This one is special. It seems you're finally awakening to your more... fascinating abilities. Like the ones you demonstrated back in the sewers of Platto.'

'The sewers of...' Sebastian murmured, trying to remember clearly.

He saw the gates closing, his friends running further ahead, fingers brushing Ariana's face through the bars. Those same fingers tightened as the crashing sounds of boots spoiled the calm waters. Sebastian felt a rage bubbling as he turned to face his captors. Then all was black, accompanied by a guttural fit of laughter...

Sebastian jerked against his bindings. 'I don't remember what happened in the sewers,' he said, trying to keep his body steady.

'Interesting.' Doctor G mused, grabbing a pen and clipboard. He began writing intently, taking breaks to glance at Sebastian's bound body.

'Were my friends captured? Are they here as well?'

'Darius Blake and Ariana Lane. They both *somehow* escaped the ever-watchful eyes of Blackout with minimal effort. They are both hiding away in a secluded town a few hundred miles east of our location. The two have already lost the scent of the stuffy-nosed dogs in black. But it seems they are lying low just to be safe.'

'How... do you know all of this?'

'I am Doctor G, Subject. I see all. I know all. And contrary to what Blackout would have you believe. I *control* all.'

The next few hours had been spent answering questions. They were basic, simple facts that the doctor should already have known; his name, height, eye colour, shoe size, and the list went on. Seb's head was beginning to hurt by the time Doctor G asked his next question.

'And your age?'

'Seventeen,' Sebastian answered, 'wait... maybe eighteen? I haven't kept track of the days lately. I'm not sure.'

'Very interesting.'

The doctor jumped out of his seat and waddled towards the computer. He began tapping upon the keyboard before stepping a few feet back and cackling menacingly to himself. 'That could be it! It comes alive when the subject comes of age.'

'What are you talking about, Doc?' Seb sighed.

'You're breaking the rules. I believe it's still my turn to ask the questions.'

'You know what, no! I'm not answering any more of your questions until you tell me why Blackout is after me?'

Doctor G scowled at Seb for a moment, before throwing his arms up with a shrug. 'Fine, Subject. If telling you makes my job easier, then I am happy to oblige,' Doctor G remarked, making his way over to the chair. The doctor cleared his throat. 'Legends tell of a time before the world was plunged within shadow. A natural world, one of both light and darkness. But a change occurred. One that tore our planet apart, leaving an empty husk to drift aimlessly through space and decay. We were nothing more than maggots eating away at that carcass.'

'What has the Blight got to do with me?'

'I'm getting to it, Subject. Have patience.' Doctor G turned back and cleared his throat. 'When all seemed lost, a light rose from the darkness, shining a torch over our dying planet. A group of people found salvation from the edge of the world. From there, they discovered a way to rid the poison from Endura, bringing back the remnants of humanity from the brink and building a new society on top of the old.'

'Who were these people?' Seb asked.

'You know them as Blackout.'

Sebastian's eyes widened, and a jolt ran down his spine. 'You're wrong,' he told the mad doctor.

'Am I?' The Doctor asked with his slimy grin widening. 'Named after the day our world was swallowed by shadow, the group known as Blackout appeared. They brought with them a means not only to survive but to also thrive. They taught the denizens of our ruptured planet to stop living like maggots and to claw back some semblance of life. Leading them was their master, the soul who had studied the Blight to the point of becoming one with it. *The Black Beast.* No longer man nor creature, the beast was an entity. An energy. Raw and unsustainable power, too chaotic to control, too precious to kill. Blackout was chosen to keep this monster at bay, or risk dismantling the planet that they had sacrificed so much to save.'

When the doctor was finished, Seb allowed himself to breathe. 'And they... no, you believe I'm this Black Beast?' Seb asked with a quick laugh. 'Don't you see how ridiculous that sounds? I'm not the monster here. Blackout is. You are!'

'You truly don't remember what happened in the sewers, do you?'

'I told you. I said I-'

'Think back, my entity of cruelty. Let your rage take you there.'

'No, I can't remember, I...' Sebastian turned away and closed his eyes, gritting his teeth as his head sent pulses through his body. His bones ached, his stomach seized...

Seb let out a roar of pain. He released his grip on the bars, leaving them bent and misshapen. He turned and laughed at them all. The lights exploded around him. They tried to run. He stopped them, making sure they would never run again. Sebastian looked into the blood-red face of the mask as he squeezed the life from its wearer, thrilled that he looked more terrifying at that moment. Shaking violently, he felt the bullet pierce through the skin. Obliterating his hand and leaving a bloody stump. Next came fire, and ice soon after. More bullets tore away at him until he was mangled. He saw the face of Vincent Vale looking down upon him. His eyes filled with sorrow.

Seb's body convulsed. The doctor injected a syringe into his neck. It dulled the pain, allowing Sebastian to breathe and fall limp. He looked down, realising why he hadn't been able to move his body. 'I remember...' he uttered in a dried gasp.

'And now you will never be able to forget.' The mad doctor grinned wickedly.

Sebastian could still feel his fingers twitching as he squeezed them into fists, an itch on the bottom of his foot, a chill stretching over his legs caused by the icy room. He could even feel the sensation of pain shooting up his arms.

The doctor lifted a mirror above Seb with an impish smile, finally revealing his body for what it was.

Sebastian shook violently when he took witness to the craven image. He saw a demon staring back at him, hair longer than it had ever been, black as night and almost completely covering its scarred face. Burns and deep cuts ravaged the beast's skin, leaving it blistered. Bandages covered its torso, reaching across to wrap around the shoulders and down the arms to end at amputated elbows.

Sebastian tried lifting his hands to wipe away the tears. But he could see nothing, feel nothing. Just useless stumps that sprouted from his elbows. His legs were the same past the knees; broken, useless, corrupted. Sebastian winced, averting his eyes from the mirror and sobbed pitifully to himself.

'What are you waiting for? Just kill me and be done with it.'

'Why all the fuss, Subject? It is a nasty sight to be sure. But it is only temporary,' Doctor G said, removing the mirror.

'Don't joke with me, you sick freak! I've lost everything!' Sebastian shook violently on the table, unable to move. 'Everything...'

'You think the blackness inside will allow its host to succumb to such a pitiful display? The thing that lives just below the surface has already begun regenerating your lost limbs. Weeks ago, you had no bones or skin past your shoulders or pelvis. Half of what you have lost has already been rebuilt - better than before.'

Sebastian raised his elbow and noticed something bubbling under his skin. 'What is this?' he asked as his pupils dilated in ever-widening eyes. Seb's elbow began to tremble as he slammed what was left of his arm down hard on the table and turned away, feeling hot bile creep up his throat. 'It's impossible!'

The doctor took a moment before continuing.

'Normally, yes. But this creature has a precise map of your molecular structure, it can reshape your base design whenever you happen to lose a limb, or even get a scratch. Your face was completely unrecognisable from the burns it sustained when you were brought here. In only a few short months, it has healed astonishingly.'

'I don't want this.' Seb retched as he turned away from his craven body. 'Why is this happening to me?'

'Because you're needed for a higher purpose, Subject. Meaning, your life is no longer yours to end,' Doctor G nonchalantly said. 'You're nothing more than a tool. A shell for the parasite that lives inside.'

'You're wrong. This thing that's inside of me. Whatever it is.' Sebastian turned slowly to lock eyes with Doctor G. 'It will die along with me.'

'How dare you,' Doctor G said through clenched teeth, slapping Seb hard across the face. 'You've been given the gifts of a god. The ability to regenerate, to destroy! The power to rule this corpse of a planet and you would rather die?' The doctor raised his hand again, forcing Sebastian to wince. 'This gift is wasted on you, Subject,' Doctor G said with a sigh, lowering his hand. 'However, that makes my job easier.'

'What do you mean?'

Doctor G leaned in close and grinned, showing his slimy yellow teeth. 'I'm going to extract whatever it is that lives inside of you, Subject. Unlike you, I will appreciate its *gifts*.' He rushed out of the room, his cackle lingering down the halls long after he had made his exit. Sebastian was left alone, staring at the mirror. Reflected, the demon gazed back.

Broken, useless, corrupted. That is how the abyssal light described Sebastian. The only thing he could do now - other than sob pitifully to himself - was to repeat those words in his head.

'Can you hear me?' Seb asked aloud, staring at his reflection.

He was met with silence.

'I don't know what you are. To be quite honest, I don't think I want to know. But whatever you are, you're a part of me. That must mean we want the same thing, right?'

Again, there was no answer.

'I remember you saved me before - or tried to, at least. That lunatic out there said you're fixing my body. So, thanks, I guess.'

Sebastian continued to stare at the craven image of the mirror. If the thing within him could talk, it was an awful conversationalist.

'There's this girl. I'll do anything to find her. So, if you know some way to get out of this place, let's hear it. I'm pretty sure you hate being experimented on just as much as I do, anyway.'

Nothing.

'Well, it was just a thought,' he said, finally looking away.

After some time, the door creaked open. Sebastian twisted his neck to see what the madman had planned next. But the silhouette was new. Tall and slim, the complete opposite of the doctor.

'Hungry?' a frail voice called out.

'Who's there?'

'I'm Irvine,' he said, shuffling over to Sebastian with a bowl of steaming soup. 'The doctor said you wouldn't need to eat, as the...' He gulped. '*Thing* inside provides you with all the nutrients you require to survive. But I thought it would help you recover.'

Sebastian squinted up at the man, although he was more of a boy than an adult. Pale skinned like the doctor, but blemishes and acne smeared Irvine's face. He wore thick glasses that made his head look longer than it was, with the faintest shadow of a moustache forming above his quivering lips. The man smiled and lifted the bowl towards Seb.

'What is it?' Seb asked.

'Glitches special recipe. My mother taught me how to cook before she... before I left home.' Irvine spooned up some of the soup and placed it before Sebastian's mouth.

Seb could see the bubbling grey sludge in front of him. It smelled like the fish market back in Lora - or perhaps the back alley where they would throw out the rotten food. Seb hesitated for a moment but opened his mouth, wishing his hand would suddenly grow back for him to hold his nose. He gagged as the colourless soup touched his tongue, but swallowed the bile out of instinct. 'Are you trying to poison me?'

'Sorry, I told you my mother taught me how to cook. I never said I was a good student.' Irvine placed the bowl on a nearby table and scratched his face. 'And where we are, there aren't many options.'

'In that case, I'll eat it.'

The gangly man smiled once again and continued.

Sebastian gulped down the grey sludge and smiled. 'You know, this isn't that bad. After the initial shock, at least.'

'Well, there's plenty of it. I'll make sure to bring more down and join you next time. It would be good to share my meals with someone.'

'You don't eat with the Doctor?'

Irvine shuddered. 'Never,' he said, shaking his head.

'So, what's up with that guy? How does he-'

'I've got to go,' Irvine said, shooting up from his chair. 'But it was nice to make your acquaintance, Sub... Sebastian.'

'My friends call me Seb. It was good to meet you too, Irvine.'

'My friends call... I mean, they *called* me Glitch.'

'Then, Glitch it is. Don't be a stranger now.'

'I won't, Seb. Now get some rest.'

Irvine turned off the lights and closed the door, leaving Sebastian in the darkness. It was here that Seb felt safe. No clinical lab equipment or computer screens flashing, nor the eerie blue and green lights displaying needle-like tools. Seb could even feel his arms and legs within the darkness. It was almost like the shadows wrapped around him like a blanket. Sebastian felt warm. He felt secure. Letting himself drift into a peaceful slumber.

As the weeks turned into months, Sebastian's limbs sprouted further. His arms now stretched down to form wrists, and his legs stopped at the ankles. Within this time, Seb had made himself a home within the prison. His electrified cell held a bed and a change of clothes. Glitch had even provided books for him to read, although turning the pages was a cumbersome task.

Irvine would join him in the cell most days, providing Seb with some much-needed conversation. However, he would fade into silence when

Sebastian would ask of the outside world, his friends, Blackout, or what Doctor G was planning to do with him. Seb knew that Glitch was under strict orders not to speak of such things, but he also saw how it tore at the young scientist when he couldn't answer. Because of this, Sebastian tried his best to avoid such subjects.

'So, still working on that photon displacer?' Seb asked.

'Sure am,' Glitch answered eagerly, tinkering with the device. 'Once I work out all the kinks, this puppy will be ready for testing.'

'Explain to me again what it's meant to do.'

'How many times do I have to go over it with you?'

'Just one more time, promise.'

They both laughed and sighed, with Sebastian placing his wrist on the back of his neck.

'The photon displacer is a device that I'm hoping to use much like a gun. But instead of killing its targets, it immobilises them humanely and without injury.'

'By shooting light bullets?'

'That is an apt description, yes,' Glitch said, adjusting his glasses. 'It uses the particles produced by the light and condenses them to a specified area. The flash will not only blind its target but nullify their other senses also - in theory, at least.'

'Well, you've always got a willing test subject right here. That's if Doctor G is kind enough to share, of course.'

'I wish you would stop talking like that, Seb.' Glitch frowned, turning away.

'Look at me, Irvine. I'm a lab rat. I know it, the doctor knows it, and you know it too.'

'Sebastian... you're not-'

The doors whooshed open, and a maniacal whistle filled the room with a diabolical tune, accompanied by the screeching of wheels. Doctor G walked through, pushing Sebastian's wheelchair in front of him. He entered the passcode on the locks of the cell and stepped inside.

'Morning, Irvine. Morning, Subject.'

'Good morning, Doctor G.' Seb and Glitch spoke in unison, as they often did when addressing the doctor at the start of the day.

'How are you feeling today, my little cocoon of unspeakable power?' The doctor asked, shining a light into Sebastian's eyes and placing a wooden stick on his tongue.

'I'm fine, doctor,' Seb tried to say with a wide-open mouth. It all came out as incomprehensible gargles, but it didn't matter to Doctor G. The madman didn't care how Sebastian was feeling.

'Good. Well, there are no noticeable changes from yesterday. But it would seem that you will be fully healed in the next few weeks.'

'Then will you finally let me leave?' Seb asked.

'In time, Subject. All in good time.'

Sebastian felt his phantom hands mould into fists. But he forced a smile. 'Thank you.'

The doctor smiled back and turned towards Glitch, noticing the device in his hands. 'Irvine, what have I told you about tinkering with your toys during work hours?' he asked, picking up the photon displacer.

'I apologise, sir. However, I have performed all of the morning tasks successfully and thought-'

'You thought what? That you would take advantage of my good nature, wasting your working hours and my laboratory's resources to craft your ridiculously half-baked contraptions?' Doctor G snatched the device from Glitch's hands and threw it against the electrified cell, smiling as it burst into pieces.

'I'm... sorry, Doctor.'

'Now pick up this mess before the subject uses the pieces to kill itself somehow. Then prep it and wheel it out into the main hall. I am eager to show it something *I've* been working on.' Doctor G stormed out of the cell and through the doors laughing to himself.

Glitch sighed deeply and proceeded to pick up the pieces from his destroyed photon displacer.

Sebastian watched for a moment, before bending down to help. 'How can you let him treat you like that?' Seb asked, adding another burnt piece to the pile, awkwardly with his wrists.

'He's my boss. It's not like I can stand up to him.' Glitch shrugged, eyes watering as he inspected each broken part.

'He's a lunatic,' Seb corrected, pushing himself up to balance on his ankles. 'How did you ever end up working for a nut like that?'

'I'm sorry, I can't say.'

'Why not? He doesn't control you.' Sebastian fell back onto his bed and hit the pillow with his wrist. 'Why do you work for these people, Glitch? Doctor G is just as insane as the rest of Blackout. By working for them, you're just as bad.'

'You don't have to tell me. I already know.' Glitch dropped the pieces of his device to the floor and turned away. 'If anything, I'm worse. I know that all of this is wrong, but I help them anyway. I'm nothing but a coward.'

'Then why don't you leave?' Seb asked, pushing himself upright.

'They know everything about me; the town I grew up. Where my family...' Glitch grabbed hold of a book he had given Seb and hurled it against the electrified bars, disintegrating it.

'What happened, Glitch? How did you end up here?'

'My family. They're the reason.' He turned and sighed at the confusion on Seb's face. 'We were poor. One of the poorest of the city where I grew up. Everything I owned I had to make myself. Turns out, I had a knack for it. Before long I was creating all kinds of nifty gadgets from whatever I could find on the streets. I was able to sell them, and it kept my family from starving. For a time, at least. One day, they came. The Ender Knights of Blackout. They had caught wind of my inventions and gave my parents the offer to live lavishly upon the Crimson Cloud. But to do so, they would need to sign my life over to them.'

'How could your parents do that?'

'To spend your life on the Crimson is a fleeting dream for all Endurians. And they were hungry, Seb. They had my brother and sisters to think about. They had already lost one child that year. I understand why they did it.' Irvine's hand balled into a fist as he continued picking up the pieces of his Photon Displacer. 'I may not have an electrified cell, but I'm a prisoner, same as you.'

'I didn't know. How could Blackout do something like that? Steal a kid from their family.'

'They weren't always like this. Something happened a few decades back. I don't know what. But since then, they've taken what they want without regard for human lives.'

They stayed there for a time. Sebastian consoled Glitch as he sobbed pitifully on the floor over his dismantled device. Before long, Irvine wiped away his tears and picked Seb up, placing him in the wheelchair.

'You sure you're okay?' Seb asked.

'I'll be fine,' Glitch said through snot-filled sniffs.

'I wonder what the *good* doctor wants to show me.'

'I think I know,' Glitch answered solemnly, wiping the sweat from his brow. 'It's best if you prepare yourself, Seb.'

15.

Man, Made Monsters

Seb and Irvine met Doctor G outside of the cell, his unsettling grin gleaming up at them. Glitch sighed and followed, pushing Sebastian along with him. After some time travelling through the underground labyrinth, the doctor stopped at a door. It was different from the rest - large, circular and made of thick steel. Doctor G placed his face on an indent in the wall, and soon after, gears and pistons hissed from the other side, and the door groaned open.

A green light peered out from the open entrance, spilling into the large hall. Sebastian gulped as he was wheeled into the unusual room. Inside were many blinking lights from machines covering the walls. Seb's eyes followed the tubes slithering along the floor towards the centre of the room. All of the cables were connected to a tank at the heart of the laboratory. A large cylindrical vat filled with a green transparent liquid. The tubes became smaller once inside the structure as they connected to a strange creature sleeping within. It had the body of a man but was almost three times the size. Its skin was pale grey and ravaged with scars that seemed to stretch across the monster's entire body.

'Incredible, isn't it?' Doctor G asked as he stepped through.

'What is that thing?' Seb asked.

'Subject, meet Alpha. The first genetically engineered human.'

'It's grotesque!' Seb wailed, trying to wheel himself back.

The creature opened its bright yellow eyes and locked onto Sebastian's.

'Careful, Subject. It can hear you.'

'Please, sir. Can I take the subject back to his – I mean, *its* cell.'

'Nonsense, Irvine. I like to show off my toys just as much as you do.' Doctor G pushed Glitch aside and wheeled Sebastian's wheelchair forward.

Seb's neck arched up as he was thrust ever closer to the substantial, hairless being in the tank. The monster eventually lost interest and continued its slumber, allowing Seb to breathe a sigh of relief. He looked closer at it now - the tubes were pumping chemicals in and out of its body. One masked its mouth, allowing tiny bubbles to escape. Sebastian wheeled himself ever closer to the thing in the vat and placed a stump on the glass. 'It's in pain.'

'I didn't think you would have that reaction,' Doctor G said, taking a step back. 'But you are kindred spirits, after all.'

'This is barbaric. How could you do this to a person?' Seb asked, turning to face him.

'Not a person, Subject. *People.* Alpha is an amalgamation of many.'

'It can't be,' Seb uttered, looking towards Glitch who had hung his head.

'And not just any ordinary people.' The doctor continued. 'A collection of the greatest specimens that humanity has produced within the last few decades. Men and women who were skilled in combat, individuals who had mastered their User abilities, and even great scientists. Their knowledge and expertise would have been otherwise lost to the world if they were not preserved within our dear Alpha. Their bodies, brains, and their hearts live on within it. Maybe even their very souls burn through its chest. They are once again able to stand, to think, to feel and-'

'Become your slave.' Sebastian cut in. 'You think Alpha and I need to be caged, but you're the one who should be locked away. *You're* the monster here, Doc.'

'Come now, Subject. I'm not that bad. I waited for all those people to die before I united their parts.' The doctor said, wheeling Seb away from

Alpha. 'Well, most of them, at least.'

'Let go of me!' Seb yelled, elbowing at the doctor's mitts.

'You should know the end goal of all our little medical examinations, Subject.' The doctor chuckled, moving closer to Sebastian's ear. 'You're the last piece of the puzzle that my Alpha needs. Its skin is already infused with the toughest substance I could create, but once the god living within you is extracted and bestowed upon my greatest creation. It will be the strongest living being on the planet. Perhaps even more powerful than *him*.'

The doctor wheeled a screaming Sebastian out of the eerie green laboratory. Glitch stood frozen, watching the doctor as G cackled maniacally. Seb called out for him and looked back, only to see that Glitch had removed his glasses and was now staring back at the creature in the vat.

As Sebastian neared the doorway, he heard Glitch's muffled voice moan, 'We're all monsters.'

'You're wrong!' Seb screamed as he was wheeled out of the room. 'This isn't you, Glitch. Please... you have to-'

'You think Irvine cares for you, Subject?' Doctor G asked, chuckling to himself. 'You're nothing more to him than Alpha is. An experiment.'

'No. He's my...' Seb breathed, taking one last look towards his friend.

Glitch had tears in his eyes, pulling something from his pocket. The young scientist stared longingly at whatever he was holding, before squeezing it within his fist. His gaze wandered around the room and finally landed on Seb the moment Doctor G turned a corner. Then he was gone. Sebastian was wheeled through the underground labyrinth, lost in the maze until Doctor G stopped at an old, dilapidated room. Cobwebs and rust surrounded the walls. It was the room Sebastian woke up in all those months ago.

'This is where you will be staying for the foreseeable future,' Doctor G told him.

'Please, doctor,' Sebastian pleaded, trying to stop the wheels from moving with his pitiful stumps. 'Just let me go back to my cell. I'll do anything, I promise. I'll never question your genius again, I swear it. Please!' A needle pierced Sebastian's neck. His eyes widened, then closed, as he slumped back into his wheelchair.

'Be still, my vessel of unspeakable power,' Doctor G whispered tenderly into Sebastian's ear. 'We have much work to do.'

Sebastian felt the bubbles rushing past his face when he took another long deep breath. They were screaming, clawing at him from within his mind, desperate to escape. Seb sensed himself drifting through unconsciousness as he floated in the gelatinous substance. He felt the gentle push of chemicals pumping into his body through many different tubes, interconnecting like a river into the ocean of his being.

The woes of anguish wouldn't stop. The painful cries were not his own. The agony was theirs - the many souls trapped within him, forever screaming. Sebastian wanted to join them. He wished to scream as they did, to give voice to their suffering. Sebastian wanted to end their pain. But he could not. Whatever it was he was floating in, it held him in place. Like a statue in a lake without borders, he drifted.

'It's grotesque!' Wailed a muffled voice from beyond the lake that submerged him.

Sebastian's eyes shot open and stared down upon the source of his torment – a boy in a wheelchair, with no hands or feet.

The short, fat one spoke next, his voice muffled. Then the taller one from further behind. Sebastian ignored them and focused on the child. His skin was pale and his body feeble, but darkness blackened his eyes as if it were seeping out of the boy.

Sebastian closed his eyes again. Opening them had become too painful.

It made them all scream and scratch with more vigour. They hated the people who weren't trapped, wanted them to stop talking – wanted them all to just stop.

Seb wished that everyone within him would take their own advice and allow him a moment of silence. But they just kept on screaming at him – demanding their freedom.

'It's in pain.' He heard the child of darkness say once more between the wails of eternal torture before drifting back into the black silence - the nothingness where all of the screams became a lullaby.

'It is time to wake, Subject.' Cackled a voice from the darkness.

Sebastian gasped back into the waking world as freezing water struck him. Coughing and flailing, Seb struggled against the binds that wrapped around his body.

'The screaming!' Sebastian wailed. 'Why won't they stop?'

'Another bad dream.' Doctor G smirked. 'Be glad that it is over. You're back in the land of the living, where the real nightmare can commence.'

Sebastian heard the vicious spinning of one of the doctor's torture devices and braced himself for the worst. He felt the ice-cold flash of pain, fast becoming red hot and unbearable as it drilled into his chest. Seb roared in pain, only to have the doctor stuff his mouth with a dirty rag.

'Do you know what day it is, Subject?'

Sebastian didn't answer.

'It is the day of your complete recovery. It took longer than I thought, but your hands and feet are back. Every digit accounted for.'

Seb's eyes widened. He tried to look down but was unable to move his head from the strap tightened around it. Was this another of the mad doctor's cruel lies? Sebastian rolled his hands and feet in a circular motion, squeezing his fingers and toes - and not just a phantom memory, these were the real things. Seb made a muffled cheer through the rag in his mouth. Tears began streaming down his face as he rubbed his fingertips together and squeezed his toes. He started bobbing his head and humming a tune through the rag.

'It is quite sweet to see you so cheerful,' the doctor said, turning towards Seb. 'It almost breaks my heart, knowing I will have to remove them once more.'

Sebastian stopped abruptly from his muffled tune and made a noise that sounded like it could have been a question.

'You didn't think I would let you keep them, did you?' The doctor asked. 'I have proven data that it is through your very hand movements that the power inside is released. If you think I'm going to trust you not to kill me, then you really are a fool.'

Seb begged incomprehensible words through the rag and shook his head wildly, all the while keeping his eyes locked on Doctor G's

'And your feet?' the doctor continued, with a shrug. 'Well, I kind of like the idea of wheeling you around.'

Seb shook his head slowly, squeezing his hands into fists and shivering violently against the operating table. He looked up to see the doctor holding a dull, rusty saw - the edges didn't even look sharp.

'It will take a while to get through each limb with this. But they take so long to grow back that we might as well savour the experience.'

Sebastian closed his eyes, taking a faint breath. He finally stopped struggling and allowed his body to go limp as the doctor readied his blade. Suddenly, a loud slam echoed across the room. Sebastian and the doctor both turned to see Glitch, panting by the open doorway.

'You're just in time, Irvine. I was just about to perform the amputation. Be a lamb and fetch a bucket for the discarded limbs, won't you?'

'No... I won't,' Glitch uttered, his body trembling.

'Irvine?' Doctor G asked, his eyebrow raised high into his meaty forehead. 'I must have misheard you. It almost sounded like you were defying my orders. I said, can you-'

'Get away from him, you freak!' Glitch screamed, pointing a trembling finger towards the doctor. 'Leave my friend alone.'

'Friend?' The doctor looked back at Seb in amazement. 'You think this... *thing* is your friend? Irvine, you fool! This is a monster. It is a thing of horror and hate. Somehow it has manipulated you into caring for it.'

'I *have* been manipulated,' Irvine said, raising his other hand from behind his back. 'For as long as I can remember, I've been controlled by you and your twisted mind.' Glitch held a large device in his hands – it looked familiar, but Sebastian couldn't place it. Glitch pointed the device at Doctor G and told him. 'That changes today.'

'Irvine, what is that?' The doctor asked, raising his arms.

'I call it the photon displacer. Do you want to know what it does?' Irvine stepped further into the room, never dropping his aim. 'Please, Sir. Ask me what it does.'

Doctor G gulped. 'What... what does it-'

Before he could finish, Glitch pulled the trigger, unleashing a flash of pure white energy around the doctor. Both Glitch and Seb averted their eyes as the white ray exploded into the room. When the light faded, they both looked upon the doctor - now a slobbering mess of a man sprawled out on the floor. Glitch removed the rag from Sebastian's mouth and proceeded to loosen his bonds.

'You saved me,' Seb said feebly.

'Maybe,' Glitch said with a grin, 'or perhaps it's the other way around.'

Sebastian met his smile and held out his hand.

'Now we have to be quick,' Glitch said, pulling Seb up to his feet. 'This place will go into lockdown once he regains consciousness.'

'I Can't believe this is the first time we've shaken hands,' Sebastian said with a strained smile.

'Let's hope it's not the last,' Glitch said, pulling Sebastian towards the door.

It was as if Sebastian had all but forgotten how to use his feet, stumbling as he ran with Glitch gliding him through the long and winding halls. Finally, they stopped at a door. Irvine began typing at a nearby computer. Within moments the door whooshed opened and he pushed Seb inside before darting to a nearby keyboard.

Sebastian breathed heavily as he looked around this strange room. The walls were filled with many screens depicting landscapes. In some, he could see the vast expanse of the sandy wastes where he had awoken. In others, the village hidden in the sands that once housed the Oasis pub - now, as demolished and discarded as the rest of the wastes. Another showed the ashen forest where he spent that night with Ariana. Sebastian saw screens that showed Platto and other cities he hadn't yet visited. Some were incredibly different from anything he had witnessed.

'That ought to do it,' Glitch said, facing towards the largest of the screens that now depicted a town with several spherical stone buildings and a castle built into the face of a cliff.

'Where's that?' Sebastian asked.

'That's where your friends are hiding.' Irvine grinned, wiping the sweat from his forehead. 'That's where we're going.'

Seb smiled, leaning back against a pillar, and letting out a deep breath. His eyes became drawn to a smaller display further down the room. As he approached, his eyes widened at the image. It was a village, or what was left of one. The ruins were left scattered and broken. Amidst the chaos, a lone structure stood tall - the remnants of a marble fountain. The white statue atop it remained pristine, as if untouched by the surrounding destruction.

It was *Lora.*

'Glitch?' Seb uttered, pointing towards the screen. 'How do we get there?'

Irvine stared at the image, scratching his head. 'I don't know. It doesn't look familiar'

'Can you find it?'

'I'll have a look, but I'm not sure if-'

Before Glitch could finish, a high-pitched sound rang out from the walls. Seb covered his ears, noticing the lights fading in and out, turning red, flashing with the alarm.

Glitch ran to another computer and typed in some codes. That's when the large screen flashed onto the dusty operating room they had escaped from. Only now, Doctor G was not in there. 'We have to go,' Glitch said, stepping back from the screen.

'Glitch, please,' Seb pleaded, pointing to the remains of his village. 'You have to find out where it is!'

'Seb, you won't be seeing that place or any other if we don't leave immediately.'

Sebastian stared at the image of his lost home a moment longer before nodding and reaching out his hand. Glitch grabbed hold of it and ran back out into the halls, now flashing red before giving them a second of complete darkness. The fleeting moments of shadow provided Sebastian with an unexpected sense of comfort. He moved more confidently in the dark, no longer clumsy on his feet, sprinting ahead, seemingly guided by an instinctive knowledge of his surroundings. Glitch struggled to keep up, urging Seb to watch out.

Turning the next corner, an explosion erupted from the floor at Sebastian's feet. He leapt back into cover. Irvine, catching up, nearly collapsed against the wall, gasping for breath.

'The defence grid,' Glitch wheezed, 'it won't let us pass this way. We have to find an alternate route.'

Seb peered out and noticed two automated rifles attached to the ceiling. One began firing at him the moment he peeked at it, and he moved back behind cover. 'Don't worry, Glitch. I think I've got this.'

'What are you-'

Seb inhaled deeply, tensing the muscles in his newly formed calves as he propelled himself from behind the corner. Glitch's voice blended with the blaring alarm, drowned out by the screeching turrets and their low hum as they unleashed a barrage of kinetic shots. The heat of plasma and the crackling static of electricity surrounded Seb as the shots whizzed around his body. Spinning through the air, Seb dodged the projectiles, leaping from wall to wall until he closed the distance. He tore one turret from the ceiling and hurled it at the other. The collision resonated with a forceful blast, leaving behind only smoke and severed wires.

Glitch peered out from behind the corner, seeing Sebastian's shadow obscured by fire and smoke. 'What did you do?'

'I don't know exactly. I just lost control for a second and...' Seb said through panted breaths. He looked around to see the debris and shook his head.

'Come with me,' Glitch said, putting a hand on Seb's shoulder. 'There's one thing that must be done before we leave.'

Glitch guided Sebastian through the labyrinth for a time, avoiding detection from the automated security, eventually arriving at the thick steel door that Seb remembered all too well.

'Why are we here?' Seb asked.

Glitch paused briefly, allowing himself to take a breath. 'We're going to put Alpha out of its misery.'

'You're going to kill them?'

'I have to, Seb.'

Sebastian turned away, before nodding glumly. Glitch pulled out a small device from his pocket and used it to remove the face scanner next to the door. He then brought out a small glowing screen from his other pocket and connected a wire from inside the wall. Seb peered over his shoulder to see a constant stream of text flowing through the screen. Irvine then started typing a code into the device.

'What is that thing?'

'I call it the Codebreaker. It can allow anyone to hack into the most secure locks in all of Endura. If they're smart enough to know how to use it, of course.'

'Of course,' Seb repeated, rolling his eyes.

'Sadly, Blackout also thought it was a great device. Which is why they forced me to create more for each of their Ender Knights,'

'Well, at least they let you keep one.'

'Actually, they didn't. This was simply the prototype.'

The gears behind the door hissed at them before groaning open, allowing the lucid green light to pour out. Glitch stepped through, with Seb closely behind. Irvine began the process immediately, moving from screen to screen, punching codes and hitting buttons faster than Seb's eyes could follow. The tubes hissed at them as steam began pouring from the vents. The green liquid in Alpha's vat began to drain, and the wires connected to it began breaking away with sparks of electricity. Seb watched on, unable to look away. He put a hand on Glitch's shoulder when he saw the anguish on the young scientist's face. Alpha began shrieking, throwing wild and clumsy punches against the tube, causing cracks to appear.

'What's happening?' Seb asked, taking a step back as the cracks grew wider.

'It's not working,' Glitch answered, continuing to punch upon the keyboards. 'All life support systems are down, but Alpha is fighting against it.'

'Is there anything we can do?'

'I can only think of one thing. But it's risky.'

Sebastian took another look towards Alpha. It had ripped the cables from its body and was staring back at him, continuing its relentless punching and flailing at the reinforced glass.

'Do it,' Seb told Irvine.

Glitch nodded and returned to the computer. 'Once the countdown commences, we'll have less than ten minutes to escape this place.'

'What do you mean?' Seb asked, never taking his eyes off the monster.

'We can't kill it, Seb. The best we can hope for is that it gets buried along with everything else.'

'You don't mean…'

'Laboratory G houses many secrets that the doctor would rather see destroyed than fall into the wrong hands. It's funny to think there could be grubbier fingers than his own. But there's a failsafe. A self-destruct code.'

'You sure we can make it out in time?'

'I reckon we'll be able to get far away enough to get a good view of the fireworks,' Glitch said with a smirk.

'You're starting to scare me.' Sebastian smiled, planting a hand on the back of his neck.

'You ready? Glitch asked with a strained gulp.

Seb nodded, and with trembling fingers, Glitch tapped at the keyboard. The ringing finally stopped but was replaced by a synthetic female voice - repeating itself.

'*Self-Destruct process engaged.*'

Glitch and Seb sprinted into the halls, and through the long winding corridors that eventually lead to a spiralling staircase. They ran, wheezing up the never-ending steps.

'The exit!' Glitch yelled, pointing ahead.

Seb's eyes became filled with tears when he heard those words. Soon he would be free from this place, free to be with his friends, free to find out the truth of what happened to Lora, free to-

Sebastian froze. Glitch came to a stop behind him, mouth agape and eyes wide.

It was Doctor G, clutching his chest and hunched over like he was about to collapse. In his hand, he held onto a small vial of black liquid. Delivering his signature slimy grin. 'I was wondering when you two would show up,' he said through clenched teeth.

'It's over, G,' Glitch yelled. 'Every terrible experiment you've ever had a part in is about to be lost.'

'Not just my great deeds, Irvine. They were yours also.'

Glitch stepped back, looking behind his shoulder towards the facility. 'You're right. That's why it's my responsibility to make sure these sins never see the light of day.'

'And what about the sin that stands beside you?'

Sebastian and Glitch glanced at one another.

'He's my friend,' Glitch breathed, nodding at Seb. 'You're the only monster here.'

'Not yet...' Doctor G growled. 'But with the help of your *friend*, I soon will be.' The mad doctor held the tube of black bile high above his head. He grinned wildly as he poured it down his throat, smashing the glass container to the ground.

'What was that?' Sebastian asked.

'The creature that lives within you has found a new home, Subject!'

'No,' Irvine uttered.

'What are you talking about?' Seb asked again, taking a step back.

'The conclusion of all our experiments. The powers you neglected now rest within me!'

'You're insane,' Glitch said, shaking his head.

'I can feel its power... coursing through my veins.' Doctor G threw his arms up in the air, before coughing slightly. 'Now Endura's crowning power will be bestowed upon the greatest mind of all...' He grabbed at his throat and collapsed to the floor. 'Wait... what... is this?'

Sebastian and Glitch stood motionless as Doctor G flailed helplessly on the ground.

'What's happening to him?' Seb asked, peering closer.

'It would seem that Endura's crowning power didn't agree with him,' Glitch answered, adjusting his glasses.

'Should we... do something?'

'Yes. We should leave. Who knows how much time we have left before this place goes under.'

Sebastian nodded and followed Glitch as they stepped past Doctor G, making their way towards the exit. Seb could see it, the light at the end of the tunnel - bright and brimming with colours Sebastian had not seen in a long time.

They were finally free.

The two managed to find Glitch's vehicle he had named the zoomer. The machine couldn't fly but still managed to hover a few feet from the ground. It was small, made from rusted metals and looked almost like the bikes people used to ride back in Lora. The zoomer allowed them to drive to a safe enough distance, surrounded by rocky cliffs, overlooking a thick black ocean. Sebastian stopped when he saw it. It was the same one from his journey to the void.

'Terrible, isn't it?' Glitch asked.

'What am I looking at?'

'It has many names; the Black Sea, Ocean of Oil, Blight Tide. Whatever you wish to call it doesn't make a difference. It'll swallow Endura all the same.

Seb turned to him with a questioning look on his face. Glitch could tell it was there without needing to turn. Instead, he continued staring out at the abysmal body of water.

'Year by year, the pit surrounding Blight Tide grows a little larger. The decay that poisons the land spreads a little further. The creatures that live in the surrounding areas grow a little more deranged. Blackout had done well for humanity when they purified the lands of that toxicity. But this chasm was something even they weren't able to solve. It's why I became a scientist. I wanted to stop the spread and help mend this world. Instead, all I did was create more misery.'

'There's still time,' Sebastian nodded with a feeble smile, but it soon faded. He held a hand in front of his face and stared hard at it, inspecting every molecule as it squeezed into a fist.

'You're okay. It's over now.' Irvine said, patting Seb on the shoulder. 'We're free.'

Sebastian shrugged the hand from his back. 'I don't think it will ever be over, Glitch.' He let his hand fall back to his side and stared at the ocean. 'I'll never be free. Maybe I never was.'

Irvine stepped away for a moment to look back at the underground facility. 'You know, from above ground, it's just a steel door built into the rocks. Only we know what lies beneath the surface.'

Sebastian didn't answer.

'I don't know about you, but I'm going to rest easy knowing that we freed the world from the secrets and sins that were hidden in laboratory G.'

Sebastian looked up and met Glitch's eyes.

'You could say we just saved the world, Seb. And your powers helped us do it.'

'Okay, I get it.' Sebastian laughed, shaking his head.

'That's more like it.' Glitch smiled. 'Now get up here so we can watch the fireworks.'

Sebastian grinned and ran up beside him. Together they sat and watched as a stream of flames burst from the steel door, ripping it loose and sending it flying into the ocean. The ground trembled beneath them as the underground lair was incinerated within. When the smoke cleared, and the sun began to set beyond the darkening sea, Sebastian and Glitch prepared themselves for the long drive ahead.

'You think everything down there was destroyed?' Seb asked.

'Nothing but ashes and ghosts,' Glitch answered as he whistled a tune, tinkering with the engine of his zoomer.

'And what about Doctor G and Alpha?'

'There's no probable chance they could have survived,' Irvine uttered, wiping his brow. He turned to look at the crumbled entrance once more, watching for any sign of movement. Finally, he shook his head and turned towards the vehicle. 'You ready to pay your friends a visit?'

Sebastian couldn't hide his grin. He nodded, and before long, the two were off. As they left the smouldering cliffs, Seb's eyes were drawn to the black ocean, wondering if Zara was on the other side waiting for him.

16.

Stonehaven

Thoughts of Zara drifted the further they travelled from Blight Tide. Sebastian tore his eyes away and looked ahead, squinting at the salty sea wind lashing at his face. When Glitch eased on the speed, Sebastian managed to open his eyes fully, noticing strangely shaped boulders in the distance.

'There it is!' Irvine shouted, removing his face mask and pointing towards them.

'I can't see anything but rocks,' Seb yelled.

'Use your eyes. It *is* the rocks.'

Seb stretched his neck out for a closer inspection, making out the dome-shaped structures before him. Behind them was a small cliff shaped like a castle, jutting out from the very rock in which it resided.

'We've made it, Seb. Welcome to Stonehaven.'

As they pulled into the dusty town, Seb noticed many burly-looking men and women hauling large stone carts of metals from cavernous tunnels that ran deep beneath the ground. Others hammered away at the metals over roaring fires, stopping as their attention turned towards the noise of the zoomer. Seb smiled shyly and gave a stiff wave. However, when nobody met his greeting, he turned to Glitch.

'Don't look at me,' Irvine said, watching nervously. 'If I was a people person, I wouldn't have spent half my life underground.'

Sebastian sighed and rubbed the back of his neck. A group had now formed around them. Their skin was as dark as Ariana's. Some of the women even looked like her, with surreal hairstyles and well-toned bodies. The men all had blue tattoos that spread across their large puffed-out chests. They all wore simple garbs made from cloth that barely covered the skin. These people didn't look threatening or hostile, but something about the way they stared made Sebastian feel uneasy.

He stepped out from the zoomer and took a few steps forward, scanning their faces and puffing out his chest to match theirs. With a deep breath, Sebastian addressed them. 'We come in peace!' Seb yelled, waving his hands in surrender. 'We mean you no harm. We're just trying to find our friends.'

The grizzled citizens looked at Seb for a moment, then at each other. Before Sebastian realised, they were all laughing. Some even fell to the floor with tears in their eyes. But others picked up their weapons and casually strode towards the two.

'Your skills in diplomacy could use some work,' Glitch hissed.

'Shut it, Irvine. At least I said something,' Seb snapped behind gritted teeth.

'Yes. You've just announced to them that we're no threat. Do you know what savages like this are capable of?'

'And just what are we *savages* capable of?' A muscular brute of a man at the front of the group asked. His voice was deep, yet soothing. His words felt forced as if Seb's language was new to him.

'No, Sir. I wasn't talking about you,' Glitch squealed, holding up his trembling hands. 'I would never say anything so brutish about a fine upstanding fellow like yourself. I was merely-'

'Enough,' he said, before turning his attention to Sebastian. 'We don't like strangers in our town. If you're not seeking trouble, then leave, now.'

'Please, we have nowhere else to go,' Seb told him.

'Look around you, boy. Nowhere is where all our journeys lead. Take your frail friend, your offensive machine, and fly back to where you hail from.'

'Well, technically it doesn't fly,' Glitch said, ignoring the man's eyes burning into him. 'It uses steam-powered compulsion to-' Before he could finish, Irvine was lifted out of the zoomer by his lab coat and thrown to the ground. As Glitch tumbled, his codebreaker fell out of his pocket. 'Okay, okay, no talking.' Glitch said, clutching at his bruised sides.

'Hold, Baskay!' A woman yelled from behind them with a thick accent, pointing at Glitch's codebreaker. 'This device. It is the same that *they* wield. These strangers - they are with Blackout!'

The weary group began hissing at the two, with some even throwing stones. Seb managed to duck and swat away the ones that flew at him. But Glitch was not so lucky. He was struck on the head and fell to the ground. The man called Baskay raised an arm, halting the barrage. He sidled up to Sebastian and pointed his curved blade towards him. 'Is it true, boy?' he asked, shifting his body into a fighting stance, his scimitar edging ever closer.

'We're not with them,' Seb answered with a cool breath, standing his ground and staring deep into Baskay's eyes. 'That's why we've come. We want to help.'

'Lies,' scoffed someone in the crowd.

'Kill them!' Another urged. Followed by people yelling in a language Seb had never heard. Although, he could tell they weren't being complimentary. Seb gulped, taking a step back, all the while keeping his eyes locked on Baskay's.

The bronzed warrior's scowl dropped gradually. He stroked his brow and softened his cold stare for a moment before turning back to his people. 'Listen to yourselves!' Baskay roared, slowly spinning to look upon every one of them. 'Is this what we have become? Killing strangers on sight?' The crowd fell silent, with many turning away from their leader. 'We must be better than they are. Or else what are we fighting for?' Baskay threw his weapon to the floor and extended a hand towards Sebastian instead. 'I apologise for our hostility. Please, let us start over.'

Sebastian blinked, staring at the man's hand. Then without further hesitation, he grabbed onto it with both of his and shook hard. 'Don't mention it, Baskay,' he said with a wide grin. 'My name's Sebastian, but my friends call me Seb.'

'Seb?' Baskay almost yelped, jumping back. '*You're* Sebastian Travis?'

'Erm... yeah?'

'How foolish of me,' Baskay breathed to himself, giving Seb a long and formal bow. 'She's going to rip my head off for this.'

'Who's gonna rip your head off?' Seb asked, scratching his face.

'Miss Lane, of course. She's been quite vocal about taking down anyone stupid enough to lay a finger on you.' Baskay laughed uneasily.

'Ariana?' Sebastian asked, grabbing Baskay by the shoulders. 'She's really here? Darius too?'

'Calm yourself, boy. They're both here.' Baskay smiled, patting Seb on the shoulder.

'Should I notify the two, Sir?' An eager young warrior ran up to ask.

'I think it is best if the boy announces himself.' Baskay said with a wink. 'I cannot wait to see the look on her face.'

By the time Glitch had regained consciousness, Baskay had already led Sebastian into the stone castle. Everything inside was made from the cliff it resided in; chairs, tables and even doors were created from the same grey stone.

The scientist awoke to find he was being carried in the arms of a large muscular woman. 'Am I dead?' Irvine asked, adjusting his glasses. 'Is this Etheria? Are you an angel?' He raised a limp hand towards her and stroked the woman's face.

She huffed and shook him away with a scowl. 'Only strong and brave are permitted into Etheria, frail man,' she said, looking ahead.

'How're you feeling, Glitch?' Seb asked, gazing at the incredible stone structure.

'Seb, what's happening? Please, don't tell me we've become prisoners again so soon.'

'We're safe. These guys are on our side.'

'Well, they have a funny way of showing it,' Glitch huffed, stroking his bruised head. The woman carrying Glitch sighed and dropped him to the floor. He landed, rolling and feebly clutching at his sides. 'Yep, that's a bruise forming, right there,' he wheezed.

'What is the meaning of this, Vulga?' Baskay asked, stopping and turning back to her.

'Weak man has woken, Sir. Let him gain back what little honour remains.'

'Very well.' He shrugged, gesturing for her to return outside. She bowed and took her leave.

'I'm not great with women so I couldn't tell,' Glitch said, crawling towards Seb. 'But do you think she likes me?'

'What's not to like?' Seb laughed, pulling Glitch back up onto his feet and dusting him off.

Baskay escorted them through the many halls of the castle. It seemed like an entire community was living within the massive structure; with a school for children, a training dojo, even a pub and talk of a hot spring hidden somewhere within the stone palace. Sebastian's eyes widened at the thought of living in this place, with a huge grin to match.

'And where is the laboratory?' Glitch asked.

'The what?' Baskay asked with a puzzled look on his face.

'You're kidding, right? The room you conduct vital research in.'

'Ahh, you must mean the *war* room.'

'No, that's not remotely close to what I meant,' Glitch said, stamping his foot, making more of a tapping sound than a stomp. 'I'm talking about creating technology, setting up surveillance, making this place run at full efficiency!'

'You mean, making the Gizmos that our enemies use? Their strange weapons?'

'Well, yeah. I can do that too, I guess.' Glitch shrugged feebly.

'Then it is settled!' Baskay yelled with a booming laugh, patting Glitch hard on the shoulder. 'Whatever you need, we will provide. You will have your lavatory in no time.'

'It's 'labo-ra-tory',' Glitch said, trying his hardest not to laugh. 'Thank you, Baskay. You won't regret it.'

'What am I thinking?' Baskay huffed, hitting himself on the head. 'This is no time to talk strategy. This is a time for reunion! Come, follow.' Baskay began sprinting, almost as eager as Seb was. Glitch and Sebastian ran with him, following the mountain of a man through the many halls. Finally, they stopped outside of a grand set of stone doors. The bronzed warrior stood to attention beside one, and then with a simple tap on the ground with his boot, they both opened. Sebastian jumped back. He turned to Baskay, who stifled a laugh and winked.

'Earth User,' Baskay said, squeezing his hand into a fist.

Seb smiled and let out a short breath before turning his attention towards the open doors. 'Is she…'

'Just inside, boy. She's been waiting for you,' Baskay said, winking again.

Sebastian nodded and took another breath. He slowly stepped inside, peering around the large room. Rugs and drapes were scattered throughout. Comfy chairs and sofas littered the inviting place, with a fireplace built into the centre. It was empty, except for one other person. She sat with her back to him, her nose deep in a thick, dusty book, warming herself by the fire.

'Whoever that is, can you shut the doors? The draft is distracting.'

Sebastian froze when he heard her voice. No words came to mind. He simply stood, watching her as she read. 'Hey, Ariana...' he said, rubbing the back of his neck.

Her eyes shot up. The book fell from her hands and onto the floor. Its withered pages flew out, scattering across the room. Ariana slowly turned towards him, her grip tightening on the armrests.

'I'm back.'

They stood there for some time, both staring at one another from across the room. Ariana trembled as she looked over his body. She was a mirror at that moment - a reflection of himself. Finally, she allowed her soft hand to reach across to him.

'Is it... is it really you?' Ariana asked.

Sebastian's throat tightened. His head tilted as he nodded, watching the tears glide down Ariana's cheeks - sliding past her scar. Ariana bit her lip and shook her head before leaping towards him. Sebastian grabbed hold of her and held on tight, feeling Ariana squeeze back.

'I thought I'd never see you again,' she whispered into his chest.

'I'm sorry,' Sebastian told her, catching his breath so as not to let out a whimper.

'I should be the one apologising. I can't stop blaming myself for leaving you in that disgusting place.' Ariana looked deep into his eyes as tears filled her own.

'It wasn't your choice to make,' he said, wiping her cheek.

'What happened? How did you escape?' she asked, clutching onto his newly formed arms.

'It's a long story. One I'd rather not get into now.'

Ariana closed her eyes and nodded. 'I understand,' she said, biting her lower lip. 'Whenever you're ready.'

'Thanks, appreciate it,' he said, noticing her attention darting towards the open door.

'Stay down,' Ariana whispered, brow furling as she spun away from him in a flowing motion and blasted a ball of water at one of the solid stone doors - slamming it shut. 'Whoever you are, show yourself. I could sense you creeping from a mile away!'

Baskay jumped out from behind the open door, bowing repeatedly.

'Please forgive me, Miss Lane,' he wailed through teary eyes, 'try as I might, I could not deny my ears the beauty of such a touching reunion.'

'Baskay?' Ariana tilted her head. 'That's strange. I could have sworn I sensed a kind of creepy, pathetic presence.'

'Oh!' Baskay clapped, laughing loudly. 'You must mean-' He pulled Glitch into the room and presented him to her.

'Who's that?' Ariana frowned, folding her arms.

'Ariana, this is Irvine. He's the reason I'm here.' Sebastian turned to Glitch, nodding at him. 'The guy saved my life.'

Glitch smiled at Seb. Yet, it soon faded when he noticed Ariana marching towards him.

'Let's just get one thing clear,' she told Irvine, wagging a finger in his face. 'Rescuing Seb is usually my job.' Her eyes squinted at him hard, watching the beads of sweat drip down his forehead. Her frown turned into a grin as she threw her arms around Glitch and squeezed him tight. 'So, thanks for filling in while I was away,' she said, kissing him on the cheek.

'It's no... no problem, miss,' Irvine said, his cheeks beginning to glow red.

Baskay stamped his foot and pulled Glitch away from her. 'What do you think you're doing, Irvine?' he yelled, dragging the still-blushing scientist out of the room. 'You can't be stealing kisses at a time like this. Gate-crashing this ceremony of young hearts, I can't believe-' The booming voice turned into muffled sounds as Baskay closed the stone doors. Leaving Ariana to turn around to find Sebastian. His throat became dry when their eyes met. She smiled softly and sauntered towards him, rocking from heel to toe when they were close enough to touch.

'Sebastian?' she asked, staring at her feet. She looked into his eyes briefly before sighing and looking back at the ground. 'I'm glad you're back to kick butt with us again.'

Seb grinned, laughing a little as he shook his head. 'Thanks, Ari. Me too.'

Ariana gave Sebastian a playful punch to the chest. 'Speaking of kicking butt, let's go surprise Big Daddy D. I can't wait to see the look on his face!'

While Baskay escorted the group into the training dojo beneath the castle, lit up with a thousand torches, Ariana had been filling Sebastian in on what had happened since escaping Platto. Stonehaven was a mystery to many. Even Blackout didn't know of its existence. Darius had trained there in his earlier days and knew it would be the best place to lay low. Ariana wanted her nana to join, but she refused. Instead, Viola decided to stay and train recruits from Platto and help the people there. The last time they had corresponded, Viola spoke of getting a group together to the unnamed sand village in search of survivors.

'And we've been training ever since,' Ariana finished with a shrug. 'I hardly even see Darius these days. He's been so focused on getting the recruits ready for the big showdown with Blackout.'

'I don't understand' Sebastian said, 'I thought Darius was finished with all this saving the world stuff.'

'He was,' Ariana answered, turning to him. 'But something must have changed that day in the sewers. By the time I woke up, the big lug had told me he was ready to fight back. He won't tell me what changed that day. But I have a feeling that you had something to do with it.'

'I doubt it.' Seb laughed, placing a hand on the back of his neck.

'The man speaks highly of you, Sebastian,' Baskay interjected with his booming broken voice. 'And the Darius I knew growing up was never quick to compliment.'

'You grew up with Darius?' Sebastian asked.

'Are you kidding, Seb? This is Baskay Crane!' Ariana shouted, pointing at the man. 'Son of Buano 'The Rock' Crane. His dad was a legend. He built this very castle we're standing in with his bare hands - in a single evening!'

'My father was a great man. It cannot be denied,' Baskay smiled softly, stroking his fingers along the stone walls. 'It would seem I have a pair of large boots to fill. Master Blake was my father's protege. I was too young to fight back then. But his son, Dillon and I were the closest of friends.'

When the descent ended, Seb was faced with a wondrous cavern. Fiery lights danced for miles around. A river connected to the ocean ran through the sides. Hundreds of men and women were battling one another, some with wooden sticks, others with swords, shields, lances and a mixture of many different weapons. The sounds of clashing steel and battle cries filled the large hall, becoming a chaotic orchestra. Sebastian watched them all with wide eyes, feeling their determination as they fought one another. He turned to find Glitch, who had since retreated into himself, looking around nervously and twiddling his thumbs. He smiled at his new friend and gave him a nod before realising what was taking place past the river behind him. Seb squinted to make out the many Users. They spun to create water, sliced the air to cause flames, or even pounded the ground to manipulate the very rocks beneath them.

'What do you think?' Ariana asked.

'It's incredible,' Seb blinked, not knowing where to look.

'I'm glad you think so. My water students are getting better by the day, I can't believe their improvement.'

'Wait, you're a teacher?' Seb asked, turning to face her.

'Me, Baskay, Darius and many others. What, did you think we've been resting the whole time you've been away?'

'No, I didn't - It's just... how did all this happen? I thought the world had given up.'

'So did I. I guess Blackout finally went too far when they started hunting you. Nana has even sent letters letting us know Platto is a free city again.'

'You can only push a man down so far before he pushes back,' Baskay said aloud, nodding at the two.

'By trying desperately to prevent an uprising, Blackout has, in turn, caused a true rebellion.' Glitch said, stroking the wisps of hair on his chin. 'You could say that they were the reason for this chain of events.'

'An interesting theory,' Baskay noted, patting Glitch on the back. 'Which reminds me, I would like to take you to see our blacksmiths, Irvine. We must get that lab-o-ra-tory of yours up and running.'

Glitch nodded eagerly before looking towards Sebastian.

'It's fine,' Seb told him. 'I'm pretty sure all this fighting isn't really your thing, anyway.'

'An astute hypothesis,' Glitch smiled, shaking his head slightly. 'But I'm glad you've found your friends, Seb.' Irvine held out his hand for Seb to shake it.

Seb looked at the hand and knocked it away, hugging him instead. 'Thanks for all your help, pal. We'll catch up soon.'

Glitch nodded as he left with Baskay. Leaving Sebastian alone with Ariana.

'You know, I don't think I agree with what your new friend said earlier,' Ariana said, folding her arms. 'Blackout didn't start this revolution. I think it was you who kicked it off.'

'Get real,' Sebastian said, pushing her back. 'I didn't do any of this, and neither did Blackout. It was all you and Darius.'

'Well, we might have played a small part in it,' she said with a wink. 'And speaking of the big guy, how about we mess with him a bit?'

Passing the many students and masters, they made their way to a group of young fighters, struggling to even lift the colossal weapons they were wielding.

'You call yourselves warriors?' a gruff voice yelled, echoing across the cavern.

Sebastian looked past the recruits to see Darius, standing tall among them, weaving in and out of their pitiful strikes.

'Feel the blade in your hand. It's an extension of who you are!'

A young cadet started swinging towards Darius, his bastard sword spinning like a disk. Darius jumped above him and threw his giant knife into the stone ground. The trainee's spinning sword knocked into it, sending him flying onto the floor, hands trembling. Two others took the opportunity to rush Darius as best they could. They pointed out the tips of their swords like spears, struggling to keep them steady as they ran. Darius simply smiled and leapt upon both blades, driving them to the ground. He then grabbed one of the men and threw him into the other.

'That was hopeless,' he told them, shaking his head and wiping a hand over his face. 'Come on, people. We've been at this for months. Now, is anyone gonna muster up the courage to actually hit me?' As he turned around, a projectile whirled through the air and struck Darius in the back of the head, soaking him in cold, icy water. 'That's not exactly what I had in mind, missy,' he sighed, shaking himself dry.

'Maybe your students could benefit from lighter weaponry,' Ariana said with a smirk, watching some of his men collapsing under the weight of their broadswords. 'How many times have I told you that?'

'They knew what they were getting themselves into when they signed up to train under me.' He huffed, turning to face her. 'Maybe you should concern yourself with your own-' His words stiffened along with the rest of his body when he looked past her. His expression softened. 'Kid?' Darius breathed, making his way through the crowd of exhausted recruits. 'What the blight are you doing here?'

'I thought you'd be a little happier to see me,' Sebastian said with a smirk.

'You kidding? Just looking at your useless mug is giving me a headache,' Darius laughed, slamming a hand down on Seb's shoulder. 'I'll be counting down the days waiting for the trouble that's sure to follow ya.'

'Let it come,' Ariana chimed in, patting Seb hard on the back. 'I've been getting bored cooped up in this place. It's been too long since our last big fight.'

'Can everyone stop hitting me?' Seb asked, stroking his bruised shoulder.

Ariana and Darius looked at one another before breaking out into laughter. She wrapped her arms around Sebastian's shoulders, and Darius grabbed Seb's head and ruffled his hair. Seb began laughing with them, struggling to break away from the two.

Darius' face turned fierce again as he looked back at his pupils, who were now sniggering at the three of them. 'I don't know what you lot find so funny,' he yelled, walking past them to collect Xerxes. 'None of you are ready for a fight. So, I'm gonna need a hundred more downward strikes before you even think about having a rest.' Darius performed the move himself so that his recruits could mirror him.

Ariana grabbed Sebastian by the arm. 'Best leave him to it. Only the gods know when he'll be finished.'

'I didn't think I'd be so happy to see him,' Seb said, scratching his head as he watched the once-retired hero.

'That will pass. Trust me. Come on, I'll show you to your room.'

'Good idea. I could use some sleep after today.' Seb said with a yawn, only now realising the fatigue that had been building since his arrival at Stonehaven.

'You can rest later. But first things first, that mop on your head ain't gonna cut it. We've gotta give you a new look.' She grinned wickedly, pulling him towards the stairs.

'Could we not go back to the old look?'

'Come on, Seb. Where's your sense of adventure?'

Sebastian gulped as Ariana whisked him through the castle. He watched as she glided elegantly up the steps, with him tripping over himself on his newly formed feet. Maybe a new look was just what Seb needed. He had changed so much since he had last seen her. Perhaps it was time to finally accept it.

17.

A New Day

A brisk breeze woke Sebastian from Slumber, drifting in through the hole in his room that Ariana had affectionately referred to as a window. The clean air filled Sebastian's lungs, refreshing him in a way he hadn't experienced in a long time. He sat up, absorbing the simplicity of a moment as mundane as waking up to a lazy Sunday morning. The straw-covered stone slab beneath him felt like a luxury compared to the sterile steel he had grown accustomed to sleeping upon. Still, his bones ached as he lifted himself off the mattress and scratched his head, watching loose wisps of hair fall. Sebastian winced as he touched the graze on his ear from where she had nicked him.

He stepped forward to finally see his reflection in the polished copper mirror in the light of a new day. He gazed at the aftermath of the intense battle that had unfolded on his head. The sides and back were now cleanly shaved, giving a stark contrast to the longer hair on top. As his fingers ran over the prickly skin, he could feel the remnants of the struggle he had endured. The hair on the crown of his head, though still long, had been brushed back and artfully tied into a bun. Sebastian pulled the tie loose, allowing his hair to cascade freely. As he brushed the strands to the side, he couldn't help but marvel at the changes.

A smile played on Sebastian's lips as he admired himself. The reflection staring back at him was one of resilience, a culmination of the battles fought and won. The new hairstyle, chosen by Ariana, was a symbol of taking control of his destiny in a way he hadn't been able to before. In that fleeting moment, as Sebastian stood before the reflective surface, he found a sense of calm. Yet, the smile that adorned his face carried a weight of sadness, and his eyes reflected a deep longing. The copper mirror became a silent witness to his metamorphosis, capturing a new chapter in his life.

Sebastian's eyes drifted towards a package in the reflection that had been left in the corner of his room. As he unveiled the contents, a grin spread across his face, realising that Ariana had taken the initiative to pick out a new wardrobe for him. He tore off the rags Doctor G had provided and changed into his new outfit. The charcoal jeans were thick, durable and adorned with chains, and the belt equipped with a sword holster was a nice edition. Eager to complete his ensemble, Sebastian slipped into the dark blue duster jacket that hung past his waist, giving him a certain cloak-like appearance. It mirrored Ariana's style, yet carried its own unique flair with more zips and pockets than Sebastian could fathom needing. Sebastian admired himself in the copper mirror, appreciating the transformation. The jacket felt heavy but comforting. He adjusted the sword holster and checked himself out from different angles.

With a final look in the mirror, Sebastian made his way towards the open window, appreciating the fresh breeze that had roused him from slumber. The outside world beckoned, and he couldn't help but feel a sense of liberation. The battle scars on his shaved head served as a reminder of the ordeal he had overcome, and the change in his appearance symbolized a new chapter in his life. Seb couldn't help but wonder about Ariana. He was grateful for the unexpected kindness she had shown, from the makeshift bed to the carefully chosen wardrobe. She had put thought into his well-being, and Seb couldn't help but smile at the gesture.

Sebastian felt the weight of the room's attention as he entered the mess hall, a mix of recruits, teachers, guards, and everyday citizens sat with their backs to him, more interested in their conversations and meals than the newcomer. The echoing slam of the stone door behind him abruptly hushed the room, and in that moment, every eye pivoted to Sebastian. A nervous smile touched his lips as he navigated past the long stretch of tables. Most of the occupants maintained their focus on their discussions, some acknowledged his presence with whistles, while others diverted their attention just long enough to share a laugh.

Caught in the spotlight, the red hue of embarrassment began to creep across his cheeks, the collective gaze of the room intensifying the feeling. Amidst the scattered reactions, he noticed one individual laughing louder than the rest. He sighed, following the sound, his feet as heavy as his stone mattress. The laughter was accompanied by thunderous slams of a fist pounding upon a solid table. Sebastian could see him now - the great Darius Blake, and the tears streaming down his face as he pointed, still howling uncontrollably.

'Morning,' Seb said, trying his best to ignore the giant.

'Sorry, but... it's even funnier up close,' Darius wheezed, slamming his head on the table, trying to stop himself.

'Good morning, Seb!' Ariana cheered, jumping up and dancing around him. 'What do you think, it's good, right? Does everything fit okay? I took your measurements while you slept. I hope you don't mind.'

'It's perfect, Ariana. Thank you,' Sebastian said, his cheeks reddening further. He gave her a quick hug and sat down. 'Have either of you seen Glitch?' he asked, hoping to steer the conversation away from his new look.

'He's with Baskay,' Ariana told him. 'They're building some kind of lab or something.'

'I got a look this morning,' Darius added, having composed himself. 'That pasty guy you brought back is quite the technician. Everyone's talking about the breakthroughs he's already making. Good work, kid.'

Sebastian grinned. 'Thanks, Darius.'

'You still look ridiculous though.'

Sebastian's smile became a scowl.

'Ignore him, Seb. Darius is just jealous that I haven't updated *his* look,' Ariana said with a wink, brushing the dust off the hero's red cape.

'What you wear means nothing on the battlefield, Girly.' Darius shook his head, taking a bite of his meal.

'Not even if it's adorned with Rachni silk?' Ariana asked, stretching her arms out and smiling to herself.

Darius choked on his food, his eyes darting to hers.

'What's Rachni silk?' Seb asked, looking down at his suit.

'*What's Rachni silk?*' Darius repeated, spitting bits of food onto Sebastian's new clothes. 'It's only one of the strongest materials on Endura. Tougher than steel, yet weighs next to nothing. It can stop knives and even bullets.' He then turned to Ariana and grabbed onto her hands. 'How did you find it?'

'There's a Rachni nest deep within the caverns. The scouts discovered it while they were exploring.'

'Rachni are dangerous. Why wasn't I informed?'

'You would have known if you didn't spend all your time training.'

'Were you gonna wait until I was cut to shreds before you told me?'

'Look around you, big guy. Everyone's wearing it.'

Darius scanned the mess hall while Seb glanced over his shoulder and noticed the men and women who wore thick, sleeveless beige jackets.

'So, that's why everyone's wearing those things. I thought they had all lost a bet...' Darius rose from his seat and slammed his hands on the table. 'You have to make me one!'

'I'm sure you'll find one in your size if you rummage through the armoury,' Ariana told him, keeping her eyes on her meal.'

'I don't want what everyone else is wearing. I want what you made the kid.'

'I thought you said I looked ridiculous.' Seb raised an eyebrow.

'You stay out of this.'

'I'll think about it.' Ariana shrugged.

Darius stood motionless for a moment, before sitting back down with a grumble.

Sebastian looked away and tapped his fingers on the table, waiting for the air to settle. 'Anyway, what are you guys up to after eating? I thought we could catch up or something.'

'Sorry, Seb. The big guy and I have to teach a class soon. They usually last a few hours.'

'Not mine,' Darius smirked, stroking his greying beard, 'my classes last until nightfall.'

'I swear you're killing those kids,' Ariana told him, 'You should at least save a few for Blackout.'

'My boys will be ready for anything once I'm through with them.'

'And your girls,' Ariana added.

'So, what am I supposed to do?' Sebastian asked.

Ariana and Darius both glanced at each other.

'Seb, you only just got here. Maybe you should rest,' Ariana said with a gentle smile. 'Take a walk around the castle. There's a hot spring somewhere around here.'

'Forget that!' Seb stood up, slamming a fist down on the table. He quickly regretted the decision as he clasped it with his other hand, letting out a pained moan. 'If everyone else is training, then I want to join.'

'You do, huh?' Darius asked, a sinister grin spreading across his cheeks.

'Wait, I didn't mean...' Seb said, shaking his head, 'Ariana, maybe I could sit in on one of your classes. I bet you're a fantastic teacher.'

'I am pretty good,' Ariana said, looking up at him. 'But I don't know.

Maybe it will be more beneficial to study under a great hero, like Darius.'

Sebastian jumped back, waving his arms in front of him. 'No, please. Anything but that.'

'Maybe I don't wanna train a squirt like you.' Darius huffed, facing away from Seb. 'Only real men make it in my class.'

'And real women,' Ariana reminded him yet again, shaking her head.

'Yeah, yeah, Girly. A woman is as strong as any man,' he agreed, closing his eyes and rubbing his temple. When he looked back at Seb, he added. 'But the kid ain't fit for my class.'

The insult cut a little too deep for Sebastian, but it was greatly outweighed by the wave of relief washing over him.

'That's a real shame.' Ariana shrugged, prodding at her food with a fork as a mischievous smile formed on her lips. 'I would have totally made you a new outfit if you took Seb on as an apprentice. But I get it. You like your old gear. What material is that made from again?'

Darius slowly shook his head with a groan before turning to Seb's terrified face. He stood up and pointed at the boy. 'Sebastian Travis, you are now a disciple of the great Darius Blake. I hope your hard life has conditioned you for the world of pain you're about to enter.'

Sebastian gulped.

'Right, well, thank the gods that's sorted,' Ariana said with a yawn, getting up from the table. 'Good luck, Seb. I'm sure you'll do great.' With a spin, she bounded away from them humming a tune.

Sebastian couldn't help but smile at Ariana. Yet in the wake of her departure, a sense of unease lingered in the air. Seb turned his attention back to the giant staring scornfully back at him.

'Well, kid,' Darius said with a groan. 'Looks like you're coming with me.'

Night had already fallen by the time Sebastian limped back to his room, falling against the door as it closed and rubbing the two bruises that were once his arms, hoping he wouldn't lose them again. For hours, Sebastian had struggled under Darius's demands, lifting a heavy chunk of metal above his head. The giant had pushed him to the limit, yelling for Sebastian to keep swinging, to focus his strikes. But despite the demands, Sebastian eventually faltered, dropping the weight to the ground and collapsing on top of it. All the while, Darius berated him to get back up.

As he sat gazing out of the window at the pure white moon of Etheria, the celestial glow contrasted with the darkness surrounding him, Sebastian wondered why the power he once possessed hadn't yet revealed itself. The pulsating energy that once coursed through his body had abandoned him. He longed for a taste of that strength, a connection to the force he had lost. The lifeless moon seemed to stare back at him, silent and unmoving. Images of the void, as bright as the ethereal sphere in the night sky, flashed before Sebastian's eyes. The memories of that otherworldly realm threatened to engulf him, but he shook the thoughts away, determined to focus on the present.

With aching limbs, Sebastian dragged himself to his stone bed, wincing as he settled in. Staring at the ceiling, he whispered a promise to himself, the determination evident in his voice. 'Tomorrow,' he said, 'tomorrow, I will strike Darius down.' The echoes of his resolve lingered in the quiet room, mingling with the distant sounds of Stonehaven castle.

Days turned into weeks, and weeks melted into months. Sebastian's eyes snapped open as he awoke. With a quick breath, he seized his arms, running his hands over them for reassurance. The same routine followed for his legs. He exhaled, falling back onto the stony surface, reminding himself that his time in the laboratory was behind him. Sebastian stretched his aching muscles and pushed himself up from the stone mattress. Wincing, he rubbed his bruised arms before dropping to the floor, commencing his morning push-ups. This had been Seb's routine since that night when he stared up at the troubling moon, promising he wouldn't gaze upon it again. Not until he was ready.

It was better this way. His physical pain now outweighed what had been raging within his mind. But Seb could still feel it lingering within him. He had kep his training a secret from everyone. Seb had become adept at keeping secrets; the pain that ravaged his body, the demon energy nesting within him. Seb had only spoken of the void to Nana Viola, and she was back in Platto, recruiting allies for the cause. That cavern of pure light terrified even her. No good would come from revealing the eternal place to anyone else. Only Glitch knew of Sebastian's time in the underground prison, and they had decided that was how it was going to stay. Nobody would accept what Glitch had done; they would see him as a criminal. And if they would think that of Irvine, then how would they ever accept Seb? Would they see him as Doctor G had? Some kind of monster?

'One eighty-five, one eighty-six, one eighty-seven!' Sebastian huffed aloud, staying focused on counting. Pushing the ever-creeping thoughts back down where they belonged.

When he had finished training, Seb stood up and gazed into the copper mirror. In the short time he had been living in Stonehaven, Sebastian had grown a few inches taller. His hair suited him more now that his jaw had become more angular and strong - as did the rest of his body. Seb ran a hand down his abdomen to see if the image wasn't a trick of the mirror. His chest felt as tough as the rock he'd been sleeping on. His shoulders had become more broad, and his arms flexed involuntarily. His eyes rose to meet themselves in the mirror, and that's when Seb leaned forward and glared at his reflection. 'Today, I strike Darius down!'

It had become routine for Sebastian to eat breakfast early in the empty mess hall before running laps around Stonehaven castle. He smiled and nodded to the miners and blacksmiths as he jogged past them. The young children of the village would run with him, laughing and jumping in circles. Seb slowed to match their speed, faking that he was out of energy. He would keep his eyes on the ground, staying focused on his breathing. However, Seb was often distracted by the young women of Stonehaven, brazenly watching him with eager smiles. Sebastian broke into a sprint, hoping they wouldn't catch him blushing.

As he rounded a corner, Seb noticed Glitch standing by one of the mines, tapping away at his codebreaker. 'Long time, buddy. Thought I'd never catch you outside your lab these days.'

'It has been,' Glitch said with a faint smile. 'You could always come visit now and then.'

'I know, I know. I've been busy.'

'I could tell.' Glitch shook his head with a whistle. 'Darius must be a great teacher for you to improve in so short a time.'

'Yeah, I guess,' Sebastian said with a mumble. 'So, what are you doing out here? I thought you hated the sun.'

'Even the heat of our closest star can't negate my research,' Glitch replied with a sly smirk on his face and the light reflecting from his glasses. He pointed far into the distance. 'You see those poles way out there?'

Seb looked out to see small white rods had been placed around the perimeter of the village and nodded.

'This is our security line. If anything large enough to be a threat crosses from the outside, we'll know about it. It's hooked up to my recently implemented alarm system. We'll be ready for any sneak attack now.'

'That's great, Glitch. Glad to have you on our side.' Seb said with feigned excitement as he patted the scientist on the shoulder.

'Yeah, me too.' Irvine sighed and stared out into the horizon for a moment. 'Seb, how are you holding up? I mean, we haven't spoken much since... well, you know.'

'I'm fine,' Seb answered sharply, his eyes darting away.

'Are you sure? Because honestly, I don't think I am.'

'Glitch, please don't,' Seb urged, shaking his head.

'Every night I get these nightmares where I'm still there, working on these horrific-'

'I told you to stop.' Sebastian glared back.

'I'm sorry, but I can't help it. Everything keeps building and building until I feel like I need to scream,' Irvine said, taking off his glasses to wipe his brow. 'I thought that maybe focusing on my work would help - but it doesn't. Please, I just need to talk about-'

'You haven't told anyone what happened, have you?' Seb asked, cutting him off.

'No. I promised I wouldn't say a thing,' Glitch answered, lowering his gaze to the floor.

Sebastian turned away from him and took a few steps back. Just looking at the guy was enough to remind him. 'Good. Because nobody here will accept it, Glitch. We're both monsters, remember?'

'You don't have to remind me, Seb. I know.'

Seb broke into another sprint, creating as much distance as possible - not only from Glitch but the demon that had been chasing him ever since he left that dungeon.

Turning the final corner of the castle, Sebastian skidded to a halt. In front of him was someone else he hadn't seen in a while, standing with her hands on her hips and staring him down.

'Ariana, what are you doing here?' Seb huffed, leaning on his knees.

'I'm surprised you remember my name,' she said, unable to look him in the eyes. 'So, this is what you've been busy doing while avoiding me and everyone else.' She finally looked up at him - something she would need to get used to now that he was taller than her.

'I haven't been avoiding anything,' Seb answered with a faint shrug, his eyes glancing away from hers.

'Well, it sure does feel like it. I hardly ever see you anymore. And when I do...' Ariana's eyes slowly drifted down Sebastian's body, her cheeks blushing slightly. 'It's like you're a different person.'

'What are you talking about?' He looked down at Ariana and lifted her chin. 'I'm still the same old Seb.' He tried his best to muster up a convincing grin. His cheek began to twitch when he realised it was just another lie.

'I want to believe that.' Ariana smiled faintly, looking into his eyes. 'But I don't understand what you're doing to yourself.' She grabbed his hand and clutched it on her chest. 'What happened when we got split up? Please, you've got to-'

'Nothing happened,' Seb told her, pulling his hand away.

She shuddered slightly. Tears masked her face as she stared towards the ground.

'I'm sorry, Ari. I can't.' He wrapped his arms around her and felt hers squeeze around his waist.

'I'm sorry too, you idiot. You don't need to tell me what happened. Just like how I don't have to tell you about my past.' she pulled away to look him in the eyes. 'But you can't let it affect you, okay? We've gotta live for the future now.'

Seb grinned back at her - the first authentic one in a long time. 'I promise. Now stop worrying. It's been a while since I've seen you conjuring water,' Sebastian said, wiping a tear from her cheek.

'That's not funny,' she replied with a playful shove.

Their attention was stolen by a group of giggling girls passing by. Whispers and glances emerged when they noticed Sebastian and Ariana.

'How embarrassing,' Ariana said, shaking her head. 'We're out here gearing up for war, and all they ever do is ogle all the boys training.' She folded her arms and looked away.

'So, how is training going?' Seb asked, trying his hardest to change the subject as he began to blush.

'Really good, thanks!' Ariana squealed, eyes beaming. 'My coven of Water Users has grown so much these past few months. We've even gotten to the stage where we can start *pooling* our abilities together.' She laughed to herself. 'I can't wait to get out and cause some serious carnage. What about you?'

'Good to hear,' Seb said with a smile before letting it fade as he thought about Darius' class. 'Honestly, it's not going as well as I had hoped. I've been training every day, and I still can't swing that sword properly. Have you tried lifting that thing?'

'I've been watching. I was worried your arm would fall off.'

Sebastian laughed, thinking, *it wouldn't be the first time.*

He wanted to tell her everything - his newly grown limbs, the creature living within him, all the fear that raged through his mind. But looking down at her dumb grin - he couldn't. Why would anyone want to take away that smile?

'His classes are relentless,' she continued, leaning up against the castle wall. 'I've told him many times; not everyone's like him. People can't wield swords twice their size, no matter how hard they train.'

'Then why is he doing it?' Seb asked, almost collapsing on the wall beside her.

'I don't know, but remember it isn't just you who's struggling. It's everyone in his class. We have other teachers here, Seb. You don't have to suffer Darius.

'I know,' Seb sighed, shaking his head. 'But I can't quit. I just need to get stronger.'

'No, Seb. Doing this alone isn't working. A heavy burden is easier to lift when you have someone there to help carry the load,' Ariana told him, giving him a playful punch to the shoulder.

'You're starting to sound like Viola,' Seb told her, rubbing his sore arm and getting up to stretch.

'Don't let her hear you say that. She'd never let me live it down.' She smiled, looking up towards the castle. 'I've written to her about your return. Nana was overjoyed to hear that you're back with us. You seem to have made quite the impression with her.'

'I guess I have that effect on people.' He pushed past her, winking as he did.

'Yeah right.' her eyes rolled as he broke into another sprint, before calling out, 'And don't be a stranger!'

Sebastian waved over his shoulder. letting the smile fade the instant he turned away. How could he ever tell her what he was? Nothing he could say would make it better. Nothing he could do would change the fact that he was a monster. But isolating himself hadn't worked. He felt a pit in his stomach and wished he could run back and tell her everything. Instead, he kept his eyes on the ground, staying focused on his breathing. Repeating that same mantra.

'Today, I strike Darius down!'

18.

The Immovable Object

A symphony of clashing steel sang throughout the underground cavern, accompanied by a choir of anguished grunts. Seb sat on his knees with the other students, struggling to listen as Darius yelled. The others were panting, staring as the sweat from their brows dripped upon heavy slabs of metal before them. Sebastian watched the brute standing above them, twirling his sword with ease as some form of insult.

Darius' words had faded into white noise, filtered by the clanging and scraping orchestra of the hundreds of other students training. Seb waited for that one phrase - the order that would allow him to finally strike. His thoughts drifted into memories. The things they had all said about him. Was it all true? It weighed heavier than the sword in front of him. Sebastian winced as he tried to block out the words, overlapping and repeating like they would in the void. When he closed his eyes long enough, the white abyss would filter through, as if the nothingness was now a place within him.

'...The boy is a menace to the society we are trying our utmost to protect...'

'...The people are not safe with him walking the streets...'

'...This is real life, Seb. It's pain. It's suffering. It's losing everyone you've ever loved. It's doing things to survive - things that make you want to kill yourself...'

'...You're broken. A fractured soul converging between fantasy and reality...'

'...Broken, useless, corrupted. This is your story...'

'Shut your damned mouths!' Seb screamed within himself, his muscles tightening as he pushed back and lashed out at them - punching, kicking, biting and tearing their bodies as they exploded into particles of light.

'So, if any of you weaklings think you're ready. Then, by all means, come at me!'

Sebastian's eyes fluttered open, finding himself once again in the familiar dojo. Around him, fellow students sighed as they struggled to lift their cumbersome weapons. His gaze fell upon the sword neatly laid out before him, and then his eyes lifted to meet the stern face of Darius.

'I mean, come on,' Darius said, shaking his head. 'You guys are all useless!'

Sebastian's primal roar echoed through the dojo as he seized the sword with both hands and charged towards Darius. The other students scrambled to clear a path as he closed in on his mentor, lifting the blade high. With a swift motion, Sebastian swung down in a powerful vertical slice, the impact shattering the stone floor beneath. Darius had leapt backward just in time, gripping Xerxes at both ends like a shield. Sebastian picked up his blade and continued wailing upon his teacher.

'What... the blight... is this... kid?' Darius asked with panted breaths between each blow.

Seb only answered in a rage-fuelled cry, changing the direction of his sword as it flew in from all angles. Darius finally pushed back, swinging Xerxes with the blade flat like a paddle. Seb leapt away with a skid and instantly rushed back, his heavy slab swinging horizontally. Darius ducked and swept Sebastian's legs, only to have Seb flip up once again and kick him in the chest. A hush fell over the dojo as spectators, including Users and warriors, gathered to witness the intense confrontation.

Despite the audience, Darius remained focused, spreading his feet firmly on the dusty ground. 'Calm yourself, kid,' he said, watching Sebastian's chest rise and fall. 'You're not yourself. Take a deep breath and find your-'

'I said, shut your mouth!' Sebastian dashed on quick feet towards his teacher.

The battle wore on. Seb's unrelenting speed and strength had returned, yet he still couldn't land a blow. He grew more violent with each failed swing. The lust for blood caused his own to boil. Finally, with a frenzied roar, Seb smashed his sword into Darius' and watched as Xerxes flew from his teacher's hands. It spun through the air. A moment's silence occurred before the clatter of heavy steel on stone. Seb stopped abruptly, unsure of how to continue. He looked at Xerxes, discarded upon the ground and then up at the stern face of his master, before hunching forward and coughing as a fist caved into his stomach. Darius picked him up by his collar and threw him several feet back. Sebastian landed with a thud, his sword embedded into the rock just inches away from him. The other students gasped, watching Seb for signs of movement. Darius, however, laughed and clapped his hands.

'Okay, everyone. Shows over. I think we should finish today's-'

Before Darius could finish, a primal scream unleashed itself from Sebastian. He jumped up, lifting his sword by the hilt with both hands, before dashing at Darius - dragging the tip of his blade along the stone, causing sparks to fly from the ground.

Darius turned around in shock. His body was stiff, unable to react. He could only watch, mouth agape, as Sebastian charged towards him. Darius sighed and extended his hand to Xerxes, which seemed impossibly out of reach. The massive blade quivered, as if the very ground were trembling, and lifted itself off the stone floor. Soaring through the air, it landed perfectly in Darius's grasp just as Sebastian reached him.

A loud chime resonated through the halls as the swords clashed.

Sebastian froze. His eyes widened as he gazed upon the blade that parried his own. Confusion countered his rage and Seb dropped his weapon, he took a few steps back, almost cowering before the giant.

Darius bared his teeth, glaring down. His stare then wandered to the other students. 'Class... dismissed,' he said with a heavy breath as he rested his sword onto the holster on his back.

The students got up to leave, none of them uttering a single word. Sebastian tried scurrying away with them, but he felt a large hand fall hard on his shoulder. He turned and looked up at Darius, his eyes more tired than they had ever been.

'Not you, kid. We gotta talk.'

Sebastian hadn't stepped foot in Darius' study before. He didn't even know the warrior had a study. If he had, he would have suspected it would have been stocked with weapons, booze, and even a barkeeper. But it was all very ordinary. The room, though mostly bare, held a certain charm. Row after row of extensive bookcases lined the walls, their shelves groaning under the weight of dusty tomes. At a stone desk, Darius sat. His sword, Xerxes, rested atop the surface.

Sebastian stood across from him, staring at the sword, watching the colossal blade to see if it would move once more. His gaze then stretched over to Darius, also watching the slab of metal before him.

'I'm guessing you want me to explain what happened earlier,' Darius said, his eyes falling upon Sebastian.

Seb took a moment to answer. 'I wasn't going to ask.'

'You wanna know how I did it,' Darius said with a heavy breath. 'I'll tell you. But first, you've gotta explain what in the blight that was back there. I looked into your eyes when you came at me. That wasn't you.'

Sebastian hesitated, feeling his stomach tighten. He knew there was no hiding from it now. He opened his mouth and took a deep breath.

'You're a User, ain't ya, kid?' Darius asked with a sly smirk.

'What?' Sebastian asked, blinking dumbly.

'You can't hide it from me. The way you picked up that sword like a butter knife, I could hardly believe my eyes. I knew there was always something special about ya.'

'No, there isn't. Darius, I'm not a User. I've... been training every day. I'm stronger now, that's the only reason I was able to lift it.' Sebastian's eyes fell to the floor as he dropped his shoulders, ashamed that he had to keep up the lie.

Darius took a moment to collect his thoughts. He stood up from behind his desk and gestured for Seb to take a seat. Sebastian slumped into the chair. Darius sighed, leaning on the desk with his back facing Seb. 'I've noticed your progression lately, kid. You've near enough worked yourself to death with your little exercises. But do you think you're the only one? I've been keeping a close eye on all my students. Like you, they're all so busy focusing on getting stronger that they've failed to realise the actual point of my class.' He turned to face Sebastian, seeing now that the kid's head had tilted to the point of being on its side, with his eyebrow raised to an almost comical degree. Darius shook his head and pulled on his ear. His mouth twitched as he tried to convey his next words correctly. 'Well, the thing is... the weapons I made for all of you. Nobody could ever hope to wield them. I'm surprised that some of you can even lift 'em, let alone swing those oversized dumbbells around.'

Sebastian stared blankly at him.

'The point of my classes was to teach you that some battles can't be won. The fate of the world is a heavy burden that nobody can shoulder alone. You can't keep fighting when that weight is on top of ya. And yet, you can't give up. It's a cheap trick, I know. But it's the same one that made me the man I am today.'

'So, this whole time you haven't been training us. You've been *testing* us?' Sebastian asked, mouth agape.

'Call it what you like. What's important is you've passed, kid. You all have.' Darius said with a faint smile. 'I mean, look at you. You're no longer the snivelling brat I met back in the Oasis. You've all grown into fine warriors, and not one of you has given up on my classes. Tomorrow I'll let the others know and give them their real training weapons.'

'This isn't another joke, right?' Seb asked, trying to hide his grin. 'We can have lighter weapons?'

'Not you, kid. I'm afraid I can't teach you anymore.'

'Why not?'

'Because you're a User. The only way you could have wielded that sword the way you did was if you manipulated the very atoms within. Skills with a blade are important. But you have something real powerful within ya. It's time you-'

'I'm telling you, I didn't. I'm not a-' Seb's eyes widened. 'Wait, does that mean... *you're* a User?'

'It's a little more complicated than that.' Darius sighed, wiping a hand over his face.

'So, let me get this straight. All this time, you've been using magic so that you could *pretend* to lift your sword?'

'Watch your mouth, kid. I told you, it ain't like that.'

'And then you force your students to a class they have no hope of ever passing just so you can act like you're better than us?'

'I said it runs deeper than that, damn it!' Darius slammed his fist down on the desk, chipping away at the stone.

'What have we even been training for?' Seb continued, ignoring Darius' outburst. 'All the months of hell you put your students through was for nothing?'

'Shut your blighted mouth!' Darius roared, his body shaking. He picked up his desk and hurled it into the bookshelf, sending rocky debris and loose pages scattering across the room.

'Unbelievable,' Seb muttered under his breath, folding his arms and looking away.

There was a knock at the door.

'About bleeding time,' Darius said, stroking his temples with his thumbs. 'Come in!'

Seb turned as the door opened, seeing Ariana at the entrance. Her cheerful grin disappeared as soon as she looked at the two of them.

'Is this a bad time?' she asked, surveying the room.

'Quite the opposite, in fact,' Darius answered with a mocking smirk forming on his lips. 'Because as of this moment, I will no longer be training the kid.'

Ariana sighed and ran a hand through her hair, 'What did you do this time, Seb?'

Seb dropped his eyes to the floor, unable to answer.

'Actually, he passed with flying colours. There's nothing more I can teach him.' Darius shrugged.

'He what?' Ariana asked, almost falling back. 'But how, what did he... what?'

'It would seem that young Mr Travis here has shown signs of being a User.'

'You're kidding, right?'

'Far from it, missy. I've witnessed him manipulate the elements of earth first-hand. So, I'm having Baskay teach him from now on. But I need you to find out what else he's hiding.'

'Seb... is this true?'

Sebastian looked up at her, then at Darius. 'I don't know,' he said, burying his head in his hands. 'I hope that's what it is.'

'Sebastian, it's okay,' Ariana said, running to his side and holding him in her arms. 'We're gonna get through this together. Look to the future, remember?'

Sebastian stroked her arm and looked up at her with a weak smile.

'Then it's settled,' Darius said with a clap of his hands. 'From this day forward, Sebastian Travis. You're a User in training. And officially not my problem.'

The moaning wind tunnelling through the caverns beneath the dojo was marred only by the crackling flames of Baskay's torch. The stalactites throughout the labyrinthian structure of caves had been dripping for some time, leaving the floor wet and glassy.

'Concentrate,' Baskay said, emphasizing each syllable. 'Your mind is clouded, this I can tell.'

Seb gritted his teeth and focused harder, pushing down on the craggy ground. Sweat dripped down his arms and was swallowed by thirsty cracks in the stone.

'You're trying too hard, boy. The earth is a stubborn and hardy element. Meet it with force and it will break. Instead, nurture and shape it as you would yourself and it will grow life anew.'

'What does that even mean?' Seb asked, collapsing onto his back.

'It means to push your consciousness further than your body,' Baskay said, planting his hand upon a nearby jagged wall. 'To see the world around you as nothing more than an extension of yourself.' He closed his eyes, and soon the surface of the cave began to change. The wall then pushed back, creating more space within the cavern. Baskay lifted his other hand, forcing a chair to form from the very stone itself. He took a deep breath and wiped the sweat from his brow before taking a seat. 'It means, *concentrate*.'

Seb peered up at Baskay to see the warriors' eyes burning brighter than the torch's flame. He nodded and returned to his previous position. With a deep breath, he focused, clearing his mind of everything; his doubts, fears and his anger, all were swept up and whisked away, allowing Sebastian to sink into himself. The stone was rough and icy to the touch. Seb forced his mind to drift beyond and somehow found himself beneath the very ground itself.

'Very good.' Baskay smiled. 'Now, you may think of these caves as only one solid structure. Created by nature in her infinite wisdom to become what you see before you. But remember this, nature herself is a User who shapes the world to her will. She is like us, Seb. To be a User, you must be one with nature. Like her, you must see the world as ever-changing energy that can be shaped. Focus on the particles that make up Endura and accept that you are made up of the same materials.'

Sebastian let his subconsciousness linger within the ground. Only seeing darkness wherever he focused. Allowing Baskay's words to sink in, he could start to feel himself drifting through the molecules packed tightly together in the ground - like tiny bubbles moving erratically, vibrating against one another but leaving just enough room for his mind to seep through.

'When you are ready, you may push against these fragments. But be gentle with them, as they are the very building blocks of life itself.'

Sebastian's mind moved between the atoms, weaving through them. When he was ready, Seb began to push. His will brought a force that started to draw the particles closer together. But they resisted, pushing back. Their vibrations became erratically violent. Seb locked himself in place and with a burst of pure determination, he swept them out of his way, only to have them rise like a wave and smash into him in the form of pure energy.

Sebastian's mind shot back through the ground and emerged in his head once again. Gasping for breath, Seb dropped to the floor, trembling and talking to himself in a foreign tone. Baskay rushed to his side and opened his eyelids. He removed a flask and splashed water over Sebastian and began slapping him lightly on the cheek.

'It's okay, boy. Let your mind relax,' he whispered, placing the flask in Sebastian's hand.

Seb's fingers gripped the bottle and instinctively poured the water down his throat, drinking every morsel until the flask was empty. He dropped it, clawing at his head. Trying to unsee everything as a combination of particles continually colliding.

'Breathe...' Baskay told him, taking Seb's hands and placing them back on the ground. 'I know it is hard coming back to reality when you first see the truth.'

'The walls... they won't stop moving.'

'It will take time to adjust,' Baskay said, patting the boy on the back. 'Keep breathing, and the world will be as it should.'

They sat there for some time. Seb flinched nervously every so often, afraid to open his eyes. Baskay watched over him, patient as ever. Eventually, Seb began to calm himself and finally scanned the cave around him, relieved that everything was back to normal.

'How are you feeling?' Baskay asked.

'Better.'

'I am glad. You did well today, especially for someone who isn't an Earth User.'

'You're saying I couldn't do it?'

'I'm sorry, Sebastian. But you showed great concentration when communing with the particles. Perhaps there's something inside you yet.'

'Yeah, I bet,' Seb said with a sigh, fearing whatever it was would someday rise to the surface.

'Just like Darius, your true User abilities are yet to be revealed.'

'Just like... Darius?'

'A story for another day.' Baskay sniffed and turned away, leaning back in his newly formed chair.

'Why is it such a secret if the big guy is a User or not?'

'Like most things, it is complicated. Master Blake can never be an Earth User. Or any User for that matter. The man cannot see the world as an extension of himself - just a separate and cruel place he can never again be a part of.'

Sebastian sat on the ground, staring up at the dripping stalactites, listening to the mournful wails of wind echoing through the cavern.

'My father was a scholar above all else,' Baskay said, rising from his seat. 'Buano Crane believed that training a body was useless if you didn't train the mind. And so, he began the teaching of the immovable object. It conveyed to his students that some battles cannot be won and that some adversaries are too great to overthrow - like trying to move a mountain. He gave each of his students impossibly heavy weapons and-'

'Your father came up with that trick?' Sebastian interrupted, shaking his head.

'It was not a trick. It was a teaching. It was to show the young acolytes that some fights cannot be won. That no matter how strong one's will, the body cannot compete.'

'So, where does being an Earth User come into this *teaching*?'

'That was a happy accident,' Baskay laughed, scratching his bald head.

'Some students surprised my father and revealed that they too had powers like him. Those students would move on to becoming great Earth Users in their own right.'

'So, if it wasn't about finding Users then what was the point? Wouldn't it have been easier just to tell us these teachings?'

'A teaching told is never taught,' Baskay said, with a proud smirk.

'You just came up with that, didn't you?'

'Maybe there is more of my father in me than I knew,' Baskay laughed loudly, grabbing the back of his head. 'But to learn a hard lesson, you must first truly experience it for yourself. And the teaching of the immovable object was to bend one to the point of breaking, only for them to snap back with more power than they ever thought possible.'

'Okay, I think I get it. But it's still a sneaky trick.'

'Yes, however after the students passed and moved onto lighter weapons, it was as if they were wielding particles of air - as if their tools were a part of their body.'

'An extension of one's self.'

'Now you're getting it.' Baskay laughed again, ruffling Seb's hair.

'So, come on, out with it.' Seb shook off the warrior's mitt. 'How can Darius lift Xerxes so easily?'

'Okay, okay. So, Darius, as with many of my father's students, showed no signs of becoming an Earth User. He had no hope of lifting his weighted weapon with will alone. But like no other, Master Blake never gave up on trying to lift the blighted thing. Even after my father had seen his resolve and switched him onto lighter tools, Darius refused and returned every day to swing the immovable object.'

'Yep, that's Darius alright. Never knows when to give up.'

Baskay's smile faded as he brought the torch closer to his face. 'Tell me, Sebastian. Have you ever come into contact with a Surphite?'

'I haven't. But the name is familiar.'

'An offshoot of humanity. Poisoned by the Blight. Stories say that when the calamity struck, most of humanity survived by hiding in caves deep underground such as this. Unable to seek shelter, the Surphites endured the Blights' curse and over time, became what they are today. *Monsters*.'

'I remember now. On our way to Platto, some were hiding out in the wastes.' Sebastian shifted uncomfortably on the hard stone. 'Ari was more sympathetic towards them. But Darius shared your thoughts.'

'He had every reason to, lad. Before Blackout's shadow loomed over us, those reptilian beasts were Endura's greatest menace. They would pillage villages, leaving a trail of destruction. Fires, death, and the abduction of the innocent. Our town suffered the same fate when they arrived. I was just a lad back then, playing with Darius' son, Dillon. While Darius and the village protectors battled the Surphite invasion, my father worked tirelessly, conjuring formidable walls from the earth to contain the flames.' Baskay leaned away from the torch in his hand, staring into it as if it was the fire from his tale. 'Dillon started running. Not knowing what else to do, I followed, unsure of where he was leading us. Soon, I realised. Dillon's home - it was burning, collapsing with his mother still inside.' Baskay's features softened and he turned away, wiping a tear from his face. 'Dillon ran in to save her. And I... I stood there and did nothing.'

'Baskay...' Seb uttered. 'You were just a kid. There was nothing you could have done.'

'This I now know. But it took some years to learn.'

'A teaching told is never taught,' Sebastian said, smiling when he saw a smirk appear on the bronzed warrior's face. 'So, what happened?'

'Darius appeared. He ran into the crumbling building and moments later, emerged with his wife and son in each arm. Thankfully, Dillon survived with minor injuries. But his mother was carried out and laid to rest outside their crumbling home. When the fighting was over, we simply sat and watched as the place we called home burned to the ground.'

'I had no idea.'

'Darius never spoke of what transpired within his burning home, but Dillon was more than willing to divulge. He told a tale of how he and his mother were pinned down by a fallen girder, so heavy that the weight almost crushed them. Darius somehow lifted that beam high above his head to free them with no effort at all.' He shook his head and laughed bitterly. 'I always believed the love of his family gave him the strength to match his will. Somehow, Master Blake passed the teaching of the immovable object in a way my father thought impossible. Many moons later, Buano gifted Darius a new sword, heavier than even his weighted training weapon. That sword, named Xerxes by my father, was forged using the same melted-down steel as the girder that once held up his home.'

'I don't understand. Surely, he could only lift it that first time because he needed to save his family. How can he wield it now?'

'You're asking a man who questions very little and seeks fewer answers. All I know is my father taught his students that some battles were not worth fighting. That there would always be an immovable object. But he was wrong. Darius was the one student who managed to teach the master scholar that *every* battle can be won, even when all seems hopeless. As the only thing that could beat an immovable object, is an unstoppable force - that was Darius, through and through.'

'I had no idea.'

'Act like you still don't. Master Blake would skewer me if he knew I told you.'

'I won't say anything, I swear. But what happened to Darius' son?'

'What always happens. He died.'

Sebastian looked away. 'I know that. I was asking *how* he died.'

'I wasn't there to witness it. The tragic events unfolded years later, amidst our conflict with Blackout. After the Battle of the Black, I was sent home to Stonehaven. Darius, Dillon, and many other freedom fighters remained in Platto. However, betrayal stained our cause. One among us divulged the location of our hideout to Blackout, leading to their capture. Darius and Viola were away on a separate mission when the betrayal occurred. When they returned, it was too late. Dillon, along with everyone else, had fallen victim to Blackout's brutality. They were displayed as a gruesome spectacle for all of Platto to witness. By the time I received the heart-wrenching news, Darius had vanished. Until his unexpected return outside the castle those many months ago, I had believed he perished with the others.'

'The Gallows…' Seb shook his head, fists tightening.

'Those were dark times,' Baskay said, standing up and gesturing for Sebastian to follow. 'I'm sure darker days are yet to come. And that is why we need my father's teachings now more than ever.'

Neither of them said much during the journey back up to the dojo. Sebastian did ask about the Battle of the Black, but Baskay simply said it was a story for another time. When they emerged in the brightly lit halls, they took note of Darius. He had since given his students lighter weapons to wield. After months of using such heavy swords, the trainees danced around each other as if their blades weighed next to nothing.

Seb turned to Baskay and bowed, thanking him for the lesson. Baskay smiled and placed a finger to his lips. Sebastian nodded, taking one last look at the great Darius Blake.

19.

A Dark Secret

Sebastian stared longingly at the stone door before him. Ariana's room resided on the highest floor of the castle, far away from the clanging of miners and blacksmiths, hidden away from the commotion of the soldiers fighting in the dojo. Sebastian looked to his left and smiled at the only sound to venture so high - two doves had perched themselves on the edge of an opening to the outside, singing a tranquil tune. Wiping sweat from his palm, Seb knocked at her door and breathed in deeply.

'Just a minute,' Ariana sang out. When the door opened, she greeted him with a coy smile and bowed. 'Welcome, student. I hear you wish to learn the ways of water,' she said in an overly elegant tone.

'Please, drop the act, I got enough of that from Baskay.'

'Relax, Seb. I'm messing with you.' She winked, standing upright. 'Word is, you're showing great promise with your User abilities.'

'What abilities?' Seb asked with a shrug. 'I couldn't do anything.'

'That's not the point, dumb-dumb.' Ariana knocked on Sebastian's forehead and laughed. 'You were able to commune with the atoms in the stone. That's a big step.'

'But what good is talking to those weird bubbles if they don't want to listen?'

'Now, that is the question,' Ariana said with a huge grin forming from cheek to cheek. 'It's all about who you are as a person. So, let's say...' She stopped herself and shook her head. 'What am I doing? I'm starting the lesson without even having invited you in. Get in here quick before I forget what I'm saying.' Ariana stepped aside, holding her arm out for Sebastian to enter.

When he did, he noticed that the room was completely bare. No bed or window, nothing apart from the two of them. 'I like what you've done with the place.'

'What, you think I'm gonna get all of my stuff wet?' Ariana answered, folding her arms and raising an eyebrow. 'Besides, I don't think you've earned the honour of being invited into my bedroom just yet.'

Sebastian felt his cheeks redden as he looked away from her. 'So, you were saying?'

'Oh, right! Gods, where was I?' Ariana asked herself, tapping her foot and looking up to the ceiling. 'Okay, so you couldn't move the earth because the elements are tied to our personalities. Your abilities as a User are connected to who you are on the inside.' Ariana looked towards Seb and saw the confusion that clearly labelled his face. She sighed and explained further. 'So, let's say Earth Users are strong-willed and determined individuals who never crumble. Their resolve is the same as the particles of the earth, and as such, they can work together.'

'So, you're saying that I'm not strong-willed?' Seb asked with a raised eyebrow. 'And rocks *do* crumble.'

'Idiot. I'm not *saying* anything.' Ariana said, tapping him on the chest. 'But you couldn't move the atoms in the stone, so the evidence clearly speaks for itself.'

'Last time I checked, you couldn't break rocks either.'

'I don't need to throw stones when I can wash 'em away.' Ariana began to sway rhythmically. 'User abilities don't just come from will alone. We need movement to help manipulate the particles around us.'

'Like your dancing?'

'Like my dancing.' She confirmed with a nod. 'Earth Users stomp and tap the ground.' Ariana jumped and slammed her feet hard on the floor. 'Or they clap. This is to create a ripple that resonates through the stone,' she said, bringing her hands together hard in front of Seb's face, forcing him to flinch. 'Fire Users are different. They click their fingers or make strange stiff movements.' Ariana clumsily emulated the technique.

Seb couldn't help but smile at her.

'The trick with their ability is creating friction. If you can ricochet particles against one another fast enough, they ignite, creating flames.'

'Stomping and cracking. Got it.' Seb grinned, giving her a thumbs up.

'Now, when it comes to water.' Ariana began to spin around the room. 'The trick is to feel the moisture in the air and let it flow within you.' As she danced, balls of water inflated around her and began to move rhythmically.

Seb shook his head, 'I had no idea that so much effort goes into it. You make it look easy.'

'It's far from easy, Seb. It takes years of dedication to learn. And even then, some never perfect these abilities.'

'But not you,' Seb said, taking a step closer. 'I've not seen many Water Users, but I can tell you're special. I've watched you create tidal waves and even liquid tornadoes. How did you get so good?'

'You know how to make a girl blush.' She laughed, rolling her eyes. 'Honestly, I couldn't tell you. I practised just as hard as anyone else during my youth.' She stopped spinning and slowly waved her arms, allowing the spheres to connect above her to become a gravity-defying pool.

Seb became entranced with the floating stream until something in Ariana's voice prompted him to look back at her.

'My story isn't a happy one,' she said, her eyes glistening.

'I'm starting to get the feeling that all stories are like that,' Seb said with a shake of his head. 'But they don't have to be. We can create our own narrative. Write better stories.'

'You can't promise that. Nobody can.' Her eyes darted to his, and he watched the sadness in them fade, being replaced by anger. 'Everyone who's ever told me something like that always ended up-' Ariana's words caught in her throat as Sebastian wrapped his arms around her shoulders. She hesitated for a moment. Her hands moved to his waist, holding him tightly.

Seb felt a breath upon his breast as Ariana moistened his shirt with tears. 'I'm not going anywhere,' Sebastian said, telling himself it wouldn't be another lie.

Ariana's grip tightened before letting go. He felt her arms swaying behind his back as the pool of water around them expanded to submerge the entire room, shielding the two of them in a pocket of air. He held out his arm and slid his fingers along the translucent walls.

'You've gotten stronger,' he told her, wiping a tear from her cheek.

'Thank you, Sebastian,' she replied, arching her neck up. She stood on her toes to match his height, bringing her face closer to his.

Seb closed his eyes and leaned in towards her. All he could hear was his heart pounding against his chest, followed by a burst of a bubble as the invisible dam broke. The wave washed Seb away from her, slamming him against the stone wall. With a groan, he opened his eyes, looking up at a dry Ariana leaning over him.

'Don't think you can get out of training that easily,' she said with a wink.

The class continued after Sebastian received a towel and a change of clothes - Ariana somehow knew he would need them.

When he was ready, she told him. 'Concentrate, as you did with Baskay.'

It came naturally to him now. He could sense the pulsing balls of energy bumping together in the stone.

'Even the air around us is filled with atoms. They aren't as tightly packed as the particles in solid objects. Meaning, they're harder to make out. Just keep breathing until you can see them.'

Sebastian struggled as he looked around the empty room. Then he saw it, a tiny bubble drifting through the air, almost invisible. He widened his gaze until he could witness countless particles floating around him.

'I see them,' he said with an excited breath.

'Good. Now watch how they dance and move with them.'

Embarrassment washed over him as he waved his arms, trying to match the sway of the erratic atoms. As he waved, Sebastian realised that he was no longer copying them. They were following his movements.

'I sense a change in the air,' Ariana said, trying her hardest to hide a smile. 'They're listening to you, Seb. Now *use* them.'

'How do I do that?'

'There is no simple answer to that. It's something you just have to do.'

Seb nodded and continued swaying gently, watching the particles dancing with him. As he moved, he noticed the air begin to change, darkening. The almost invisible atoms turned black and stopped abruptly, becoming still and lifeless. Sebastian winced and gritted his teeth, commanding them to move once more. Millions of black particles collided together and rushed towards him. He held out an arm to stop them, but they wrapped around it, like a bubbling black goo - cold, yet leaving a burning sensation that spread throughout his body as it enveloped him. Out of the black cocoon came four shadowy tendrils, releasing themselves from Seb's shoulders. He roared in pain as they exploded out of him. There was screaming. It was Ariana. Her voice was a distant echo to him now. Sebastian looked down at his hands and tightened them, grinning wickedly to himself. He could feel it now - the raw, unrelinquishing force that resonated within him. The strength he had been so afraid of. The strength he had yearned for. With a loud grunt, he tensed his muscles, letting the energy explode out of him, the tendrils on his back swung erratically, breaking through the floor and ceiling. With wild eyes, Sebastian could see the black particles that bowed to his will, finally understanding his power. Turning towards her, his grin faded.

Ariana was huddled in the corner of the room - her eyes locked on him in fear. Finally, she saw him for what he was.

The strength drained out of him as the darkness rushed back inside - deep down where it couldn't hurt anybody. He closed his eyes and fell to his knees, listening to the faint whimpers coming from the girl who never showed fear. 'Ariana,' he breathed her name like it was his last. 'Now you know. This is why they're after me.'

It took some time for Ariana to stop trembling. When she did, Sebastian told her his story - his whole story. The scattered memories of home, the frequent trips to the void and the mysterious white entity who resided there. Eventually, Ariana stopped shaking. Her fear became curiosity. Seb continued with what had transpired after breaking away from them in the sewers under Platto. How he used his twisted powers to tear apart the Blackmasks before being ambushed by Ender Knights. He finally told her the story of waking up without his limbs, and how he had to regrow them while being held captive as a test subject in that underground laboratory. The place where he met Irvine.

'We escaped Laboratory G, watching as every dark secret of that place was buried. We came here and... well, the rest you know,' Sebastian told her with a heavy breath and scrunched his face tight, tilting his head to the ceiling. It felt good to finally talk about it. When he opened his eyes, he saw that Ariana was still speechless. She stroked at the scar that ran down her cheek, staring at the broken floor with tired eyes.

'I had no idea,' she said, looking up at him.

'I wish it could have stayed that way,' Sebastian answered, rubbing the back of his neck.

'You've had this uncontrollable power the whole time and never even told us?'

'I'm sorry. Really, I am. I didn't want to believe it myself. And saying it out loud would just-'

'Do you know how incredible this is?' she asked, jumping up and grabbing his arms. 'Seb, this means we don't have to hide anymore. We have the weapon they fear the most on our side. With you, we can kill every last one of them vile scumbags!' she grinned wickedly, shaking him by the shoulders.

'I'm not a weapon, Ari.' Sebastian furrowed his brow, turning away from her.

'C'mon, you know I didn't mean it like that.'

'And I don't want to *kill* anybody. This thing inside me takes over whenever it wants. Every morning I wake up wondering if it will be the day I take someone's life,' Sebastian buried his head in his hands. 'I can't control it.'

Ariana crawled over to him and cradled Seb's head in her arms.

'I'll help you,' she told him, stroking his cheek. 'Whatever it is, it can be used like any other element. We'll figure it out together. It will be our little secret.'

Sebastian wanted to smile. Instead, he held on to her hand and gripped it tightly, weeping softly. Eventually, his whimpers faded into heavy breathing - then to silence. As the morning sun began its rise, a faint smile swept over his grim face.

20.

Ariana's Scars

Sebastian and Ariana stood tall amidst the vast expanse of scorched earth, their gazes locked in a silent challenge. A fierce wind spiralled, beckoning her hair towards him. She followed the breeze on quick feet with streams of crystalline energy surging forth from her fingertips, slicing through the air with deadly precision.

With a pained groan, Sebastian planted his feet firmly into the cracked earth, his muscles coiled like springs ready to unleash their power. With a wave of his hand, a translucent screen appeared before him - a shadow hanging in the air. It protected him from the piercing water, cracking further with every collision. The translucent shield shattered, allowing the last spike to break through, striking the boy in the ribs. He clutched at his side as air escaped his lungs, stretching out his other arm with a roar. Tendrils burst from his shoulders - black, oily, bubbling snakes that slithered towards his open palm, before leaping erratically across the plains.

Ariana had only just landed when she saw them approaching - the same black tendrils that had terrified her only a few short weeks prior. She shook her head clear of festering thoughts and leapt back into the air, using a torrent of water to propel her further. She landed with a roll and rushed at him, avoiding the tendrils that tore through the plains with wild frenzy. When she was upon him Ariana twisted into a somersault, threw her hands down and screamed. A beam of liquid energy erupted from her hands.

Sebastian gritted his teeth and dug his feet further, bringing up his arms as the blast struck. His body trembled as dark veins sprouted from his skin.

The ground around his feet cracked and became as black as his ever-growing shadow. With a strained bellow, Seb spread his arms apart as dust and wind scattered, escaping the blast of electric energy surrounding him. He collapsed, falling back into a black and brittle patch of dirt, panting as he tried pushing his body upright, only to crumble back down to the earth. After a few failed attempts, he found a hand extending towards him. He looked up to see her sweet face smiling down at him.

'I think it's time we head home,' Ariana said.

'Sounds good,' Sebastian agreed, taking her hand.

The ride back to Stonehaven was oddly peaceful. Ariana handled the zoomer better than Glitch ever had. She travelled at a leisurely pace, allowing them time to take in the emptiness of Sebastian's new world. 'You're getting stronger,' she said, keeping her eyes towards their destination.

'Thanks.' Sebastian grinned, leaning back in the sidecar with his arms behind his head. 'Still, it's gonna be a while before I'm at your level.'

'Don't sell yourself short, Seb. These fights have been some of my hardest,' Ariana admitted, turning to him. 'You'll surpass me in no time.'

'I hope you're wrong...' Sebastian said without thinking. He slowly turned towards her and noticed that subtle look of hers. 'I mean, I just like having you as a teacher,' he said, shifting and rubbing the back of his neck. 'I'd hate for it to end so soon.'

Ariana continued staring, almost like she sensed what he was thinking. 'You've got to stop worrying, Seb. Your powers are just as much a gift as they are a curse. The end result will be what you choose to call them.'

Sebastian sighed, staring up at the cloud-covered violet sky. A drop of water hit his cheek, causing him to flinch - his training with Ariana had almost given him a fear of the substance. She must have sensed this too, as she started laughing to herself.

'Relax, dummy. It's just a bit of rain.'

Sebastian smiled and calmed himself as the shower began its quenching of the barren plains. Ariana breathed in the fresh scents and turned her wrist to give the zoomer more speed.

On returning to Stonehaven, the shower had become a storm. Seb jumped in his seat as lightning struck and thunder crashed upon the rocky dunes. Ariana stopped just outside the castle, keeping close to him until they entered. Sebastian shuddered as the doors closed. Looking out to find one last beam of light hammering down in the distance. Ariana wrapped her arms around his waist, instantly bringing Sebastian back to her.

'I'm glad you both made it back,' a deep voice called out. It was Baskay, peering out from an open door. 'I honestly don't know why the two of you insist on travelling so far for your training.'

'I told you before,' Ariana stepped in front of Sebastian as if to protect him. 'Seb needs to be far away from all sources of water. If he gets thirsty, he'll have to make his own,' she lied - another in a long line of lies Sebastian had burdened her with.

'The boy looks as far from thirsty as one can get,' Baskay said with a coy smile.

'Actually, I could do with a drink.' Seb laughed.

'Gods, same!' Ariana sighed. 'Where is everyone?'

'Funny you should ask. Work has been snipped small today due to the storm. So, many are in the tavern.'

'Sounds good to me,' Ariana said with a stretch. 'But first I gotta get into some dry clothes. I may be a Water User, but that doesn't mean I like getting wet.'

'I'm growing to hate it quite a bit myself,' Sebastian agreed, shaking his head at Ariana.

The Stonehaven pub looked nothing like the rest of the castle. It stood as a sanctuary within the formidable walls of the castle, a haven of warmth amidst the cold stone. Unlike the rest of the fortress, every corner exuded rustic charm. Despite its stone construction, the pub emanated a welcoming atmosphere, from quilted rugs covering the hard floor to delicate drapes billowing gently from the ceiling. Above, chandeliers cast a soft, inviting glow, their flickering light dancing playfully across the room. Yet, it was the stained-glass windows that truly set the pub apart, their vibrant hues filtering in the sunlight and casting the room in a cornucopia of colours. As the light shifted and danced across the walls, it imbued the space with an ethereal beauty, transforming it into a sanctuary of warmth and serenity amidst the fortress's cold, imposing exterior.

Sebastian often came here when he wanted some normalcy in his ever-changing life. Yet, as he stepped into the bustling den, Seb had never seen it so alive. Nearly every citizen of Stonehaven was packed within the spacious tavern, their laughter and chatter echoing above the roar of the storm outside. Navigating through the throng of people, Sebastian's eyes scanned the crowd in search of familiar faces. He spotted his comrades from Darius' class, and with a smile, he joined them at their booth. His classmates welcomed him with cheers and applause. Sebastian had become quite the legend in recent weeks after the news of his fight with Darius spread throughout the castle. He accepted a mug of ale with gratitude and drank it down before being handed another. As he engaged in spirited arm-wrestling matches and shared laughter with his companions, Sebastian couldn't help but feel a sense of peace wash over him.

That's when she entered. Ariana stepped into the bustling tavern, wearing an emerald gown, glinting in the ambient light. Sebastian's breath caught in his throat when he saw her enter. She tugged at her dress nervously as she scanned the room. That changed when her eyes landed on his. Ariana smiled and made her way over to him. She moved with a grace that commanded attention, her dress dancing as it reflected every glow of the room. Sebastian continued staring, the energy of the tavern fading into the background as if they were the only two souls in the world. As she finally reached his side, Sebastian felt his heart pounding in rhythm with the music that filled the air.

'I'm not interrupting anything, am I?' she asked, surveying the booth.

'Not at all,' a tall, burly lad stood up to greet her, knocking his pint over the table and trying desperately to clean the spill, the others laughing as he did.

'Actually, Seb. I was hoping to steal you away. You boys don't mind, do you?' she asked again, her voice like honey.

They said nothing but bashfully shook their heads. Ariana smiled and took Sebastian's hand, whisking him towards the bar. She leaned over and shouted for the bartender. Sebastian couldn't take his eyes off her. She had changed her hairstyle from the usual ponytail. Instead, it flowed elegantly, covering the shaved sides of her head and resting playfully upon her bare shoulders. Her gown glided to her ankles with a tear that ran down from her thigh, showing off her legs.

'You look incredible...' Sebastian thought, before realising he was speaking out loud.

'You say something? she asked over the roaring patrons, leaning into him.

Sebastian simply smiled and shook his head, she grinned back as the bartender asked what they wanted to drink. Ariana was in the middle of ordering when a large pair of arms wrapped around their shoulders.

'I was wondering when you two would show,' Darius said, slurring his words and spilling a foul-smelling beverage over Sebastian's arm from a large jug in his hand.

'Gross!' Seb yelled, pushing Darius back. 'What is that stuff?'

'Just the strongest hooch ever made,' Darius answered, taking a huge gulp and retching at the taste. 'Wanna try some?'

'We're good, thanks,' Ariana politely refused, grabbing two less toxic-looking drinks from the bartender. 'Seb and I want to remember what happens tonight.'

'Suit yourself, girlie. I'm hoping tonight will be a memorable one too,' he said, looking towards a booth with two women giggling and stealing glances at the giant. 'Now if you kids excuse me.' Darius turned back and nodded before making his way over to them.

'Forget what I said,' Ariana told Seb, shaking her head. 'I want to forget everything that just happened.'

The night continued as Sebastian and Ariana were joined by Glitch. The young scientist had brought another one of his inventions along with him, spilling screws and wires across the bar as he worked on it. Seb scratched his head and stared deeply at his glass. Realising how harshly he had treated Glitch the last time they had spoken. He glanced at the scrawny scientist, who was utterly absorbed in his latest toy. Sebastian sighed, knowing that he had to apologise.

Ariana must have picked up on this also, as she pushed her stall from the bar and slid off. 'I'm gonna hit the lady's room, don't miss me too much, boys.' She winked, leaving the two alone.

'So, Glitch...' Sebastian hesitated as he turned, wondering how he could say the words. 'Tell me what you're working on.' He closed his eyes, ashamed that he couldn't go through with it.

'This baby is something I like to call *the beacon*,' Irvine, said proudly, lifting the small black box towards Seb. 'It's a signalling device that I'm hoping to mass produce. Provided I get enough materials, that is. It's so our scouting parties can call for help if they run into danger. Their whereabouts will be transferred to our hub so we can send backup.'

'Impressive.' Seb nodded, taking another sip of his drink. 'You're gonna save a lot of lives with this one.'

'Let's hope,' Glitch said, laughing awkwardly before hanging his head. 'Not that it makes up for much.'

'You've got to stop beating yourself up over the past, Glitch. You're a good person. You can't be held responsible for the things you were forced to do. What matters is what you're doing now. How you choose to live.'

'Why are you telling me this?' Irvine uttered, placing a hand on the bar and adjusting his glasses. 'I thought you hated me.'

'Of Course, I don't hate you,' Seb told him with a smile and a pat on the shoulder. 'The last time we spoke, I... I was in a dark place. I thought that it didn't matter what we did, we wouldn't be able to escape what we were. But we never had a choice before - now we do. That gives me hope.'

Glitch smiled and grabbed Seb by the shoulders before embracing him. 'Thank you,' he said, his eyes beginning to glisten.

'Anytime, pal,' Sebastian said, pushing the scientist away. 'Remember, I'm always here if you need to talk things out.'

'As am I,' Ariana said, placing a hand on both their shoulders.

'Oh, Ariana.' Glitch turned to her with a yelp. 'We were just... discussing science, yeah that's all,' he said, masking the tears that had been forming.

'It's okay, Irvine,' she said sweetly, placing her hand on his. 'Sebastian told me everything. What happened wasn't your fault.'

The tears began spilling from Glitch's specs. He stood and hugged her harder than he did Seb. 'You have no idea how much I needed to hear those words.' he sobbed into her shoulder.

'Okay, big guy, take it easy. This ain't the best look for a crowded tavern.' Ariana laughed shyly, trying to pry him off her.

Glitch pulled away but still held on to her shoulders, a huge grin forming on his face.

'My life is mine to do as I choose,' he said, turning and giving Sebastian a thumbs up. 'Now on that note, I don't suppose either of you have seen Vulga anywhere around here?'

'Vulga?' Seb repeated, remembering the large muscular woman who had carried Irvine into Stonehaven on their first arrival. 'Why do you-'

'Actually, I just saw her on my way back from the little girl's room,' Ariana said, cutting off Sebastian. 'She was obliterating all of Seb's old classmates at arm wrestling last time I checked.'

'Well, if you would both pardon me,' Glitch said graciously, making his exit.

'Go get 'em, tiger.' Ariana winked, giving him a playful shove in Vulga's direction.

'What was all that about?' Seb asked, finishing his pint.

'So clueless,' Ariana said under her breath, shaking her head with a smirk.

'You say something?'

'Nothing.' She laughed, joining him on the stool. 'Looks like you could use another drink.'

As the night wore on, Stonehaven Tavern began to empty. Many of the townsfolk tried braving the horrific storm, only to return when the force of the wind and heavy rain proved too strong. Baskay had allowed them to take refuge within the castle until the rain cleared, asking Sebastian and many others to offer their sleeping quarters for the evening.

'Looks like you're coming back with me tonight.' Ariana winked, nudging Seb with her elbow.

'Does that mean I've earned the right to enter your room?' he asked, leaning into her.

'I'd say you've more than earned it.' She smiled, her gaze drifting from his eyes to his lips.

The surge of energy from earlier had calmed. The tavern was almost empty, save for a few patrons unwilling to let the night end. The band had moved on from their songs of merriment some time ago, allowing a sombre yet tranquil tune to flutter through the air.

Sebastian found himself swaying on his stool to the music, his eyes gently closing.

'You're not passing out on me yet, are you?' Ariana asked, softly shaking Seb's shoulder.

'Sorry.' He yawned, rubbing his eyes and groaning when he noticed his glass was still full, pushing it away. 'I thought drinking was meant to make you feel good.'

'You've only had a few pints, Seb.' She laughed, grabbing his glass and taking a sip. 'Trust me to get stuck with the lightweight.'

'Leave off. I'm still new to this.'

'Guess I just have a lot more to teach you,' Ariana said, waving towards the bartender. 'Can we get a jug of water here, please?' When it arrived, Ariana smacked herself on the forehead. 'Why did I ask for this? I'm a Water User!'

'Looks like you're not as hardened a drinker as you think.' Seb winked, his head collapsing onto the table.

Glitch had remained in the tavern. He was one of the last to stay - and without a single drop of alcohol ever touching his lips. He sat beside a stained-glass window, staring out into the storm with his head propped up in his hand. He had tried to talk to Vulga earlier, only to have the foreboding woman berate him for being weak and pitiful, loud enough for all the tavern to hear. And so, the young scientist solemnly drifted to a booth and remained.

'Should we go over and say something?' Sebastian asked, turning back towards Ariana

'I think it's best we leave him alone. Rejection is tough. But he'll feel better come morning,' Ariana answered, circling her finger in the air and filling up the empty jug with fresh water. The young scientist fell asleep in his booth soon after.

More time passed, and the tavern emptied further. Even the bartender had left, leaving those remaining to pour their own drinks. Darius stumbled out with his arms around the two women from before. It looked as though they were holding the warrior up, but he was still clutching onto the large jug of strong alcohol - he hadn't taken his hands off it all night.

'Did I ever tell you, girls, how I took out a hundred men... with just one swing of my... sword?' Darius asked, hiccupping between each breath.

Sebastian and Ariana laughed as they watched the mountain of a man get escorted out. They shook their heads and clinked their glasses together.

'Here's to a moment's peace.' Ariana toasted.

'May it last forever,' Sebastian added.

Ariana's smile faded as she took another sip. She turned back to the bar, running her fingers along her scar.

'How did you get it?' Seb asked, watching her.

'How'd I get what?'

'Your scar. You touch it whenever you're thinking about something.'

'I do?' Ariana asked, moving her hand away from her face. 'I hadn't noticed. It's not something I like to remember.'

'Well, I've told you my deepest darkest secrets. It's only fair you tell me yours.'

'I don't know if I...' She hesitated, noticing Seb had placed his hand on hers.

'Trust me. Talking helps.'

'Okay... I'll try. Honestly, I can hardly remember anything of my life before seeing that floating city.' Ariana stared at him with a haunted look in her eyes. 'The Crimson Cloud blotted out the sun, shrouding my village in darkness.' She turned towards her glass of water and scratched the rim. 'The light returned as fire rained from the sky.' The tavern flashed white as lightning struck outside. The crashing of thunder came soon after. Ariana shuddered, pushing her water away and leaned over the bar to grab a bottle of something stronger. Once she had poured herself a glass, she continued. 'My entire world was covered in flames. I heard the screams of people who were singing just moments before,' Ariana said, shaking as she took another gulp of ale and filled Sebastian's glass.

He felt as though he couldn't drink anymore, but dared not object.

'I remember my mother and father hugging me, telling me to run through the forest and never turn back. I didn't want to, so my mother took me by the hand so tightly and dragged me out with her.' Ariana squeezed her wrist and shuddered. 'I can still feel her grip, sometimes.'

Sebastian glumly looked ahead, nursing the drink in front of him. A more sober and less exhausted Seb would have said something by now. He would have tried to calm her. Instead, he closed his eyes and let her talk.

'She ran with me in her arms as the trees around us burst into cinders. The fire seemed to follow us, no matter how far we ran. Before long I realised it wasn't the fire coming after us - but a man. He was covered from head to toe in horrific tattoos, shooting flames from his fingertips.' Ariana's hands turned to fists as she slammed them down on the bar. 'I never forgot his face. Now I finally have a name to match.'

'Reid,' Seb said with a heavy breath, remembering the short, dark and sinister man from the Gallows pub.

'He looked different back then. More hair, fewer tattoos, but his slimy smirk was the same.' Ariana shuddered. 'When he realised the fire wasn't enough to stop my mother, Reid started throwing knives.' Ariana grabbed the side of her face and dug her nails in, almost tearing the skin. 'They tore through the hot air and ripped right through her. That's when I felt something glide across my cheek.' Ariana let go of her face, leaving nail marks that broke the skin. 'I remember screaming as the blood seeped into my eyes. My world became red.' Ariana lifted her head, staring at the chandelier above her. 'I looked up and saw my mum smiling down. She was covered in cuts and burns. But still, she smiled. She bent down to kiss me and told me to keep going. She told me that I had to be strong. I can still see her turning away as that bald freak launched another ball of fire towards us, only for it to fizzle out.' Ariana's lips finally stretched into a smile. 'My mother was a Water User - like me. I had seen her stir before, but this was something different. She danced beautifully, creating waves that extinguished the flames around us.' Ariana's eyes glistened, and she quickly wiped them. Her smile faded. 'But she just kept screaming for me to go, her voice filled with pain. So, I ran. Even when I heard her final cry - I never turned back.' Ariana slumped over the bar, throwing her hands behind her head. 'I was found by her coven soon after. My mum belonged to a group of Water Users who came to help when they saw the smoke rising from my village. I was the sole survivor, so they took me in and eventually trained me to become a Water User, like my mother before me.' She lifted her head and placed the glass to her lips. 'That's where I met Miller. And then... well, the rest isn't worth mentioning,'

Seb breathed deeply, placing his hand on her back, only now realising the faint markings of many more scars on her skin. 'I had no idea,' he uttered.

Ariana shook her head and laughed. 'Everyone has a story like this. I'm nothing special.'

'That doesn't make it okay,' Seb told her, rubbing his forehead.

'I don't even know why I'm telling you this. Maybe I'm drunk,' Ariana said, staring at her almost empty glass before turning to Seb. 'Or maybe it's because you're-' Ariana's words caught in her throat as she stared at him. Suddenly her hands were around Sebastian's neck, pulling him towards her.

Before Seb could think, her lips were on his. His eyes widened as Ariana wrapped her arms around his shoulders and brought her body closer to him. Not knowing how to react or where to put his hands, Seb moved his mouth with hers, feeling her tongue. He could taste the bitter alcohol on her breath, the touch of her hands on his skin. The tavern, Stonehaven and the storm raging outside all melted away until all he could see was her. Finally, he closed his eyes and leaned into her, putting his hands on her hips and pulling her closer. Their hands explored effortlessly as they took short deep breaths like crashing waves on a shore. Sebastian picked Ariana up off her stool and sat her on the bar, his fingers sliding up her waist. She leaned down and smiled. He stopped, realising there were tears in her eyes. Sebastian took his hands off her and leaned back.

'What's wrong?' she asked.

Sebastian hesitated before telling her. 'This isn't right.'

'Seriously, Seb?' Ariana tilted her head. 'This is probably the only chance we're ever gonna get.'

'I'm sorry,' he uttered, stepping back. 'I can't do this.'

'Why not?' She pushed herself from the bar.

'Because you're upset,' he told her, rubbing the back of his neck and turning away. 'And we've been drinking. It feels wrong.'

'This has nothing to do with me.' Ariana closed her eyes and shook her head. 'This is about Zara, isn't it?'

'What?' Seb asked, his brows furling as he spun towards her.

'Come on, Seb. The only reason you agreed to come with me in the first place was so you could go back to her,' she said bluntly, her tone becoming sharper by the syllable. 'You never cared about me, or Darius, or our pointless war. All you cared about was going home.'

'How can you say that?' Seb asked, his mouth agape. 'Do you see me leaving to go find her? I'm here with you. Ready to fight *our* war!' he yelled, throwing his arms up, before sighing pitifully and running a hand down his face. 'Wherever she is, she'll have to wait. This fight is more important than what I want.'

Ariana leaned back against the bar. 'So, she *is* what you want,' she whispered, trembling and watching the ground. 'Sebastian, when will you realise? She's dead.'

'Don't say that,' he warned her, stepping closer.

'She's dead, Seb! That's what people do to us. They barge into our lives, make us fall in love with them, and then they die!' Her words began sputtering as tears crept down her cheeks, sliding past that scar. 'Who knows, you and me, we'll probably be dead soon enough. Just like your Zara... like *my* Miller. So, why did you have to ruin a perfectly *wrong* moment? Just for a second, it would have been nice to forget everything and pretend I remembered what it was like to actually feel something.' Ariana wiped her face free from tears and looked up at him.

Sebastian stared at the broken girl before him - the strongest person he had ever known. He moved towards Ariana and held her in his arms. 'We're not going to die.'

'Funny, that's exactly what *he* said.' She said, smiling.

He smiled back, watching as she gently closed her eyes and inched her face towards his, opening her mouth ever so slightly. Sebastian leaned his face close to hers, closing his eyes.

Alarm bells rang out the instant their lips touched.

Seb and Ariana didn't hear the siren at first, not until Glitch shot up from the booth in a mad panic, taking out his codebreaker. The two turned as the horror spread across Irvine's face.

'It... can't be,' Glitch uttered.

'Blackout?' Ariana asked.

'No,' he answered, his gaze locking onto Sebastian's. 'It's worse.'

Seb stared blankly at him, 'What do you mean?'

'Everyone, panic!' Glitch screamed, covering his face with his lab coat, and running out of the tavern.

'Another moment lost forever,' Ariana sighed, glancing back at Seb. She then elbowed him in the ribs before running for the door. 'Well, what can you do? Gear up, Doomsday. Better hope that training pays off.'

Sebastian watched her vanish through the doors, his hand reaching towards her. He peered through the stained-glass windows as another flash of lightning brightened the darkness outside, he caught a glimpse of something he couldn't comprehend. A thing he had all but forgotten. The ringing of alarms and crashing of thunder gave way to the screams of Stonehaven citizens and the ferocious roar of something inhuman.

21.

The Storm

Sebastian burst through the tavern doors and into the scream-filled halls. The townsfolk were panicked, huddled throughout the walkways and clutching onto the soldiers rushing past. Seb's eyes darted around the tightly packed halls, watching their pitiful sobs, hearing their woes. Something about their cries drilled into his brain along with the alarms piercing through his ears, Sebastian gritted his teeth, almost screaming for them all to stop.

A nasally, high-pitched squeal broke through the crowd, causing Seb to lift his head. He pushed past them to find Glitch crouched in a corner with his lab coat covering his face, shouting incomprehensible sentences. 'He always said it! I didn't listen. Thought he was lying. But it came. Just like he told me,' The scientist said, babbling to himself.

Sebastian pulled the coat away from him, only to be met with a yelp. 'Glitch, take it easy. It's just me,' he said, kneeling beside Irvine.

Glitch lunged for him, grabbing hold of his collar. 'This is the end! He always said this was how it would happen.'

'What are you talking about?' Seb batted Irvine's hands away from him.

Glitch slammed himself back into the corner, watching the frantic mob. 'It was G,' he whispered as his eyes drifted back to Sebastian's. 'His spirit has come to haunt us.'

'You're wrong, Glitch. You're a man of science. You know as much as anyone that ghosts aren't real. And that mad loon couldn't have survived the explosion.'

'*Something* could have.' Glitch gulped. 'The Doctor may not have survived. But his ghost - his demon, it's still alive. And it's come for revenge.'

Seb felt a familiar chill run down his spine - the same as when his bare back was placed on the cold operating table of Doctor G's Laboratory. He already knew what was out there.

Alpha.

The sounds around him faded. The erratic crowd began to slow, their screams drifting into echo. Sebastian felt his legs buckle as if they were no longer there, and before he had realised, he was lying on the floor with Glitch kneeling over him. Irvine's lips were moving, but Seb could only hear a high-pitched chime ringing in his ears. Glitch slapped Sebastian hard across the face, allowing the sounds of panic to come flooding back.

He sat up, clutching Irvine's coat. 'Where?' Seb asked.

Glitch looked away. 'Just outside the main doors, Baskay and Ariana have already left to face it. I tried to stop them, but they wouldn't listen.'

'Help me up.'

'Seb, there's nothing you can do. That thing is-'

'What the blight is all this?' A gruff voice asked from above them.

Seb looked up to see Darius, still gently swaying and holding onto his jug of strong rum.

'We've got a situation,' Seb told him.

'You're damned right we've got a situation. All this noise has completely killed my chances tonight.'

'It's a monster!' Glitch wailed, standing up to meet the giant.

'Say no more.' Darius raised his hands, reassuring the scientist. 'Thought as much, that's why I brought this.' He gestured a thumb towards Xerxes resting on his back. 'Just point me in the direction of what's ruining my evening.'

'You don't understand,' Glitch said, stepping in front of him. 'This thing can't be hurt through basic means. We must evacuate everyone immediately. Otherwise, there's no telling what that thing could-'

'Loving the pep talk, Poindexter,' Darius said, pushing him aside. 'You can worry about the outcome all you like. Me, I'm going to decide it for myself.' Darius stepped past him, walking proudly through the townsfolk. They all stopped screaming when they saw him - some even cheered.

Sebastian nodded and followed him, only to be grabbed by his sleeve.

'This isn't going to work, Seb,' Irvine told him. 'I helped create that thing. It's indestructible.'

'I don't care,' Seb said, tugging his arm free. 'Darius is right. The point of this place is to stand up to monsters. That's what the people outside believe, and they're willing to die for it.' He took a few more steps, then called over his shoulder. 'We were meant to bury everything in that place, Glitch. They're out there fighting right now because something got out. That's on us.' Seb sighed and hung his head. 'If you want to run, then go ahead. Get these people to safety below the caverns.'

'I will,' Glitch said with a firm nod. 'But you have to come with us.'

'Sorry, pal. I can't.' Sebastian turned back and tightened his fists, following Darius into the storm.

The wind and rain tore through the night air, allowing only flashes of lightning to break through as thunder littered the landscape. Sebastian slid across the ground now wet and glassy, gazing upon the carnage. It didn't take long for him to find the mammoth beast - trudging through the muck on its arms and legs like an animal. Alpha's bare, grey skin almost glowed in the rain as Baskay and his men surrounded it. They threw spears and hurled rocks as they circled Alpha. The creature feebly resisted them, confused and moaning.

Sebastian stopped running when he noticed the look in Alpha's eyes. Its stitched-together face had creased, and its disjointed jaw dropped open - quivering.

It was scared.

Some of Baskay's men had found an opening to attack, only to have Alpha swat them away with a simple swing of its arm. One soldier managed to land a blow, but the blade bounced off Alpha's tough skin. The beast wailed in frustration and turned to face the recruit who instantly dropped his dented blade and backed away. Alpha grabbed the warrior and squeezed him within its fist, before throwing him into the growing crowd. Sebastian watched as the monster shielded itself, moaning as more warriors swung their weapons around it. Reaching a single hand out at the beast, tears escaped Seb's strained eyes, becoming lost in the wind and rain.

Baskay yelled for his men to retreat, falling back towards the castle. Seb sprinted past them as hundreds of bright lights shot across the sky and at the beast. He turned back to the stone towers as bowmen with flame-tipped arrows littered the slits in the castle, with Fire Users standing beside them, lighting their arrows.

Alpha made a sorry attempt to protect itself as the arrows bounced off its skin like twigs, the fire almost extinguished completely within the harsh rains.

'He's just protecting himself…' Sebastian said aloud, yet silent in the chaos. He slowed to a stop and watched fire light up the rain-filled sky. 'Alpha *isn't* our enemy.'

'Get down, boy!' Baskay yelled as he knocked Sebastian onto the ground. A giant boulder followed, whirling through the air where Seb had been standing. Alpha lifted more debris made from the oval stone houses and hurled them towards the castle. Baskay pulled Seb to his feet before turning back and placing his hands on the ground. With a strained yell, he punched through the stone, erecting a wall. Other Earth Users joined, constructing smaller defences around the castle.

'You should get to safety,' Baskay told him, his body trembling as he struggled to maintain the barrier.

'This is a mistake. Call your men off, Baskay,' Seb pleaded, watching as the beast hurled another boulder.

'What you're asking is impossible. This monster attacked our home.'

'Please, you have to stop. Alpha is only defending itself.'

'As are we,' Baskay said through clenched teeth, his veins almost popping out of his skin as he struggled to keep up the walls. 'Wait… you know this fiend?'

The wall exploded as somebody's home crashed through. Seb and Baskay barrelled to safety, as gravel rained over them. When Seb looked towards the beast, he witnessed the drunken hero walking barefoot across the battlefield.

Darius had stopped in front of Alpha, almost standing tall against the mammoth creature. 'So, you're the party crasher?' he yelled through the storm with one hand on the hilt of his sword - the other, still holding onto that jug of strong alcohol. 'It's a pity. This hooch is the finest I've had in a long time. I'd say it's wasted on you.' Darius hurled the jug at Alpha, the clay container breaking on impact, and drenching the beast in the foul-smelling liquid.

'No…' Sebastian urged, breaking into a sprint towards the grizzled warrior.

Darius lifted his head, now smiling with a cigar hanging from his mouth. He took out a lighter and lit the cigar, throwing the flame at the beast. An explosion sprang from Alpha, knocking Darius back. The beast shrieked in pain as it flailed helplessly across the wet ground, trying to put out the fire. Darius sat up, almost bewildered. When he noticed the beast's pain, he screamed with laughter. Seb skidded beside him and dragged Darius to a safe enough distance, all the while watching the poor creature rolling around in fear.

'Where's Ariana?' he asked, never taking his eyes off Alpha.

'That girl,' Darius groaned with a shake of his head. 'Said to keep that thing busy while she prepared. Can't believe she's missing the show. I should've bought sausages.'

Sebastian turned and grabbed Darius by the collar. 'Where is she? Alpha's gonna burn to death if she doesn't get here quick.'

Darius raised an eyebrow. 'How much did *you* drink tonight, kid?'

Sebastian let go, turning his head in all directions. But then, as if by magic, the rain stopped. Seb looked up, as did Darius and everyone else. The weather hadn't cleared. The droplets of rain still hung in the air. Suspended, as if time had frozen. The wind had calmed, leaving a gentle breeze.

When Sebastian's eyes drifted back, he noticed a group of Users from Ariana's class in the distance. They glided elegantly across the battlefield, making their way towards the burning creature. Ariana walked among them. She wasn't dancing like her students. Instead, the girl held out her arms, observing the particles around her. When she was close enough, Ariana began dancing, allowing her followers to circle her, swaying rhythmically. The drops of rain resumed their heavy fall. But now, they fell to Ariana, gathering above her into an ever-increasing orb of water.

Sebastian watched as the translucent sphere grew more substantial. The look in Ariana's eyes was desperate. Alpha was still smouldering but managed to cover itself in just enough mud to put out the flames.

'Well, I'll be,' Darius uttered.

'She's gonna kill it,' Seb breathed, shaking his head.

'She just might.' Darius smiled. 'You know, after all this time. I-'

'I have to stop her!' Seb yelled, clawing the ground as he pushed himself to his feet.

He began running, watching as the warriors around him retreated to the castle. The flame-tipped arrows continued raining down. Sebastian weaved in and out of the way as they lit up the ground.

Alpha rose its body up high on its legs, ignoring the flames. It looked out towards Ariana and her coven. The rain had been building to form an incredible ocean suspended within the sphere, matching the size of Stonehaven castle. Seb screamed for her to stop, but she couldn't hear him. Ariana was only focused on killing the beast that ruined her evening. Finally, a tear opened from the floating globe above her. A jet of water tore through the sky, so powerful, that it dispersed the black clouds overhead. The rapid beam rocketed at Alpha, too fast to make a sound.

Without time to think, Sebastian threw himself in front of the beast, turning and planting his feet into the brittle stone. Seb bared his teeth and focused all of his energy, feeling the black bile creep out of him. He held out his arms and closed his eyes as the oceanic beam tore through him.

In a single moment, everything had stopped. The bowmen lowered their aim, the fighters slowed their assault, and the Users relinquished their flames and allowed their stone barriers to crumble. All were left staring at that suspended ocean. From the centre, a torrent of water -using the pressure harnessed from the night's storm- shot through the sky. No longer formed from water, but an overwhelming, translucent energy.

The roar escaping Sebastian's lungs was no longer human. His arms formed into a cross, protecting Alpha from the power surging against him. His muscles contracted, burning and breaking down, replaced by something stronger. Seb felt the energy within him rival even Ariana's seismic beam. The wet ground around him hardened and cracked. Tendrils broke through the broken earth, wrapping around Seb as his rage-filled screams became ever-increasing. Finally, he threw his arms down, causing smoke to explode around him.

Ariana finally broke free from her trance as she realised it was Sebastian standing against her. She spread out her hands and slammed them upon the ground - bursting the orb above her coven. The ocean fell from the sky, crashing towards them. The Users in training all screamed, only for the tidal wave to become suspended once more.

Ariana danced, lifting her arms to keep the raging sea from descending further. With a flip of her wrist, the ocean exploded back into rain, giving Stonehaven one final shower. When it was over, she let out a quick sigh, before turning her attention back to Sebastian.

He watched her. Trembling, yet still holding his stance to protect Alpha. His clothes were torn and smouldering. His body beneath was left bruised and bleeding. He panted heavily, slowly turning to the beast behind him. Alpha was gazing down with curiosity. It sat with a thud, breaking the cracked earth.

'Leeee…' It spoke, reaching a hand out towards Sebastian.

'Stay back, Alpha!' A frail voice yelled. It was Glitch. The scientist was shaking, more soaked from sweat than the others had gotten from the rain. He stood behind the creature, readying his photon displacer - the same weapon he had used on Alpha's creator.

'Glitch... don't,' Seb warned.

Irvine pulled the trigger, blinding Alpha. The beast let out a roar and rose to its feet. Covering its face with its grotesque claws. When it removed its hand, its eyes were bleeding, and glaring down at the frail scientist. Glitch dropped his weapon and fell to the ground.

'You had to choose this moment... to be a... hero.' Seb laughed as best he could.

'It's like you said. Alpha is our burden. It's only fitting that we're the ones to end it,' Glitch replied, staring into the milky green eyes of his greatest sin.

Alpha snarled at the two of them, raising its fist. Glitch grabbed hold of Seb and squeezed his eyes shut as it brought its mighty mitt down upon them. Sebastian watched on, feeling a strange sense of tranquillity wash over him. Alpha seemed to fade from view, as did everything else. There was someone, however. A lone prospector, standing atop the castle. This stranger wore a white hooded robe and leaned casually upon a pillar. He raised an arm out to the skies, and in a flash, a bolt of lightning descended from the heavens, landing in the stranger's hand. They slowly moved their crackling palm towards Sebastian and the bolt shot out across the valley.

Seb finally closed his eyes, hearing a monstrous wail. When they opened, Alpha was before him, smouldering, trembling. Its hardened skin was left broken, oozing green slime. The beast whimpered, pulling its broken body away from the castle. Alpha trembled as it stood, taking one last pained look at everyone and snarled, before trudging away into the empty wilderness.

The people of Stonehaven watched silently as it disappeared into the wastes. Sebastian's eyes drifted from Alpha, and then to the top of Stonehaven castle where the bolt of lightning came from. The hooded figure had disappeared.

Ariana rushed to his side and grabbed hold of his shoulders. 'Seb... what was that?' she asked. He could see the look on her face - the same one she wore when he had first revealed his powers to her.

'I'm sorry, Ari,' he said, making a poor attempt to stand. 'I couldn't let you...'

Sebastian looked around desperately, his eyes gazing upon the faces of Darius, Baskay and the rest of his comrades. They all looked at him with the same fear in their eyes.

'Seb, you've got to understand,' she said in a whisper. 'The way you're acting. It isn't normal.'

'Ariana, that was Alpha. The bioengineered creature from the lab,' Glitch told her, getting up from the ground. 'I don't know how it escaped, but-'

As Glitch's speech drifted into echo, Sebastian got to his feet and reached a hand out towards the castle roof. He felt a strange urge building within him. A rage like he hadn't felt before. A longing. Sebastian's fists tightened, almost shaking.

'Seb?' Ariana asked, cutting Glitch off. He could sense the uncertainty in her voice as she uttered his name.

'I have to go,' he told her, breaking into a sprint.

The people of Stonehaven backed away as he rushed past, staring at him like the freak he was. Seb ignored them. Avoided them like the debris littering the ground, making his way behind the castle.

Ariana rushed after Seb, only to have Darius grab hold of her. 'What are you doing? I need to go after him!' She screamed.

'Let him go, girly,' Darius sighed. 'Just... let him go.'

A vengeful sun had finally broken free from grey clouds. Sebastian sprinted past the puddles, sending explosions into the air. He clutched hold of his bruised arms and chest, only just beginning to register the pain from Ariana's attack. He looked down to see the jacket Ariana had made for him, almost torn to shreds, revealing his bruised and scathed skin. His arms had inflated like red balloons, feeling as though they were about to pop.

The stranger in the hooded robe dashed across the rooftops, leaping from one to the other as if he could fly. The outsider must have felt Sebastian's presence trailing behind, as he would weave in and out of the many districts without a sound. Sebastian followed, his body screaming at him to stop, begging for him to topple over and fall unconscious. He wished to forget himself, if only for a moment.

The robed figure vaulted from the last roof, almost soaring through the sky, landing with a quick roll and was instantly back on their feet, escaping into a dark tunnel under a bridge. Seb skidded through the underpass, feeling his pain cease as he entered the soothing shadows. With his second wind, he closed the distance between them, throwing up his arms and forcing black tendrils to shoot across the tunnel. As the spiny shadows approached, the stranger spun around and a flash of light illuminated the tunnel, eradicating the tendrils. Sebastian fell back, shielding his eyes. In the corner of his vision, Sebastian glimpsed at the hooded silhouette walking casually towards the exit.

'Alex!' Sebastian screamed, reaching out to him.

The robed stranger stopped abruptly as the name echoed across the tunnel. His body became stiff as he turned back towards Sebastian.

'I know it's you...' Seb uttered, quieter this time - with faith his voice would still be heard. After all, Alex's ears never missed a thing. 'You can run, but you'll be forever looking over your shoulder.' Seb tried getting back to his feet, only to fall forward and land on his knees. 'I'll never stop chasing you....' He leaned back, held his head up to the ceiling and inhaled deeply. 'Not until you give her back to me.'

The robed stranger sighed and pulled back his hood, finally revealing what Sebastian already knew. Alex ran a hand through his blonde hair - now golden in the light of the sun. 'It would seem you've caught me. It has been some time, Seb. I wish I could say that it is good to see you again,' Alex spoke plainly, his face remaining expressionless.

'What are you doing here?' Seb asked, lifting his arm once more. 'I've travelled so far to find you - to find all of you.' He scrunched his eyes shut, determined not to show any tears.

'I know. I've been watching since your awakening in the sands.'

'You were there?' Seb uttered, shaking as he glared. 'I remember now. I saw you in Platto. I was captured and you did nothing! You were watching the whole time and *now* you decide to show yourself.'

'You left me little choice. I couldn't allow you to get yourself killed. Not when you were so close.'

Sebastian could hardly register the words coming from Alex's mouth. His old friend was drenched in the sunlight, made all the brighter from where Seb knelt in the dark tunnel. His gaze dropped to his lap, and he could see the tears drop upon his torn jeans.

'So, you just watched. When I was stranded in the wastes. When I was captured and amputated. Held prisoner and tested on like some lab rat. Where was your help then?' Seb asked, his shaking hands clenched into fists.

'I couldn't show my hand, Seb. The risk was too great. Even now, secluded as we are, the ramifications of my involvement could be detrimental to everything I've sacrificed.'

'Everything *you've* sacrificed?' Seb uttered, his body trembling as he struggled to get the next words out. 'I thought I was truly alone, Alex. I thought I'd never see any of you again.'

'There's no excuse for the mistakes I have made.' Alex placed a hand over his face with a subtle shake of his head. 'For what it's worth, I did it all for your protection.'

Sebastian shook his head and breathed deeply, wiping his face free from tears. 'We were always meant to leave together.'

'I was never a part of your journey. Neither was Zara.'

'My journey?' Sebastian asked, frowning up at Alex. 'Is that what you call the torture I've gone through?'

'Your life was destined for tragedy long before we met.' Alex hung his head and turned away from the darkness. 'Leaving Lora was always your destiny. However, instead of the planned departure, I decided to give you something different - a chance to fight.' He turned back, an ounce of sadness breaking through his expression. 'I needed to see what you would become.'

'So, that's why you left me in the wastes. To test me?'

'I didn't leave you in that desert to *test* you, Seb. I left you there to die.'

Sebastian's eyes widened as the last words slipped from Alex's tongue, echoing through the tunnel and bouncing across the spherical walls.

'Left me... To die?' Seb repeated, joining the echoes of the cavern. How could you say that? You're supposed to be my friend!'

'It would have been a mercy. I walked away and allowed nature to take its course. And somehow, against all odds, you survived.' Alex said with a shrug.

'Is that why you followed, so you could finish the job?' Seb sniffed, wiping the newly formed tears from his cheeks.

'My reasoning was unknown even to myself.' Alex sighed and wiped a hand across his face. 'For so long I've been following orders with little agency to speak of. At first, it was mere curiosity. Only now are my decisions beginning to make sense.'

'I'm glad you're making sense of them, at least.' Seb shook his head and spat. 'Whatever your reasons. I don't care. I just want to go home.'

Alex was silent for a moment. He looked upon Sebastian and groaned. 'Far to the north. Mountains surround a village.' Alex turned away and walked closer to the exit. 'You'll find it there, along with the answers you seek.'

'You mean, Lora. And what of Zara, is she still there?' Seb asked, almost stuttering as he pushed himself onto his feet.

'She never left, Sebastian. None of them did.' Alex waved as he walked, his voice growing louder as it resonated along the tube. 'To find them, I suggest borrowing a cruiser from those who still believe they hold any semblance of power. Sadly, they're the only ones who desperately cling to that primitive technology. Your new friend, Irvine, has a device that will show you the way.'

'How do you know all of this?' Seb yelled, clutching hold of a wall to steady himself.

'Those fools, giving up their humanity to save this barren rock.' Alex continued, now speaking only to himself as he disappeared into the light.

'Alex, wait!' Sebastian called out, limping towards the exit.

'They sacrificed everything. And in the end, it changed nothing.'

Sebastian stumbled out of the tunnel, struggling to keep up. When he emerged into the light, he was met with the vast nothingness of the outside world. Alex had somehow vanished. Seb scanned the area, hoping to find something. His eyes narrowed until he finally managed to make out mountains looming in the far distance. Sebastian tightened his fists and turned back around to Stonehaven.

The rains had finally ceased upon Sebastian's return. He drifted back towards the castle, clutching at his sides and leaning on the walls of the buildings as he passed, leaving trails of bloody handprints. Ariana was the first to spot him. She shouted for help as she ran to his side, catching Seb in her arms before he fell to the ground. The clouds had fully dispersed, allowing the sun to make its triumphant return, bringing with it a glorious light. Sebastian looked up to see her silhouette. He smiled, brushing his thumb across her cheek.

'Seb,' Ariana said sweetly, as she grabbed hold of his arm.

'Za...ra,' Sebastian uttered with a heavy breath as he closed his eyes, allowing the light to envelop him.

22.

Thunder and Light

Sebastian opened his eyes hoping to see Zara standing above him. Instead, he was alone. Seb crept out of bed and peeked outside the window. It was the dead of night, and the streets were bare. All the surrounding houses were dark with curtains drawn. He shrugged and turned towards his bed, suddenly realising where he was.

It was his bedroom back in Lora; the rough wooden floorboards, the poorly stuffed mattress, the desk with paper strewn across it. Seb took a step closer. There was handwriting scrawled haphazardly across the sheets. His handwriting. He picked up one of the papers and began to read.

'...Tell me. What is the meaning of existence?'

The room flashed white - lasting less than a second, yet it left him with wide and wild eyes. He slowly turned to the window, the paper slipping from his hand. He remembered this night. Parts of it, at least.

'...Is the point of being, to simply survive?'

The next second brought with it a thunderous boom, bouncing Sebastian to the rattling floorboards. He scrambled to the window with loose limbs. His eyes lit up, reflecting the home opposite. As if crushed beneath some divine weight, the cobblestone cottage before him had disintegrated. Even the dust burned up in the flames. Sebastian stepped back, unable to avert his gaze. His throat shuddered as it garbled incomprehensible prayers. The flames had grown as high as a tower, dancing with the harshening winds, ripping their way through the surrounding homes - nothing more than kindling for the hungry fire.

'...Living long enough to pass some irrelevant data down to your offspring?'

Another flash lit up the darkening sky, raining forth a pillar of light that obliterated the black clouds beneath. A devastating crash followed as white beams descended upon the unsuspecting ground in the distance. Seb's room shook as if it were encased within a snow globe. The wave of destruction spread out, tearing through all in its way. Leaving everything else wrapped in thick flames.

'...Who in turn, follow the perpetual contract of sustaining some meaningless genetic code...'

Sebastian dragged his lead-laden feet to his mother's room in a panic, tripping over moving furniture as the house rumbled beneath him. Once inside, he pulled off the bedsheets to find nobody beneath. He looked under the bed and checked the closet but found nothing. She was gone. He screamed for her but heard only the crashing waves of the storm outside.

'...This is how primitive lifeforms justify existence...'

He ran to her window - the rain now hammering against it. Black clouds loomed overhead as smoke filled the sky. Despite the downpour, unrelenting flames swept through Lora, the pillars of thunderous energy ripping away any structure still standing. Sebastian watched on, shaking his head in disbelief. He turned to face his mother's empty bed. 'Where were you?' he asked, hiding his head in his hands.

'...It is how your forefathers justified theirs...'

Turning his attention to the horrors outside, Seb surveyed the streets and noticed someone. Opening the window to call out to them, he realised that this person wasn't running or screaming. No, they were walking, maybe even strolling, completely unphased by the hellfire his village had become. The hooded person was short and round - a shape that didn't match any of the villagers in Lora. And yet, something about them seemed all too familiar. This outsider wore a distinctive black robe, with a hood obscuring their face. Sebastian backed away from the window, the floorboards wailing with every step he took. Smoke had clawed its way in from the open window, filling the room. Seb took a deep breath, swallowed some bile that had been creeping up his throat and ran out of his home.

'...I found a better answer to the question. A new way of being...'

Like stepping through the gates of hell, Sebastian crept out from the veiled security of his home. Smouldering debris littered the broken cobblestone paths, blurred only by grey mist escaping into the clouds. He put his arms out to protect himself against the fierce winds, mixing with the shards of glass and smouldering splinters cascading from the fire's prey. Seb ambled across the street in a daze, turning back when he heard the groan of his home. He watched, mouth agape as the flames licked at the straw roof, erupting into a wave of red, yellow, and orange.

'...Do you truly believe you are deserving of existence?'

Seb spun around and shook his head, grabbing hold of it with both hands before dropping to his knees. He cried a gut-wrenching scream as black smoke filled his lungs. He vomited upon his lap, hands shaking as he pushed himself up. Watching the grim nightmare once more, Sebastian laid eyes on the shadowy-robed figure in the distance - now accompanied by someone else. This new arrival was incredibly tall and unrealistically slim. Much like their shorter friend, they wore black robes, strolling through flames like they were merely an illusion. He gulped, taking one last look at his home as it crumbled before him.

'...Is the blade of grass you trample upon as worthy?'

The two strangers drifted through what used to be the market district. Sebastian had to rely on barely intact walls and debris large enough to duck behind. Between the glowing flames and pillars of light. It was almost impossible to stay hidden. Not that it mattered. The hooded individuals hadn't turned back once or stopped to check their surroundings.

'...All you did was take from true existence. Used and consumed her. Until nothing was left...'

Eventually, they stopped in front of Avalon Fountain. The open area around the village centre was untouched by the chaos that Lora had become. The rounder of the hooded robes dropped to their knees and threw their hands up to the sky. The taller of the two stepped into the fountain and submerged themselves in the water. Sebastian watched on, shaking intensely as the thin one got up and started splashing the other.

'...To think otherwise is arrogant...'

Becoming still, his breath caught when Seb realised that the two were frolicking in the fountain just as he and Zara had done only hours prior. Seb balled his hands into fists and stepped out from cover.

'*...Selfish...*'

Before he could confront them, another flash illuminated the sky. A white pillar careened from the heavens, obliterating the bridge above him. Wood and stone exploded around Sebastian, knocking him against a nearby wall.

'*...Seb... You know I can tell when you're lying to me... right?*'

Sebastian felt the harsh wind, the heavy rain and the shaking ground beneath him.

'*...And that cheesy face you pull can't fool anyone...*'

He felt the heat of the growing fire, the smoke filling his lungs, the bruises and fractured bones, and the intense agony that planted him to the concrete.

'*...It's okay... you don't need to be strong for me...*'

The orchestra of crackling electricity, crumbling buildings, and blasts of desolation came from all around him. But then, all was quiet. The only sound he heard was her voice.

'...I'm just happy you're here...'

'Zara...' Sebastian gasped, his hands clutching onto anything he could find. Seb dragged his limp body away from the fountain, clawing at the brittle ground. He pulled himself further, screaming in anguish. 'Zara, please...' Sebastian was coughing up blood every time he called out for her. But he couldn't stop. He had to find her, even if it killed him. A screech from high above forced Sebastian to take witness. Union Tower was still standing, swaying against the harsh winds. Wilting from the fire, it began to collapse. Sebastian let out a gasping breath just as the world slowed around him. He watched as the flaming structure descended upon him. He dropped his head to the ground and closed his eyes. 'Zara... I'm sorry.' He kept his eyes closed for a time, awaiting the tower of glass and steel to topple.

He waited a moment, only for nothing to happen.

'It's tiring, always having to watch over you.'

He lifted his head to find the tower suspended, along with the rain and beams of light. All had frozen around him. All except for Alex who was standing over Sebastian, holding out his hand.

'Alex... what's happening?'

'This is the fall of Lora, Seb.'

Sebastian winced, faintly gasping for breath as he watched the still flames and floating stones. 'The fall... of Lora?'

'They've found you,' Alex said, grabbing hold of Sebastian's throat and lifting him into the air. 'So, it's time to leave, just like you've always wanted.'

'I don't know… what you…' Seb tried to speak, the grip on his throat growing tighter. He clawed at Alex's hand, only for his friend to punch him in the stomach and drop him to the floor.

Alex stepped away to survey the black hoods at the fountain. There were more of them now, and they had started chanting some strange language. 'It's time to put this place behind us.'

Sebastian pulled himself to his feet and grabbed Alex by his shirt. 'Where's Zara? We need to find her.'

'Relax, she's safe. I got to her just in time.' Alex looked away as he said the words. 'I wish I could have done the same for you.'

Sebastian winced, pushing himself from the rubble littering the once-paved ground. Alex held out an arm to keep him steady.

'She's safe...' Sebastian repeated as he grabbed on for support, 'that's good.'

Alex laughed and shook his head. 'We're pretty far from good, Seb. Look around you. Our way of life is over.'

The flames began to flicker once more. The tower came crashing down. glass and steel exploded upon the broken ground. Alex grabbed hold of Sebastian's collar and wrapped an arm around his shoulder. 'Looks like that's all the time we have. I'll see you on the other side, pal. Good luck,' he said, and with a forceful push, he propelled Sebastian through the air and onto his back, atop broken bricks and hot stone.

Sebastian's head pulsed. Looking up, he witnessed the chaotic white beam of light ripping through the clouds, making its way towards him. Within an instant, it struck. The intensity of pure white burning through his retinas, that high-pitched chime bursting his eardrums, his flesh melting away, his bones crunching under the weight of the immense pressure. In but a fraction of a moment, he had disintegrated into nothing.

'...And yet, you continue to live. Each day, more futile than the last...'

Was this the first time he had travelled to this realm? Sebastian looked at his hands. They were missing, brushed away by white paint, disappearing into the abyss.

'...Searching for meaning in meaningless...'

Lines of static electricity flashed across the eternal sky, illuminated more so by the looming darkness hanging above the empty canvas. Storm clouds erupted, bringing heavy rain. A hand materialised before Sebastian. He held it out, allowing black droplets to land upon his palm - a sticky burning substance. It pooled together and hardened quickly. Sebastian squeezed his hand into a fist and broke free from the brittle muck. More rained down as another echo reverberated across the void.

'...But fear not, child. There is still hope...'

The droplets congealed and clung to his skin, hardening like cement until Sebastian was covered entirely in the putrid jelly. He tried to run, but a puddle made from the black bile began to emerge, growing deeper, and expanding indefinitely. The liquid stuck like glue and dried into clay.

Sebastian could do nothing but gaze down at the reflective surface to look upon himself. A black beast stared back at him with wild eyes - pupils dilating and shaking rhythmically, with a grin so wide it looked inhuman.

'...When your world bleeds back into mine...'

Sebastian dropped to his knees when he felt the words ripple across the black waters. He looked up with a squint at the glorious light above, obliterating the flickering clouds. The enigmatic entity looked down at Seb, descending from the heavens and touching the frozen black lake, causing it to crack. It walked elegantly towards him, each step chipping away at the cement encasing Sebastian.

'...Our journeys will end. Our memories to be forgotten...'

The glowing one gazed across the cavern before lowering its head and melting away into empty space. Leaving the black oily substance to rise from the ground as a sea of shadows. The sky was white, and the ground was black. Both coexisted peacefully within the nothingness. Seb closed his eyes and took a deep breath, allowing the ocean of oil to engulf his being. He sunk to the depths, looking up at the white being drifting towards the heavens. Its unsettling grin was finally free to form a frown.

'...Existence as we know it will fade into myth...'

23.

Eternally Bound

Echoes of whispers filtered through the air. Sebastian winced at the light and sounds attacking his senses, lifting him from the black ocean in his mind.

'How do we know the boy isn't working with them.' A deep but clear voice echoed through the air.

'Don't be ridiculous, Baskay. He's one of us.' A softer tone sprang forward.

'The boy knew the creature by name - protected it even. And let's not forget, he stood against you, Miss Lane.'

'You've got it all wrong!' A different voice cried out, nasally and high-pitched. 'Alpha was an experiment. Seb and I... tried to destroy it. Somehow it escaped.'

'That's enough out of you!' The first voice growled, silencing all of them. 'I let you into my home. Crushed bread with you. If I had known what you were...' A loud clap broke through the air.

Sebastian opened his eyes, only to see blurred colours and shapes around him. The room was small and dark - allowing only a sliver of light to peer in from a small opening. The pain suddenly became overwhelming as Sebastian's mind reconnected with his body. He groaned and made a feeble attempt to stretch, but something snagged hold of his wrists.

'The kid's coming around, people. We close to a decision?' A familiar gruff voice came from the corner of the room, followed by a yawn. Seb peered towards it, his eyes settling on a shape larger than the rest.

The room swayed and tilted, causing the bile within Seb's stomach to slosh about as he blinked himself back to consciousness. Sebastian could finally make out the shapes before him. Darius, Baskay and Ariana were all standing above him.

'Welcome back to the land of the living, kid,' Darius said with a shrug, facing away the instant their eyes met.

'How're you feeling?' Ariana asked, her tears betraying the smile she gave him. She stepped closer and placed a hand on his shoulder.

'Get away from him, Miss Lane!' Baskay yelled, his face red with anger.

'Stop it. Can't you see you're just making things worse?' Ariana sighed, staring back at the bronzed warrior. She gave Baskay a cold glare before returning her gaze to Sebastian's vacant face, smiling softly. 'What happened out there, Seb?' she asked, brushing the hair away from his face.

'I... I can't move,' Sebastian said with a feeble breath, dropping his head to the floor.

'This is ridiculous,' Darius said as he lit a cigarette. 'You're scared this kid is gonna explode or somethin'? He can't even break through them ropes. Untie him, Baskay.'

'Or is that just what he wants us to think?' Baskay asked, tapping his chin. 'This could be another ploy to deceive us.'

'He's not deceiving anybody!' Ariana yelled, spinning to face the proud chief. 'He's already told me everything. His powers and Irvine's past were kept hidden because they knew people would react like this!'

The room fell silent. Sebastian peered up again to find Glitch sitting opposite, tied to an uncomfortable-looking chair.

'Glitch? What's happening?'

'Seb, I'm sorry. We had to tell them,' Irvine said, struggling against his bonds. 'They think you're some kind of-'

Baskay stepped forward and struck Irvine across the face with the back of his hand. 'I thought I told you to shut your cage.'

'Baskay, stop it!' Ariana jumped in front of Glitch, shielding him. 'Back me up here, big guy,' she said, turning to Darius.

'Can we at least untie the scientist, Baskay? We all know he's no threat,' Darius asked with a sigh as he stubbed out his cigarette.

'I feel like you're not taking any of this seriously.' Baskay turned to him with a scowl.

Darius rose to his feet and glared down at Stonehaven's leader.

Baskay averted his eyes. 'Fine... he's told us everything we need to hear.'

Sebastian had finally become aware of the situation. He pushed all the air from his lungs, staring down at the hard floor. He was a prisoner once more.

Baskay removed the binds on Irvine and shoved him off the chair.

'Right, thank you.' Ariana exhaled, wiping the sweat from her brow. 'Now, free Seb.'

'I can't do that, Miss Lane,' Baskay replied in a sombre tone.

'Why not?' I get that Seb has these crazy powers, but don't we all? I've been called a freak more times than I can count for *magically* conjuring water.' She pointed at Baskay. 'You can create towers by punching the ground. Even Nana Viola can read people's thoughts.' Ariana turned to Seb one last time and hung her head. 'We're all freaks, criminals, terrorists. Call it what you want. They give us these names because they're scared of what they don't understand.' Ariana whispered, tightening her fists before shooting her eyes towards Baskay. 'This world has enough monsters without you creating more. Sebastian is one of us.'

Seb could no longer lift his head, but he managed a smile.

'Ariana... I understand your frustrations,' Baskay told her. 'But I'm afraid it's more serious than that. You don't know what Sebastian truly is.'

'And you do?'

'You want to explain, Master Blake?' Baskay asked, turning to Darius. 'After all, you are the only one here who's seen what this power is capable of.'

Darius remained silent.

Baskay sighed and scratched the top of his head. 'Fine,' he said, grabbing a stool and sitting down. 'Where to even begin? It may sound ridiculous. I scarcely believe it myself, but there are worse threats to Endura than Blackout or Surphites. The thing I speak of isn't a man or beast. It's a demon, born from the very Blight that consumes Endura. It is the embodiment of corruption. The reason for this broken world.'

'Hold up. You mean the Black Beast?' Arianna scoffed, folding her arms. 'That's just a fairy tale, Baskay - a dumb story to scare kids.'

'The legend may have fallen into myth. But all that tells us is that the creature is cunning and elusive.'

'Or that it doesn't exist.'

'We all wanted to believe that the legends were mere stories.' Baskay exhaled, placing a hand on his neck. 'But whispers kept spreading throughout the years. Settlements engulfed by shadow - swallowed whole. Never to be heard from again.'

'That could have been caused by anything,' Ariana answered, shifting uncomfortably.

'There are documented accounts from the survivors of these events. Their voices are few and spread out in both time and distance. But all speak of a being formed of shadows - more animal than man. In the last few decades, these rumours have only grown. Even today, some have seen the creature on the field of battle, not twenty years passed.'

'Seventeen years, two months and twenty-nine days,' Darius corrected, tightening his fists.

'Well, I wouldn't know exactly,' Baskay said, leaning back against a wall. 'I wasn't there.'

'You wouldn't be alive today if you were.' Darius smirked, taking out a flask and unscrewing the lid with shaking hands.

'Darius?' Ariana asked, raising an eyebrow. 'You've seen this thing?'

'It's a day I don't care to remember. And yet, it's the one I can't seem to forget.'

'What happened?'

'It was the fight to decide the fate of Endura - The Battle of the Black. We had finally amassed an army large enough to stand against Vincent Vale, his Ender Knights and the whole of Blackout itself.' Darius took a long swig from his container. 'You should have seen it. Thousands of warriors in a single fight. Together, we could have taken out the whole blight-ridden operation.' Darius cleared his throat and lit his cigarette. 'Amidst the battle, a bell rang. A strange tune - almost hypnotic in a sense. And not soon after, a black cloud descended from the Crimson Capital. A man appeared from that shroud, almost like he was born from them shadows.'

'The Black Beast,' Baskay clarified, staring down at Sebastian.

'It tore across the battlefield, ripping through anyone in its path. Our troops, and even its own. Our army fell back. Hell, half of Blackout fled. I've not seen a thing like it. The look in its eyes.' Darius turned upon Seb, staring down at him. 'It was the battle to change the fate of the world. But that beast just saw it as sport.'

Glitch and Ariana glanced up at one another, before slowly turning towards Sebastian. He was shaking, his gaze glued to the giant.

'I often overheard Doctor G speak of the Black Beast,' Glitch said, gulping as he stepped forward. 'Although there is no concrete evidence to prove its existence, he seemed intent on finding it. And when Sebastian arrived, he...' He shook his head and furrowed his brow as he stared Baskay down. 'He was a madman. His theories were based on an illusion of attaining godlike power. He would have believed anything to achieve that dream. Seb isn't the Black Beast'

'How could he be?' Ariana shouted, tears breaking from her eyes. 'You said it yourself. You saw that thing a long time ago. Sebastian would have been a baby at that point. It can't be him...' She looked back towards the bound boy, shaking her head.

'I did see the beast that day,' Darius told her. 'Long black hair, eyes of a killer, a body that could have been mistaken for something inhuman.' Darius breathed uneasily, scratching at his greying beard. 'That thing, whatever it was, died on that battlefield. I watched the darkness spill out like ash, drifting higher than their floating fortress.'

'So, it's dead then.' Ariana breathed a sigh of relief. 'Then what's the problem here?'

'The darkness is a leech,' Baskay said, folding his arms and facing away from Seb. 'It's a corruption that takes over its host, turns them hollow, before rushing off to the next victim when the current shell becomes a husk. It is an eternal creature that can't be killed. But Sebastian can at least give us a time of peace by making the ultimate sacrifice.'

'You want to *kill* him?' Ariana asked with a shudder.

'I want peace for my people,' Baskay answered. 'Blackout will stop at nothing to get hold of this boy. And eventually, Sebastian will be no more than a puppet. A suitcase made from skin and bone, carrying the greatest threat of the world - unleashing it where our enemies see fit.' Baskay removed his scimitar from its holster and held it up to Sebastian's throat. 'I take no pleasure in this. But it must be done.'

Sebastian gazed up at the bald warrior, his eyes glistening. Baskay's face matched his own, allowing a tear to slip through. Ariana screamed for him to stop. Glitch threw himself back against the wall. Baskay winced and closed his eyes, reluctant to do what must be done. Sebastian gulped, his eyes following the curved blade towards his throat. Then with a heavy breath, he closed his eyes.

'We shouldn't make such rash decisions.' Darius said, placing his hand on Baskay's shoulder. The proud warrior's hand trembled. 'The kid will still be here in the morning. We'll have the rest of the night to think about the best solution.'

'Master Blake, if we let him live, who knows what-'

'I'm not saying we're gonna let him live,' Darius said, his lips curling into a smirk. 'I'm saying we can use the kid as bait. Maybe set up a trap for Vincent and his knights. We could take out all our enemies in one fell swoop.'

Sebastian's chest tightened as he looked up at the cold, uncaring eyes of Darius. He felt the black bile creep up his throat and swallowed it back down. That's when the sounds around him faded into echo once more. His vision blurred yet again as tears blotted his view. He thought he could hear the cries of anguish from Ariana as she was dragged from the room. But soon enough, he was alone with his demon.

Sebastian sat waiting for death. His last hours were spent listening to water dripping from a crack in the roof of his cell, as he tried to make sense of the storm that changed everything. Another layer of sound broke the monotony. Almost unnoticeable scuttering feet from outside the stone cell. There was a bang at the door, followed by a pained groan. Moments later, a key turned within the lock, and his cage opened. The quick feet rushed to his side, immersing Sebastian in a warm embrace. He looked up to see her smiling down at him with tears in her eyes.

'Ariana? What are you doing here?'

'I'm not waiting around for you to die,' she told him, hopping behind his chair to release him from the restraints. 'You're getting out of here.'

'You can't. You heard what I am - what I'll become.'

'You're not a monster. You're Seb.'

'Ari, you don't understand. I can feel it inside of me. It's only a matter of time before I...' Sebastian trailed off into thought, hanging his head.

Ariana stopped and stepped back, holding her hands to her chest. Then she shook her head and jumped in front of him. 'Shut up, you idiot! You're not the Black Beast, so stop panicking.'

'You don't know that. Everyone saw what happened out there. I stood against you. Just so I could protect some stupid creature.'

'Yeah, about that,' Ariana rubbed the back of her neck and looked away briefly. 'Why did you protect Alpha? Glitch told us about what it was. But he was just as confused as everyone else.'

'I don't know,' Seb answered, turning away.

'Come on, Seb. You know why.' Ariana grabbed his knee and squeezed it softly. 'I thought we weren't keeping any more secrets from each other.'

Sebastian faced her. She smiled softly, but Ariana's shaking eyes betrayed her expression.

'Alpha must've been walking endlessly for weeks, perhaps even months. It was frightened and completely alone, looking for sanctuary. Instead, it found us. We attacked without even thinking - assuming it to be a threat. I don't know how, but I could sense how Alpha felt. It wasn't there to harm anyone.' Sebastian let out a breath and shook his head. 'And now, I'm the threat. So what's the point of arguing? They won't listen.'

'Seb...' Ariana uttered, leaning back.

'Does it matter why I protected it? Alpha's still out there because I helped it escape. Whatever it does next will be on me. Don't make the mistake I did. If I become... that thing they think I am. If I hurt someone, you'll never forgive yourself.'

Ariana grabbed Sebastian by the shoulders. 'I swear it, Sebastian. If you ever become the thing you're so afraid of, then I'll put you down myself.' She lifted Seb's chin with a finger. 'But until then, you have to keep fighting.'

'The fighting never ends. I'm tired.' Sebastian said, turning away.

'No. You don't get to give up. Zara's still out there somewhere. I told you I'd help you find her, and that's what I'm going to do. No matter what.'

Sebastian lifted his head and stared deeply into her eyes - her quivering smile. Ariana jumped behind the chair and freed Seb from his bonds. The instant he was no longer tied, he wrapped his arms around her. 'Thank you,' Seb said, burying his face in her neck.

'What are friends for? Now put this on, quick.' Ariana handed Seb some folded clothes. He unwrapped them to find another dark blue Rachni jacket, much like the one she originally made for him.

'How did you...' Seb began to ask.

'I knew the old one would end up getting torn apart. I just didn't think I'd be the one to do it.'

Sebastian laughed and put the jacket on, wincing as he moved his bruised arms.

'How're you feeling?'

'I'll live.' Sebastian sighed before giving her his signature grin.

There was a knock on the door. 'What are you two doing in there?' Seb heard Glitch hiss from the hallway.

'We're coming,' Ariana called back, before taking Sebastian's hand and pulling him towards the exit.

Once outside, Seb was embraced yet again by the tall, pale scientist. 'I'm so sorry, Seb. We had to tell them. I would never have predicted they'd react like this,' Irvine cried out, squeezing the life out of him.

'It's okay, Glitch. You were only trying to help. I'm sorry I dragged you both into this,' Seb said, patting him on the back.

'I thought we were supposed to be making a break for it,' Ariana chimed in, folding her arms.

'Right,' Glitch agreed, taking out his codebreaker and tapping away at the screen. 'The zoomer is just outside. Now if we take the road west, we should arrive at the next town by daybreak.'

'What's that?' Seb asked, pointing at a blinking dot on Glitch's radar.

'That's the location of an Ender Knight.' Glitch answered with a gulp.

'How long will it take to get there?' Seb grabbed hold of the codebreaker and pulled it closer.

'Maybe a couple of days, but that would... wait. Why would you want to get *closer* to those people?' Glitch asked, pulling the radar back.

'We should be focusing on escaping first, Seb,' Ariana hissed, peering behind a corner. 'We can take out those scumbags later.'

'You don't understand. We have to get hold of one of their metal birds,' Sebastian told them, looking back and forth with pleading eyes.

'An air cruiser?' Glitch asked, 'I understand the benefits of procuring such a vehicle. But surely we have more pressing matters to-'

'Get down.' Ariana dived from the open hallway, grabbing both Seb and Glitch by their sleeves.

Sebastian heard footsteps from around the corner, and the hushed tones of guards growing closer. They retreated further and turned to find a dead end. They could hear the guards shouting for reinforcements, noticing his escape. Sebastian looked down at his hands, and as he blinked, he could see that they were as black and oily as they had become in the void. His gaze drifted to the thick stone wall and a feeling washed over him, almost as if he was hearing someone else's thoughts. 'Maybe...' he pondered to himself, moving stealthily towards the torches and extinguishing one.

'What are you doing?' Ariana asked with a hushed voice, turning back to the hall and preparing herself for a fight.

'We need to get rid of the lights.'

Glitch and Ariana nodded and proceeded to suffocate the remaining flames. Soon, they were submerged in the pillowy soft darkness. It wrapped around Sebastian like a blanket, soothing his aches and pains. Seb turned his attention to the wall in front of him and placed his hand on it. He smiled when he realised that it had worked. He crept back to Ariana and Glitch, taking them by their hands.

'Close your eyes, I've got an idea,' he told them.

'Why does that not fill me with hope?' Ariana asked, a faint smirk forming.

'You're gonna have to trust me,' Seb said as he gingerly pulled them back with him towards the wall and pressed his back upon it - shaping their particles to be that of shadow, fading seamlessly through the cracks in the porous stone. Sebastian focused on the atoms around him - the molecules within him and his friends. Before Ariana and Glitch knew it, they were standing outside on the other side of the wall. 'Okay, you can open them now.'

'Umm Seb, what just happened?' Ariana asked as she blinked, staring up at the night sky.

'It's just like you taught me, manipulate the particles around us and bend them to our will.'

'You... changed our atoms?'

'Incredible,' Glitch said with a gasp, patting down his chest and arms. 'You deconstructed and then reconstructed our entire molecular structure. You have to tell me how you did it!'

'I don't know, I... just knew,' Seb began to wonder aloud.

A siren sounded off from the castle, two alarming notes overlapping and bringing with it fearful yelling from the Stonehaven troops.

'We gotta go,' he said, stepping away from the prison wall and gesturing for them to start running. 'Now where's the zoomer?'

'Don't worry. It's just over...' Ariana smiled and pointed as they ran up to the vehicle. That's when they slowed to a stop, noticing a large foreboding shadow standing in front of it. '...there,' she finished, her smile fading.

It was Darius. He leaned upon the zoomer, with Xerxes resting over his shoulder - his hand on the hilt. The giant's face was as stern as ever, staring steely brown eyes towards the three. 'So, it's come to this,' the old hero said with a heavy breath, lifting his blade high above his head before pointing it down at Sebastian.

'Darius, please. Don't do this.' Ariana stepped in front of Seb and stretched her arms wide to protect him.

'You have any idea what you're doing, girly?' Darius asked, lowering his sword slightly. 'If you go through with this, you'll be a traitor.'

'I don't care,' Ariana told him, closing her eyes. 'What you're doing is wrong. I won't let you hurt him.'

'Ari,' Sebastian uttered, looking past her to see Darius' lip begin to quiver. 'Go back home.' Seb stepped past her. 'Where I'm going... there's no coming back. I don't want you to give up on everything you have here.'

'Seb,' she squeaked, grabbing hold of his hand.

'You too, Glitch. If you both go back now, you can still have a life here.'

Glitch opened his mouth to speak, only to close it again and slump his shoulders forward, looking back at the castle in the distance.

'We're all going home,' Darius agreed. 'That means you too, kid.'

'Sorry, we'll have to reschedule that execution of yours. I have somewhere to be.' Sebastian smirked, turning towards the giant with a glare.

'You've got some nerve. You think I was gonna let 'em kill ya?'

'I'm not waiting around here to find out. I won't be a prisoner again,' Sebastian told him, walking closer to the large blade until he was only inches away. 'And I won't let you kill me. Not until I make it home. I need to know if my people are safe, and why my friend betrayed me.' He looked up to face Darius. 'Once I know the truth, you can do what you want with me.' Sebastian closed his eyes and tensed his body, only to open them when he heard the whoosh and scrape of the sword being sheathed.

'Friend betrayed ya, huh?' Darius asked with a groan as he leaned back upon the zoomer. 'You know where he is?'

'Yeah,' Seb said, breathing a sigh of relief. 'The mountains to the north. The place I used to call home.'

'And you finally found your home. That's real special, kid.' Darius whistled, taking out a cigarette and lighting it. 'But those mountains are pretty treacherous. You have any idea how you're gonna climb them rocks?'

'We'll need a Blackout cruiser.' Glitch interjected, stepping forward and taking out his codebreaker. 'We have the location of an Ender Knight stationed at a church down south.'

'A church?' Darius gasped, grabbing the device from Irvine and staring hard at the image. He laughed and shook his head. 'Fate, you fickle fiend.'

'What's so funny?' Ariana asked with a pout, folding her arms.

'I know the place,' Darius said, his excitement waning. 'And I know the Ender Knight we'll be hunting.'

'*We?*' Seb asked, taking a step back. 'You're coming with us?'

'Well, we can't have an escaped fugitive on the loose. For now, just think of me as your warden.' Darius laughed, patting Sebastian hard on the back. 'And I've missed the open road. Being pent up in one place plays havoc on these old bones.'

'Thanks, Darius. It wouldn't be the same without you.' Sebastian grinned.

'So, we're all going?' Ariana asked, an eager smile forming on her lips.

'The old gang, back together.' Darius smiled.

Ariana squealed with joy as she ran to Seb and leapt upon him with a forceful embrace. Darius laughed gruffly, picking them both up and swinging them around in the air. When he placed them back on the ground, even Sebastian was laughing. Seb stopped as he looked over at Irvine, who was gazing mournfully towards Stonehaven tower, his eyes glistening through his spectacles.

'Glitch, are you okay, buddy?' Seb asked.

'Yeah, I think I am,' Irvine said, taking a deep breath. 'I'm going to stay. You were right, Seb. If I go back now, I can still have a life here.' He turned to face them and removed his glasses. 'I like Stonehaven. It's the one place I've ever truly belonged. And... I'm not giving up on Vulga.'

'Glitch, you can't.' Ariana said, grabbing hold of his sleeve. 'If they find out you helped free Seb, they'll arrest you. Maybe even kill you.' Ariana said, grabbing hold of his sleeve.

'I didn't think I'd have to convince you, Ariana. Risking your life doesn't matter. Not when it's for someone you love.'

Ariana's cheeks flushed red. 'Well, when you put it like that. I guess I understand,' she spoke faintly, shuffling her feet.

'I hope you find what you're looking for, pal.' Sebastian smiled, extending his hand.

'You too.' Glitch grinned, patting Seb's hand away and going in for a hug. 'I don't care what anyone says. You're the furthest thing from a monster I've seen.'

Seb felt the warm wet tears of his departing friend moisten his cheek. 'I'll miss you, Glitch,' Seb told him, grabbing the scientist by the shoulder.

'Then you should have this.' Irvine handed Sebastian his codebreaker. 'As something to remember me by.'

'I don't think I'll need much help there.'

'I trust you'll take good care of him, Miss Lane.' Glitch turned to Ariana and gave her a regal bow.

'You can count on me.' Ariana curtsied and laughed, giving Irvine a quick hug and kiss on the cheek. 'You take care of Vulga. I just know she'll come around when she sees how brave you are.'

Glitch smiled, wiping a tear and placing his glasses back on his long head. 'And Master Blake...' He turned towards Darius, clearing his throat and keeping his head firmly on the ground. 'While we're being honest. I want to say that I've never liked you. You've acted as nothing more than a brutish oaf and a bully for the entire time that I've been here.' He took a deep breath and looked up to stare the goliath in the eyes. 'But saying that... I know you're a good person, and want to... thank you for helping my friends.'

Darius shook his head and smiled at the scientist. 'You're gonna make me cry.' He laughed. 'Gonna miss you too, Poindexter.'

They all stood there for a time, not saying anything. That is until the yells from the guards drifted closer.

'That's our cue,' Ariana said, jumping behind the handlebars. 'Let's go, boys.'

Sebastian nodded and jumped on behind her, placing his arms around her waist. Darius squeezed into the sidecar, grunting and swearing as he did.

'The great Ariana, hopeless Seb, and big daddy D, back together again!' She yelled with a triumphant tone, turning the ignition and revving up the engine. 'Now let's snag us an Ender Knight!'

And with that, they were off, throttling through the wasteland at high speeds. Sebastian looked behind his shoulder towards Glitch and waved goodbye. His smile faded as he watched his tech-savvy friend drifting from view along with Stonehaven. A place that Seb was close to calling home.

24.

From Hollowed Ground to the Heathens Above

For hours they had travelled in silence, anticipating the fight that was sure to come. Rocky cliffs soon gave way to fresh dirt and dense woodlands. It was the first living forest Sebastian had seen since leaving Lora. Red leaves covered the violet sky as they passed beneath tall trees. Many small creatures ran along the branches and even a strange six-legged animal that looked much like a deer skipped past. Sebastian grinned for a moment before it slowly faded. Eventually, they arrived at an old church hiding in a clearing within the forest. The place of worship had been constructed from thick wooden beams and coarse stone bricks - clearly made without an Earth User's influence.

'What is this place?' Ariana asked, scanning the environment as she pulled the zoomer into the open area.

'Somewhere I thought I'd never return.' Darius sighed, squeezing out of the sidecar - cursing under his breath as he struggled to do so.

Sebastian and Ariana glanced over at each other, trying their best not to laugh. When the giant was free, he kicked the zoomer before turning towards the church and staring up at the old building.

'You didn't answer my question, big guy.' Ariana huffed, jumping from the vehicle. She held out her hand for Seb and pulled him close.

'This is Remerxia chapel,' Darius uttered, taking in every inch of the structure. 'A Church of Unification. It's been governed by the Homulls for hundreds of years. I'm surprised it's still standing, considering what Blackout usually does when discovering one.'

'What's a Homull?' Seb asked, half-paying attention as he stretched his body free from the long ride.

'Look!' Ariana squealed, completely ignoring Sebastian's question and pointing at a Blackout cruiser, partially hidden behind the church. 'Well, that was easy. But I don't understand,' Ariana said, peering closer at the cruiser. 'If this is a Church of Unification, why would Blackout be here.'

'Who cares? Let's take the bird and fly out of here while we still can.' Seb strolled past the two of them, heading towards the ship.

'Not so fast, kid. I have business here,' Darius told the boy, his eyes still glued to the old chapel. He tightened his fists and took a long drawn-out breath before making his way to the main doors.

'You're not going in there, are you?' Ariana asked, running up in front of him to block his way. 'Have you forgotten that there's an Ender Knight inside? And who knows how many creepy face-painted goons they've got with 'em!'

'I can assure you, he's alone.' Darius brushed past her and grabbed hold of the door handle. 'If he's here, his pride won't allow him to bring an audience.' He opened the doors and went inside, leaving Ariana to turn back towards Seb with a worried look, before beckoning him to follow.

Once inside, Seb gasped at the surroundings not knowing where to look. Large paintings hung across the recently polished, vibrant room - with many sculptures and symbols moulded into the woodwork by hand. That was when his eyes drifted up to a tall person with the snout of an animal standing over him, with a smile wide enough to match his own. 'Woah!' Sebastian shouted, jumping back and pointing up at the almost-human creature. 'What is that thing?'

The strange animal raised an eyebrow towards the boy, still managing to hold its cheerful expression.

Ariana rushed to Seb's side and punched him hard in the stomach, forcing him to keel over and drop to the floor. 'I'm so sorry about him. He doesn't get out much.' Ariana laughed out of embarrassment as she bowed her head multiple times to the peculiar person. 'He didn't mean any disrespect. We ask for your forgiveness, Father.'

'Can't... breathe.' Sebastian winced, clutching at his ribs.

'It is quite alright, my child,' the tall creature reassured her, lifting an unsettlingly long arm towards Ariana and placing a hand on her shoulder. 'I fear our form is quite the shock to those who are not used to seeing our kind.'

'Not at all,' Ariana urged, shamefully bowing her head several more times.

Darius stepped between them and bowed before the animal. 'It is good to see you again, Father Baelith.'

'Well, if it isn't young Darius Blake. Not so young anymore, are we?' Baelith spoke in a soft and soothing tone.

'I'll never be as old as you, ya relic,' Darius replied, standing up straight and smirking at the peculiar creature.

Baelith smiled before giving Darius a quick pat on the back. The two laughed as they stepped out into the halls. It was strange for Sebastian to see a thing larger than Darius that didn't want to fight him. He watched in awe of the bizarre person as they walked out of the room. Father Baelith had an almost human body, but the proportions were all wrong, like looking at someone from the reflection of a spoon. Sebastian peered closer at the creature's face, trying not to make it look as if he was staring. Its snub nose didn't protrude far like some long-faced animals. It was more akin to something like a rabbit or a cat. Seb finally felt the pain fade from his stomach when he was lifted by the collar and pulled to his feet.

'Why do you always have to talk?' Ariana hissed at him, giving him another punch in the shoulder.

'Take it easy,' Seb said, holding his arms up in defence. 'I didn't know it was friendly. For all I know, it could have been an Ender Knight, or another monster cooked up in some-'

Ariana covered Sebastian's mouth with the palm of her hand. 'I'm gonna stop you right there. First of all, Father Baelith is a *he*, not an *it*. And second, just... shut up from now on, okay?'

He nodded slowly.

Ariana breathed a sigh of relief and removed her palm.

'But seriously, what was that thing?' Sebastian asked, rubbing the back of his neck.

'Seb!' Ariana yelled, instantly covering her mouth. She looked across the halls and pulled Sebastian to the corner of the tranquil room. 'The Father and his coven are Homulls. They're a gentle and kind race who pray to Etheria. Now can we drop this?'

'So, that's a Homull,' Seb said with the snap of his fingers, remembering the strange creatures he saw in Platto being evicted from a church. 'Wait, why do they pray to the moon?'

'I'm not having this conversation with you,' Ariana said, heading for the hallway.

Sebastian slumped his shoulders as he followed her down the halls and back to Darius.

'I take it, he's here too.' Darius stated his question as if it were fact.

Either way, it had been answered by the priest, who looked into the old hero's eyes with soft sadness. 'The Inner Sanctum, to be precise. He asked to be left alone. But I suppose you cannot accept those wishes.'

'I'm afraid I can't.' Darius bowed his head. 'Forgive me, Father.'

'Forgiveness is a light that shines in all directions, my boy. To receive, one must also bestow.'

'Those are some fine words. But these days, I'm more inclined to bestow justice than forgiveness.'

Baelith glumly nodded before taking his leave. He passed Ariana, who smiled respectfully at him. Then Sebastian, who kept his eyes glued to the floor.

'Who is it, big guy?' Ariana asked in a soothing tone, placing a hand on Darius' arm. 'Who have we come to kill?'

Darius couldn't help but smile and shake his head. He gestured for them to follow him into the sanctuary before passing through the gilded curtains that hung in the archway. Stained-glass windows illuminated the marble arches, reflecting many vibrant colours. A gentle hum reverberated around the vast open sanctuary, made by the rhythmic melody of the many Homulls, each singing a prayer. Pews were lined across the area, all facing in on a glorious statue made from the whitest of marble. Sebastian stepped past Darius and Ariana. His eyes had become focused on a foreboding statue hanging from the ceiling. Its skin was so white. Its face - so familiar. Seb reached out towards it, almost in a trance.

'Seb!' Ariana hissed loudly, breaking him from his thoughts. He turned around to see her bright red face - possibly from frustration or perhaps embarrassment, as many of the Homulls stopped their songs to glare at the three.

Sebastian grinned awkwardly and rubbed the back of his neck before joining them. They sat silently for a time. Darius gazed at the stained-glass windows. Ariana watched him with a gentle sadness. Sebastian however, kept his eyes on the statue standing tall and glaring down upon him, holding a ball in its hands that resembled the moon.

'I used to come here often,' Darius said aloud, his voice sounding softer than usual. 'My comrade and I would sit right here and pray for a better future.'

Sebastian turned towards the old warrior.

'Everything changed when the Black Beast revealed itself to the world. All that I believed in before that moment turned to dust as I saw those I called family being torn apart. That day, I lost my reason to fight.' Darius continued, shifting uncomfortably in his seat.

'But you killed the Black Beast,' Ariana urged him, tapping him on the shoulder. 'It was a victory. Not a defeat.'

'Nobody won that day, girly. And I wasn't the one to strike down the demon. That curse fell to an old friend.'

'Friend?' Ariana asked.

'Curse?' Seb added.

'The man I used to visit this very church with, he was the one who killed the beast,' Darius answered, his head falling to his lap. 'I watched helplessly as the Black Beast approached him, hoping his death would be quick. But in an instant, his blade pierced the demon's chest. And then... it fell to the floor.'

'I thought this thing was meant to be unstoppable,' Seb said, scratching his head. 'How could it have died so easily?'

'I guess a pierced heart kills eternal demons just the same as any creature.' Darius shrugged, raising his head to look upon the white statue that lifted the giant sphere. 'He gazed into the eyes of the Black Beast as it crumbled into ash. With that, the battle ended. Blackout dispersed almost immediately. And those of us who were left alive returned home.'

'Why didn't you continue fighting? Ariana asked, raising an eyebrow as she leaned into the solemn giant. 'Blackout was retreating. You could have finished them off.'

'The demon changed everything, girly. None of us believed it existed before it started ripping through us all. The will to fight simply drifted from that battlefield. But the fighting didn't end there. Not for the hero of the hour, at least. He became torn apart by fear. Any form of darkness would send him into shock, even the faintest of shadows would leave him petrified or screaming. He came to believe that the Black Beast would return seeking vengeance someday. The fool even took to wearing gold suits in a mad attempt to ward off the demon.'

Ariana and Sebastian glanced at one another, wide-eyed.

'You don't mean...' Ariana began to ask.

'Brandon Frost,' Darius answered. 'The Ender Knight we're here for.'

'What?' Seb and Ariana both shouted, jumping up from their seats. Once again breaking the gentle songs of the Homulls, who now looked to be growing quite impatient with their presence. Ariana quickly bowed and sat down discreetly, leaving Sebastian to grin and wave sheepishly at the holy folk.

'How can it be frickin' Brandon?' Ariana asked in a hushed tone. 'He's the most vile person I've ever met. There's no way you could have been friends with him.'

'He wasn't always that way, Ari. Brandon was born into a wealthy family who lived in the Crimson Capital.'

'Yep, that sounds like Brandon,' Ariana chimed in.

'He renounced his titles and that floating paradise.' Darius continued, folding his arms across his chest. 'He even offered to give up his life for the cause. He felt such guilt that the misfortune of so many had paid for his comfortable life. Brandon gave up everything to do what was right.' Darius sighed pitifully and wiped the sweat from his brow. 'Me, on the other hand, I came from nothing. I fought only because I was bitter and angry with what I didn't have. He was a better man than I'll ever be.'

'I'm sorry,' Ariana said, 'I had no idea.'

'So, what happened?' Sebastian asked. 'How could he have gone from that to... well, Brandon?'

'As I said, his fear got the better of him,' Darius stated, leaning forward in his seat to stare down at the ground. There were no survivors that day, not truly. All of us who came home left a piece of ourselves on that battlefield. But Brandon... he lost himself completely.'

Silence filled the room as the Homulls made their exit, leaving the three of them alone in the sanctuary.

'Sometime after, upon returning to Platto, Viola and I discovered that Blackout had taken siege of her grotto - the freedom fighter's base of operations. Even my son, Dillon, was...' Darius leaned back once more, finally revealing the tears in his eyes. 'They had all been taken. Paraded through the town as a warning to those who would dare think about going against Blackout again. Gallows had been placed across the main square. And as soon as a large enough crowd gathered, they were executed one by one. Some were hung, others were burned, drowned, and pelted with stones. Blight, some were even frozen. It was like some sick show as well as a message. Viola and I arrived too late. Blood spread across the sand like wine on a dusty old map. Bodies were piled higher than that gods forsaken pub they built as a constant reminder of what happened there. I remember seeing Vincent Vale standing proud over the corpses with his Ender Knights and masked army. By his side was Brandon.' Darius shook his head and sniffed as he placed a cigarette in his mouth, only to grumble when he remembered where he was, placing it back in his jacket. 'I left my life behind that day and found a place in the middle of nowhere so I could drink myself to death.' He looked over at Sebastian and Ariana with a warm smile. 'And I would have succeeded if you two brats hadn't shown up.'

Ariana smiled, almost laughing when she noticed Seb wiping a tear from his cheek.

'It's as if fate herself had brought us together.' Ariana winked at the giant.

Darius laughed and stood tall with a stretch before stepping into the aisle. He turned to Seb and nodded. 'If your friend betrays you, do whatever it takes to settle the score. You got that, kid?'

Sebastian looked up with sharp eyes and nodded back, joining Darius. Ariana jumped to her feet and skipped to their side. From there, they made their way to the inner sanctum.

The tortured wailing tore through the halls, almost harmonising with the gentle song of the Homulls. Darius marched towards the inner sanctum with Seb and Ariana close behind. At the end of the hall, a thick cloth hung. The old hero reached out to pull back the curtain. He froze, his fingers grabbing the cloth tightly. Ariana stopped beside him and placed a hand on his shoulder. He turned to her and gave a strained smile. His gaze then drifted behind his shoulder at Seb, who nodded in return. He ripped the sheet to the floor to find Brandon Frost, kneeling before a marble sphere with his back to them.

'What else must I do, Lord?' Brandon wailed, throwing his arms around the stone ball. 'I've done everything you've asked. I betrayed the ones I loved. Joined those I despised. Just so I could get close enough to the child. I became what I hated most to bring you that foul creature. And still, you keep me trapped here - away from your radiant light.' His once golden hair had lost its shimmer and become matted. His gilded armour had begun to rust. The blue cape that had once flowed elegantly behind him dragged limply across the dusty floor, sweeping up the dirt. 'I was a mere puppet you promised to protect, just so long as you could pull the strings.' Brandon punched the stone ball with his gauntlet, causing a crack to form down the centre. 'You manipulated me. Controlled me.' He stood up and kicked the orb, chipping away at its layers with his steel boots. 'I was never guided by fate. It was your string that pulled me. Not that it matters. Any piece of me worth protecting was ripped away many years ago. So let the beast come for its revenge. I welcome it!' Brandon unholstered his revolver and began blasting away at what was left of the marble, exploding smoke and white shards across the inner sanctum. The golden knight laughed maniacally, becoming louder and more unhinged with each pull of the trigger.

Darius unsheathed his blade, pointing it towards the once-golden knight. Ariana twirled her hands in a circular motion, conjuring pools of water to form around them. Seb ducked behind a pillar and watched on with wide, fearful eyes.

The gun clicked as the last bullet made its exit. Brandon's cackle dwindled, becoming a pitifully pained chuckle. The smoke cleared as the golden knight turned around, his crazed grin drifted into confusion when he saw them. He stepped back, almost tripping over the shattered stone. 'Da...Darius?' He croaked, dropping his revolver.

'Brandon.' Darius nodded with a grimace. 'It's been a while.'

Brandon gritted his teeth, glaring at his old friend. That stare spread to Ariana, before finally falling upon Sebastian. His eyes widened. Brandon dropped to his knees and began frantically picking up the pieces of the broken orb. 'I'm sorry, my Lord!' he shrieked, trying desperately to fit them back together. 'I didn't wish to anger you. I was merely asking for your kind-' Brandon's words caught in his throat as the hilt of Darius' blade struck the back of his head. He slumped forward to the stone-littered floor with a thud.

Darius picked the Ender Knight up by the belt and made his way out into the halls. 'We're done here,' he told the others.

'What's Darius gonna do with him?' Seb asked glumly, watching as the giant stomped past the audience of Homulls who had congregated in the halls

'I don't know,' Ariana answered weakly. 'But... I guess he's gotten what he came for.' She made her way out of the destroyed room and down the hall.

Sebastian watched as she turned away from him and followed Darius out into the sanctuary. He scratched his head, making his way out of the church. As Seb walked, he felt the Homulls watching with contempt. He picked up his pace just to give them the satisfaction of never having to see him again. One pair of eyes burned into the back of his head worse than the rest. Sebastian winced, his head pulsating. He turned around, and before him was the white, marble statue, hanging high above him. Sebastian backed away and spun around, only to find Father Baelith blocking his path.

'Our Lord is the saviour of Endura, my child,' he said with a gentle smile.

Sebastian nodded quickly, stepping past the priest.

'He is the light that eradicates the bile.' Baelith continued, his voice growing louder and more strained. 'The blackness that sleeps within you.'

Sebastian stopped, remembering those words. He slowly turned around and raised an eyebrow at the priest, only to be met with that calming yet creepy smile. He backed away, not taking his eyes off Father Baelith until he turned the corner. From there, he picked up the pace until he left that church and joined back up with the others.

As the trembling aircraft lifted itself from the hallowed grounds to the heavens above, Sebastian watched the church and the land below becoming little more than a memory. Endura expanded and Seb realised that the green forest was as rare as the creatures it held. They continued over barren soil and rocky terrain, making their way towards the mountains. Darius hadn't said anything for a while, leaving a painful silence that Sebastian didn't wish to be the first to fill. Ariana rummaged through several containers before lifting out a pair of handcuffs. She sidled up to Brandon, now slumped forward in a peaceful daze and secured his hands behind his back.

She turned to Seb and gave him a thumbs up.

He shook his head, but couldn't help but smile at her. 'You remember how easily he can get out of them, right?' But when his eyes found hers, all he could see was a vacant expression. There was no excitement from her, no yearning for adventure. Just an exhausted girl, working a job she knew would never end.

'I thought this felt familiar,' Ariana said, managing a strained smile. 'Kind of reminds me of how we all met.'

'Forget about Bran,' Darius called from the cockpit, 'He's no threat to us. Not anymore.'

Sebastian stepped closer to the front of the ship and stared far out into the barren landscape below. The cracked earth almost looked tranquil from so high up. As the sunlight escaped from the clouds, Seb could see Darius' reflection on the windscreen. The old hero's head hung low. His eyes glistened in the light, his lip twitching. Before Seb could gauge Darius' expression, he felt a hand slide down his arm. Ariana moved past him, fastening herself in and patting the seat beside her for him to join. As he did, she immediately rested her head on his shoulder and slumped into his chest. Sebastian lifted his arm and placed it around her. He held her body close, his eyes growing heavy. Sebastian began drifting with the clouds. The hum of the air carrier and its ceaseless shaking seemed to melt away. Eventually, all he could feel and hear was the gentle breathing of the girl resting beside him.

'So, you're going back to that place, I see.' A voice spoke from within the darkness.

Sebastian opened his eyes to see Brandon standing with his arms folded - one of his hands had been freed from the restraints. He tapped his boot upon the floor and frowned as he stared outwards towards the front of the ship. Seb followed his eye line, until finally landing on what was outside.

Mountains, hundreds of them. Breathtaking, tall peaks pierced the sky, cutting through the heavens. Sebastian nudged Ariana awake before unfastening his seatbelt. He got up and approached the front of the ship, watching in awe at the countless cliffs.

'You live somewhere in all of this, do ya?' Darius couldn't help but laugh when he saw Seb's face. 'It's no wonder you know so little of the world.'

'There are so many.' Seb uttered, glancing at each new behemoth spike they passed. 'It would have been impossible to climb over all of this on our own.'

'You're telling me.' Ariana answered, assuming he was talking to her. She stepped beside them with a whistle, shaking her head as she took witness. 'Thank the gods for old-age technology,' she said as she patted the walls of the ship.

'There's only one god you should be thanking, girl,' Brandon sneered, brushing a tangled knot of hair away from his face. '*Lucian Avalon.* The self-proclaimed, Eternal Light.'

'I think you bumped his head a little too hard back there, big guy,' Ariana told Darius as she turned back towards the golden knight.

'I don't think I hit him hard enough,' Darius replied with a groan. 'He came around a while back and hasn't shut up since. I'm surprised you two managed to sleep through it all.'

'I've been trying to warn you, Blake!' Brandon said in a soured tone. 'He's fooling you, much the same as he fooled me. This place you're approaching. It's his domain. His slice of Etheria upon Endura. Brandon's words fell flat as he slumped his shoulders and hung his head, looking down at the sharp peaks. 'I suppose I wasn't his only puppet.'

'You want me to put some tape over his mouth or something?' Ariana asked, gesturing towards the supply crates.

'Do what you want with me. It matters not,' Brandon answered glumly, falling to the floor.

Sebastian watched as the usually pompous knight gazed down, and made his way over. 'Who is this Eternal Light?' he asked, kneeling to face Brandon. 'You said he had a name.'

'Lucian *"The Unifier"* Avalon,' Brandon said with venom in his voice, spitting on the metal plating beneath him. 'His fame is almost as widespread as yours, monster.'

'Don't listen to him, kid,' Darius called out across his shoulder. 'The guy has completely cracked. He believes the Lord of Light is actually talking to him.'

'You've felt his presence for as long as I have, Blake,' Brandon hissed, lifting his head to glare at his former ally. 'Why else did you pray for forgiveness at his house with each life you took?'

'I learned a long time ago that gods don't exist - only madmen and monsters,' Darius answered, briefly looking at the two of them.

Sebastian felt a twinge in his stomach as he turned away from the retired hero, he looked upon Brandon once more and placed a hand on his shoulder plate. 'Tell me what this Lucian is after. What does he want?'

'I thought that would be apparent by now,' Brandon sniffed, shrugging Seb's hand away from his shoulder. 'You've felt him too, haven't you? The grand shining light. The holy spectre. *The white entity.* What he wants is *you*, beast.' Brandon laughed and threw his hands up 'It's the only reason he allows this pitiful rock to keep spinning. And here we are, delivering you straight to him.'

'Give me a break, creep,' Ariana said with an exhausted sigh. 'Seb, please don't tell me you're listening to this crap.'

'He knew we'd come to the church, didn't he?' Seb asked, ignoring Ariana, grabbing the golden knight by his steel collar. 'You were bait so we could get here...' Seb let go and turned around, watching the mountains scatter past. '...to Lora.'

'Seb, stop it!' Ariana yelled, rushing towards him. 'Can't you see, he's just trying to make you-' Her words halted abruptly as she closed in, only to have Sebastian swing his arm at her as if in rage rage-fuelled trance. Ariana collided with the side of the ship and landed on the seats.

'What the blight, kid?' Darius yelled, momentarily losing control of the cruiser.

Sebastian immediately turned back to Brandon and picked him up by the throat.

'All this time, everything that happened, was it planned from the start? Seb asked him, his voice plummeting into a fierce growl. 'Why Alex had been following me? To make sure I didn't stray from Lucian's path.'

Brandon's face turned purple. His mouth opened fully, trying to suck as much air into his lungs as he could. Sebastian's grip tightened further, almost crushing Brandon's neck.

'It's why you didn't want Blackout to capture me back in the wastes.' Seb growled, glaring into Brandon's eyes and seeing his reflection - a pale boy with black eyes and black smoke lapping out from his skin. 'You, Alex and this *Lucian*. You did all this, just so I would return. Why? What's waiting for me down there?'

Brandon's face had become twisted, unable to break eye contact with the shroud of darkness in human form. Snot and tears ran down his trembling face. Sebastian finally let go of the golden knight and rose to his feet. Turning, he noticed Darius still controlled the ship with one hand, yet the other was gripped onto the hilt of his sword. The old hero's eyes were fixed on Seb's reflection on the windscreen.

Sebastian looked down at his hands, seeing grey skin and black nails - not dissimilar to claws. 'Land the bird,' he said.

'I... I don't think that's a good idea, kid. This terrain is too uneven.'

Sebastian punched the side of the ship, denting it.

'Dammit, land the ship! Going any further would be exactly what he wants.' Seb yelled, his breathing becoming erratic as he punched the side panel yet again.

'What who wants?' Ariana asked, glued to the seat he left her in.

'The entity. It's followed me since the day I washed up on Endura. Haunting me - leading me here with... you two.' Seb stopped and looked back at them. 'Wait... were you a part of this?'

'You're not serious,' Ariana said as tears broke from her eyes, slipping past her scar.

'How else could you have found me in the middle of an endless desert?' Seb asked, backing away from her, clutching at his hair. 'It sent you there to find me, didn't it? You've been leading me to it this whole time.'

'Have you completely lost it, kid?' Darius roared in anger, letting go of the controls as he stood to confront the boy.

'Get away from me!' Seb roared, grabbing hold of Brandon's neck and lifting him off the ground. 'I'm not falling into your trap. Not until I know what's waiting for me down there.' With that, Sebastian threw Brandon towards the door panel, sending the golden knight smashing through it. Brandon screamed as he fell from the ship. Sebastian leaned out, watching as the Ender Knight disappeared into the mountains below.

'If you know what's good for you, you won't follow me.' Sebastian didn't hesitate as he took one last look at his comrades and leapt out into the open sky, letting the wind guide him towards his fate.

25.

Goodbye, Old Friend

It was calming, falling through the tranquil expanse of the violet sky. Sebastian closed his eyes and embraced the strong winds that carried him, their gentle caress reminding him of home. He could almost feel the cool dew of the grass licking the nape of his neck, the whispers of Zara's laughter dancing in the air. It was as if time itself had slowed to a standstill. In that suspended moment, memories flooded his mind like fragments of a fading dream. As he drifted through the endless expanse of the sky, Sebastian couldn't help but yearn for the familiarity of home, for the comfort of Zara's presence beside him. In the quiet depths of his heart, he half-expected her to wake him from this dream with a playful kick to the ribs.

But as the winds carried him ever closer to his destination, Sebastian opened his eyes and knew the memories were nothing more than distant echoes. The once-green fields hidden within the mountains had since turned brown and lifeless. He could see a barren forest and scattered debris from an old forgotten ruin. It was Lora - Sebastian was finally home.

A solitary tear traced a path down Sebastian's cheek, its journey mirroring his descent towards the village below. With a trembling hand, he brushed it away, only to catch sight of a glimmer in the distance - a distant peak bathed in the golden hue of the sun, its surface adorned with shattered remnants of sparkling armour. A surge of rage coursed through Sebastian's veins, the darkness within him bubbling to the surface. Gritting his teeth, he felt the tendrils of shadow erupt from his skin, melting into monstrous wings that tore through his jacket with brutal force. With a primal roar,

Sebastian unfurled his newly formed appendages, their ebony feathers scattering through the air like shards of night.

Mid-air, he paused, suspended on the brink of fury. Sebastian glanced over his shoulder, his gaze tracing the sinuous tendrils spiralling down his arms. His breath caught as he watched the torn jacket and shirt crafted by Ariana, gently descending towards the earth below. With a powerful beat of his wings, Sebastian propelled himself forward, his eyes fixed upon the shimmering mountain that loomed ahead.

Sebastian landed forcefully on solid ground, crushing the rocks beneath his feet. He made a pained groan as the wings exploded into black smoke, covering the mountaintop in a dark shroud of mist. He waved his arm to clear the fog, following the trail of golden breadcrumbs until he came upon the heavily breathing heap on the ground that once adorned them.

Brandon was shaking intensely. His arms and legs were mangled and twisted into something unrecognisable as human limbs. A pool of crimson seeped out from where he lay. The once golden knight made a pathetic sound as the blood crept from his mouth.

'You're still alive,' Seb said, circling Brandon. 'Your god must love you. That, or he wants to see you suffer.'

'Get on with it. Kill me, beast' Brandon said, straining with each word.

'Not until you tell me what's waiting for me down there.'

'I can't. The truth... it will...' Brandon managed a pained cackle as he looked up at Sebastian. 'It will break you... monster.'

Sebastian knelt upon the trembling man and grabbed him by the throat, lifting him from the ground. 'Look at me! Look into my eyes and tell me I'm not already broken. Nothing you say will change that.'

A crash sounded from behind. Seb looked over his shoulder through the mist and saw the shadow of a metal bird. Then came the silhouettes of Ariana and Darius. Sebastian released his hold on Brandon and let the

Ender Knight slump back into a heap on the blood-soaked ground.

'You broke the damned cruiser, kid!' Darius yelled through the smoke.

'I told you not to follow me,' Seb yelled, snapping his neck to face them.

'We're not following you.' Ariana stepped closer, forcing her eyes closed. 'We're here to stop you!'

'Why are you doing this?' Seb asked, hanging his head. 'I just want to go home.'

'You're not right, kid. None of this is.' Darius said, pulling out a large silhouette from behind his back.

'You can't... stop it, Blake.' Brandon's voice gurgled with blood. 'The boy is simply... fulfilling his purpose.'

'What purpose?' Seb asked, kneeling to hear his whispers.

Brandon laughed feebly. 'It would take all day... to explain it.' He coughed up more blood and gritted his teeth as his body seized up yet again. 'I just wish I could have... been down there when you found out for yourself.'

Sebastian's glare bore into Brandon as he loomed over the fallen knight, raising his foot high before stomping it upon the gilded knight's chest, forcing Brandon to release a blood-curdling scream. Seb lifted his boot yet again, but as he brought it down, he felt something strike him from behind. It knocked him off his feet and hurled him through the air. As he scraped across the ground, he felt the wet surface, his body drenched. Sebastian sprang to his feet and twisted towards Ariana, who was now spinning on her feet, her eyes glistening. He raised a hand and watched as black tendrils burst from the ground beneath her, wrapping around her arms and legs, and lifting Ariana in the air. She screamed as the black vines constricted around her limbs. Darius rushed forward, his blade pointing at Sebastian.

'Have you gone insane?' the old hero yelled as he closed in.

Seb held out his other arm, allowing a purple mist to seep from his skin and form into a sharp and solid object - an ebony sword, long and jagged. He swung the blade down, clashing with Xerxes.

'I didn't want to believe it, kid. But it's true. You are the Black Beast!' Darius shook his head and spread his feet, ready to lunge yet again.

Seb simply raised his hand once more and allowed the tendrils to break through the ground around Darius. The giant dodged out of the way of the vines, cutting them down as they exploded into smoke - creating more mist to fill the area. Soon enough, one managed to snag around his neck and lifted him into the air. Another wrapped around his arm before he could cut himself free. Many more burst from the mountain, wrapping around his legs, waist, and shoulders until he was completely immobilised. Darius roared in pain, releasing his grip on Xerxes. Sebastian sighed pitifully, turning towards Brandon - still clinging to life like he had some grand purpose.

'What's waiting for me down there?' Seb asked with little emotion left in his voice - no expression on his face. He pointed his blade down, pressing it against Brandon's stomach.

'Your fate... that's what's waiting.' Brandon spat blood on Seb's boot. 'Now stop wasting your time with me and see it for yourself.'

'Fine. I will.' Seb slowly pierced the blade deep into Brandon's gut, and further still until it pierced the rock beneath him.

Brandon's guttural cries rang out across the mountains. Echoes of pain bounced back, filling Sebastian's ears with a high-pitched ringing that wouldn't dull. Seb stepped away, his sword dispersing into a puff of purple smoke. He looked down upon the hand he used to puncture Brandon's stomach. Turning towards Ariana and Darius, he saw that they were screaming at him. He couldn't hear them. The ringing faded as he faced the edge of the peak, stepping closer. Sebastian looked upon the land below - a place once filled with wonder and merriment. Now lifeless and hollow. A place Sebastian belonged to now more than ever.

Sound gradually returned. The tendrils disintegrated into dust. Ariana fell to the ground covering her face when she saw Brandon. Darius landed, crawling towards his former comrade, clutching Brandon in his arms.

'Darius...' Brandon breathed his name like a secret.

'It's okay. Don't talk now, Bran. You need to save your strength.' Darius told him, holding onto Brandon's shoulders.

'No... lady fate has made an exception for me for far too long.' Brandon feebly lifted his hand and let it fall on Darius' back. 'I died many years ago... on that battlefield.'

'We both died that day, Bran.' Darius laughed as tears muddied his face. 'Now look at us. Two old ghosts haunting the world we failed to save.'

Brandon clutched onto Darius' shoulder and brought the giant closer to him. 'Darius, your son...'

Darius leaned back, looking away for a moment and sighed, sniffing as he returned to look upon Brandon. 'It's okay. I forgive you.' He winced, forcing a smile onto his cracked lips.

'No, Darius... Dillon... he's alive.'

Darius dropped Brandon, almost falling back himself. 'He can't be. You're lying.'

'I couldn't let them... kill him. Not after everything else I did to you - to everyone.' Brandon began convulsing, voice shuddering. 'But... he belongs to *them* now. I'm... sorry. Maybe death would have been... better.'

'Why did you do it, Bran?' Darius asked, tears streaming from his face, falling upon his old comrade. 'We could have regrouped - finished them off while they were down. We could have saved this pitiful rock!'

'I was more concerned with saving... myself,' Brandon laughed feebly, lifting his mangled arm to rest it upon Darius' shoulder. 'And in turn, I

311

sacrificed the only part of myself... worth saving.' Brandon shook his head and laughed. 'You can't change destiny.' He turned towards Sebastian and spat more blood upon the crimson ground. 'And you can't hide from your demons, either. No matter how hard... you try.'

'But we have to keep trying, right?' Darius asked, gently shaking Brandon, watching the golden knight's eyes close. 'We can't let the past consume us. We can still fight!'

'Goodbye... old friend,' Brandon said, his body falling limp.

Darius held on to Brandon's slumped shoulders for a time, trembling as much as Brandon had been just moments before. He hugged Brandon and rested him on the ground, looking down at the sincere smile on the once-shining knight's face.

'My son... my Dillon. He's still out there somewhere,' Darius told himself, wiping the tears from his face. 'Thank you. Old friend...'

Darius removed a pack of cigarettes from his jacket and tried lighting one with his trembling fingers. After a few failed attempts, Darius roared and threw his lighter from the peak, crushed the box in his hand and let it fall to the ground before turning to face Sebastian. 'You killed him...'

'He was our enemy. Isn't that what we do to our enemies?' Seb asked with a shrug.

'Not like this,' Ariana answered faintly, slowly turning to Brandon. 'He was our captive, Seb. He was defenceless.'

'Are you saying what I did was wrong?'

'It wasn't your choice to make.' Darius growled, his muscles seizing as he stomped towards the boy. 'It was *me* he betrayed. *My* people he killed, not yours! If anyone had the right to take his life it should have been me.'

The strong winds spread throughout the barren peak. It was the only sound heard as Sebastian's gaze drifted between Ariana and Darius as they glared at him.

'You're right,' Seb finally said, rubbing the back of his neck. 'I shouldn't have killed him. This is your fight - your war. I don't want any part in it.'

'Seb, this is your war too,' Ariana said, stepping closer with her hand on her chest.

'You're wrong,' Sebastian told her, turning to look down upon the ruined village he once called home. 'Everything that is mine was once down there. And I'm going to take it back.'

'Sebastian, please wait!' she yelled, running towards him.

'Go home, Ariana. You have no place here,' Sebastian growled, hanging his head. 'And there's no place for me with you.'

'Sebastian,' Ariana breathed, allowing a single tear to trickle down her cheek, running along that scar of hers, just like it always did.

'I'm sorry,' Seb told her as he stepped backwards from the cliff's edge and dropped from the peak, hoping it was the last tear she would shed on his account.

The ebony wings unfurled from his shoulders once more, allowing Sebastian to soar through the turbulent sky. He made his descent towards the brown patch of broken land that used to be Lora. Sebastian thought about looking back at Ariana, maybe even returning and embracing her in his arms. He dreamt of taking her to a place where they could hide away from the world and live out the rest of their days in peace. But Sebastian continued his descent, letting his heart choose who it always had. He focused on Zara, allowing the vision of her fiery red hair and moonlit pale skin to fill his mind. He promised himself that he would find her. It no longer mattered if she was alive or dead. Sebastian would be with her soon.

26.

Crumbling Mountains

The oily feathers scattered, dissolving into ash the moment Sebastian's feet touched down on barren soil. With a heavy heart, he raised his head, fixing his eyes upon the ruins that stretched before him. In that fleeting moment, amidst the wreckage of his former home, Sebastian caught glimpses of what it once had been - blades of grass swayed gently in the breeze, while birds soared high in the azure sky. The land teemed with wildlife, bounding across verdant meadows, with a tranquil river winding its way through the valley, its waters reflecting the golden hues of the sun. Memories of laughter and joy flooded Sebastian's mind.

Seb winced, as the clouds above dispersed and light pierced his eyes. He scanned the land once more and reality had set in. The fields were cracked and barren. The echoes of laughter and the warmth of smiling faces had vanished, replaced by a haunting wind pulling on the tattered remains of Sebastian's clothes, beckoning him home. With a deep breath, he steeled himself for the journey ahead. With each step forward, Sebastian embraced the path that lay before him, ready to confront the shadows of his past.

The once familiar groan of the bridge leading into Lora now wailed as Seb crossed. With each tentative step, the rotten beams and crumbling stones threatened to give way beneath his weight. Suddenly, his foot plunged through a brittle beam, sending Sebastian tumbling into the putrid muck below. As he lay amidst the decaying remnants of the bridge, Sebastian gazed up at the shattered structure above him, his mind drifting back to the days when the creek had flowed beneath it. Sebastian would often leave Lora to spend a night or two in the vale, for the chance to return and see his community through the eyes of an outsider. For the first time, he truly knew how that felt.

'...Don't rest yet, Seb...'

Sebastian jolted up at the sound of a voice. Yet, as he scanned his surroundings, he found himself alone amidst the desolate landscape. With a heavy sigh, he dragged himself out of the mud and trudged towards the shore beneath the bridge - the very spot where he and Zara had shared countless moments together. As he emerged onto the riverbank, Sebastian cast his gaze to what had once been the bustling market district of Lora. He could still hear echoes of the vibrant chaos that had once filled the streets - the laughter of children, the chatter of merchants, the lively exchanges between neighbours. Those sounds were nothing more than ghosts of a bygone era, haunting the empty streets. With each step he took, Sebastian felt a weight pressing down upon him. He stopped to stare at the broken ground, imagining Zara's comforting presence casting a shadow over his every move as she guided him through these streets.

As Sebastian left the market, he passed a mound of rubble as ordinary as any other in the dilapidated village. He gazed upon the heap of shattered memories. His heart clenched with a mixture of grief and rage. It was Sebastian's home. Drawing closer to what remained of his former cottage, he reached out and grasped a discarded brick, feeling its rough surface beneath his fingertips. With a trembling hand, he lifted the brick high above his head. Closing his eyes, Sebastian let out a primal scream, a torrent of anguish and frustration pouring forth as he hurled the brick into the air. The distant sound of shattering stone echoed through the desolate streets of Lora. He pulled back his leg and kicked through a patch of rubble, sending clouds of soot and dust billowing into the air, releasing the pain that threatened to consume him whole.

Sebastian's voice was barely a whisper as he sank to his knees. With trembling fingers, he traced aimless circles in the dirt, each motion a silent plea for forgiveness. 'I'm sorry,' he said, his words carried away by the mournful wind. 'I should never have left.' Pushing himself upright, Sebastian brushed the tears from his cheeks, his gaze lingering on the remnants of his former life. 'Goodbye, mum,' he uttered, almost choking. 'I... I've missed you.'

Sebastian turned away from the ruins of Lora, each step a painful reminder of the home he had lost and the family he could never reclaim. Yet, as he walked, a glimmer of determination flickered in his eyes, a silent promise to those he had left behind.

Sebastian trudged through the corpse of his village, his steps heavy with sorrow and regret. As he pressed on, the distant murmur of flowing water reached his ears, drawing him towards the source with an almost magnetic pull. Sebastian's heart quickened as he approached the tranquil oasis of Avalon Fountain. Despite the devastation that surrounded him, the fountain remained as untouched as it had always been.

Sebastian gazed upon the shimmering waters, its surface reflecting the faint light filtering through the canopy above. For a fleeting moment, he allowed himself to be transported back to simpler times. Closing his eyes, Sebastian let the soothing sound of cascading water wash over him. He sank to his knees beside the tranquil pool, his gaze fixed upon the rippling surface. His reflection stared back at him, a haunting image of weariness and despair etched into his features. Dirt, ash, and streaks of blood marred his pale, scarred face. With trembling hands, Sebastian reached out towards the soothing water, yearning for its cool embrace. Yet, it sputtered and fell back into the fountain before being given the chance to touch his face. He closed his eyes as he realised, Avalon Fountain could not wash away the stains of his past, nor heal the scars that ran deep within him.

'...They say the waters of this fountain are a source of protection...'

As the pool's surface shimmered and danced with the strong breeze, Sebastian caught a fleeting glimpse of her reflection. He glanced above the pool, hoping she'd be sitting beside him. But once again, he was alone.

'You can hear her, can't you?' A familiar voice called out from behind, cutting through the silence like a blade.

Sebastian twisted to find Alex leaning against a crumbling wall, his arms folded within the white robe, flapping against the breeze.

'I was wondering when you'd show yourself,' Seb muttered, his gaze returning to the fountain.

'She talks to me too.' Alex stretched, pushing himself from the wall. 'Not the same as you hear her, but she's been with us both.'

'I wouldn't have returned if that were true.' Sebastian's expression hardened as he rose to his feet and faced Alex. 'Now tell me where she is so we can leave this place.'

'Terrible, isn't it?' Alex turned to scan the districts of Lora. 'Who would ever believe that this was where it all started.'

'Enough games, Alex. Whatever you've got planned, get on with it already.'

'I see you've come alone. Can I assume your friends won't be joining us?'

Sebastian shook his head. 'It's just me.'

'That is fortunate. The two you've allied with seem quite formidable. I'm sure the proceedings will run more smoothly without their involvement. Still, for what it's worth, I'm sorry you've had to return alone.' With a slow, deliberate turn, Alex surveyed the ruins of Lora, his gaze lingering on the shattered remnants of what was once a thriving community. 'This must be hard to witness.'

'I expected as much,' Seb said, his gaze drifting across the devastated village. 'Lora is gone. I know that now. but you still haven't told me why.'

'Why indeed. I often ask myself the meaning of things. But in the end, the why rarely matters.'

'I'm starting to realise I don't care much either. I'm here for the people, Alex. Where are they?'

'They never left.'

'You don't mean... they're not-' Sebastian's voice caught in his throat.

'They're not dead, Seb. They're... still here.'

'Still here?' Seb scoured the broken buildings. 'But there's nothing left!'

'There is one place that survived the Cleansing,' Alex replied, removing a device, much like Irvine's codebreaker. However, instead of a screen, an image appeared above the device.

Seb tilted his head and blinked, reaching for the floating pictures displayed before him, only for his hand to pierce through them like smoke.

'It's a hologram,' Alex told him, tapping the images suspended in the air. 'If this is enough to alarm you, then perhaps you should prepare yourself.'

The fountain suddenly stopped the flow of water. The pool began to drain through an opening in the centre. Seb stepped closer and peered into the emptying basin to find a set of stairs leading underground.

'The answers you seek are waiting below,' Alex said, stepping into the fountain and descending the staircase. 'You want to see her again, don't you?' Alex asked, turning towards him.

Seb took a step back and stared up at the sky one last time, his eyes became drawn to the statue standing proud atop the fountain, its features strikingly familiar. Sebastian's eyes widened as he finally realised - it was a sculpture of the entity from his dreams, the same statue from Remexia Church, staring down at him just as it always had. The visage of Lucian Avalon.

Sebastian shook his head and turned towards Alex, who had already vanished within the black depths. He sighed and rubbed the back of his neck before jumping into the draining waters and making his descent.

The rushing tide swept past Sebastian's ankles as he placed one cautious foot in front of the other. He spiralled further, and further, comforted only by the flame torches that lit the way before him.

"I've heard stories of what this world once was," Alex's voice echoed from the darkness below. *"An untouched paradise, filled with life and harmony. I know, it almost sounds like a fairytale. The Human race was once young, but never innocent. Our ancestors were just one of the countless species that walked these lands. But for whatever reason, we were deemed the fittest. And as so, we hunted the others to extinction."*

Sebastian ignored him, following further until the wet marble walls gave way to clear glass. Colourful lights emerged within the translucent arch. Sebastian slid his hands along the walls - smooth like glass. Splashes of yellows, blues, and reds burst from his fingertips and began eagerly painting the cavern. Sebastian almost lost his footing as he became enraptured by the fireworks of colours forming around him.

"Caves turned to settlements, then to kingdoms. The fight for survival became archaic for our race, but a lust for blood still boiled in our hearts.

That's when the war of men began - a war that would span throughout time and change the world forever."

The sparkling colours began to morph into what looked like a child's picture; Crudely drawn people without faces were hunting animals, making fires and camping beneath the stars. Sebastian couldn't help but marvel at the moving painting as it developed. A society was built before his very eyes, from humble huts to a bustling metropolis. Horse-drawn vehicles became flying ships and buildings grew tall, ascending further than the very wall depicting them.

"The prophets state that as the world changed, we were altered also. Suddenly, man couldn't simply defy nature, but the nature of the universe. They deemed this phenomenon as science and used its power to strengthen our tools, our way of life, into a new golden age."

An explosion of crimson light illuminated the arching staircase, casting Sebastian in a blood-red shadow. Silhouettes danced frenetically on the walls as buildings collapsed in a torrent of steel and fire. Amidst the chaos, people ran, cried, and tore each other apart. Sebastian watched in horror as the scene unfolded, feeling a sense of dread creeping over him.

The paintbrush morphed into a pencil, sketching erratic symbols within the glass, adding to the surreal atmosphere. Leaning against the wall for support, Sebastian recoiled as a powerful slam shook the glass by his shoulder. He spun around, stumbling back onto the steps, only to find a white hand pressed against the surface. Alex's words had become a lingering echo now. With a deep breath, Sebastian pushed himself upright and placed his hand on the opposite wall. As he withdrew it, a black mark remained, its edges oozing down the glass like thick oil.

"Technology was far from reaching its peak. However, our intelligence of this continually evolving power was bleak at best. We abused this influence of the gods. And what was our punishment? It was becoming that

which we feared, that which we couldn't comprehend."

Sebastian continued his descent down the staircase, his gaze fixated on the ever-growing patterns of black claw marks and white handprints that adorned the walls on either side, piling atop one another and fighting for dominance. His eyes darted to every newly formed print - a canvas of light and darkness. With each step, the glass seemed to tremble and shake, as if unable to contain the conflicting forces at play. Sebastian quickened his pace, slipping on the slick steps and fell, landing with a thud on level ground. Pushing himself up, Sebastian realised he had finally reached the bottom of the staircase.

"We became gods ourselves, and the planet went to hell…"

Alex stood above him, leaning against a sealed door, his eyes transfixed on an old, leatherbound book. 'Texts of the old world are all but extinct. It's better that way, I feel. It was their knowledge that gave them hubris. It is the reason you and I find ourselves here.' He stared down at Seb and closed the journal, placing it in his robe. 'Knowing the truth behind this world can help you understand your purpose, Seb. Beyond this door lies the answers you seek. Use them to help mend the planet.' He stepped past Sebastian and made his way back up the staircase. 'Or help end it, if you wish.'

Seb raised an eyebrow, watching Alex ascend the steps. The black and white handprints faded as Alex approached them, allowing for the vibrant colours to drift back through the cavern. When he was alone, Sebastian placed a palm on the handle. He bit his lip, and with a cold breath, opened the door.

27.

Re-union

Sebastian's eyes widened as he stepped into the room. Curved walls projected an eerie white glow that bathed the entire dome in an otherworldly light. Creeping within the ethereal space, it was as if he were stepping into the heart of the void itself. As Sebastian moved forward, his gaze was drawn to the floor, where translucent orbs protruded from the glass panels. They hovered weightlessly, their gelatinous forms undulating and shifting in a mesmerizing dance. Each orb seemed to pulse with a faint inner light, casting strange shadows against the walls. Sebastian approached cautiously, stopping mid-step as they moulded into screens and turned to face him. In a flash, the displays switched on with a resonating buzz. Sebastian flinched, only to realise they were projecting simple images. He loosened his muscles and let out a sigh, stepping closer to the monitors.

Familiar landscapes filled the room. Seb found the village hidden within the sands where he first awoke. The other monitors depicted the city of Platto, Stonehaven, and all the other places he had visited throughout his journey. Sebastian stepped past the images to find more displays further within the white room. The screens guided him to the centre where a cylindrical vat rested. It reminded him of the tank in which Alpha was created, with an aqua-blue, jellified liquid floating within. Sebastian placed his hand on the surface, feeling the warmth radiating from inside.

An orb moved towards him, the light in the walls fell to the same blue of the tank, and on the screen was Alex, yawning, eyes twitching, and wearing some form of a white clinical jacket, much like Glitch and Doctor G would wear in their lab. Alex stifled a cough and spoke.

'Lora project, day four-hundred fifty-two. The vessel has broken free from the program for the ninth time now. No signs of integration with the current software. Doesn't respond well to the artificial intelligence within the system. AI needs work. I have decided to enter the program myself. Hopefully, this effort will distract the vessel from breaking out.'

'Vessel?' Sebastian repeated as his brow furrowed. He took in the scene before him. The room was a hive of activity, with screens displaying intricate designs and blueprints for the reconstruction of Lora. Images of strange creatures flickered across other monitors, accompanied by detailed information about their biology and behaviour. And stranger yet, he saw frameworks of the villagers, standing straight with arms spread horizontally. Sebastian reached for Glitch's codebreaker, his fingers deftly manipulating the dials as he attempted to unlock the secrets hidden within.

The sight of a familiar face sent a chill down Sebastian's spine. Among the images flashing on the screens were numerous pictures of himself, each one capturing a different moment from his past. He turned to face each of them, finally stopping at one image of a small child with short black hair and pale skin. The young boy was floating within the aqua vat in this very room. Sebastian tilted his head and touched the image with a frail hand, only to hear the door behind him open, with Alex's voice emerging.

'I once believed my actions were justified,' he spoke softly, closing the door behind him. 'But this place is proof of how far we've fallen.'

'What is this?' Seb asked, still watching the strange gelatinous machines displaying his portraits like a nightmarish art gallery.

'These are the archives of your life, made possible through the wonders of Etherian technology.'

'This kid... It's me, isn't it?' Seb asked, peering closer as his fingers traced over the young boy's face. 'Why don't I remember this place?'

'Not remembering was the whole point.' Alex sighed, stepping closer. 'I hoped that bringing you back here would help clear your memory. I hoped that it would help you come to terms with what I'm about to say.' He turned away from Seb and stared at one of the images of their home. 'The Lora you remember is a place that hasn't existed for thousands of years.'

Sebastian flinched, his chest tightening.

'It's hard to believe, I know.' Alex stepped past Seb and tapped at one of the gelatinous screens. 'We wanted you to believe that Lora was the only place to survive cataclysmic event that split the old world apart. But it was swallowed, along with the rest.'

'I don't understand, Lora was fine until that night. I saw what happened, and I remember what you did to me. What has the Blight got to do with any of this?' Seb asked, feeling his body tremble, his heart beating hard as his gaze drifted to the soft blue glow of the glass beneath him.

'You call it the Blight on your world. On mine, we call it the Cleansing.'

Sebastian stopped shaking. His eyes darted back up to meet Alex. 'Your world?'

'I... think we're getting ahead of ourselves.' Alex turned quickly towards Seb, rubbing his forehead. 'Let's just get back on topic before-'

'You're deranged.' Seb said, managing a laugh. 'You really expect me to believe any of this?'

'I knew this would be too much for you,' Alex said, shaking his head. 'How could it not be? You'd have to be mad to understand what I'm about to tell you. Maybe not believing is the only way you've kept yourself sane.' Alex allowed himself to think for a moment. 'I brought you here because it was the only way to show you evidence of what I planned to say. But I can't. The truth will break you, Seb. Maybe it would be best if we just forget about-'

'Don't you dare,' Seb growled, tightening his fists. 'I came here for answers. And I'm not leaving until you tell me everything.'

'If you want the truth so badly, I'll tell you.' Alex groaned, rubbing his eyes as he turned away. 'But just know I warned you. The things I'm about to say will seem impossible. I understand that my secrecy thus far has given you reason to doubt me. Nonetheless, I'll tell you everything. All I ask is that you don't interrupt. I can't have you asking questions, as there would be too many to answer, and we haven't the time. Do you understand?'

Sebastian's eyes narrowed but with a pained sigh, he nodded.

'Very well. Then I shall begin where I did. I'm not from Lora, Sebastian. The fields in which I was raised were paved with cement, the cottages consisted of concrete boxes stacked upon one another to form pillars in the sky. Our air was thin and bitter. The villagers - loud and violent. Places like *your* Lora had all but vanished by the time of my birth, to make way for more paved roads and concrete cubes. Resources were limited. Food and water, especially. I was still only a child when I realised that provisions would all but cease within my lifetime. It was around then that I decided that change was needed. I had grown tired of watching the people around me lose their hope and humanity.

In my teenage years, I travelled the globe on an expedition of scientific knowledge. I studied the known ways of sustaining our species and worked on constructing some techniques of my own. I knew that something was waiting to be created - something that would push humanity past its expected extinction. In my travels, I discovered Lucian Avalon, a gifted physicist who understood the complexities of photon particles like none before. He had discovered how to create matter from the very light around us. With this, we could use photons to wrap around particles and create perfect replicas. Like fire giving way to electricity, his research would be

325

the next step in humanity's evolution.

It wasn't long before Lucian took me on as an apprentice. Together, we grew enough crops to feed a city from a single seed, the energy we provided gave people a means to live more comfortably. And yet, it was never enough. Humanity's survival had been extended, but only by a fraction. Photon energy wouldn't be enough to save us. We needed something more. And after years of searching, we found it. A substance discovered in the farthest reaches of space. An alien material that could only be assumed to be anti-matter.'

Alex reached into his robe and removed the old tome from before, brazenly flipping through the pages.

'An interesting fellow, if not a little odd. Bartholomew Barker had hidden away for most of his life, working with a specimen retrieved from a space expedition. He was obsessed with it - an otherworldly element that had previously been thought of as simply a myth. A formless substance that affected the very atoms in the air, changing them, bending them to its will. Bart discovered, with the help of anti-matter, that he could shape these particles through his will alone. Manipulate and change them. This was the birth of the phenomenon you know today as *User abilities*.

When Lucian heard about Bartholomew and his elusive particle, he wished to create more. Lord Avalon wanted to use the power of light to mass produce dark matter so that the entire world could pull water from the air and terraform new lands without the need for any primitive technology. It was to be the torch that would free us from the darkness. The very birth of magic!'

'Stop talking,' Sebastian spoke in a whisper.

The robed boy stifled. He had been pacing the dome, his hands shaking. Alex slowly turned; head low, eyes trembling, a quiver upon his lip. It was a look he had never given Sebastian. 'I told you not to interrupt.'

'You expect me to stay silent through this nonsense? You couldn't have been alive before the Blight,' Seb told him, unsure of each word as soon as it was spoken. 'How could any of what you're saying be possible?'

Alex looked past Seb, staring somewhere else entirely as though he was watching something that wasn't there. 'Lora was to be the testing ground. Union Tower, more specifically. Built to house the most dangerous experiment in human history. The moment when true light enraptured total blackness. Needless to say, complications occurred. A surge of energy, too great for our childish minds to comprehend, swallowed the tower. It wasn't destructive. Not in the common sense, at least. Instead, it seemed to change the particles of all it enveloped. All I can recall was Bart and Lucian being torn apart at the atomic level. Both men turned to dust before my eyes by the very particles they had dedicated their lives seeking to understand. A fraction of a moment later, the rest of us disintegrated along with them.

I awoke in a different place - a different time. A land that glowed brightly with radiant energy. A floating island on a white ocean of air. For a moment, I believed it to be a place we old-worlders once called heaven. Instead, I had arisen in a place you Endurans wish to one day awake. A new heaven, one *he* had named Etheria.

A radiant light washed over me, extending its hand. I mistook it for God, and it laughed. I soon realised that it was Lucian. And yet, it wasn't. His body retained its shape but little else, replaced by the particles of glimmering light at the molecular level. No longer did the professor require sustenance or sleep for energy. He *was* energy. Limitless, unrelenting power enveloped his entire being. And even with his omnipotence, he gently extended his hand. I took it, feeling the electricity coursing through his veins. He laughed again and said, "Perhaps I am god, as I have just created life." I hadn't realised it at the time, but he was referring to my awakening.

It had taken Lucian many centuries, but he had perfected his cloning technology to create biological specimens. In all respects, I had died on that old world. But he found what particles remained, my essence, and restructured my entire being as he had done for himself. I was the first to be born on Etheria but far from the last. Before long, we had created a new society from what remained of the old world. Still, some survived on your broken planet. A world that had been ravaged by the antimatter we tried to replicate. A planet its new denizens had named *Endura.*

'Enough!' Seb roared, slamming his fist back against the vat behind, causing cracks to appear and grow. 'You think I care about any of this? That's not what I came here for. I don't believe in your god, and I don't care what it wants with me. Enough games, Alex. Tell me where she is!'

The low hum of the white room was marred only by the heavy breathing of Sebastian. His fist remained half embedded in the fractured vat, with more cracks forming and growing further along the cylindrical tube. The glowing blue liquid had begun to drain from within, seeping past his hand, and dripping onto the glass panels. The liquid was warm and thick, almost soothing. He wanted to close his eyes and drift someplace else, but he stopped himself and stared hard at Alex.

Alex gazed back, his eye twitching slightly. 'I'm not here to lecture you on what does and does not exist. I'm here to explain what lies beyond your comprehension. Lucian didn't bring you here, Seb. I did.' He rubbed his eyes and turned away. 'Lord Avalon believed you were dead. That's what I lead him to believe, at least. Yet, all this time, his lapdog had been watching you as I have. Not that it matters now. Brandon Frost is dead.'

Sebastian stiffened, removing his fist from the cracked glass and staring at his bleeding hand, unsure of how much of it belonged to himself or the golden knight.

'Tell me, how did it feel?'

'I... I didn't mean to.'

'Didn't mean to what? Kill him? When you live as long as I have, you discover that meaning doesn't matter. The outcome remains the same. Every action becomes another burden to bear. Brandon understood this. You may too someday.' Alex shook his head and smiled to himself. 'Although I must admit, it is intriguing to see his prediction come true.'

'What prediction?' Seb asked, looking away from his bloodied hand.

'Lord Avalon's. He made Brandon his pawn by offering protection, fabricating a story that the next Black Beast will want revenge for the prior being vanquished. I thought it to be another lie, of course. So seeing it come to fruition leads me to question a few things, that's all.'

'I couldn't control myself,' Seb said to himself, lowering his gaze to the floor. 'It was as if someone else was working through me.'

'Maybe some part of you remembered him. It's been said that all fate requires to bond two souls for eternity is one single act.'

'Brandon was a murderer,' Sebastian said with a frustrated groan. 'What does it even matter? It's like you said, he's dead now.'

'What Brandon did is of great importance, Seb. For you in particular.'

'I just want to know about Zara.' Seb growled, stamping his foot down and shattering the glass panel beneath. The room flashed static grey. 'And... the rest of them. The other villagers. My mother... you said they were down here. Tell me where.'

'Telling you is proving to be impossible,' Alex sighed, taking out his advanced codebreaker and pointing it towards the centre of the room. 'But perhaps I can show you.' A projection of Alex appeared with noticeably dark circles below his holographic eyes.

'Lora project, day seven-hundred eighty-nine. He is still breaking out! I have tried everything. The vessel knows he is in a simulation. We need something that will hold him here. Something more sophisticated than the

basic AI you've created. We need something that feels real!'

'A simulation?' Seb asked aloud, scratching the back of his head and turning towards Alex.

'*Our* Lora - the one in which you spent your formative years, was a... fabrication.'

'What are you saying? That it was fake?'

'More of a constructed reality,' Alex corrected.

'That's not true. You're lying.'

'You know it to be true, Seb. Deep down you've always known.'

More screens emerged displaying data on animals, villagers and structures that had been recreated from the ruins of Lora. 'You didn't like its people - never trusted them. I even placed my consciousness inside to convince you it was real. But like the entitled prince you are, you needed more. That's when my master constructed *her*.'

The floating screens all turned to face Sebastian. His cracked lips parted, and a breath slipped out. He slowly twisted, gazing at every image. They were all the same; moon-lit skin, fiery-red hair, Sapphire sky eyes.

'Zara...'

'She was the perfect girl, wasn't she? Sweet, kind... *pure*,' Alex asked, looking down at his watch. 'The image of her had been burned into your memory like a photograph. But tell me, what do you remember of the others in Lora?'

'The others?' Seb pried his gaze away from her and turned back to Alex.

'Your neighbours, classmates, teachers. Do you remember their faces so fondly?

'I...' Seb thought back, putting a hand to his forehead, wincing as a pain shot through his temple. 'I don't know what you-'

'What about your mother?' Alex asked, beginning to circle Seb. 'You don't remember her at all, do you?'

'Of course, I do!' Seb screamed, stamping another foot down, sending shards of glass to explode into the air. 'She was... she...' Sebastian began shaking his head, scrunching his eyes shut, trying to force a picture of her to appear. 'I... don't remember,' Seb urged as he exhaled. 'Why can't I remember?'

'The answer is simple. It's because she didn't exist. None of them did.'

Sebastian's chest constricted. The muscles in his legs seized, bringing him to his knees, swinging his arm down upon the shards of glass as the vibrant colours faded to many different shades of static grey.

'If you don't believe me, then maybe you'll listen to *her*.' Alex slid a hand down his face, staring at the ceiling.

The white gooey screens all drifted towards the centre of the room, merging into one. Sebastian looked up at the large display that filled the dome with tears in his eyes, reaching a trembling hand towards it.

'Zara?' Seb whispered, 'is it really you?'

'Of course, it's me, Seb.' Zara smiled back sweetly before hanging her head and looking away. 'It's good to see you.'

'I'm coming to get you, Zara!' Sebastian yelled, feeling a burst of adrenaline pump through his veins as he jumped to his feet. 'Tell me where they're keeping you, I'll be there before you know it.'

'Seb... I've heard about your journey. It makes me so happy to know that you, Sebastian Travis, travelled this desolate world to rescue us.' Zara laughed as tears swept past her cheeks. 'The same boy who could never even find the energy to get out of bed before noon.'

Sebastian smiled, looking up at her, somehow managing to laugh a little as he rubbed the back of his neck.

'You don't have to search for me any longer, Seb,' she told him, wiping a tear from her cheek. 'Because I'll always be with you.'

'Zara, what are you saying?' Sebastian asked, shaking his head. 'I've not come all this way to turn back now. Just tell me what I have to do. I won't stop until-'

'Sebastian, you have to!' Zara snapped as more tears spilt from her eyes. 'You're never going to find me. At least... not how you had hoped.'

'You're not making sense.' Sebastian shuddered, reaching towards her. 'Quit messing around, Zara. We're leaving together this time!'

'You don't get it, do you?' Alex asked, covering his face in his hands.

Sebastian's arm trembled as it continued reaching out to her. His eyes strained and a hollow sensation swept across his body.

'She's not real, Seb.'

Sebastian's eyes widened as he slowly turned towards Alex. The robed boy was now trembling just as much as he was. 'Not... real?'

'She's... a computer program,' Alex continued, looking up at her with straining red eyes. 'Although a highly intelligent one. She even had me fooled at times. Zara was created for the singular purpose of convincing you to stay within the confines of Lora. She even encouraged you to break free from it as a true friend would. It's almost unimaginable how-'

'No!' Seb shouted, pointing at Alex. 'It's not true. You're lying!'

The room fell silent.

Alex took a deep breath and widened his stance. 'The only lie here is the one you've been living.'

'Alex, please,' Zara begged, her screen drifting closer to him. 'You said it wouldn't turn out like this. You promised!'

'I promised what?' Alex turned towards her, waving his arms. 'That we would save Seb, and everything would go back to how it used to be?' He stopped himself and turned away. 'Things can never be like how they were. I wish we could have gone on pretending forever. But you know as well as I do that *he* would have given the order soon enough.'

'You don't know that,' Zara told him, shifting uncomfortably.

'That was the whole point of the Lora project.' Alex sighed, sliding a hand down his face. 'Once Seb was of age, Lucian would have made the call, and Seb would have been...'

'How is this any better?' Zara asked, turning to face Sebastian. 'Look what you've done to him.'

Alex turned to Sebastian, who was now struggling just to keep himself from collapsing. He held his body up with weak, trembling arms, sobbing pitifully to himself.

'Maybe revealing everything was too much for you to handle.' Alex sighed, stepping closer towards Seb, planting a hand firmly over his face. 'I can't imagine what you've been through.' His hand lifted, revealing teary eyes. 'I'm sorry. I shouldn't have left you to die in that desert to die.'

Sebastian shuddered, pushing himself up to face Alex.

'No. I should have killed you myself.' Alex reached within his robe, pulling out a long, curved and glimmering blade.

'Alex, what are you doing?' Zara yelled, her screen shaking.

'You were right. Look at him. He's broken,' Alex stated, eyes wide, blade trembling. 'He's no help to anyone like this.'

'Stop! Please, don't do this!'

'Trust me. It's kinder this way,' Alex reassured her as he lifted the curved blade. He closed his eyes and propelled himself forward, the katana whirling as it closed the gap between him and Sebastian.

A sharp clang of scraping metal filled the dome.

Alex opened his eyes. They became full and frenzied as he looked upon Seb. The boy had risen, repelling the blade with a smoking black sword of his own.

'Sebastian... you're...' Alex uttered, the shining blade wobbling in his mitts.

'You've taken everything from me…' Seb winced, pushing back against him. 'I have nothing left to give!' He kicked through Alex's shin and spun around, slicing the blade deeply into his arm.

Alex roared with pain and tumbled to the floor, quickly scrambling to his feet and pointing his blade back at Seb, watching as the black and purple tendrils sprouted from the dark boy's shoulder, skin becoming pale, eyes darkening.

'The blackness is enveloping you, Seb. You think it can be controlled. But it can't. If you continue, I'll have no choice but to-'

Sebastian simply growled, the glass beneath his feet cracking further, sending sparks to flash within the dome. 'My whole life has been a lie...' He briefly faced Zara before returning to Alex. 'All that I ever knew, everything I ever cared for. Each thought and feeling I've had was dreamed up by you!'

The grey static faded, and the room dimmed. Alex sheathed his blade and grabbed hold of his arm, blood seeping through the white robe.

'You're right,' Alex uttered, releasing his grip, allowing the blood to drip down his sleeve and onto the floor. 'Maybe I'm the one who deserves death. But like you, I won't fade willingly. If you want to end this properly, we'll require some space.' Alex turned away and removed a metallic ball from within his robe.

Before Seb could react, Alex threw the marble between them, filling the room in a flash of light. When it faded, Alex had disappeared. Sebastian shook his head and made his way towards the exit.

'Sebastian, please don't do this,' Zara called out to him.

Seb stopped and turned to face her screen. She reached a hand to him with tears in her eyes.

'You know, I've played this out in my head a thousand times. The moment I finally found you...' Seb sighed, looking down at the ebony sword in his hand. Tendrils protruded from the hilt and crept up his forearm, pulsating like a heartbeat. 'Never was it like this.'

'Seb...'

'Was it all a lie? Sebastian asked her, turning back. 'Everything we did together? Everything I felt?' Seb turned back towards the door with a shudder before swinging his sword at the grey light panels, causing the room to fall to complete darkness.

The glow from her monitor was the only light that remained. 'I... I'm sorry,' Zara whispered, her voice breaking. 'I know you can never forgive me, but please-'

'Tell me where he is.'

Zara paused briefly before answering. 'He went where he always goes,' she told him with a heavy breath. 'It should be easy enough to find him.'

Sebastian shook his head, managing a strained smile. 'Why does it always have to be Moth Forest?' he asked with an exhausted laugh, stepping over the shattered glass in the doorway.

'Seb!' she called out once more, watching him ascend the steps. 'What you said before. You're wrong! If life here was real to you back in Lora, then it couldn't have been a lie.'

Sebastian gritted his teeth, harbouring all of his energy as he forced himself away from her.

'Everything you did. Everyone you loved. If all it takes is believing, then Lora was real! And if that's true... maybe I could have been real too.'

Sebastian heard her final words linger, fading into echo as he made his way up the spiralling staircase. He scrunched his eyes tight, breaking into a sprint and tripping over himself as tears spilt onto the already wet steps. His chest tightened as he breathed, yet he kept moving forward, blocking out the thoughts that raced through his mind. They were never his thoughts, so what did it matter now? It was time to end it all.

28.

Full Circle

Sebastian would have to give a new name to Moth Forest. The previous residents of the crawling wilderness had long since passed, leaving only the husks of once-mighty trees. Brittle and broken, their gnarled branches reached out like skeletal fingers towards a mist-shrouded sky. The fog remained, however, coiling around his feet, caressing his skin with a ghostly touch.

As the cloud entered his lungs, Sebastian heard echoes of a deluded past come to life. Through the haze, he glimpsed the idyllic village of Lora nestled in the valley below, bathed in the golden light of dawn. He could almost feel Zara taking his hand and beckoning for him to leave this forest, her laughter dancing on the breeze, before falling to the silence of the mist. Sebastian winced, stumbling, reaching out a hand and holding on to a nearby tree. The fossilised wood crumbled to his touch, falling to ash, revealing hollowness within. Seb gazed down at his soot-covered hand and balled it into a fist.

It didn't take long to find Alex. Sebastian simply followed the trail of blood before it was swallowed by the thirsty soil. The crimson path led him to where Alex leaned against a gnarled tree, surrounded by withered branches and ash.

Alex clutched onto his limp arm, blood seeping through to his white robes. 'Remember what you told me the last time we were here?' he asked through clenched teeth as Sebastian stepped into the clearing. 'You told me that all this life and energy can be wiped off the face of the planet. Well,

336

here it is. Just what you always wanted.'

'I never asked for this,' Seb told him, taking another glance at the decayed wilderness. 'You knew what I was from the beginnng, didn't you?'

Alex remained silent.

'I get it now.' Seb shook his head, almost managing a smile. 'You were always so distant - so angry. I never understood why. But how could you not have been? Having to befriend a monster.'

'You're wrong.' Alex scoffed, pointing at Seb with his crimson sleeve. 'You have no clue of what you truly are.'

'I'm a demon.' Sebastian spat with anger, feeling the hate flooding through him. 'Something born from the Blight, destined to plunge this world further than it already has.'

'Is that what they've been telling you?' Alex laughed menacingly, almost unhinged. 'You're no demon, Seb. You weren't born from the Blight. *You are the Blight*. A being created as punishment for our malice. Our greed. Our sick lust for survival. No. You call yourself a demon, a monster, but you are something far worse. You're a *god*.'

'I'm a what?' Seb gasped, stumbling back into the mist.

'I'll never understand the people of this world,' Alex continued, beginning to circle Seb. 'To hunt you down, time and time again. Slaughtering you like some deranged animal. They forced you into hiding and turned you into the very beast you're so affectionately known as.'

'A god?' Seb repeated, looking down at his hands.

'On my world, our god is revered. Worshipped by all. Some even pray to him on *this* pitiful planet.' Alex stopped pacing and gazed up at the darkening clouds. 'I once believed in him myself.'

Sebastian continued staring at his soot-covered hands as they trembled in the light. He pressed them upon his face, gripped his fingers over his head and squeezed tightly.

'When Blackout had finally found you, Lord Avalon commanded me to wipe all data from Lora and bring you to him.' Alex sighed, releasing the pressure on his bleeding arm, letting the blood glide down to his hand and drip upon the dead dirt. 'He wanted me to erase her, Seb. I couldn't let that happen.'

Seb removed his hands and stared up at Alex. 'All of this, you did... for Zara?'

'Not just for her. I guess living in Lora all that time didn't only change who you were.' Alex turned back, looking Sebastian in the eyes. 'I've been alive for countless aeons, seen the death and rebirth of worlds and deities. And yet, those few short years living with you and Zara taught me more than the countless thousands before.' Alex managed a soft laugh as he shook his head. 'There I was, living with a clueless child with no memories, and a girl created from a computer program, and somehow, you were both more real than I had ever been. That's why I did it. It's why I sent your location to Blackout. It was the only way. I know it was. It had to be.'

Seb shook his head, taking a few uncoordinated steps back, almost falling. 'What was it all for, Alex?'

'Sebastian, I know you're angry - angry at the world, at Lucian, at me. And you have every right to be. I've kept so much from you, things I hoped you'd never have to know. I've done things, terrible things, that I can never take back. And for the longest time, I thought that was all there was to my existence. But then, I found Lora. I found you. Zara. For the first time in centuries, I felt something I'd forgotten I was capable of feeling - hope. Hope for a different life, a life where I wasn't just a tool for destruction. You and Zara... you gave me a glimpse of what it meant to live, not just survive. And it terrified me... because I knew, deep down, that it couldn't last. I knew Lucian's plan, Sebastian. I knew that he would come for you - merge with you, and in doing so, he would merge our very worlds. It may have ended the Blight, but it would have given him a power so unspeakable, that it would give him absolute control. I saw the madness in him growing, the obsession consuming him. And I knew, in my heart, that he had to be stopped.' Alex turned away from Seb and reached out his arms to the surrounding trees. 'I'm going to bring life back to these desolate worlds. Yours and mine.' He spun around and faced Sebastian once again. 'But I can't allow it to be done his way. To stop him, I'll need you - your unnatural power.'

'You want me to help you? After leaving me to die?'

'I *allowed* you to die.' Alex corrected, throwing out his arm and letting the crimson paint spray around him. 'You're right. I betrayed you, Sebastian. I thought it was the only way to save you - to save us all. I hoped that by breaking you free from that false reality, I could buy us more time. But when we were flying through the wastes, when I looked at you sleeping with no clue of your fate, I couldn't bring myself to tell you the truth. I couldn't bear to see the pain it would cause you. So, I made the hardest decision of my life. I left you there, praying that you would die as the boy from Lora, with some semblance of peace, I wanted you to leave this world secure in the knowledge that you were Sebastian Travis from a village hidden within the mountains. That you had a simple life with good friends. People who loved you.' Alex gritted his teeth as the tears glinted. 'Seb, doesn't it kill you to breathe this bitter air?'

'You were wrong, Alex. I'm glad to have woken up in this world,' Seb spoke softly as a tear ran down his cheek. 'I've made a new life - better than the one you created.' Seb stared into the fog and let out a sigh. 'And now you expect me to help you after hearing what happened - what you did to me?' Seb sighed as he watched Alex's haunting stare. 'Coming here was a mistake. I was so concerned about finding a home that didn't exist, I hadn't even realised that I'd found something *real* along the way. Now, if you don't mind, I'm going to find my friends and hope that they can forgive me.'

Alex wiped his eyes with the red wet sleeve, covering his face in blood. 'I thought bringing you here would make you understand why I did it.' He removed his katana from the hilt on his belt. 'Help you understand what I must do.' Alex pointed the blade towards Sebastian, and as elusive as the wind, he propelled himself forward. 'I'm sorry. But if you're not under my protection, it won't be long before you're Lucian's puppet.'

Alex flashed in front of him and thrust his katana through the air. Sebastian clumsily ducked and hurled himself back, weaving in and out of the white blade's reach as it sliced through the air around him. He jumped onto a thick branch, leaping from tree to tree. Alex followed him, smashing the withered husks to dust.

Sebastian could hardly register Alex's attacks. But still, he dodged out of the way. After a few messy dives, he tripped and fell to the ground. Alex was upon him, the tip of his blade pointing down. Sebastian closed his eyes and somehow knew his body would disintegrate into shadow, evaporating away from Alex's pursuit.

'Everything I did, every lie, every betrayal, was because I believed it was the only way to keep you from a fate worse than death.' Alex yelled into the trees, sheathing his blade as his gaze stretched across the forest. 'But fate, or whatever cruel force governs our lives, had other plans. That girl, Ariana found you, saved you, and brought you back into this nightmare. And I followed, watching from the shadows as you grew stronger, as the beast within you started to stir. I told myself I was doing the right thing, that by staying close I could still protect you, guide you, stop you from becoming what Lucian wanted. But I was wrong. I saw it too late, Seb. You were changing, becoming something that terrified me. The rage, the power - it was too much like *him*. Too much like your father, the Black Beast before you.'

Sebastian re-emerged from the shade and brought with him a black blade that curved to a jagged edge. 'Fine. If you want a fight, I'll give you one,' Seb said with tendrils sprouting from his shoulders. He rushed towards Alex on quick feet, yelling in pain as the ebony wings sprouted from his back. Bubbling black vines reached down his arms and he lifted the jagged edge of his sword at the crimson-robed boy. Alex planted his foot deep into the dead earth and held out his katana, calmly waiting. Sebastian's blade collided with Alex's, creating a flash of energy that disintegrated the surrounding trees in an instant.

Alex jumped back and lifted his bloody arm, allowing a bolt of lightning to burst down from the heavens and into his palm. 'Too late I've realized that the only way to truly protect you - to protect everyone, is to end it. To end you.'

Seb stopped abruptly, lowering his curved sword. He observed Alex as the robed boy slowly brought his arm back down, with electricity crackling around his fingertips, before pointing them towards Sebastian. Bursts of electricity filled the forest, decimating any tree left standing. Sebastian mimicked the mystical energy, moving like lightning as he closed the distance between them. He leapt high in the air, lifted the blade above his head and screamed as he swung it down.

Alex simply repelled the black sword with his own. He showed little expression as he ducked and dodged, tapping away Sebastian's blade as if it were little more than an annoyance. 'You were the closest thing to a friend I've had in centuries, Seb. And I failed you. But there's still a chance, a slim one, that we can end this madness. If you can find it in yourself to forgive me, if you can see beyond the rage and the lies... maybe, just maybe, we can stop him together.'

Sebastian replied with a monstrous roar, swinging with both hands gripped onto the hilt. Forcing the bile's speed and strength to seep out like it always had when he needed it. But each strike seemed more sluggish and uncoordinated than the last. He bared his teeth, growling as he took another swing.

'Have it your way,' Alex said with a wince, as he repelled Sebastian's blade. 'I won't ask you to trust me. I don't deserve it. But know that whatever happens next, I never wanted this for you. I wanted you to be free. I wanted you to live.' Alex suddenly stopped. Stepped back and rushed towards him.

His speed caused Seb to freeze. A cold flash nipped along his arm. Followed by a hot wave of pain. He fell back, his sword bursting into a purple cloud.

Alex stepped closer, pointing his katana down. 'You've become too powerful, Seb. You're changing, evolving into something far more dangerous than even Lucian could have imagined. That beast inside you - it's not just some dark force you can keep locked away. It's growing stronger every day, feeding off your anger, your pain. And when it fully takes over, there'll be no stopping it.'

Seb raised his arms in defence. Realising too late what had happened. He could only see one hand before him. The other was still on the floor where it had landed. Seb's breath had trapped within a tightening chest. He screamed, watching the blood pump out from the hole where his elbow should have been. He gripped hold of his arm with the other trembling hand to no avail. The burning ache wouldn't leave. He couldn't look away. The blood spilt - his tendons hanging like stringy meat. Sebastian hunched forward and wretched uncontrollably, releasing the bile from his stomach.

'I tried to find another way, I really did,' Alex remarked, wiping the blood from his katana. 'I thought maybe I could help you control it, maybe even help you use it against Lucian. But it's too late for that now. I was a fool to believe you would be the one to bring an end to his reign,' he said, raising his blade above the mist.

Sebastian lifted his head and instantly leapt back before the sword made contact. With a quick flap of his wings, Seb flew high into the air. Alex simply lifted his hand, splintering the sky with bursts of lightning. Seb dodged between the explosive torrent of energy and lifted his remaining arm to pull tendrils from the dead soil. They wrapped around Alex's leg, only to have him slice through them with ease. He kept his aim on Sebastian, continuously shooting electricity.

A stray bolt struck. The pain travelled through Seb's entire body, his muscles seizing. He couldn't even scream as he plummeted towards the earth and smashed into the black soil. His wings disintegrated to dust, allowing the tendrils to retreat within him. He lay trembling - broken. All he could do now was listen to the footsteps as they grew closer. He closed his eyes, his shaking body trying to lift itself once more. Sebastian shuddered as he felt Alex's eyes bearing down upon him.

'Please forgive me, Seb. But this power of yours goes against nature. Just as *his* does. Our worlds will not be appeased until you are both gone.'

Seb could almost hear the katana being lifted above him. The wind passed along the blade like a bittersweet symphony. Sebastian opened his eyes one last time to take in the beauty of his decrepit world before closing them tightly, awaiting to return to the never-ending abyss.

The sound of an engine broke through the clouds above them. Sebastian lifted his head to see the battered cruiser jittering towards the forest while Ariana stood ready at the opening. The girl jumped out of the ship as if she was diving into a pool. Her body spun through the air, becoming submerged in water gathering around her - enveloping the girl as she formed into a torpedo that crashed into Alex and sent him flying back through the trees.

She landed on her feet and turned to Sebastian. 'I won't let you disappear on me again, got that?' Ariana's sights darted towards the soaking wet and bloodied Alex who had emerged from the broken trees - katana in hand. His fingers crackled with electricity, as hers waved around the air to form the translucent liquid of life.

Seb couldn't make out most of the battle as he listened intently, his body still convulsing. His eyelids became heavy as he urged them open to witness the cruiser touching ground and Darius emerging with Xerxes drawn. He closed his eyes, allowing his body to go limp. Faintly struggling to stay awake, Sebastian clawed feebly at the dead dirt beneath him and rubbed the black soil between his fingertips. He found it strangely therapeutic. He felt his mind drift below the ground, surrounded by the atoms that formed around him. He fell further still until all was white, and yet, all was black. Sebastian was finally safe again, within the void.

29.

Fractured Reality

Sebastian opened his eyes, yet the world was still black. The ground bubbled like oil as it wrapped around his body, dragging him under. Seb pushed himself up from the muck to emerge into a realm of light. A blinding whiteness surrounded the shadows of trees sinking into the putrid muck. Insects buzzed past him, some consisting of ebony ink, and others, with mystical glowing energy. Within the fog, he found apparitions. Silhouettes formed from smoke leapt and danced between the trees. He could even hear their voices.

'...Let me handle this punk, girly. Watch the kid!'

The large shadow yelled as it glided past Sebastian and into the wilderness. Seb turned to the other ghost, now kneeling in the mist, and watching over some hideously shaped creature that lay in the dirt. It was the form of a person, yet bubbling from a substance so dark that Sebastian thought he was staring into the deepest reaches of space.

'...Leave some for me, big guy. I've just gotta make sure he's okay...'

The soft shadow answered as it cradled the black creature in its arms. Sebastian circled the two of them as the silhouette gently swayed the thing back and forth, stroking its round head. The apparition whispered into the black entity's ear.

'...Sebastian, can you hear me?'

Seb's breath caught in his throat. He fell backwards, looking upon the creature once more. This being had no eyes or ears, not even a nose. All it possessed was a large, unsettling grin. Sebastian's eyes drifted along the beast's body before they flashed wide - its arm was missing. He shuddered and turned away from the ghosts and monsters of the forest, wiping a hand across his face. He looked upon his one remaining shaking palm. It was as infinitely black as the thing lying behind him.

Sebastian slowly fell to his knees and took a deep breath. He closed his eyes, calmly raising his chest as the emptiness filled his lungs. He screamed - snapping his head back and roaring into the boundless sky. The sound sent vibrations to ripple across the void, shattering it like glass. With the world bending and breaking all around him, his cry faded into echo, allowing the shards to reshape into nothingness.

When his eyes opened, Seb could see an alluring glow, brighter than the rest of the white void. He pushed past the dense wilderness, swatting away at the white and black moths as he followed the light. Sebastian knew what would be waiting for him. Brushing past some vines, he finally made it to the end of the forest. The white light dispersed all of the trees and insects around them. In the clearing stood the glowing white creature. It faced him, eyes bulging, scanning the emptiness as if many things were hiding that

Sebastian couldn't see.

'...From one world. Two were created...'

The glowing one croaked, its grin motionless as it turned towards Sebastian. The shaking pupils on its bug-like eyes moved independently, scanning the forest before falling on Seb, and holding out its hand.

'...Entirely separate. And yet, they reach towards the other...'

Sebastian backed away into the safety of the forest only to realise there was nothing behind him. The endless white void had returned - just as the entity preferred.

'...These worlds built a bridge where we created barriers. Forcing us to cross...'

The glowing one bowed before Sebastian, snapping its fingers and bringing colour into the void. Particles of browns, blues and greens exploded around them.

'...Tell me, child. How many times has your consciousness bled into

mine?'

Sebastian hesitated as the guardian waited patiently. 'Enough times to know not to trust anything here,' Seb finally replied, stepping forward, ignoring the colours seeping back into the trees and shrubs like the world was being painted anew - his gaze locked on the elusive white creature. 'You, least of all, Lucian Avalon.'

'...This blank canvas is a place that lives within you, just as it does me. To not trust in it is to not trust in yourself...'

'If this place is a part of me, then what does that make you?'

'...I am the light that eradicates the bile, the blackness that-'

'Enough!' Seb yelled with a wave of his arm, scattering the colour from the painting. 'For once, please speak without these senseless riddles. Tell me what you want from me! Why do I always find you here?'

'...It is the same reason I find you. It is a strange feeling to fear the thing you most desire. To forget what you were once part of. And yet, we find one another. Just as your forefathers found me...'

Sebastian shook his head and folded his arms. 'I wouldn't call this the most coherent of conversations. But it's a start, at least.' He looked to the grass, watching as the gentle breeze compelled the blades to dance elegantly, the green had crept back somehow. 'You said my forefathers once came here - the Black Beasts before me. But for what purpose?'

'... You've not been a part of this plane long. Your eyes have yet to adjust. The infinite whiteness surrounding me. You may not see clearly, but every inch is a memory. Of mine, of yours, of theirs. Another dream, another nightmare. They play an infinite loop...'

The white being flashed its sinister grin before pulling back the branches behind it, gesturing for Sebastian to proceed. Stepping into the clearing, Sebastian was momentarily blinded by the brilliance of the white sun overhead. As his vision adjusted, he beheld a sprawling village unlike anything he had seen, its grandeur stretching far and wide. Paved roads crisscrossed the landscape, lined with towering buildings that reached towards the sky. Some structures dwarfed even the largest in Platto, their spires disappearing into the clouds above. In the distance, Sebastian could glimpse other villages dotting the countryside, connected by vast networks of roads and bridges. Beyond them lay the expanse of a boundless ocean, its azure waters stretching to the very edge of the horizon. Amidst this bustling metropolis, people of diverse races moved about, their attire and technology vastly different from anything Sebastian had encountered before. They carried devices akin to Glitch's codebreaker, their clothing adorned with intricate designs and vibrant colours that spoke of a culture far removed from his own.

'What is this place?' Sebastian asked, his head turning in all directions.

'...This is Lora as I remember it...'

Seb's brow lifted as he scanned the village once more. 'But... there aren't any mountains.' He turned to Lucian and asked, 'What happened to the mountains?'

'...The question you should be asking is, what happened to everything else?'

The glowing one tapped Sebastian on the shoulder and pointed up towards the tallest building of Lora - Union Tower.

'...Even after countless aeons, this day still haunts me...'

As the pulse erupted from the glass tower, Sebastian shielded his face from the blinding white energy that surged forth. One side of the land was engulfed in light, while a black, oily blast erupted from the other, scorching the planet instantly. Shockwaves reverberated across the land, sending tremors through the very earth itself. Sebastian stumbled backwards, losing his balance, but to his astonishment, he found himself suspended in the air next to the creature, floating above the devastation below, he watched as the once-blue sky turned a menacing shade of red.

'...This is how the world ends...'

Sebastian's heart clenched as he extended a trembling hand towards the distant villages, witnessing their inevitable demise as they were consumed by the relentless blast. Tears streamed down his cheeks as despair etched upon his face. When he turned to face the glowing demon beside him, gone was the eerie grin that had haunted his nightmares, replaced instead by a frown that mirrored the profound sadness reflected in the creature's eyes. In that moment, amidst the chaos and destruction, Sebastian sensed a shared sorrow between himself and the enigmatic being.

'...Playing with forces older than time itself...'

In the blink of an eye, the once-vibrant land had been consumed by the relentless onslaught of light and shadow. The energies surged forth, extending their reach across the vast expanse of the grand ocean, devouring it with ferocious intensity, with steam billowing into the sky as the waters evaporated. Turning his gaze back towards the disappearing horizon, Sebastian watched in silent anguish as Lora was swallowed by the unforgiving depths of the earth. It vanished beneath the relentless tide of black and white energy, the very fabric of the land reshaped and transformed before his eyes. Towers of jagged rock rose from the fractured terrain, encircling the area like silent sentinels bearing witness to the destruction that had befallen them.

'...Light and shadow, creation and destruction...'

As the titanic clash reached its climax, the radiant brilliance of the light and the ominous shroud of darkness crashed into one another, exploding into a form Sebastian's eyes couldn't comprehend. For a moment, these powerful energies almost seemed to be alive, fighting for dominance over the other's territory. With a deafening roar, the very ground beneath Sebastian's feet trembled and convulsed as the energies rended the earth asunder. A jagged crack split across the widening terrain, tearing through the fabric of reality itself. From the gaping fissures, a seething torrent of molten red and yellow fire surged forth, casting an eerie glow upon the desolate wasteland.

'...By our hands, the world was ripped in two...'

As the cataclysmic storm subsided, Sebastian found himself once more surrounded by vast mountains on all sides. Where once a vibrant world had thrived, now only echoes of its former splendour remained. Sebastian watched as Lucian descended alongside him. The luminous monster kicked at the dirt. Sebastian sank to the ground, his hands clutching a handful of ashen soil.

'So, that was the Blight,' Seb said, letting the dust fall from his closed fist like an hourglass. 'Why are you showing me this?' He looked up to see the entity still watching the tower intently. The glass had shattered, and the steel had melted and bent out of shape, but it was still standing. The only structure left.

'...The black bile on your hands, and the light engulfing mine. It is the blood we can never wash away...'

Another explosion rang out from the heavens, darkening the sky evermore. Sebastian jumped to his feet and arched his head up to the sky. There, a full moon had appeared from the darkness of space, glowing with the same intensity as the creature of light.

'...We can bring it back, you and I...'

Lord Avalon wailed a screeching hiss that sent ripples across the void, breaking the landscape and allowing nothingness to return. Seb stepped back, watching the thing shake intensely and tear at its white, fluorescent hair.

'...It will require sacrifice, wisdom, and a willingness to embrace the very forces that tore this world apart...'

Suddenly the creature was upon him, towering over Sebastian like the many crumbled buildings once had. Its grin - wider than ever.

'...Become part of me, my child...'

Sebastian turned and ran from the giant as it wailed behind him. Each booming word caused shockwaves of static energy to spread throughout the white void. Seb hopped from one pocket of darkness to another, trying to create as much distance as possible.

'...Let me fix it...'

The being of light flashed before him, swiping at Sebastian with glowing claws. Its erratic eyes popped from its skull as it gazed upon the boy. Seb tripped as the last platform of brittle blackness crumbled beneath his feet.

'...Leon...'

Sebastian froze when he heard that name. He turned around, but instead of facing the glowing god, Seb only found a campsite. Three small tents pitched beside two comfy-looking logs and a roaring fire blazing brightly in the centre. With every blink, the world shifted from black to white and back again. But still, he smiled. Sebastian drifted past the nothingness and floated onto one of the logs where a pocket of colour had returned.

He turned towards the girl sitting beside him. 'So, what happens now?' Sebastian asked, his body leaning into hers.

'Let's just enjoy the fire,' she answered with a strained smile. Her eyes glided to his. 'I don't know how long it will stay burning.'

Sebastian sighed and nodded his head, straining to show his signature grin, ignoring the tears in his eyes. Seb turned his attention back to the warm glow of the fire and wrapped his arm around her shoulders. 'It's funny. After all that's happened - all I've seen. I should be angry... but I'm not.' Sebastian turned to her and grabbed hold of her hand. 'We're together now. The rest can all be a bad dream.'

'Then stay here with me,' she told him, squeezing his hand.

'I want to. Really, I do.' Seb sighed, pushing himself to his feet. 'But I have to go back.'

'Back to what?' she asked, voice breaking. 'You know as well as I do. There's nothing left for you out there.'

'That's not true.'

'You're a monster in their eyes.'

'They're my friends.'

'You're a stranger to that world.'

'It's where I belong, Zara.'

'Sebastian, look at me!' she yelled, allowing the fire to burst before fading into cinders.

The moon fell from the sky in mere moments. Daylight spread across the still starry night. Sebastian blinked as he turned towards her, his eyes scanning the beautiful hills and peaceful mountains before landing on hers.

'What do I have to do?' she asked him.

'Zara, please. Don't make this any harder.' Seb knelt beside her, placing a hand on her shoulder.

'Tell me what you want. Do you want to see what's past the mountains? Then I'll show you. Just please... don't leave me alone out here.'

Sebastian watched the desperation in her eyes as she stared out towards the mountains and lifted her arm. Zara swept her fingers through the air and the mountains rumbled, moving with her. She lifted the other hand and lowered it, pushing the remaining peaks deep into the earth. He slowly turned, watching the world open up around him. Sebastian could see it all. He could finally leave. Go anywhere. And yet, the only place he wished to be was by her side. He turned towards her and grabbed her hand, squeezing it.

'See that, Seb! I'll move mountains just to make you smile,' she told him, tilting her head with a wink. 'Now where's that cheesy grin hiding?'

Sebastian began to laugh. She joined him and they fell back onto the log, overlooking their new horizon.

'Seb?'

'Yes, Zara?'

'Can you hear me?'

'Of course, I can hear you.'

'Seb, please. Why won't you wake up?'

'What are you talking about?' he asked, raising an eyebrow. 'I am awake.'

'Seb! What's wrong with you?' Zara pleaded, grabbing him by the shoulders.

'I don't understand... what's… happening...'

'...Seb...'

'...Seb...'

'...Seb...'

'...Seb...'

'...Seb...'

'...Seb...'

'...Seb...'

'...Seb...'

'...Seb...'

'...Seb...'

'...Seb...'

'...Seb...'

'...Seb...'

'...Seb...'

'...Seb...'

'...Seb...'

'...Seb...'

'...Seb...'

'...Seb...'

30.

Farewell

'Seb... Seb... please wake up.' Ariana breathlessly urged, holding onto his weak shoulders, squeezing and shaking him, staring deep into his vacant gaze. 'Can't you hear me?' she asked through cracked lips, gliding her hand down his arm before landing upon that empty space where his hand once was.

How long had it been since they had returned to Stonehaven? The days might have well been minutes for how quickly they fell into the next. She glanced upon the hollow sleeve and quickly averted her gaze towards his other hand, interlocking her fingers between his. He stared with dull eyes, gazing at nothing. She tightened her grip around his fingers, wincing when he didn't squeeze back.

'Please wake up! You have to. We're safe now... we're home.'

'It would seem the child is far from anything resembling home.' A frail voice appeared from behind her.

Ariana turned to find Viola standing behind her in the small, unkempt room. Without realising, tears had begun to spill down her cheeks as she crawled towards the old woman on her knees, embracing her. 'Nana, I don't know what to do,' Arianna squeaked, sinking her face into Viola's waist.

'Hush now, my dear,' Viola whispered, stroking the back of Ariana's head. 'You've done everything you can.'

'But it wasn't enough. It never is.'

'Ariana!' Viola snapped, grabbing hold of the girl's shoulders and pulling her to her feet. She looked upon the girl's blotchy face and shook her head. 'I've not seen you this defeated since the day you first turned up at my door. And if I remember correctly, it was over a boy back then, too.'

'This has nothing to do with Miller.' Ariana scowled.

'It has everything to do with Miller. Him and everyone else you feel responsible for.'

'He's dead because of me, Nana. They all are. And now, even...' Ariana drifted into silence as she turned back towards Sebastian.

The boy had since slumped forward in a seemingly uncomfortable position. His neck craned to the left, causing his head to drop, staring at the empty sleeve.

'You can't keep blaming yourself for the people you've lost, my sweet girl.' Viola pulled Ariana back into a warm embrace. 'I know your pain. But feeling guilt for someone's sacrifice only diminishes their final act.'

'I know. I'm sorry.' Ariana sniffed, wiping her face free from tears. 'I'll make sure their sacrifices weren't wasted. I'm going to kill every last one of those-'

'And enough of this mad quest for vengeance!' Viola interrupted, shaking the girl as a tear ran down her wrinkled face. 'Is that what they wanted for you? Is that what they died for?'

Ariana hung her head and shrugged.

'Besides,' Viola continued, leaning past her and inspecting the boy sitting against the wall. 'There are some you haven't lost. Not yet.'

'Can you do anything for him?' the girl asked, afraid of the answer.

'Well, let's see.' Viola stroked the grey hairs on her chin and stepped closer, staring Sebastian in his vacant eyes. 'I don't understand...' she uttered, before fading back to silence for a moment. 'The child is hiding in a place so deep within his mind, it's as if he's separated from it entirely.'

'What does that mean?' Ariana asked, spinning around and running to their side. She placed her trembling hands on both Seb's and Viola's arms.

'Please, Nana. Try harder. You have to find him.'

'I'm trying, my dear. I'm...' Viola suddenly wailed, snapping her neck back.

'Nana!' Ariana screamed, gripping hold of her.

'I... I cannot find Sebastian. He is an island lost in an ocean of confusion and despair. However, I did find someone else.'

Ariana turned towards Viola with an arched eyebrow.

'In all my years I've not seen anything like this. I don't understand how it's possible.'

'Nana, what are you saying?'

'Another soul lives within Sebastian. A unique personality. A memory. No, an identity.'

'What is it?'

'Leon.'

'It has a name?'

'Yes, *he* does,' Viola corrected, prying open Sebastian's eyelids. 'I can't be sure if this other child is the cause of Sebastian's state of being. But at this moment, I can see no other reason.'

'What should we do?' Ariana asked, giving Sebastian a soft glance.

'You know what we must do, Miss Lane.' A thick voice emerged from the veiled doorway. The two turned to find the large, bronzed body of Baskay squeezing through.

'What are *you* doing here?' Ariana asked, averting her gaze.

'I am sorry, Miss Lane. But I cannot grab my tongue any longer. Sebastian is gone. This... thing you've brought back with you is not the boy I welcomed into my village.'

'You wanted him dead long before we came back.' Ariana twisted towards him, glaring into Baskay's fearful eyes. She allowed her anger to subside and let out a deep breath. 'I've lost count of the times you've told me how you feel about Seb. What makes you think I'd change my mind now?'

'Because this time we're joined by someone whose reasoning might get through to you.' Baskay turned towards the old woman with open arms. 'Viola. I have always trusted you to make the right decision. Please, tell the girl what you believe to be the wisest road.'

'Whether we *kill* the child or not?' Viola asked.

Baskay leaned back, almost shuddering at the brutality of her words. He paused briefly, before giving his answer. 'Yes. That is what I mean.'

Viola gazed into Sebastian's eyes once more. 'This child's aura does not shine as bright as it once did. It has been submerged within a deep, dark pit. But... I can still feel its warmth.'

'And that means?' Baskay asked, scratching his bald head.

'Seriously, Nana. You've gotta be more specific when you do this.' Ariana sighed, folding her arms.

'Look, people. I can't tell you more than you already know,' Viola told them, rubbing her temples in a circular pattern. 'Sebastian may very well become what you fear, Baskay. Given time, he could turn into a deranged creature, plunging the world further into chaos.'

Ariana frowned, glancing towards Baskay who wore a matching expression. He caught her eye and his jaw tightened as he turned away, folding his arms.

'And yet, with these peculiar gifts the child possesses,' Viola continued, 'properly nurtured, they could be used to bring balance back to these lands, lifting us all from the darkness.'

Ariana looked back at Seb and smiled, brushing her fingers against the back of his neck.

'And they're not the only outcomes.' The old woman shrugged, waving a hand in the air. 'Sebastian could decide to change nothing. Choosing instead to live a simple life, far from this responsibility. And who's to say if the child will even wake?' She took Ariana's hand and looked into her eyes. 'I fear that outcome worst of all, for your sake, my dear.'

'Thank you, Nana.' Ariana sniffed.

'So, we're to do nothing?' Baskay asked as he paced around the small empty room.

'You're free to do what you want. I have predicted the child's possible future. Not yours. Although, I don't think it would take an Echo User to know what path you're heading down.'

'If I'm right about the boy then I see no other option. It may be a mistake, but it is one I am willing to burden myself with.'

'It's not for us to know what fate decides. Ending his life now will simply mean we will never know what could have been. I remember a proud and noble man who once believed he could guide fate. You knew him too when you were younger. His convictions drove him to madness and inevitably a painful death.' She slowly arched her head towards Sebastian. 'Call it fate or simply coincidence. But Brandon always feared the Black Beast would have its vengeance one of these days. Was it always inevitable? Or perhaps the outcome of a man who tried so desperately to stop something that he ended up being the catalyst for it.'

'We're in a war!' Baskay yelled, releasing his scimitar from its holster. 'And I am confident we can win without the help from some possessed demon.'

'Don't you dare!' Ariana turned, leaning back against Sebastian as she pulled a knife from her side and pointed it at Baskay.

Viola gasped, placing a wrinkled hand over her mouth and taking a step back. Baskay simply walked forward and lowered his blade.

'The boy isn't the only thing possessed. You've been tainted by his darkness, Miss Lane. Don't think I've forgotten your betrayal during his escape. And now look at him! Do you think you did him mercy? Death would have been more humane.'

'Think what you will. But I won't let you hurt him,' Ariana said through gritted teeth, the knife trembling in her hands. 'He's been through enough.'

'Are you ready to die for this creature? A boy who's proven to act with rashness and violence. A thing tainted by a disease so severe that it could potentially ruin everything we have built. Miss Lane, are you willing to *kill* for this creature?'

Ariana lowered her knife, turning towards Sebastian with tears in her eyes. Before shooting a glare back at Baskay and raising the blade once more. 'I am. And I will,' she warned him, steadying the knife.

'Okay, That's enough.' A gruff sigh broke through the silence as Darius leaned into the room, dragging Glitch in with him. 'I thought I told you to leave this matter, Baskay.'

The bronzed warrior grumbled to himself, sheathing his scimitar. Ariana allowed herself to take a breath and conceal her knife.

Glitch rushed to Sebastian's side and pulled a measuring tape from his pocket. He lifted the sleeve and inspected Seb's arm. Ariana was unable to turn away in time, shuddering when she saw it.

'That's another half-inch,' Glitch said aloud, unable to read the tension in the room. 'That makes three inches overall in the five weeks you've been back.' He stood and retrieved a notepad and pen from his lab coat and began pacing around the room. 'By my calculations, it will be a further four months before Seb is one hundred per cent back to normal. Every digit accounted for.'

Ariana couldn't help but smile and shake her head.

'Granted, the structure of the human hand is a byte more complex than that of a forearm. And that's only factoring in the growing fluctuation of intricate bone density. It's not even accounting for-'

'We get it, Poindexter. Four months.' Darius yawned.

'Am I the only one who can see the madness in all of this?' Baskay asked, his bronze complexion turning red.

'We have bigger problems to deal with right now,' Darius answered, 'an Ender Knight is dead by our hands.'

'By *his* hands, you mean,' Baskay corrected, pointing at Seb.

'Blackout isn't going to allow that to go unpunished, even if they didn't like Brandon,' Darius continued, pulling out a cigarette and placing it in his mouth. 'He was one of them. Just like the kid is one of us.'

'No smoking in here,' Ariana told him.

'The kid can grow back an arm. You think second-hand smoke is gonna hurt 'im?'

'I'm not taking any chances. I don't even like having this many people here crowded around him.'

'The girl's right,' Viola agreed, gesturing for everyone to leave. 'It's known that most disagreements stem from hunger, so how about I make a hearty meal for you lot? By the time you're finished, you'll all be too tired to argue.'

'I keep telling you, Viola,' Baskay interjected with a sigh, 'we have kitchen staff in the mess hall who prepare all the meals.'

'Nonsense! I've never trusted anyone else's cooking. Could be poison. Or even worse - vegan!' She shuddered at the thought.

Ariana could still hear Nana Viola bickering with Baskay as they left the stone hut. She had no idea how she found herself laughing, but somehow, she had. Ariana smiled and looked back at Seb, his chest slowly rising and falling, the whisper of a moustache protruding, and his eyes... even when dulled and idle, they glimmered. *Ever wonder what's behind them?* She asked herself, almost fading into a trance as she leaned closer to his face.

'Girly?' Darius asked, still standing behind her.

'Darius!' Ariana leapt up from the ground and spun to face him. 'I didn't realise anyone was still here,' she said, forcing a laugh.

'Yeah... look, I understand the kid's well-being is a priority. But we still have our duties. There are others we need to protect.'

'I know. I just...' She turned back to Sebastian and placed her hand on his lap. 'I don't trust anyone here. I'm worried that if I leave him alone, something bad will happen.'

'Then we'll take shifts watching him. You still trust me, don't you, girly?'

'Are you kidding, big guy?' She smirked, cocking her head towards him. 'We've been through enough scrapes for me to know you've got a girl's back.' She sighed and shook her head, crouching down to be with Sebastian. 'But I can't expect you to do that. It's too much to ask.'

'Who said anything about asking? I'm doing this for me. Who knows what kind of trouble the kid will get into without one of us here.' He placed a hand on her shoulder. 'Just promise me you'll start teaching classes again.'

'I promise. Thanks, Darius.'

'No problem, little lady.'

She smiled up at him and turned back towards Seb, brushing the hair from his face and sitting him upright so he was in a comfortable position. All the while she felt Darius' eyes burning into her.

'Any changes?' he finally asked.

'None,' she answered flatly.

'Can't believe that punk got away from me,' Darius spat, leaning back against the wall. 'It's like he vanished into the light or somethin'. I swear if I ever see him again...' Darius trailed off and shook his head. 'And what the blight was with that place anyway? That village looked ancient. I'll bet a year's worth of hooch that nobody's lived there for centuries.'

'I don't know what to make of any of it,' Ariana whispered, giving Seb's hand another squeeze.

'And that crazy room beneath the fountain! Girly, have you ever seen tech like that in your life?' Darius asked, finally lighting the cigarette in his mouth. 'I'm just saying, all of this seems bigger than we originally thought.'

'Everything about that place. Everything about Seb. None of it makes sense, does it?' Ariana squeezed her fist before letting it wilt open and fall to the ground. 'Am I crazy for protecting him after everything he did?' She turned to Darius with tears in her eyes.

'Ari...' Darius frowned, dropping his cigarette to the ground and stubbing it out as he made his way to her, placing a hand on her back. 'After all we've seen, I don't know what to think about the kid. All I know is with you watching his back, and with me watching yours. Well, Sebastian's gonna be alright.'

She smiled, gently closing her eyes. 'I'll hold you to that.'

'Now, I don't know about you, but I've been craving some of V's home cooking like nothing else. Want me to bring you some? Who knows, the smell could even bring the kid back if he's hungry enough. Don't think anyone's enjoyed Viola's cooking as much as him.'

'That sounds good.' Ariana laughed, unable to help the tears welling in her eyes.

Darius paused, his grin softening. 'Well, then. I'll be back soon. With *three* plates,' he told her, leaving the hut.

Ariana watched the slack sheet hanging from the doorway, listening for traces of movement outside. When she knew they were finally alone, she lifted Sebastian's head and looked deeply into his vacant eyes.

'Sebastian?' she asked, 'Who are you?'

...Sebastian's journey will continue...

...In False Reality: Of a Fractured Mind...

...Stay tuned...

Thank You for Reading

Thank you to my family, my friends and all of those who have helped me along my journey. To my mother who taught me I can accomplish anything I set my mind on, and to my father who inspired me to be creative and ask many questions. To Kea and Cerys, who helped me massively with this story, allowing me to bombard them with ideas and correct my terrible grammar. To the author, Darren Shan, whose books inspired me to become a writer. And finally, I would like to thank you, the person reading this, for your time spent with these characters. I hope that you've enjoyed this tale and continue to do so in the sequels to come.

About the Author

Joshua K Andrews is a writer and marketing strategist living in Colchester, England. His youth was spent creating games, stories and art in various forms when he wasn't climbing trees. From working behind a bar, a bookshop, and a desk at a magazine, Joshua spent his free time writing in the hopes of one day becoming an author. His journey, like Sebastian's, is far from over. With hope, he continues writing stories, to one day live a life past the mountains.